'The book is a very easy way . . . enough to shift a few
pounds' *Woman's Own*

'. . . out-loud funny, Kate Harrison's . . . deserve a place on every bookshelf'

Chris Manby

'Fabulous premise, great characters and a few surprises . . .
scarily addictive' *Daily Record*

'A poignant, very funny story, full of warmth and insight'

Sophie Kinsella

'A fun, light read for the girls' *Heat*

'Entertaining chick lit at its best' *Telegraph & Argus*

'A slick, bittersweet comedy' *Mail on Sunday*

'Fresh, feisty and fun' *Company*

'Classic chick lit . . . deeply moving' *Daily Telegraph*

Before becoming a successful author, Kate Harrison worked as a TV director on various programmes including *Panorama*. She is the author of the brilliant *Secret Shopper* series – shortlisted for the Melissa Nathan Comedy Romance Award – as well as several standalone novels. Kate lives in Brighton. To learn more about Kate and her novels visit her website at www.kate-harrison.com

By Kate Harrison

Old School Ties
The Starter Marriage
Brown Owl's Guide to Life
The Self-Preservation Society
The Secret Shopper's Revenge
The Secret Shopper Unwrapped
The Secret Shopper Affair
The Boot Camp

Young Adult Novels

Soul Beach
Soul Fire

the Boot Camp

KATE HARRISON

An Orion paperback

First published in Great Britain in 2012
by Orion
This paperback edition published in 2013
by Orion Books,
an imprint of The Orion Publishing Group Ltd,
Orion House, 5 Upper St Martin's Lane,
London WC2H 9EA

An Hachette UK company

5 7 9 10 8 6 4

Copyright © Kate Harrison 2012

A CIP catalogue record for this book
is available from the British Library.

ISBN 978-1-4091-3665-1

Typeset at The Spartan Press Ltd
Lymington, Hants

Printed and bound in Great Britain
by Clays Ltd, St Ives plc

The Orion Publishing Group's policy is to use papers
that are natural, renewable and recyclable products and
made from wood grown in sustainable forests. The logging
and manufacturing processes are expected to conform to
the environmental regulations of the country of origin.

www.orionbooks.co.uk

the Boot Camp

windy hill country house hotel and spa, devon

Dear Boot Camper,

Are you ready? Because your life is about to change for the better!

You've heard it all before, right? You've bought the book, the T-shirt, the DVD, and the hypnotherapy tape too. There've been hi-tech gyms, old-school gyms, machines that vibrate your fat away. Juice fasts, meal replacements, colonic irrigation. A thousand pain-free, easy ways to a New You.

So how come the Old You is still hanging around like a bad smell?

At Windy Hill Boot Camp, we can make you a promise. If you do as we say for one week – that's just one hundred and sixty-eight hours, or a measly ten thousand minutes – then the New You you've been longing for will *finally* make an appearance.

Don't be afraid – you have nothing to lose but your muffin top tummies! We can't wait to meet you and start you on your New You Journey. All we ask for is one thousand per cent commitment. Oh, and that you bring enough sports bras. Prepare to get sweaty.

In return, we also promise delicious, nutritious food to support your body in its new adventure. Luxury accommodation (no bunk beds or latrines!). And plenty of holistic support and massage to keep your body and soul on track.

Ready? Steady! Boot Camp is GO!

Love and good karma,

Edie Simmonds, Chief Executive & Holistic Leader, Windy Hill and Spa Boot Camp

'The celebrities' best kept booty secret'

Day 1: Sunday – The first day of the rest of your life

How you'll be feeling: excited, perhaps a little apprehensive. But don't worry. You'll love camp – and you'll love your staffs, too!

14:00   Compulsory safety & logistics briefing. Please note: there will be no refreshments provided so eat beforehand. High protein recommended.

15:00   Fitness tests and weigh-in

17:30   Snack and recreation/unpacking time

18:00   Visualisation session

19:00   Dinner: Chef's Special Chilli sin Carne, Power Grains, Spicy Apple Surprise, Sleepyhead tea

Please note all activities and meals are subject to change due to circumstances beyond our control

1

Steph

I can see them through the bay window: two blokes in black
army berets and camouflage gear, cross-armed and wide-legged,
as though they're so pumped up and muscle-bound that they
can't stand comfortably any other way.

Through the speckled glass, they look almost friendly. OK.
I'll downgrade that to *reasonable*. Or perhaps *firm but fair*. Not
the kind of guys who'd be too hard on a girl who's had the
misfortune to arrive for the Compulsory Safety and Logistics
Briefing thirteen minutes late, through absolutely no fault of
her own.

I raise my hand to rap the lion's head knocker against the
chipped black door, but my hands are shaking too much.

Bloody hell. I didn't have that khaki rash when I left London.
Stress, it must be. I need to breathe more.

'. . . punctuality is *NON*-NEGOTIABLE!'

The window rattles as one of the soldiers suddenly turns up
the volume. I shrink back.

I did everything possible to be on time. My own New You
Journey was meant to start with a gentle awakening at seven,
thanks to the Brighter Beginning Dawn Simulation Clock that
my brothers clubbed together to buy me for Christmas.

Then I'd planned some yoga stretches to loosen up my body
ahead of the week's exertions, followed by a breakfast of half
a lemon squeezed into room-temperature (*not* refrigerated)

Evian. I'd already set the sat nav to take me to boot camp via a designer shopping village where I planned to buy some knockdown exercise kit – an investment in the *new me* – before a final relaxed drive along the coast to arrive early at the Windy Hill Country House Hotel and Spa. Hey, I might even have managed a quick dip in the Jacuzzi.

I was *so* going to be Teacher's Pet this time. To prove I can change, not just to Steve but also to *myself* (not to mention lose at least two stone before the Valentine's Ball in thirty-three days' time. But who's counting?).

'Self-discipline is *NON*-NEGOTIABLE!'

Like most disasters, today's was caused by a chain of events. Despite knowing my tech-ineptitude, my brothers bought me the most complex alarm clock on the market, which failed to go off due to user error, so it was *real* daylight that woke me at a very un-crack-of-dawn-like quarter to ten.

I then downsized my yoga routine to the last three of the exercises on the *Mail on Sunday*'s 'Shake Your Booty' poster, but got locked in the Downwardly Mobile Dog and had to drive my car in a position that will henceforth be renamed as the Giraffe with Rigor Mortis.

When I got to the shopping village, it had been evacuated because the young offenders at the prison next door were rioting over the sub-zero temperatures in their single-glazed cells. The only alternative my sat nav could offer was the Happy Valley Hypermarket, a chain so downmarket that in the retail trade we call it Crappy Valley. But what choice did I have? Do seven days of workouts in kitten-heeled ankle boots and too-tight-even-before-Christmas size fourteen jeans?

'Respect for yourself and others is *NON*-NEGOTIABLE!'

So instead of weather-proof designer workout gear, my kit for boot camp consists of twenty pairs of acrylic Homer Simpson socks, two underwired sports bras so vicious MI5 could use them to extract confessions, one pair of mud-brown trainers, and five Juicy Couture-style patterned tracksuits in different sizes and colours (I cleared the entire shelf). The one I tried on over my clothes had a khaki camouflage print, which might at least help me blend into the foliage on manoeuvres.

Khaki.

Ah. That'll be the rash, then. I *knew* that fabric didn't look colour-fast. At least I worked that out before asking the squaddies for emergency medical treatment.

'If there's one thing we hate, it's **SLACKERS**! And **MOANERS**! And **WHINGERS**!'

Oh, and then the postcode I'd put into the sat nav delivered me to the wrong cliff. Sure, I had the perfect view of the whitewashed building from over there, but it took me another half hour to find a single soul to ask for directions, and drive my protesting Panda up the impossibly steep single-track road.

Twelve-foot gates loomed ahead like the entrance to a Victorian gaol, and when I tried to unbolt them, my fingers froze on the rusted metal. A padlock and chain was looped round one of the curlicues – maybe they're going to lock us in later?

Close-up, the hotel's whitewash is crumbling off like country house dandruff, and the sash windows rattle thanks to the wind and the parade-ground orders from the sergeant major.

Oh God. Maybe Steve *is* right. In life's great journey, I'm more of a passenger than a pilot. Boot camp? Who am I kidding . . .

'But if there's one thing we hate above all others, it's **lazy, LARDY, good-for-nothing LATECOMERS**!'

Shit. He's seen me. Not the doe-eyed one, but the shorter one with the World War One moustache. The one who's been doing all the shouting so far.

He's walking towards the window. No, *marching*.

I should smile. Or run. Or something. But as I stare into the abyss behind his black eyes, my body is paralysed. *That* doesn't bode well for ten hours a day of exercise.

'GIRT YOUR ... **RATTLE** ... BODY ... **RATTLE** . . . HERE.'

He's so furious that I can only make out some of the words as he rants and raves. The paintwork is flaking off the window frames, like the Puff Pastry Cream Horns I was testing on Friday for our Granny Knows Best range.

Despite my fear, my tummy rumbles.

The soldier looks hungry, too. His lips are pulled back in an expression that makes me think of the dangerous dogs you see on the news. The glass has steamed up, inside and out. He's unhinged.

No. It's just an act, isn't it? Professional women don't pay good money to be abused and bullied. God knows, I can get that at work. The brochure said boot camp takes the positive bits of military discipline: teamwork, supporting one's fellow woman, being the best . . .

The soldier's eyes widen and I realise his doe-eyed sidekick has said something to him. *Don't headbutt the window,* maybe?

'**GIRT** YOURSELF IN **HERE NOW!**'

Behind the two men, ten women are watching me with relieved expressions. As I head for the front door, I understand why, and my heart sinks even further.

They know the soldier has found his scapegoat. Which means they're in the clear.

2

Steph

I reach down and pull on the elastic band round my wrist. Then I let go.

Ow.

It hurts more than I was expecting, but that's the point. I got the idea from a magazine article about New Year's resolutions: every time I slip back into bad habits, I should pull the band, and the sting will remind me to break the cycle. I nicked a whole bagful of elastic bands from work before I left: with my track record, I'm going to need a few spare.

The bad habit I'm correcting right now is expecting the worst. I just need to take a deep yogic breath of the ozone-rich sea air and remind myself that if I didn't have room for improvement on the fitness and motivation front, there'd be no point being here, and—

'Oww . . .'

I'm lying face down on a freezing flagstoned floor. I'm too dazed to work out how I got here.

I examine the evidence.

Floor.

Door.

Hallway.

'Gosh, I'm terribly sorry! I wouldn't have opened the door if I'd known you were, um, leaning against it. Are you all right?' A cat-like woman in silky yoga gear is peering down at me.

I try to move all my limbs. 'Nothing broken. Though I might get frostbite from these tiles.'

She winces. 'Sorry. Heating the hallway isn't very eco, what with the door opening all the time. You'll soon get warm once you're inside the ballroom.'

She holds out her hand to help me up but she's so tiny I'll probably pull her over. Luckily a super-strong Yeti-sized hand appears next to hers. It belongs to the doe-eyed soldier, who is towering over me. But before he can grab me, the angry one pushes him out of the way.

'Took a tumble, **DID WE**? At least you've got plenty of padding.' There's an evil glint in his eye – just the left one; the right one doesn't seem to move much. 'You're wasting time. Join us in the ballroom, when you're good and ready. Which is sarcasm, by the way. I mean **NOW**!' And he stomps off.

The doe-eyed sidekick smiles, then pulls me up effortlessly, even though I weigh eleven and a half stone. *Ish*. That was when I last weighed myself, first thing in the morning, in my pants, before I broke up with Steve. Right now it might be a tad more.

'Staff Pepper's bark's worse than his bite,' he says. His voice is softer then I'd expected, with a hint of the Yorkshire Moors, but I'm not convinced he's telling the truth. 'I'm Staff Ryan. We're just in there.'

When he lets go of my hand, it has warmed up very nicely indeed. And the warmth seems to be spreading through my entire body.

Yoga Woman watches his taut backside as he disappears. 'He's such a softie. Both staffs are, underneath, as I'm sure you'll find out. Welcome. I'm Edie. Chief exec of Windy Hill.'

'Hi. I'm Steph.'

I hold out my hand but instead she embraces me in a cloud

of jasmine perfume. Then she mumbles something in my ear. It sounds like 'Sausage and mash with onion gravy'.

'Pardon?'

She lets go and smiles: deep grooves appear either side of her thin mouth. 'It's a welcome mantra. The boys take care of your physical development; I'm all about your *spiritual* growth.'

'Ah. Fantastic.' Frankly, I'm not here for the holistic stuff. My spiritual growth is perfectly well provided for by an evening on the sofa with *Mad Men* and a plate of . . . well, sausage and mash with onion gravy. 'I suppose I'd better . . .' and I nod towards the door, 'you know, before Staff Pepper gets even crosser.'

She smiles vaguely, then wafts off up the stairs. It's only as I struggle to pick up my over-stuffed duffel bag and carrier bags that I realise she could have helped me. I guess that doesn't come under her spiritual remit.

As I drag my luggage into the room, I feel a dozen pairs of eyes on me. The other women are judging, comparing. Thin or fat? Fighting fit, or barely breathing?

And how do I know they're doing that?

Because, however hard I try not to, I do it myself. My Compare-o-meter runs twenty-four seven. Ankle size, boob evenness, muffin top. Not to mention my own particular area of paranoia, thigh circumference.

My wrists are slim, though. The only part of my body I actually *like*.

'Are you trying to catch flies in your mouth?' says Staff Pepper.

I clamp my jaw shut and look round for the nearest empty chair. There's one next to a slim girl whose thighs *are* almost the same size as my wrists. I scuttle across the room and sit down, trying to make myself as tiny as possible, so people stop looking at me.

What the—

I'm flying through the air at high speed. Either someone has *literally* fired a rocket up my backside or—

'Oww!'

Or the seat has broken under my weight.

My hand throbs where it hit the ground. I've come to a standstill right at the centre of this massive room. The orange plastic part of the chair has broken off and propelled me along the shiny parquet, bobsleigh style, and I couldn't be more bruised if I actually *had* done the Cresta Run. But it's the total bloody humiliation that's making my eyes well up. This is *so* not me. I should turn around right now and drive back before it gets dark.

Staff Pepper is staring at me. I think he's *waiting* for me to burst into tears.

And something changes.

No bloody way am I giving him the satisfaction of seeing me cry. I ping the elastic against my wrist and I resolve here and now that whatever that thug throws at me this week – mountain climbs, dawn runs, obstacle courses over barbed wire – I will *not* surrender.

I can handle seven days, can't I? It's for the Greater Good. Everyone knows that Steph 'n' Steve are meant to be together. Everyone except Steve, that is. So if it takes a week in the back of beyond with a dozen skinny women and a psychopathic soldier to make things right again, it's a small price to pay.

'There's a seat over there that looks sturdier . . .' Pepper points to a chair next to a blonde woman with dimples and a deep crimson blush on her cheeks.

She's the first person I've seen here who looks like she actually needs a boot camp. Her wrists are bigger than mine and so's her belly. But it suits her. She looks comfortable in her skin. As I sit down, lowering my bottom millimetre by millimetre just in case this one is booby-trapped too, she whispers, 'Bad luck. I almost sat on that one too. Reckon they leave it there on purpose.'

I frown. Why would they do *that*? But before I can come up with a reason, there's a tap on my shoulder.

I swing round.

'What's your name?' Pepper barks, his lips so close to my ear you'd think he was about to bite it off.

For a second, I can't even remember. 'It's . . . Stephanie. Steph.'

He sighs. 'Last name. We don't mess about with first names, here. First names are for wimps and girls.'

'Oh, um, Dean.'

'Dean,' he repeats, like it's an obscenity. 'Dean. Well, *Stephanie* Dean, I think I can safely say I'll remember *that name*.'

He obviously doesn't expect me to answer back. So I do. 'Why's that then?'

Pepper tuts, then addresses the other women. 'Two types of people I remember on boot camp. The winners. And the losers.' He pauses. 'I think we all know which of those *Stephanie* Dean is going to turn out to be.'

3

Steph

Hallelujah! The chair holds.

'I'm Vicki,' whispers the girl with the dimply cheeks. 'Thank God you've turned up. I was beginning to think I was going to be the only –' she hesitates – '*normal*-sized person here.'

Hmm. Is that a nice way of telling me I'm fat too? I forgive her because she has a friendly smile. Before I can reply, Pepper is clapping his hands.

'For the benefit of Dean, I'll have to repeat the introductions. But in future, if *anyone* is late, the whole group get punished. My rules. My *kingdom*.' He smiles for the first time, revealing those sharp teeth again.

'So. I'm Staff Pepper. My colleague here is Staff Ryan. We don't do first names. It's a respect thing. If in doubt, call us *Staff.*'

Staff Ryan nods. 'When you're being pushed to your physical limits, you probably won't be able to remember your own name, never mind ours.'

We all laugh a bit too heartily. It won't be as bad as *that*, surely?

Pepper stops smiling. 'It's not a joke, ladies. And that's the last time I'm calling you *ladies* this week. From now on, you're not females, not individuals, not civilians. You're my platoon, God help me.'

Ryan's smile looks a little forced now.

'You all knew what you were signing up for,' Pepper barks. 'That includes permission to squeeze and squeeze until you think you've got nothing left. And then squeeze even harder.'

He mimes a testicle-bursting action with his hands. It might be scarier if any of us actually had balls to squeeze. 'I'll give you a final chance to change your mind. If anyone can't accept my rules, then bugger off. We want winners, not whingers. So, who's jacking?'

Pepper stares at each one of us in turn: first the woman with the wrist-sized thighs. She shakes her head to say, *I'm going nowhere*, and her serious chestnut bob swishes like a hair ad. There's something familiar about her but I can't work out why: I don't move in the same circles as goddesses like her.

Next there are two blondes who could be twins, identical with frozen foreheads and melon boobs that sit so high up they must have trouble seeing over them. They both shake their heads.

No one's 'jacking'. Not the wiry runner, nor the old lady with startling white cropped hair, nor the Indian girl with arms more sculpted than Madonna's.

Next to Vicki, there are two women who must be mother and daughter. The girl is in her teens, while the mother is a world-weary fortysomething, but they have the same wavy hair and the same upward-pointing noses, as though they're trying to ignore a bad smell.

Actually . . . there *is* a bad smell. Egg sandwiches? Drains? Or – I shudder – one of my fellow campers?

The hotel itself seems the most likely culprit. The 'ballroom' isn't quite what I expected from the website photos. The proportions are magnificent – if I half-close my eyes, I can imagine Victorians waltzing to Mozart, or flappers shimmying between Martinis.

But imagination can't cover up the giant cracks in the ceiling, or the tea-coloured stains seeping up the walls. Where a grand chandelier should be, there's an ugly copper pendant that casts shadows over our already gloomy faces. I know it's crazy but I feel sorry for this room. It deserves better.

Pepper is staring at me.

'What about you, Stephanie Dean? You could walk away now. Do something *nice*. No shame in it.' His words might be sympathetic, but his expression isn't. The one good eye travels down my body and his upper lip curls.

'I . . .' My mouth has gone dry, which makes me furious at myself. One quick ping of the elastic and I am back on track. 'I'm up for it if you are, Staff Pepper.'

That surprises him. Staff Ryan's Bambi eyes widen. Shock – or amusement?

'Oh, I'm *up for it*, Dean. But don't say I didn't warn you. Because this week, we're going to show you that your ability to count paperclips or answer a switchboard in a girly voice count for *nothing* in the real world.'

The Asian girl looks like she could lift an entire switchboard with her little finger. And I bet the old woman doesn't have a girly voice. But I don't think he's seeing us as people. Just as cannon fodder.

'This is how it works, you lot. We will break you. There'll be *blood*, tears, almost certainly vomit. You'll be *begging* us for mercy.'

Staff Ryan looks alarmed. 'But don't worry. Once we've broken you, we'll build you back up again. Stronger, leaner, certain that you can do more than you ever thought possible. Ready to face the world again.'

'Yeah, ready to return to your paperclips and your nice shiny reception desk with a whole new lease of life,' Pepper sneers. 'Any questions? Last chance.'

The teenager next to Vicki raises a French-manicured hand.

'On the website, it said most women lose at least half a stone. A dress size. Is that the actual, like, truth?'

She's already so waif-like that if she held a couple of helium balloons, she'd be in the Caribbean by teatime.

'We can't guarantee numbers,' says Ryan, 'but if you work hard, you will see definite changes in your body shape.'

'Great,' says the little wren girl. 'It's for my wedding, you see. My dress is modelled on Pippa Middleton's. It's not very forgiving.'

'Don't worry, we'll make sure your husband will be *very* pleased with the results on your wedding day,' says Pepper sleazily. 'Right. Enough chit-chat. Staff Ryan, talk them through the routine.'

'Our days will begin with a roll call at zero five four five hours,' says Ryan.

There's a groan from the room. 'Does he *really* mean quarter to six?' Vicki whispers.

'WHAT?' Pepper shouts. 'Was that a complaint I heard?'

We look at the floor. As Ryan recites the schedule – stretches, beach run, strength circuits, all before breakfast – I count the parquet tiles to distract myself.

But a voice keeps drowning out Ryan's descriptions of team games and bike rides.

This isn't you, is it, Steph?

Steve. Even though he dumped me five months ago, we were together so long that I know exactly what he'd say in any situation.

Come on, honeybunch. You're more of a couch potato than a runner bean. Give up now, before it gets too messy. Stay in your room and eat Green & Black's. That's your kind of break, right?

'Your diet for the week has been carefully designed to maximise energy levels and weight loss. The portion sizes might seem small, but we want to re-educate you about food. Obesity can creep up on you.'

'If you're particularly unobservant or very, very greedy,' Pepper sneers.

You can still tell your dad you finished the camp, Steph. No harm in a little white lie here and there, is there?

I shake my head. Vicki gives me a curious look.

You and institutions don't work, do they? You've got victim written all over you, and that soldier is on to you already.

I can't shut him up. I know he's not *really* here, but every word is true.

Just stop pretending to be something you're not, eh? In the end, I'm going places, but you like your home comforts. No changing that.

I ping the rubber band. No. That's where you're wrong, Steve. I *can* change. You'll see.

'There'll be times when you want to give up more than anything else you've ever wanted,' Ryan says. 'That's when your team mates will save your life. If you encourage each other, you will get through it.' Ryan smiles at us. Smiles at *me*.

Bloody hell. He's gorgeous.

How come I didn't notice before? As well as the doe eyes, there are little sun-bleached peaks in his spiky hair, and his muscled arms and chest strain the camouflage fabric of his jacket. He's younger than Pepper: late twenties, and he's less of a robo-squaddie.

This isn't good news. It's easy to hate Pepper. But if there's one thing worse than getting hideously sweaty and humiliated in front of strangers, it's getting hideously sweaty and humiliated in front of a handsome stranger.

'Staff Pepper and I are both qualified first aiders, and if you are in genuine pain, we'll help. But we're also experts at spotting fakers and slackers.'

You're the original slacker, Steph. Who but a slacker would invent a range of TV dinners called Couch Cuisine? No one cares, mate. Let's face it, when was the last time anyone but me actually wanted to see you naked?

'Shut *up!*' Whoops. Accidentally said that out loud, and Vicki heard me.

'So, fifteen minutes now to get into your kit. No special equipment but be ready to move fast,' says Ryan, and there's a mass scraping of chairs. Vicki stands up.

'You OK, Steph?'

'I—'

Tell her you're leaving. She can pass the message on. You don't even have to face those thugs yourself.

It's tempting. 'Vicki, I—'

'That Pepper's an arsehole, isn't he? But he's all hot air.'

'You think so?'

'Definitely. I've got three little boys and they all went through a phase like that just before potty-training. Staff Pepper hasn't grown up yet.' And her smile is so encouraging that I don't want her to think I'm scared of that idiot.

'He's a bit intimidating, though.'

'Nah!' She laughs. 'You can't let a squirt like that win. Have you seen how short he is? Honestly, small men are always the worst. He's only a real man when he's holding a gun.'

And suddenly I see him differently. Not powerful at all, but rather desperate. Why else would he get his kicks shouting at women?

'You're right.'

'That's a first.' She grins. 'Now, are you coming to see our luxurious bedrooms? I fancy some shuteye.'

'We've only got ten minutes,' I say.

'I'm the expert at naps,' she says. 'Forty winks, and I'm a new woman.'

A new woman. That's what we all want to be, or we wouldn't be paying the best part of a thousand pounds for a week of extreme pain. I look at the other girls; I'd die for figures like theirs, so why the hell have they signed up?

But what's the point comparing? I should focus on my own mission. This might be the only way to break twenty-eight years of bad habits – with a boot camp-sized kick up the backside.

At least we can trust Staff Pepper to deliver *that*.

Boot Camp Health & Fitness Questionnaire:

Name: Darcy Webb

Age: Over thirty, under forty

Occupation: TV Presenter

How much exercise do you do on a regular basis?
60 minutes, 3 x a week.

No, how much do you really do? Like I said,
60 minutes, 3 x per week. Seriously, why would I lie on
a confidential questionnaire? That would be completely
pointless.

Do you smoke? Gave up two years ago.

How many units of alcohol do you drink weekly
(Gentle reminder: a unit is a small glass of wine, not a *bottle*)?
On average, fourteen, as per government guidelines.

What do you want to achieve at boot camp? Include as much
detail as possible of physical and mental goals.
To look younger/better. That's it.

How do you feel about your body? For example, how would you
feel about viewing your naked body in the mirror – or showing
it off to a new partner?
I have no intention of doing either.

What difference would being fitter/slimmer make to your life?
My agent says TV is about survival of the fittest. The
fitter I am, the more likely I am to survive.

4

Darcy

I'm going to hire whoever did the photos of the Windy Hill Hotel to take my next set of PR shots.

Because if they can make this old ruin look as good as it does on the website, they'll be able to work miracles on my puffy eyes and city-grey complexion.

'I'm almost there with your room allocations, girls.' Edie the Yoga Bunny is clutching her clipboard and avoiding eye contact with any of us. 'Um, right. Now, I'm afraid there's been a teeny hitch in our redecoration schedule.'

There's no sign of *any* redecoration here for at least fifty years. The mood changes as our group waits for the bad news.

'Our interior designer is a perfectionist and alas, there have been some hold-ups on our gorgeous new Italian bathroom tiles.'

She's lying through her laser-whitened teeth. I can tell from her shifty eyes, her over-effusive gestures. The signs are the same whether it's a hotelier or a dictator trying to deceive the masses.

'What that means is that unfortunately, some of you who'd requested a single room are going to have to share. *Obviously* I'll refund your single supplement. And it'll be more fun that way. All girls together.'

Bang goes my privacy.

Though sharing a room is the least of my worries. All it takes

20

is one of these girls to realise they can make money from snaps of me rolling in the mud or exercising without full make-up.

Yes, Marian's Operation Darcy re-launch plans could backfire spectacularly if one of these women decides to turn paparazzo.

'You're so lucky; you're in the Clamshell suite, right at the top of the house,' Edie says as she skips up the final flight of stairs.

I keep looking for the hidden cameras, because I can't believe this place isn't a warped reality TV concept that Marian's signed me up for without telling me. Surely hotels like this don't exist anymore? I get it that Marian avoided the usual celebrity boot camps 'for obvious reasons, darling – this isn't a makeover we want to go public on'.

But couldn't she have found somewhere that didn't theme its bedrooms around crustaceans? It's very unsavoury. The others are sleeping in Oyster, Lobster and Barnacle. Oh, and the two blonde women who took the Crab Suite cackled like fishwives when they saw the plaque on the door, joking about trying not to catch anything between the sheets.

We should be grateful we're not bedding down in Cockles and Mussels, alive-alive-o.

'Here we are!'

We have to duck when we walk in under the eaves. Our 'suite' would have been the servants' quarters when this was a country house, and even though I'm five foot three, I must be a giant compared to the average Victorian skivvy. The space is claustrophobic but I remind myself we shouldn't be spending much time here.

The Clamshell theme is subtle, to the point of being almost non-existent. There's a painted wooden sign, a shell-shaped wash basin with a massive crack in it, and a faded clip-frame print of the Birth of Venus (now there's a girl who could have done with a week of boot camp before her portrait session).

The bathroom door has several large dents in the mahogany-effect plywood.

Edie spots us staring at it. 'Oh, that was before my time. Apparently a guest tried to kick it down during a row when his girlfriend locked herself in. It's a testament to the build quality of the door.'

The rest is what you'd expect of any clapped out B&B: no military-style bunks, thank God, but three single beds with mismatched duvet covers and worn-looking towels on top, a selection of rickety bedside tables and a travel kettle.

Best sight all day. I could *murder* a coffee.

Edie looks at me, then the kettle.

'Of course, for boot camp week, we've replaced all caffeinated beverages with delicious herbal teas! We wouldn't want to undo your good work!'

Old Sergeant Pepper and his macho posturing didn't worry me at all, but the prospect of a week without coffee is absolutely bloody terrifying. Marian talked about this week being a detox, but I thought she meant from booze and blokes. No one can expect to give up all their addictions in one go, surely?

This could all be a terrible mistake. Or not. I don't trust my judgement anymore. You're meant to learn from your mistakes but in my case, all it means is that I'm paralysed every morning by life or death decisions, like whether to use the black mascara or the brown.

I look at my two room-mates. They were sitting next to each other in the briefing session: the pretty brunette who arrived late and broke the chair, and the fair, mumsy one with the dimpliest smile I've ever seen. Though she's not smiling now.

'This is the *suite*?' she asks.

'Yes,' says Edie brightly. 'It's got a tremendous view.' And she leads us all towards the dormer window which does, indeed, offer a view of the black, uninviting sea, *if* you stand on one of the beds, on tiptoes.

No one says anything.

Edie claps her hands together. 'Right. Well, I'll let you settle in. No time to waste, eh? You've seen how tetchy Staff Pepper gets if anyone's AWOL for parade,' she says, and scuttles away before we regain the power of speech and begin to complain.

I wait for the others to pick their berths. Makes no difference to me, really. I doubt I'll sleep, and I've bedded down in worse places, and with dodgier bedfellows. The memory of some of my most recent dodgy bedfellows makes me shudder. But that's behind me. Onwards and upwards.

'Anyone have a preference?' The girl who fell off the chair – Steph, was it? – is eyeing up the bed nearest the bathroom. 'Sometimes I need to get up in the night.'

'Go ahead.' I hold out my hand. 'I'm Darcy.'

She shakes my hand but holds on a little too long, as I see recognition in her face. Better to get it over with now, I guess.

'Oh! Yes. *Darcy.* Of course you are. Um. Wow. I feel like I know you already.'

I nod politely. It's what everyone says, but if I tell her that, I'd sound like a total egomaniac. 'You're Steph, aren't you?'

Steph pulls a face. 'God, everyone knows *my* name now, thanks to my spectacular entrance.'

'He'll pick on someone else soon,' I say. 'It's how they work, men like that.'

She sighs. 'I hope you're right. Vicki told me he reminds her of her kids when they were toddlers. Didn't you?'

We both look round at Vicki, who is staring so hard at the bed under the window that I wonder if she's spotted a rattle-snake curled up on the pillow.

'Vicki?' Steph says. 'Everything OK?'

'They said *luxury*,' she replies. 'A *suite*. I was thinking slippers. Huge fluffy dressing gowns. Bubble bath.'

Steph laughs. 'Hmm, yes. Anyone who says the camera never lies hasn't seen the Windy Hill website. Still, we won't be spending much time in our rooms, will we?'

'It was meant to be a treat,' Vicki continues, her voice flat. 'That's what the magazine said.'

'Magazine?' I don't like the sound of that.

'It's my competition prize,' she says. 'David only agreed to take the week off work and look after the boys because it was meant to be, what did they say, *me* time. That's why my sister entered me in the contest. She said I needed some pampering.'

There's nothing we can say to that. Whatever's on the agenda, I can't see Pepper offering manicures or breakfast in bed.

'You won this?' Steph says.

'Could never have afforded it otherwise. But I thought that for all the money it's costing the magazine, it was going to be . . . posh.'

Maybe now's not the time to tell her that this is the cheapest boot camp Marian could find: that the truly luxurious ones start at two thousand pounds, to pay for half a sliver of smoked salmon for breakfast and the Egyptian cotton bedding you're too knackered to notice. Those are the kind of places the autocuties go to.

For a moment, the idea of India being sent here by *her* agent makes me smile. But only for a moment. Because of course, twenty-three-year-old former model India Duchamp doesn't need rejuvenation or detoxification. And if it weren't for girls like her – or, let's face it, if I'd been born a man – I wouldn't have to put myself through this ordeal in the first place.

'Three minutes!' Staff Pepper barks from the stairwell. 'If one single person is late, the whole group does fifty push-ups in the car park. No losers, no snoozers.'

The three of us exchange glances. 'He's not joking, is he?' Steph says.

'Doesn't seem to have a particularly highly developed sense of humour,' I agree.

Vicki stares at the bed, still. Her bottom lip is trembling slightly. We wait.

Then she sighs. 'Now I'm here, I'd better make the most of it, eh? The alternative is the school run, the washing, the ironing, the cooking . . . which has to be at least as tiring as a boot camp, right?'

I'm saying nothing.

She unzips her case, and unpacks her pyjamas and gym kit. Steph empties a holdall and two Happy Valley carrier bags onto her bed: a squished-up fleece explodes onto the duvet. Vicki peels off her big jumper and I see she's dressed for exercise already, in black leggings and a T-shirt that still has its packaging creases.

I lift my own rucksack onto the bed by the door. I'm more likely to sleep a little if I know I'm near the exit. I pull out a long-sleeved top, waterproof trousers and cross-terrain trainers. It's the first time I've worn my field 'uniform' in a while. It's all been packed, ready for last-minute assignments – but it's been a bloody long while since I've been sent anywhere requiring more than a winsome smile and a designer suit.

I change quickly and discreetly, another skill honed from weeks on location with stinky, sex-starved men. I'm about to put my BlackBerry into the jacket pocket, but there's still no signal at all up here. We're in the wilderness. I wonder if Marian knew *that* before she sent me. She likes to keep a tight rein on her talent.

But maybe my phone is yet another bad habit to be kicked. I tuck it under the pillow. 'All ready?' I ask.

Steph is wrestling her limbs into an ill-fitting tracksuit that will trap rainwater next to her skin like a bath sponge. I'd lend her my spare kit, except she's at least five dress sizes bigger.

'Need a hand?' Vicki scoots over to Steph, lacing up her new trainers, like a mum preparing her kid for her first day at school. 'Better sort this out too,' she says, pulling Steph's glossy auburn hair into a fat bunch. 'Have you got a scrunchie?'

Steph frowns, then takes an elastic band off her wrist. What's *that* about?

'Thanks.' Vicki fixes the bunch in place. 'And I thought I was bad for carrying everything but the kitchen sink around with me.'

I watch them giggling. They've bonded already. I've never been a girl's girl. Maybe that's why the other female presenters and I don't get along. Though it could also have something to do with them being the kind of air-headed bimbos who think Berlusconi is a pasta dish, and Guantanamo Bay is the latest A-list Caribbean beach resort.

'Ready, Clamshell chums?' asks Vicki, and then she links her right arm in mine, before doing the same with Steph to her left. And we file out of the room and down the wide, once beautiful staircase.

Maybe bonding is not an optional extra on boot camp.

In the pot-holed car park, we chat loudly to drown out our nerves, and stamp our feet to stay warm. It's only two minutes to three, but the temperature is below freezing already, with an evil north wind whipping our flesh.

And it's forecast to get worse. When I handed over to the weathergirl at the end of yesterday's last bulletin, she was so full of doom and gloom that I almost cancelled my boot camp booking.

That was until Marian reminded me of our 'agreement'.

'Fame costs, eh, and right here's where you start paying, as the woman once said, Darcy. We're facing enough of a battle as it is, what with recent events. If you're not willing to invest in your image, then you'd better start looking for another agent.'

Marian is such a bully. I only hope she's as ruthless when it comes to negotiating my next contract.

If there *is* a next contract. It's one of the many things that keeps me awake all night, but Marian says it'll be fine so long as I follow her orders.

Though Marian appears to be a pussycat compared to the fiery Pepper. I studied him when he was haranguing us in the ballroom, and I came to the conclusion that he's not pretending: he genuinely couldn't give a toss what we think.

Funny, though. After the backstabbing and bitchiness of my industry, where what people think is the *only* thing that matters, I have a grudging respect for the man. Though that might change when he's screaming blue murder at six a.m.

I count the boot campers in my head . . . seven, eight, nine. Two missing, but no punishment push-ups yet, because our two leaders aren't here either. I'd almost welcome a punishment exercise right now. Anything to stay warm.

There are more of us on this boot camp than I expected. What madness has made us all sign up in one of the coldest winters since records began? Apart from my two room-mates, everyone seems fighting fit. Like those two women from the Crab room. That skin-tight Lycra gear shows faultless muscle tone, as well as clothes-peg nipples. They want to watch that they don't freeze off.

Finally the silly girl with the Pippa Middleton wedding dress appears with her mother.

Eleven of us. Enough for a very bad football team.

The others are so busy chatting that they don't see Ryan and

Pepper emerge from a side entrance. But *I* do. They watch us for a few moments, this squawking rabble of women. Pretty boy Ryan looks amused. I guess he knows what's coming and knows it's going to be messy.

But it's Pepper's tanned face that hypnotises me. His eyes — one curiously fixed, but not false, I don't think — are hard, his dark brows are set in a brutal line and his jaws are clamped so firmly together that I worry he'll be grinding his teeth to dust. I'm used to reading people, but even so, his expression shocks me.

He absolutely despises us.

5

Darcy

Pepper waits.

So do I. How long before they notice him?

Then it happens. Silence spreads through the group, gossip stopping mid-sentence. Group consciousness is a powerful thing – I've seen the same in a riot or a warzone, the moment when everyone senses a threat at the same time. We freeze, and without thinking about it, we all stand up a little straighter.

Though judging from the upward twitch of Pepper's moustachioed lip, not straight enough.

'I've seen some bloody ugly sights in my combat days, but never such a collection of excuses for human beings. You're a disgrace to the entire species.'

We smile nervously – no one can say that and *mean* it, surely? – but he doesn't smile back.

'Since I left the army, I've been **APPALLED** by the state of the civilian population. No self-control. No sense of duty. None of the things that made Britain great. Just junk food, junk TV, junk lives. I have a mission to put that right. Starting **with you lot!**'

He means it.

I checked the two staffs out before I came. They're both former Royal Engineers: so I assumed they'd be practical, resourceful types, lacking ego. Epic fail on my part. There are

29

two types of soldier. Smart ones who lead with skill and understanding. And stupid ones who rely on fear.

Trust me to get a wannabe dictator.

'This is about respect. *Self*-respect. Respect for **AUTHORITY**. Take a look at each other – at your slumped shoulders and your dropped heads and the hands in your pockets. Then fucking well STAND **UP STRAIGHT**!'

That makes Steph jump. Without thinking about it, I've already lengthened my spine and shifted my shoulders back. I spend my whole working day having a director bark instructions via an earpiece, so I'm used to obeying orders.

Vicki's next to me, and she's straightened up so much that she seems to have totally changed shape.

'Wow, that's better. I must have grown a whole two inches,' she whispers.

Steph is on her far side, pouting like a sulky teenager. I felt sorry for her when Pepper picked on her earlier, but right now she's not doing herself any favours.

'FREEZE!' says Pepper, and we do as he says. 'Right, Dean and . . . you, what's your name?' he asks Vicki.

'Vicki.'

'Surname,' he growls.

'Whoops. Sorry. Adams.'

'Right, Dean and Adams stay frozen, the rest of you take a look at the two of them. Who's doing it right and who is **doing it WRONG?**'

Steph's gone very red and Vicki looks guilty. One of the two Crabs, the one with dirtier blonde hair, puts up her hand.

'Go on.'

'Adams is right, Staff. Dean isn't.' She sounds so proud of herself.

As if it's not blindingly *obvious*.

'Dead right.' Pepper walks right up to Steph, nose to nose,

like a comedy sergeant major. But this ain't funny. 'Head's tilted forward, neck's bowed, shoulders are rounder than a beach ball, and I haven't even started on the rest of her. See how it makes her look. like a victim.'

No, I think to myself, *you're* the one making her look like a victim.

'So let's see if we can improve things, shall we?' He puts his hand forward to move her body into position.

'Don't you dare!' Steph says.

His hand stops in mid-air. '*What?*' he scoffs.

'You're not . . . I don't want to be . . . *fondled.*'

Pepper stares at her. Obviously he's not used to having people stand up to him, but I guess even he isn't quite Neanderthal enough to laugh off the possibility of a sexual harassment charge. 'Don't flatter yourself, Dean.'

For the first time, Ryan steps forward and addresses Steph. 'It's going to be tricky if you take that attitude. We tend to be pretty hands-on. Only making sure you're doing the exercises right. We're responsible for not letting you injure yourself.'

Steph looks panicked. '*You* can do it,' she murmurs to Ryan.

Pepper laughs. 'We don't get to pick and choose our favourite soldier pin-up here, Dean. Either you let me get you into shape, or there's no point you sticking around. You can sling your hook!'

Ryan touches his colleague's arm and leans in to whisper something. Pepper's face is strained, like he's braving a chilly latrine with constipation. Then he sighs and turns back to the group.

'All right. Just to show willing, just this once I'm going to let Staff Ryan sort you out, Dean, under my guidance. But the rest of you, don't get any ideas. This isn't a bloody *male ESCORT agency.*'

Poor Steph turns an even brighter shade of beetroot. I'm sure she didn't want to be groped by *either* of them, but at least Ryan seems vaguely aware that we're human beings.

Pepper takes another step back, like a portrait painter preparing for his first stroke. Except no portrait painter would look at his subject with quite so much revulsion.

'Let's start with the turkey neck and the wobbly chin.'

6

Steph

Staff Ryan moves my head as though I'm a stiff shop mannequin (a bright red mannequin from an *outsize* shop).

He places one strong hand on my forehead and another
at the base of my skull, where it meets my neck. *That* place. It
took Steve two years to find it, and he used it against me
whenever he wanted to butter me up.

It's been five months since anyone touched me there. I'm
blushing brighter than ever but I don't want it to stop . . .

Too soon, Ryan lets go.

'How's that looking?' he asks Pepper, avoiding eye contact
with me. Probably just as well. I'm agog. He really is the most
beautiful man I've ever been this close to.

'Slightly better,' admits Pepper grudgingly. 'Now the shoulders. Square 'em off and pull 'em back.'

I steel myself for what sounds like a painful manoeuvre, but
Ryan's hands are gentle. His thumbs dig in somewhere just
above my shoulder blades, and it's like flicking a switch. My
back lengthens and my arms move down and I feel stronger and
more solid on the tarmac.

Pepper nods. 'Good job, mate. Now, you lot, look and learn.
Doesn't take much, does it? Dean looks like a different woman.
Well, almost.'

Staff Ryan steps back, but I can still feel heat where his
thumbs were. Good job, as it's perishing. He looks up, long

eyelashes sweeping up towards his brows. I feel my cheeks reddening.

I haven't had a crush since I met Steve, but as a teenager, I had them all the time, on the unlikeliest, cutest boys. My best mate Annie would tell me that they'd be lucky to have me, but I knew they were unattainable. Till Steve showed up, and that was my happy ending.

Well, it could have been, if I'd worked harder. Relationships take work, don't they? Only an idiot believes in love at first sight.

'Problem, Dean?'

I cringe. When Pepper calls me by my last name, it reminds me of the teachers at boarding school. Which then reminds me of the other girls, who were far scarier.

'Dean?'

I realise everyone else is standing in two rows, one behind the other. While I'm standing in my own *special* row, further forward than anyone else.

'Shall I explain again, Dean? Obviously the flexible fingers of Staff Ryan have screwed up your CONCENTRATION.' His breath condenses in the air like a dragon's.

I try to shuffle into line. No one makes room. It's definitely déjà vu, straight back to my days as the Girl Least Likely to Succeed in Class 3B.

'What we have here, Dean, is a *rank*. Facing me, in two ranks. Whereas when I say TWO FILES— '

At his shout, the other girls turn ninety degrees towards the road, so they're in pairs. I'm the odd woman out, with no partner.

Ain't *that* the truth?

'—then that's what should happen. Since there are eleven of you, you can come to the front with me as we take a light jog towards the seafront. At least with you as the pace-setter, it'll be a bloody easy run for everyone else. And it's downhill, of course.'

He beckons and I shuffle to the front of the file, seeing the sympathetic smile on Vicki's face as I pass. I don't feel like smiling back.

'Ready, Dean?' he asks. Before I can answer, he begins to run. 'Left, RIGHT, left, RIGHT, left, RIGHT . . .'

Except it sounds more like *lurft, roight, lurft, roight, lurft, roight.*

That's a *run*. Not a light jog at all. Now we're side by side, it strikes me that he's not as tall as I thought, but he's got a surprisingly long stride. I grit my teeth and gird my loins – if women have loins. I'm determined to keep up for at least the first few minutes. I'm twenty-eight, for God's sake. I should be able to run downhill.

The tarmac drive under my feet is spiteful, like hard slaps on my soles. I meant to go for the odd run before boot camp, but then I had a really bad cold and then it was Christmas and then there was the Granny product range to test and it's medically inadvisable to run with a belly full of Toffee Fudge Roly Poly . . .

Ah, enough bloody excuses. I'm lazy. End of.

And this might just be the end of me. I'm feeling faint already and we're barely out of the car park.

'Just one little tip, Dean. Remember to *breathe.*'

I grunt at him. But then I realise he's right.

GULP.

Wow. Amazing the difference oxygen makes. Very under-rated as a gas.

We're on a gritted path which slopes rapidly downhill to the Gates of Doom. Pepper races ahead, to unbolt them. The sight of the outside world makes me giddy. *Freedom.* I could make a run for it now . . .

But before I can pursue that thought, Pepper's back beside me, his boots setting the rhythm. Thump, THUMP, thump, THUMP. I look down: it's impossible to see what colour they were originally, because they're covered in mud and sand.

Is that Devon mud, or desert sand? Bad stuff must have happened to Pepper to turn him into such a psycho. People aren't born to be bullies, are they—

'Ugh!'

Something is attacking my cheek. I stop, at which point an elephant smashes into my back and I almost fall over. Yet again.

'DEAN! What the bloody hell do you think you're DOING?'

It's not an elephant that hit me, but an entire file of boot camp women who are tumbling into me, like jogging dominoes. I put my hand up to my cheek and when I take it away again, my fingers are red with my own blood.

'Didn't realise I had to make a health and safety announcement about not running into *bushes,* Dean.' Pepper sounds awed at how stupid I truly am. 'It's only a small cut. You won't die.'

The other women tut and brush themselves down but I'm the only one who is *bleeding.*

'Sorry,' I say. 'I was, well, thinking of something else.'

'Don't.'

'Don't what?'

'Think. Thinking isn't required of you this week, in fact, as of this minute, thinking is against boot camp Rules. Me and Staff Ryan are the only ones using our brains. The rest of you, SWITCH 'EM **OFF!**'

As we set off again, I exchange a look with Darcy. She raises her eyebrows at me, and I'm certain we're thinking along the same lines: if we have to rely on the combined brainpower of Pepper and Pretty-but-Dim Private Ryan, we really are in for the week from hell.

Pepper turns right and *finally* we see the sea. It stretches like a silky silver ribbon across the horizon, darker than the greying sky above it. Not a picture-postcard view at all, but powerful all the same.

'Not *thinking*, are we, Dean?'

I shake my head. Everyone has stopped for a few seconds, because this is the view we never get to see from our paperclip empires or behind our shiny reception desks.

'Enough sightseeing. We'll do a final jog on the flat, then it's time to stop idling, and do some **real BLOODY WORK!**'

Along the shore, we pass normal people out for a walk: an elderly couple walking a dog, an extended family with the ruddy cheeks only a long roast lunch can give you. The kids gawp at us – we must look a bit like a chain gang on a Sunday outing – and the adults smile. *Rather you than me.* I'd be thinking the same if I were them.

I try to focus on the sea. But on the other side of the path, there's a pub with an open fire glowing orange through mullioned windows. The smell of roast potatoes drifts my way. I should be at Dad's, now, cooking for him and Nigel and Robin. For years, Mum's special chicken, Mum's two veg and Mum's crumble have kept us on track when everything else is falling down round our ears. I don't belong *here*.

Don't think. Just run.

Now I can smell burned sugar. It's coming from a pastel-painted stall, where a woman is spinning in a mental candyfloss drum.

It makes me think of being little. Way, way back. Mum was with us; *that's* how far back. The smell, the taste, the sticky face afterwards.

'STOP!'

We stop.

37

'Right, this is where you get a chance to get back your self-respect. We want you to run a mile in your best time. Staff Ryan will go on ahead as your halfway marker. At the end of boot camp, we'll test you again. I take it there are no questions. Good.'

Ryan sprints past. For a big-built man – more rugby player than footballer – he moves bloody fast. In no time at all, he's reached the halfway point, next to a Victorian bench.

'Right then, boot campers. You can see where you're aiming.' Pepper takes out his iPhone, taps the screen and then nods. 'Ready . . . steady . . .'

7

Steph

'*GO!*'

I start *fast*. A mile? A mile is nothing, right? If you can't manage a mile, Steph, then you might as well order the stair lift and the support tights right this minute, and give up on the idea of Steve ever wanting you back.

We all start off like sprinters. My Compare-o-meter, which has been temporarily out of service due to physical exhaustion, cranks back into action.

Vicki is on my right. At least, whatever happens, I won't come last. She's super-kind, but she's no Olympic athlete. I can hear the swish as the shiny fabric of her leggings rubs together with each stride. Any faster and she'll start an electrical fire.

I might slow down towards the end, just to keep her company. I know how it feels to come in last. Darcy's way ahead, dressed in seriously dingy exercise wear, like she's ready for the battlefield. Maybe it's because she wants to stay incognito.

She got the hump when I recognised her, though it must be a bit of a pain to be spotted wherever you go. I read *Heat*. I've seen the pictures of TV stars battling terrible hangovers in Sainsbury's, or falling out of cabs outside some seedy club. In fact, one of those might actually have been Darcy.

Ugh. My lungs are beginning to protest, and my bra underwire is stabbing my ribs, but it's mind over matter, right? The old lady is at the back, moving so slowly it's more like a fast walk. Some of the other girls are beginning to reduce their pace, too.

Hey, I might even come in the top five. Steve'll never believe it when I text him.

No. I don't text Steve anymore. Annie deleted his number and the fact that it's burned into my subconscious is beside the point. His approval is as irrelevant to me and my life as . . . as . . .

As winning a silly running race?

Anyway, I want my Cinderella moment at the ball, when he sees me across a crowded room and realises I've changed. And then . . .

OK. Running is quite hard.

I can't. Actually. Breathe.

I turn my head. I can still count the hairs in Pepper's dis-approving monobrow, which means I haven't come nearly as far as I thought. And now the evil twin fortysomethings from the Crab room are gaining on me. No. Not gaining. Overtaking. And way ahead, the first two have actually almost reached Ryan's halfway point now. The doll-like bride-to-be and . . .

No! It can't be. *It's Vicki!*

How in God's name did she manage to get so far ahead? She's thumping along the path, about to pass me going the other way.

'Keep going, Steph, you can do it,' she calls out, without a hint of a wheeze. Her dimples are bigger than ever and her ponytail bounces as she runs. I attempt an answer but all I manage is a weak thumbs up.

OK. I'll try it Pepper's way. No thinking, just keeping my eye on the halfway point. Which happens to be Ryan. No, *not* at his face. That's too distracting.

At his feet, then. At the brown boots, oh, and maybe up to his long calves, and the wide, powerful thighs and the . . .

Get a grip, girl.

'Come on, Steph,' he calls as I get closer. For a second, I wonder who he's talking to. I've got so used to being called Dean. Have I succumbed to Stockholm Syndrome already?

He must see the confusion in my face because as I draw level, he says, 'Don't tell Staff Pepper, but I hate calling women by their last names. Or swearing at them.' I run round him, and I'm facing back the way we came.

Halfway. Is that all? The world's swimming a bit. Mountain-Goat-Granny is coming level, though her fast walk seems as effortless as before.

One. Step. After. Another.

The others are standing in line, now. A finishing line. Pepper is there, arms crossed, legs in swollen-testicles position again. What insult will he shout when I come in last?

'*Not far now, Stephanie. You're doing brilliantly.*'

The voice in my left ear is so soft that for a second I think it might be imaginary Steve. Though Steve has never said anything remotely like *you're doing brilliantly*. Except when he's talking about my scones.

I turn. It's Staff Ryan, smiling at me.

I almost fall over.

'Ngh,' I manage.

'No, seriously, you are. This isn't a race. The only person you're competing against this week is your old self. Be a winner, not a whinger. Simple, right?'

He says all that without taking a single breath.

'Guh.'

'Come on, then. One final burst of energy then it's time for a lie down.'

Maybe it's the thought of a lie down that does it. Or possibly it's *that* smile and the desire to convince him I'm not a whinger.

I find a reserve of energy, like the fumes left in an empty petrol tank, and I go careering through the line, and the girls scoop me up in a great big team embrace as I hear Pepper shout out, 'Twelve minutes twenty-nine seconds. Congratulations to Dean for a new boot camp record! That's the slowest mile we've had since we started running the course!'

But everyone else is whooping and slapping me on the back and if I close my eyes, I can imagine how it might feel to be a winner.

Ryan is a lying bastard.

Yes, there is a 'little lie down'. But he didn't mention that we're lying on cold, wet sand, with a partner hanging onto our ankles, while we attempt to do as many sit-ups as possible in two minutes.

When Pepper gave the instructions, I thought it'd be OK. Sit-ups, I can do. You use your hands to lever yourself up, especially when you're busty like me and your chest consists of two D-cup dead-weights.

But Pepper picked our partners for us, 'so none of you can cheat', and put me with the blonder of the two women from the Crab room.

'On my whistle, two minutes, starting *NOW*!'

I put my hands either side of my temples as Ryan demonstrated, and breathe out to prepare for my first sit-up. We did these in gym at school. How hard can they be?

'Ugh.'

I'm missing some vital technique point here, obviously. The blonde – whose name is Cat – looks down at me curiously. 'He's blown the whistle; you can start.'

'I can't seem to . . .' It's like someone has sneakily removed my stomach muscles, so there's no connection between the two halves of my body.

'Come on, Dean,' she says, pouting. Or maybe it's just that her lips have been filled to bursting point with collagen. 'I'm getting *really* bored up here.'

Either side of me, women are popping up and down like jack-in-the-boxes. Vicki's more a blur than a person, she's going so fast. I haven't even managed *one*.

Each time I try, I get a third of the way up and then I can get no further. My eyeballs are about to pop out from the effort so in desperation, I lower my hands towards the sand and that gives me the momentum to rock upwards and touch the sides of my ankles.

But as I flop back down again, Cat shakes her head. 'Can't count that one. Your fingers left the side of your head.'

'I can't do it otherwise.'

She shrugs. 'Not my problemo.'

I'm not a violent person, but I have never wanted to punch someone as much as I want to punch her right now.

Ryan and Pepper are patrolling the line. Ryan gave me a wide berth a second ago, probably because he doesn't want to embarrass me. Pepper is not so accommodating.

'How many so far?' he asks Cat.

'None at all,' she says, sounding amused.

'I did manage one. But she didn't allow it,' I protest.

'Dean cheated.'

'Try again,' Pepper says. 'Show some gumption.'

I close my eyes. I need to get this in perspective. My boss at work doesn't care about my ability to do a sit-up, so long as I can shoulder her dirty work as well as my own. And my brothers and my dad are only interested in me having the gumption to show up every Sunday to do the roast the way Mum used to.

Even Steve isn't bothered about sit-ups – though he did always want me to go *on top*.

43

Pepper's leaning over me now, so I can see red hairs in his nostrils. Unless he's breathing fire. 'I said, TRY *AGAIN*.' He holds my hands firmly against the sides of my head.

I close my eyes and his angry face is replaced by Steve's features. *Sorry, honey bunch. It's not me, it's definitely you. But it's not your fault you can't keep up with me—*

'Stop telling me what I can't fucking do!'

From nowhere I find the strength to propel myself up, despite my hands being locked in position. I open my eyes and find I'm eyeball to eyeball with Pepper, and he's half-smiling, half-sneering.

'Well, I must admit I didn't expect to hear parade-ground language quite so soon. Seems to have done the trick, though.'

He lets go of my hands and I sink back onto the sand.

'One,' counts Cat.

Ryan's at the head of the line, looking at his watch. 'OK, boot campers, counting down: five, four, three, two, one. STOP!'

I hear a group groan as the others slap back onto the sand. Ryan's holding a clipboard and coming along the line to get the scores.

'Twenty-seven.'

'Eighteen.'

'Forty-one.'

'Twenty-two.'

Cat stifles a giggle. 'One.'

Ryan's dark eyes pop open, but he doesn't say anything more.

'Some good work there,' Pepper shouts. 'And some less good work. If your figure's in the teens or below, you're failing. You need to work on your core strength and your bloody backbone.'

I never did have much of a backbone.

'Great, now swap partners. But don't get too relaxed.

Because we still have push-ups and burpees to do before we head back to base for the weigh-in. Followed by your hard-earned cup of herb tea and half a teaspoon of sunflower seeds.'

Everyone laughs.

'You think I'm joking, don't you? Ah, you've got a lot to learn.'

Boot Camp Health & Fitness Questionnaire:

Name: Vicki Jane Adams

Age: 33

Occupation: Housewife/mum to Alastair, Murray & Rudy

How much exercise do you do on a regular basis?
Running round after my little boys twenty-four hours a day is enough exercise for me!

No, how much do you *really* do? Don't have the money or time to join a gym.

Do you smoke? Not since Year 8 at school. It's the one healthy thing about me!

How many units of alcohol do you drink weekly (Gentle reminder: a unit is a small glass of wine, not a *bottle*)?
Half a cider at the pub when David and I go out as a couple. So that's one unit every two years!

What do you want to achieve at boot camp? Include as much detail as possible of physical and mental goals. Lose weight, stop feeling like the fattest mum at the school gate. I'm too lazy to do it on my own, which is why my sister entered me for the competition. Feels like my last hope.

How do you feel about your body? For example, how would you feel about viewing your naked body in the mirror – or showing it off to a new partner?
Horrible. Thank God I'm married.

What difference would being fitter/slimmer make to your life?
It'd change everything. Might even still be around to see my grandkids come along.

8

Vicki

I always tell my boys: don't be scared of anything. The dark, spiders, school. There's nothing about life for them to be afraid of.

So it's a bloody good job they can't see me right now, all shaky waiting for the moment of truth. The *weigh-in*. The words make me want to run another mile in the opposite direction.

'I hope they've got strong enough scales,' I say to Steph.

'And a big enough tape measure,' she replies. Of course, she's not nearly as massive as me. At most she's a curvy sixteen, and it kind of goes with her wavy hair and her fantastic boobs. I bet she can even buy clothes on the high street, instead of having to order tents from horrible plus-size catalogues.

That skinny bride-to-be is queuing in front of us. The silly cow even wore cotton gloves during the fitness test to protect her nails. She turns round. 'We've had to buy specially reinforced scales now. Where I work.'

'Really?' Steph asks.

'Hmm. The number of obese patients we see, we might have to invest in ones for agricultural use. You know, for livestock.'

Is she calling me a fat cow? 'I don't own a set,' I say. 'Except for the ones I use for making birthday cakes.'

'Ah,' she says, like it explains everything about me.

47

'What do you mean, *ah*?'

'Only that I always advise my patients that the best way to keep a check on those excess pounds is to weigh yourself every day. The second I go over a BMI of twenty-one point five, I simply cut down on sweets or crisps till I'm back to my perfect weight. It's not rocket science. It's about self-respect.'

I'm dumbstruck. Steph is frowning at her. 'Patients? Are you a doctor?'

'No. I'm a wellbeing advisor at a personal improvement centre.'

I stare at her. 'A *what*?'

'We improve people's appearance through non-surgical and surgical treatments. Though we're very holistic. We look at the inner person, as well as the outside parts.'

'You mean a plastic surgery clinic?' Steph says.

'That's a *very* old-fashioned term. We offer a wide variety of solutions to help you attack the unwelcome signs of ageing, over-indulgence or—'

'Next!' Pepper shouts from inside the office.

'My turn, then.' The girl smiles, then reaches into a tiny pocket in her even tinier running shorts and pulls out a business card. 'I'm sure we could help both of you fight back against obesity.'

Steph takes the card as the girl disappears. 'Natalia Greer, wellbeing advisor, Totally New You Spa and Clinic.'

'Never mind fighting obesity, I'm quite tempted to give her a good smack for being so rude,' I say, hoping *Natalia Greer* is hearing me loud and clear as she steps on the scales.

OK, so even though I don't have scales at home, I know exactly how heavy I am. The doctor even wrote it down for me, and, though I threw the bit of paper away, I've still got the numbers in my head. If only he'd left it in kilograms – they don't mean a thing to me.

But he converted it. So many stones, weighing me down. And that was before Christmas, before I hit the mince pies and the stuffing and every other bloody thing. I'm surprised the pavement didn't crack open when I was running by the beach.

'Take no notice of Natalia,' Steph says. 'Everyone knows skinny women are really boring in bed.' Then she giggles.

'Is that true?'

She shrugs. 'Maybe. Maybe not. But it always makes me feel better.'

I giggle, too, although I don't have a clue whether I'm boring in bed. David seems happy enough, though we were both virgins when we got together. Talk about naive. We might be David and Victoria, but Posh and Becks we most definitely ain't.

Natalia steps out of the office, smiling broadly. 'All done! Take no notice of those scales, by the way. If anything, they're a little too generous. They made me fifty-one kilos when this morning I was definitely fifty-one point three. Still, what's three hundred grams among friends?'

'Next!'

My turn. I really don't want anyone else to know what a lump I am.

But what do I do? Walk out, waste the competition prize, piss off the magazine, eat more, move less, grow to the size of a house, die early?

Chrissie would never forgive me for jacking.

I step into the office area: Bad Cop Pepper has a tape measure ready, and Good Cop Ryan is manning the scales. I'm not scared of *them*. I'm scared of what I've turned into.

Pepper has to stretch to get the tape all the way round my bust, waist and hips. Well, where he thinks my bust, waist and hips are. I'm more of a barrel than an hourglass. He doesn't look at me once while he's measuring or writing down the figures.

Then Good Cop Ryan tells me to 'pop' on the scales. We wait. I look at the grubby red carpet and wish I hadn't taken my shoes off.

'Don't tell me.'

Ryan frowns. 'Eh?'

'I know I'm big. I know I'm unhealthy. I'm not in denial or anything or I wouldn't be here. I'm going to work bloody hard. I just . . . don't want the number in my head all week, OK?'

Pepper raises his eyebrows at Ryan. So they think I'm a hysterical woman, now?

None of that matters. All that matters is I want to be around for as long as I can.

Ryan shrugs his shoulders. 'No problem. Hopefully if you work as hard as you say, we'll be able to give you a nice surprise at the final weigh-in.' And he smiles at me, which makes him look more like one of my boys than a big tough soldier.

'Next!' shouts Pepper, and I get out before they change their minds.

Bad Cop Pepper *wasn't* joking about the half teaspoon of seeds.

'Shouldn't they have offered a magnifying glass with our snack?' Steph looks pretty devastated.

'I don't even like bird food so it's all the same to me,' I say. 'Have mine.'

Our 'snack' is served in the dining room. Don't suppose it was always the dining room: it's not grand enough for the lords and ladies who must have lived here when the house was posh. Maybe this was where the servants ate.

Now, it reminds me of the dining rooms from seaside holidays with my mum and dad and Chrissie. The chipped

Formica table tops and the glass salt shakers that have nothing left inside but yellow grains of rice.

Good memories: Chrissie nicking the eggs off my plate when I wasn't looking, Dad proudly bringing back his catch of the day to the B&B owners and us trying not to laugh when we saw the size of the tiddlers served up in batter for our tea.

There's nothing frying here, though it smells of old breakfasts. Until I try to drink the 'detox' tea, that is. Pongs worse than the boys' football socks when they've been left in their sports bag for a week.

We're drinking it, though. How desperate does that make us?

Natalia's mother has joined us, almost sitting in Darcy's lap.

'I'm Liz! I can't wait to hear what we're doing here,' she says. 'I don't want to look too much like mutton in my gorgeous daughter's wedding photos.'

I've hid at family weddings for the last four summers, so I know exactly how she feels.

'Stop fishing for compliments, Mum,' Natalia says. 'She only says that because she wants people to say how pretty she is.'

'The family resemblance is very striking,' says Darcy.

David's never going to believe that I'm sharing a room with a *celebrity*. Whenever Darcy says something, I kind of expect to hear Big Ben. *The night's headlines, with Darcy Webb in London. Bong. Bong. Bong.*

'It's so exciting having you here, Darcy. Fancy!' Liz says. Natalia looks like she'd like to gag her mother for being uncool.

Darcy grips her mug so tightly that her knuckles go white. 'Ah, well, sitting behind a presenting desk isn't very good for fitness.'

'Oh, you look perfect, Darcy,' Liz says, and then giggles. 'It feels strange, saying your name, like we're *friends*. You're even more perfect in the flesh.'

Yes, Darcy is super-pretty, and even more petite than she looks on screen. But I wouldn't call her perfect, exactly. There are dark brown circles under her hazelnut eyes, and she has thread veins on her nose and cheeks. She looks . . . well, a bit knackered.

'You're very kind,' Darcy says, simply, and even Liz seems to realise that bit of the conversation is over, and turns to the two blonde women from the Crab room.

'What brings you two girls here?'

'We're boot camp aficionados,' the blonder one says. 'How many is it now, Caz?'

'This is our ninth. Plus the Keralan yoga thing. But the guru on that was so *square*, we won't be bothering with that again, will we? All that way and not a sniff of tantric sex.'

'Such a waste,' Cat agrees. 'He was so flexible, I can only imagine what he'd have done if he put his mind to it.'

They cackle. 'We like to go home with a healthy glow.'

'And our hubbies don't need to know how we get it.'

Are they saying what I think they're saying?

Liz hasn't twigged. 'So do you have any advice for us rookies?'

'There's always a prize for whoever loses the most weight,' Cat says. 'I don't mind telling you *now* because it's too late for you to add ballast.' She fishes round in the pockets of her top and produces a pile of metal kitchen weights.

'It's all about the competition for you, then?' Darcy asks.

'Yeah,' says Caz. 'We're winners, not whingers. But don't worry. Next time you'll be prepared with weights of your own, right?'

'Next time?' Darcy says.

'Believe me, boot camp is addictive.' Caz smiles at us. 'Ordinary life seems a bit lacking in thrills afterwards.'

'Lovely,' says Liz. 'All girls together, with one thing on our minds.'

And Cat looks at Caz, who raises her eyebrows, and they dissolve into another fit of cackling.

9

Steph

The last time I felt this hungry, I was very, very small and very, very sad.

Twenty years on, and it feels like nothing's changed since I was an eight-year-old kid, crying myself to sleep after yet another day of horrible food and horrible failures. If this is what all week is going to be like – coming last in every race and activity – it might be better to give in gracefully.

But I can't drive home on an empty stomach, so I guess I'll have to sleep on it. And at least this all-consuming hunger takes my mind off the aches and pains the fitness test has triggered.

'So, girls, how are we feeling?' Edie is dressed in David Icke purple, and sitting in the Lotus position on a yoga mat in the ballroom.

No one answers, probably because we don't think she'd want to hear the truth.

'Too tired to speak?' she says, ever so slightly too brightly. 'Well, don't you worry, because in this session, we're going to tap into your hidden mental reserves. To train your sub-conscious to get what you want, using the power of the mind.'

The power of *my* mind is focused on food. All food. Any food. When we passed the kitchen earlier, I could hear someone chopping. They're working their way through something resist-ant – potato? No, I mustn't think of potato. *Carbohydrate is evil.* It'll be broccoli, maybe, or cauliflower. I doubt there's a tuber to be found in the entire hotel.

But my potato mirage has taken hold. I'm picturing chunks of it on a chopping board, alongside the rest of the ingredients for what . . . ah, a hearty beef stew, just the thing to serve on a bitter night like this. Onions browning in a pool of hot butter. Plenty of salt and pepper. Cubes of carrot, a stick or two of celery, a bay leaf, all sweating away gloriously in preparation for the main event.

Oh, and that main event: beef steak. Good, honest meat, in generous chunks, sizzling against a red-hot pan. Then the whole lot poured into a crock-pot to bake, a great bubbling volcano of deliciousness. I'd serve it with mounds of colcannon, greeny-white leeky-potatoey. You can *never* have too much potato.

That's food to spirit away the memory of cold sand against your thighs, and soaked socks inside your trainers. Kitchen *magic.*

'. . . as human beings, we default to the familiar. The same bad habits, foods, thoughts. Our brains become stuck in a rut. And if we travel the same way all the time, we don't notice the scenery,' Edie says sternly. 'We become lazy.'

Lazy? Lazy is a delicious word, almost as tasty as sirloin or soufflé or meringue.

But it's also shameful. As shameful as the rumble in my fat tummy, the rumble that's telling the world that nothing is more urgent than the need to fill it. Lazy got me where I am today: wincing as I got on the scales, puffing along the prom.

'What we do at boot camp is try to set up new ways of being, a whole road map of new routes to where *you* want to be: fitter, healthier, *sexier.* But we can't do it for you. Research shows it takes sixty-six days to establish a new habit, so your success doesn't just depend on our two hunky staffs. So let's do some work on your lives *after* boot camp. Stretch out on those soft yoga mats, and come with me on a journey.'

The idea of lying down alarms me more than the sit-ups. I tried yoga and Pilates – as Steve said, any exercise where you get to lie down should be perfect for a layabout like me. But the first time, people tutted at my un-holistic belly gurgles, and the second time I fell asleep during the cool down. It *had* been a hard week in the test kitchen – my boss pinned the entire Salmonella Stroganoff debacle on me *and* made me take over the Chicken Kiev tasting panel at no notice. But the yoga master didn't want to hear any of that after he had to shake me awake to get me out of his pristine studio.

'Visualisation is one of the most powerful tools I know. But to get into the right state, we must first switch off negative, unnecessary thoughts.'

Surely I'm too wired to drop off tonight, though? Edie has put on some wind chime music. When I was growing up, we had a neighbour with so many wind chimes that you couldn't move without triggering a celestial symphony. She felt sorry for Nigel and Robin and me, and would invite us in for lukewarm veggie dinners made of revolting meat substitutes. But I'm so hungry right now that even the thought of a TVP rissole makes my mouth water.

'I want you to imagine you're in the most beautiful garden you've ever seen. The soft chamomile lawn gives off the most delicious fragrance with every step, and ahead of you is a weathered stone staircase, with fifty steps . . .'

'It's fine, Steph. Really. Nothing at all to be ashamed of. If anything, I'm *flattered* that you were relaxed enough to nod off during my session.'

'Hopefully your advice went in subliminally,' I say, and Edie frowns before she can stop herself, so I know it really *isn't* fine at all.

As I head upstairs with Vicki and Darcy, she calls after us. 'Don't bother to dress for dinner, girls. We're very informal.'

We're giggling before we close the door to our 'suite'. It might be hysteria – but I'm beginning to feel quite pleased now that I don't have a room on my own.

'Did you hear her when she said we should look in the mirror and tell ourselves that we're beautiful and perfect as we are at least twenty times before breakfast?' Vicki asks. 'I don't have time to comb my hair most days.'

'I missed that part.'

'Yes, Steph, we noticed,' Darcy says. 'You've got a killer snore. I've slept with guerrilla leaders who make less racket.'

'When you say *slept with* . . .' I begin.

'In the same room as.'

'Oh. I thought newsreaders got waited on hand and foot. Five-star luxury at all times.'

'Some do. But I never set out to be *in front* of the camera. I wanted to report. Tell the truth. Not to get into celebrity nightspots, or marry a footballer. That's another reason why I'm a dinosaur.' She's laughing, but it sounds fake.

I try to reassure her. 'Hey, come on. We don't want WAGs reading the news. They might be pretty, but they don't have authority, do they?'

'Hmm. Where I work, authority is another word for *old*.'

'You're not old, though,' Vicki says, 'are you? On screen you look about thirty.'

'And off it?'

Vicki tuts. 'I bloody hate guessing games where we take off five years to be polite. Just tell us.'

'God, telling you that would be worse than telling you what I get paid.'

Vicki laughs. 'Tell me that instead, then. Even though it might make me hate you.'

The giggling stops. Darcy's bound to be on megabucks and we won't be able to forget her telephone-number salary.

'I'd rather talk about food,' I say. 'I wonder what's for dinner?'

'Let me find the menu.' Darcy rummages in her backpack.

'No! Reality won't be anything like as good as my daydreams,' I say. 'I fancy hotpot. Or maybe steak and ale pie with golden pastry on top and the soggy bit on the bottom. Plus a nice hot chocolate pudding with custard.'

'Or curry!' says Vicki. 'I do it in the slow cooker on Sundays, so it's all tender by the time we get back from my parents' or David's. Though Alastair – that's my eldest – won't eat rice since he went fishing with his granddad. He thinks rice looks like maggots. So he has it with chips. *Lush.*'

'I love Sunday brunch with friends.' Darcy lies down on her bed, clearly relieved that we've moved on from salary or age comparisons. 'All the newspapers, obviously. Eggs Benedict, with fresh hollandaise the colour of sunshine. Oh, and tomato juice with so much Worcester sauce it almost goes black. Hot Turkish coffee. Phone on silent. Bliss.'

'How long has it taken for us to begin obsessing about food?' I ask.

Vicki looks at her watch. 'Less than four hours. It's going to be a bloody long week.'

No hollandaise. No eggs. Not even a glass of tomato juice.

I'm lying in bed after dinner, trying to control my volcanic stomach through a combination of willpower and shallow breathing. Windy Hill? Too bloody right.

Beans. That's what we got. A bloody great pile of beans on a chipped brown plate. Oh, sorry, let's not forget the half teaspoon of pearl barley to go with it. The menu says the dish of the day was *Chilli sin Carne*, but there wasn't nearly enough chilli to balance the gluey pulses. No fat, no flavour, no fun.

And the Spicy Apple Surprise? If there was a Society for the Prevention of Cruelty to Fruit, it would be launching an inquiry.

I hear another eruption, but unless my belly has learned ventriloquism, it's coming from Darcy in the corner. You can be as cool and elegant as anything but no one can digest oligosaccharides without sound effects.

Apart from our innards, silence reigns. It's not nine o'clock yet, but there's nothing else to do at the hotel. And it's getting colder. Before I took refuge under the extra-heavy blankets, my breath made vapour trails in the air. There's a wall heater, but all it does is make the room smell of burned dust, and something else that I've been trying to identify since lights out . . .

Ah. *Now* I remember.

It smells of loneliness.

Not to everyone, I guess. But to me, it's the unmistakeable smell of a wintry dormitory where an eight-year-old me is trying to cry herself to sleep without waking up any of the other girls.

Whatever shit there is in my life, at least I never have to go back *there* again.

The Big Fat Boot Camp Blog, in association with *Gossip!*

Dateline: 10 p.m., Sunday, Devon

Time to introduce our *Gossip!* correspondent and competition winner Vicki Adams, who is going to be reporting all this week from an exclusive luxury boot camp in Devon.

Mum-of-three Vicki, aged thirty-three, has left behind hubby David and her *other* three boys, eight-year-old Alastair, Murray aged six and four-year-old Rudy, to change her life – and her shape – for good. Vicki was nominated for boot camp by big sister Chrissie, who says, 'Vicki's been looking after other people non-stop for the last eight years. Everyone calls her Vix the Fix because she can't stop herself sorting things, helping out. Well, I thought it's her turn to have some pampering time.'

Well, we at *Gossip!* don't want to make too many predictions, but running round after the four men in her house might be a holiday compared to what's in store for Vicki . . .

After her weigh-in tonight, Vicki told us she's hoping to lose the first of three stones she wants to shift to get bikini-ready for this summer.

'I need to lose a lot of weight, for my kids' sake as much as my own. I'm going to give it one hundred per cent.'

The hard work begins tomorrow at 5.45 when Vicki will be embarking on her first dawn run. She'll be video-blogging all week – so you can get all the insider info on boot camp from the comfort of your own sofa.

Wish her luck, readers. We've got a feeling she's going to need it . . .

Day 2: Monday – or, as it's known on boot camp, Moanday

How you'll be feeling: horrified when that alarm clock goes off, or the staffs bang on your door. But excited too – your first full day of boot camp.

05:45	Parade and morning run/fitness kick-start
07:30	Breakfast: Power Porridge, Wake-up Tea
08:30	Snakes and Ladders
12:30	Lunch: Sensational Salmon with Yummy Yam
13:30	Human Obstacle Race
16:00	Ab Fab Abs and Quacking Quads
17:00	R&R
18:00	Dinner: Curry Night! Pineapple Surprise.
19:00	Talk: The Miracle of Massage with Frank 'Magic Hands' Walton

Please note all activities and meals are subject to change due to circumstances beyond our control

10

Vicki

Something's wrong.

Really wrong. It's too quiet.

My eyes pop open. Darkness. I reach out for David, but there's only cold air where his big warm body should be. My heart's racing.

And I'm aching like the boys have used my body as a bouncy castle again.

Then I remember.

Boot camp.

The boys are safe and sound with David, plus Chrissie on speed-dial in case of emergency. And I am on my lonesome for the first time in eight years.

No. Not quite on my lonesome. Steph is snoring in her corner. And I can just about see Darcy the newsreader by the door. Her bedclothes are all scrunched up in her fists like Rudy's are when he's fighting dragons in his sleep.

Shouldn't be thinking about home. Except the boys have been slap bang in the centre of my life for so long, it's hard not to be scared something will happen, without me there to look after them. But they're tough little boys, and as for me, well, there was a Vicki before they came along, and she still must be there under those spare tyres. That's what Chrissie says, anyhow.

I scrabble round on the bedside table for my phone: I can't even switch on the smart-phone the magazine gave me to record my video diaries. Can't get much of a signal on either, but I do seem to get texts *eventually*.

Yay! There's a little envelope in the corner of my screen.

TO THE BEST MUMMY IN THE WORLD. AND BEST WIFE TOO. COUNTING DOWN THE DAYS. BUT ENJOY YOUR TREAT. LOTS OF LOVE, THE BOYS

I hold the phone to my chest, like it's actually them. The message arrived at midnight, though I bet it was sent before the boys' bedtime.

I check the time now: quarter to five. It doesn't feel *that* much worse than six fifteen. Normally I get woken by three little people leaping onto the bed. I used to love my lie-ins, but I've trained myself to be an early bird since the kids came along, and now I'm awake I won't be able to drop off again.

Can't get up, either. I'm not built for tiptoeing.

Though I might be built for running! Who knew? I came fourth in yesterday's race, only just behind Natalia the bride and a stick insect triathlete called Karen. All right, so by the time I crossed the finishing line, I looked like Miss Piggy having a hot flush, but I *did* it. Dunno who was more gob-smacked: me, or Staff Pepper.

Gutted for Steph, though. Almost slowed down, so she wouldn't feel crap. But Chrissie told me before I left that this week was all about *me*.

'You're not to solve anyone else's problems. Or interrogate them.'

'I don't *interrogate* people. I want to help.'

'Maybe you won't believe me, but some people don't *want* your help. Forget Vix the Fix. Focus on fixing yourself.'

'Since when did I need fixing, Chrissie?'

She gave me one of her *looks* then. The ones I hated when I was little because I knew she was about to pull my hair. One good thing about sons: no hair pulling. They go straight for the punch.

Thing is, without someone to fix, I start thinking. And when I start thinking . . . It was the same when we were meant to be visualising last night. I wanted to put those mats in straight lines, top up the water jugs.

Bored. I move over in bed, see how much it creaks. That's not *too* noisy. I swing my legs out to the side, and my feet hunt round for slippers in the dark. I panicked when I thought I'd forgotten them last night but there they are. Soft and warm, like home.

When I stand up, Darcy gives a little sigh, but then turns away in her sleep. I see the moon through the window, a fat ball of cream cheese in a blackberry sky. It looks freezing out there, and once I've stopped worrying about making a noise, I realise my feet are the only things that are warm. The rest of me is all goose-bumpy.

I *need* tea. Not slimming tea, but builder's, the teabag squeezed so hard it nearly bursts. Might be my only chance, too, while the rest of the house is asleep.

I'm in the corridor now, all ancient wood panelling. And ancient woodworm too, probably. Could this be a haunted house? I never believed in ghosts until, well . . . I still don't, not really, though I wish I did. Might make it easier, somehow. Though can you have an afterlife if you never even had a life at all?

The stair groans underneath me. How old's the hotel? A hundred years, must be. I'm no good at history, but that's a lot of time for births and deaths.

Sometimes they're closer together than they should be.

I'm all goose-pimpled. Reach out to touch a radiator, but the metal's so cold it makes me worse, and breezes seem to whip up between the floorboards in the corridor. I go into the dining room where we ate last night. Still stinks of boiled beans in here, but the connecting door to the kitchen is locked. Sneaky. I bet I'm not the first to look for banned substances.

The dining table is already laid for breakfast but there are no ketchup bottles or jars of marmalade. God knows what they're dishing up later. It can't be any more horrible than dinner.

I look out of the windows. In the summer, this would be brilliant for a party. You could open those doors, let the kids run riot outside. But it's **grotty** in winter: there's ice *inside* the windows, making patterns on the panes like the Christmas decorations Rudy brought home from reception class. And those gales keep blowing up my pyjama legs.

Brrr.

There's a fox out there, its tail almost as long as its body. I hear Alastair's voice in my head: *not* tail, Mummy, it's a *brush*. He could be the next Attenborough, Chrissie says. He'd love it here: that fox is way better fed than the mangy town foxes. I hate them: they're always tearing our bin bags open and showing the world my boys live on ham sandwiches and pop, instead of paninis and Innocent smoothies like the other kids.

The neighbours look down on us. David says we only don't get invites to their parties and BBQs because the other kids in the close are all prissy little girls. But then I don't suppose I'd go even if I did get invited: he's away so much I'd feel like a spare part among all the couples.

Stop thinking about home. And tea.

I lean against the door to the garden – it swings open under my body weight and I only just keep my balance.

It's so bitter it hurts my throat but I go outside anyway. My footsteps are crunchy on the frozen grass, and when I look down, my pyjama bottoms are wet. I tell myself off in my head, like I do the boys:

*Look what you've done; you'll never get those dry now; you'll
catch cold . . .*

Bloody hell. Since when did I examine everything in my life
through this Mummy microscope? It's like my world's shrunk:
everything's tiny, whether I'm bundling together thousands of
pairs of mini football socks, or kissing better dozens of grazes
on bony little knees and tiny elbows.

I look up at the garden, and the not-quite-night sky. The
world is actually a giant place, Vicki Adams, and it doesn't
revolve around you, or Murray, Rudy, Alastair or even Dave. In
this ruddy great universe, you're tinier than tiny, no more
important than that fox, or a robin redbreast, or a snowflake
that will melt by morning. Nothing is under your control.

Should have cottoned on to that last year, shouldn't I?

My left sole tickles, like an insect has climbed into my
slipper. Alastair says human footsteps wake the earthworms in
the morning, tell them it's time to get up – that's why he runs
around barefoot, *in case I squash their heads with my shoes.*

Enough about the kids. Right now it's just me, Vicki Adams,
Vicki Coleman as was, and all the life below me in the ground,
and all the life above me in the skies.

And then, without meaning to, I remember the dead, which
everyone says I'm not supposed to, and I shiver, and I want to
go back to my bed—

'. . . what about that TV bird, then? She's fit.'

'Give it a rest, Pepper.'

The voices are coming from the side of the building, where
the kitchen is.

'Come on, Ryan, my son. You're not telling me you're
planning to live like a monk for ever.'

At first I'm not sure it really *is* Pepper talking, because his
voice is so different now he's not growling. Jovial, almost,
though he still ends his sentences with a bit of a shout.

'I'm not a monk. I just don't fancy any of them, if that's all right with you.'

And that must be Ryan. I don't think I heard him speak more than a few words yesterday. He has a soft accent, bit like the blokes off *Emmerdale*.

'Don't be a boring old fart.'

I hear Ryan sigh. Smoke drifts towards me. Which one of them is a smoker? Not exactly setting a good example, are they?

'People in glass houses, Pepper . . . go on. Remind me. When was the last time *you* got lucky?'

'Got my eye on those panthers this time.'

'*Panthers?*'

'Yeah. Panthers. Older women who like a seeing to from some young buck.'

'I think they call them cougars,' Ryan says, and they both laugh.

'Well, I don't care what they're called; those two blondes are well up for it. My only decision is which one to invite to share the red hot Pepper experience.'

'Why stop with one?'

'Both of them?' Pepper whistles. 'Hard work, boy.'

'Every real man's fantasy, isn't it?' Ryan says.

'Two women? Twice the hassle, more like.'

'No hassle. They're married; they know the rules. I thought they were rarer than unicorns, but looks like we've got ourselves some genuine Boot Camp Groupies.'

'They're here . . . for the sex?' Pepper sounds nervous.

'You'd better believe it, sunshine. And if you don't seize the opportunity, Foz'll be in there. And he doesn't put the hours in like you do, does he? Doesn't deserve fringe benefits.'

Foz? Who are they talking about now?

'Well, if you put it like that, I guess it's my . . . *duty* to give the customer what she wants.'

Ryan laughs. 'Shouldn't that be what they *both* want?'

'You sure you're not playing the game this time? Not that you have to do anything to get the girls flocking. They love that wounded soldier act.'

I shouldn't be eavesdropping, but it's too interesting to stop.

'Ha fucking ha. I'm a bit bored, I suppose. Like a conveyor belt, isn't it?'

'You *are* in a bad way. But maybe you look at it from their point of view, instead. You know that clumsy one? Dean? She's taken a serious shine to you. If you did *her,* it'd make her year. Her decade, probably.'

How dare he talk like that about Steph?

'Don't.'

At least Ryan's standing up for her.

'Hey, come on. You could shut your eyes. Think of England.'

'Pepper. Can you imagine what someone'd say if they heard you talking? Your career would be finished.'

'Career? Call this a career? Chasing fat birds round the beach?'

I hear another, deeper sigh from Ryan. 'Well, when you think where we've been. What we've done. Maybe there are worse things than chasing girls round the beach.'

Their laughter sounds bitter this time.

'At least this lot don't have weapons under their burkas. Right. Toast, then time to do battle again, eh, Ryan, me old mucker.'

I try to flatten myself against the wall in case they come back past me. But after what feels like hours, I smell toast. It might just be the best thing I've ever smelled in my life.

I creep towards the dining room and I can see their shapes through the frosted glass door to the kitchen. When they stick the radio on, I race to the stairs, hoping they don't hear me.

The boards creak again, but I make it upstairs without being chased by staffs or spirits. But back in our room, I'm spitting. How dare bloody Pepper talk about Steph like that? Though there's something else niggling me, something I can't work out till I climb under the covers to stay warm, and hear my roommates snoring softly.

Then I realise. Of the three of us, I'm the only one who didn't get a mention.

I might have a bum that has its own postcode, and a belly you could see from space, but men think I'm invisible.

I want to go home to the only four males on the planet who still realise I exist. I let myself imagine them tucked up in their beds. My little men, and my big bad trucker.

Don't worry, Chrissie. I'm going nowhere. I know the rules: no pain, no gain. I just never knew homesickness could hurt almost as much as labour.

11

Vicki

This bloody weather would make a polar bear want a hot water bottle, but at least it means no one but the other boot campers will see me in my workout gear. You'd have to be mad to be outside at five forty-five on a morning like this.

Mad. Yeah. That sums it up.

As we line up in the car park, we're wearing so many layers it looks like we've all come down with our bedclothes still wrapped around us.

Except the *panthers*. They're hotter than dancers in a rap video. Caz, the mousier one, has so much spray keeping her hair in place it could lift weights on its own. And Cat looks like a sports car in that silvery all-in-one. If Pepper gets his wicked way with her, I guess he'll find out just how fast she goes . . .

When the staffs step out of the door, the atmosphere changes. We straighten our backs, stamp our feet together, try to work out where to stand.

'Not bloody fast enough. What a **bloody MESS!**'

Pepper looks like he's found a half-eaten cockroach in his cornflakes.

No. If I think about cornflakes, I'll faint from hunger. We don't get our breakfast till *after* our morning run.

'Get in two ranks. If you remember what a BLOODY RANK **IS**.'

I remember one thing: it makes sense to be in the back row.

Trouble is, everyone else does too, so there are more sharp elbows being used than in the Primark sale. In the end, we organise ourselves into two very sloppy lines, facing Pepper.

'Stand to attention while we count you, or there'll be extra press-ups.'

Ryan counts on his fingers, then shakes his head. 'Nine.'

'Have we already lost two?' Pepper says, with a slight sneer. 'Who's missing?'

We look up and down the lines, trying to work it out. Has someone already done a runner? They might be in a motorway cafe right now, enjoying a full English, complete with fried eggs and crispy bacon.

Definitely *do not think of a full English.*

Eventually the sweet old lady shoves her hand in the air. I overheard her telling the Crabs her name was Agatha, 'as in Christie'.

Pepper nods.

'I think it might be the bride? And the bride's mother?'

Natalia and her 'embarrassing' mother. Wouldn't like to be in their trainers right now.

'I'll go and knock them up, shall I?' Ryan says, and Pepper sniggers.

I guess all blokes talk like Pepper on the quiet. David and his mates turn the air blue on their truck stops, and my three will be like that sooner or later. Daughters aren't like that, of course.

Stop it.

'At ease,' Pepper says, and people begin to stamp the ground, to stay warm.

'You OK?' Steph whispers to me. 'You look really worried. You shouldn't be. You were brilliant in the test yesterday. Born to run!'

The back door bursts open, and the bride-to-be falls out, her mum right behind her. They've both got the same grumpy expressions. The resemblance makes me sad for some reason. My boys all look like their dad.

'Sorry,' Liz says, 'I couldn't get her out of the bathroom.'

'Rubbish!' Natalia snaps back. 'She spent forty-five minutes in there. I hardly had time to brush my teeth.'

'You both look gorgeous, I'm sure,' says Pepper, 'but your beauty treatments have earned the group an extra fifty press-ups on the beach.'

We groan.

'Sorry,' the two women mumble.

'Sorry doesn't bloody well cut it,' Pepper says. 'Any more time-wasting and there'll be another fifty. Two files, steady jog down to the beach before you all freeze your little titties off.'

Steph winces as we turn towards the sea. 'I really don't want to think about him noticing the size of our titties, do you?'

If only she knew . . .

I am queen of press-ups. There must be Popeye arms under all my fat. I guess I got them carting around buggies and wrestling with wriggling boys.

While Steph and the others are whinging, I'm getting on with the punishment. I count to fifty and I could probably do another ten. Sit-ups aren't quite such a doddle. Do I even have any abs left after four pregnancies in eight years? But I soldier on despite the pain. No point wasting energy complaining.

'Slacking, are we?' Pepper barks at me as I lie panting on the grass. I'm quite surprised he notices me, really. Not like I'm *fit* or fanciable.

'No. I've done my fifty.'

He looks dubious. 'On your feet for some star jumps, then. Don't let your heart rate drop.'

Ow. Star jumps and fat birds don't go together, but I keep

going. If my doctor could see me now . . . Actually, he'd be cross. He advised only *gentle* exercise.

I look up after ten, catch Pepper watching. He nods with a half-smile, and I feel stupidly happy that he approves. It's so weird to feel like my body can get something right – after it failed me so badly before.

The groans are turning into whimpers. Only me, Darcy and Agatha have kept quiet. The panthers are making a hell of a racket, which is weird, when you think how fit they are. Then I see Pepper and Ryan exchanging a look, and I realise the girls are putting on a performance that's more porn film than parade ground.

'On your feet, then, you lot, and we'll take a gentle run along the beach before we head back up for breakfast,' Pepper shouts. 'Not that any of you deserve it.'

What about me? *I* deserve it.

We hit the beach in two files, struggling to keep up the speed as we sink into the sand. Steph's next to me, and she looks traumatised.

'Not . . . sure . . . I . . . can . . . manage . . . six more . . . mornings . . . like this.'

'Only five, now.'

'That's . . . not . . . much better. Everything . . . hurts.'

'You'll stay the course,' I say. 'I'll make sure. The hard bit was getting here in the first place.'

Dunno if I really believe that, but I'm ace at talking people into stuff they don't want to do, whether it's going to school, eating carrots, or working out in sub-zero temperatures.

We're heading towards the firmer sand right by the water. Thud, THUD, thud, THUD, against the damp ground. Pepper's platoon. Though shouldn't we be singing a song, like on *Private Benjamin*?

73

I look up, just as a first ray of light breaks through the flat pink sky ahead of us.

'Steph. Look.'

Her face is screwed up in pain, but she tilts her head anyway, and the light falls on her skin and hair, and just for a second, she looks all glowy, like an angel.

I didn't believe in angels before. But now I really, really hope they exist.

'Wow.'

'There are plus points to these dawn runs, eh?' I say.

'I guess,' she grunts. 'Though . . . I'm . . . more of a . . . cocktails and crisps at . . . sunset . . . girl, myself.'

'Ha. Once you've had kids, you'll eat crisps any time of day,' I say. 'But then I guess that's why I'm in the shape I'm in.'

There's an ambush lying in wait back at the hotel.

Luckily, we're not the targets. Pepper and Ryan are.

'Bloody wasters. You promised you wouldn't be late this time.'

A short, scowling woman wearing an apron with a stripper design on the front is poking Pepper's chest. Instead of fighting back, he's backing off.

'What's the point in me getting up at the crack of dawn if you're going to show up late?'

Ryan holds up his hands like a boxer, as though he's expecting to be punched any minute. 'Sorry, Hel, it won't happen again. First morning, it's hard to tell how fast they're going to go.'

'Well, don't come complaining to me that the porridge is cold,' she says, and stomps back into the kitchen.

We take our seats. The panthers are on the end, and I join them. Still can't quite believe they're 'groupies'. Wouldn't hiring a gigolo be a lot less effort?

'You two hardly got sweaty this morning,' I say.

'We're old hands,' Cat says and then gives a filthy laugh.

'Doesn't all this exercise get boring?'

Caz shakes her head. 'Nah. It's addictive. I'm on a permanent high, me.'

The cook comes in. She spins cereal bowls along the tables, like a barmaid in a Wild West saloon.

'Though the food isn't addictive at all,' adds Cat.

We peer into our bowls. Right at the bottom, like someone hasn't bothered to soak the bowl before washing up, is a grey layer. I only know it's porridge because that's what the cook shouted earlier.

'This has to be a candidate for the worst boot camp breakfast we've ever had,' says Caz.

Ryan and Pepper come into the dining room, grim-faced.

'Though the scenery is some of the best we've seen,' Cat says.

'You think they're good-looking?'

'Remember the rhyme about Jack Sprat could eat no fat, and his wife could eat no lean? We're like that with men. I like cute, she goes for rugged,' Caz says. 'Lucky, really. Otherwise we'd have fallen out a very long time ago.'

'You won't . . . do anything about it, though?'

They look at me like I'm stupid. 'Why not? They're game. Perk of the job.'

I glance at their hands: neither is wearing a ring, though both have a band of pale skin on their left ring fingers. 'You're married, aren't you?'

'Nineteen years,' says Caz.

'I've served seventeen,' Cat says, 'which I think means I have earned myself time off for bad behaviour. A little flirtation works wonders to pep up a stale relationship.'

'So that's all it is? Flirtation?'

They exchange a look. 'How long have you been married, Vicki?'

'Eleven years.'

'And you've both been *good*? That whole time?'

'Yes! David was my first love. We're really happy.' Well, he is. And it's not his fault if I'm not.

Caz shrugs. 'Good for you. Still do it as often as you did?'

I blush. 'We've got the kids now. But when we get the chance . . .' I smile when I remember how we tried to sneak some *special* time together before I left on Sunday, while the kids played on the Wii. And how we ended up falling asleep before we'd taken our socks off. 'We still fancy each other. Despite the fact that, well, I'm never getting into my wedding dress again, let's face it.'

Cat pats my hand. 'Good on you, sweetheart. But what happens on boot camp, stays on boot camp. It's harmless. Plus –' she glances up at Pepper and Ryan, who are gazing glumly into their bowls – 'anything we can do to cheer the boys up should have positive effects for the rest of us. We're morale boosters. Like Vera Lynn in the war.'

Caz nods. 'And we girls need our own morale boosting now and then. There's nothing like seeing *that* look in a bloke's eyes to make you feel fabulous again, Vicki.'

'I—'

'Vicki? I'm looking for Vicki.'

A burly bloke with a beard and a donkey jacket walks in. I stand up, flustered by what the panthers have said. 'That's me.'

He beams, comes over to me and shakes my hand: his is so big it feels like I'm being greeted by a bear. 'Hello, gorgeous. I'm here to take your picture.'

12

Steph

I was looking forward to my porridge till the photographer showed up.

'Don't mind me, ladies. I won't be stealing your grub. I've already had breakfast at the Little Chef.'

Little Chef. I can picture the cheeky chappie with his white hat and necktie, holding up a plate of something *deep-fried* . . .

What the hell? I hate the food at Little Chefs.

As the photographer takes out the camera, something unbelievable happens: I completely lose my appetite.

My fear of cameras is why there are no pictures of me past the age of ten (well, except *those* ones, and Steve swore he'd destroyed the memory card). Even at work, when they arranged a photo shoot for the corporate website, I organised a factory visit that day. So next to my name, there's a close-up of my prize-winning banoffee pies.

I slink along the table, taking my porridge with me, and watch as the photographer prepares to take Vicki's picture. She's smiling, confident despite her weight. Well, she should be: she's gorgeous. And she doesn't have time to obsess about her appearance the way I do. There's no Compare-o-meter running *her* life, while I have a kind of mirror mania.

Steve noticed it as soon as we got together: I was always checking myself in shop windows, or the back of spoons.

'You look exactly the same as you did ten minutes ago,' he'd tell me. 'Your eyes are still green and your cheeks are still red and your mascara's still smudged.'

But that's not why I look. It's more a kind of morbid fascination. Everyone in the world, except me, has something gorgeous about them. Vicki has an adorable smile, and even loathsome Staff Pepper has gloriously lush black hair.

Not me. I've got the right number of eyes, ears, lips, cheekbones, but they're thrown together like a Picasso painting. When I look at photos of Mum and Dad on their wedding day, him chunkily handsome, her slender and drop-dead gorgeous, I think the odds against them making a misfit like me must have been a million to one.

Darcy sits down next to me, out of camera range. 'What do you think of breakfast?'

She has different reasons for staying out of the pictures, I guess. Her glossy bob has gone all ratty and without make-up her skin is puffy, as though she's allergic to something.

'Haven't tried it yet.' I pick up my spoon – fighting the instinct to check my face in the back of it – and scoop up some porridge. I'm not big on porridge, unless it's been made with cream, topped with raspberries and honey, so the berries explode in your mouth. But here goes . . .

'Oh my God.' It tastes of a firebombed building. It's cold. And the texture is frogspawny, with flakes of incinerated oat. Somehow I manage to swallow it.

'Disgusting, isn't it?' Darcy says. 'I've tasted better in a famine relief camp.'

I put my spoon back in the bowl. The others are making the same grim discovery. Vicki is holding the spoon up to her mouth as the photographer flashes away, but judging from her broad grin, she hasn't actually *tasted* it yet.

Only Staff Pepper and Staff Ryan are still eating. They got bigger bowlfuls than us, but they're just shovelling it down.

Perhaps they're too scared of the chef to complain. Ryan's shoulders are slightly hunched over the table, and the food's disappearing. He reminds me of something, only I can't quite think what.

A dog barks outside, and we hear its paws skittering against the door.

'Karma! Karma, shhh. You shouldn't go in there.' Edie's high-pitched voice is coming from the entrance hall, but the dog keeps barking and butting the door until it gives way.

I was expecting something bigger than the snow-white terrier that races in. He's a jowly Scottie dog, with a diamante-studded collar slightly too tight for his thick neck. Karen the runner leans down to fuss over him, but he snaps at her hands.

'Do you think he might want our porridge?' says the older lady, Agatha.

'He's welcome to it,' Darcy whispers, as four bowls are placed on the floor simultaneously.

'Karma, you know you're not supposed to eat human food, bad boy,' Edie says. But she doesn't sound very fierce and the dog ignores her and begins to sniff around the food. 'Karma is my baby, girls. I keep him away from guests on the first day, as he hates change. He has a very sensitive spirit. And an even more sensitive digestive system,' she adds, eyeing the porridge suspiciously.

His digestive system can't be *that* sensitive, as his belly is as round as a barrel. He sticks his nose into Agatha's bowl, before jumping backwards with a whimper.

'What's wrong, Karma?' Edie races over to him. She finds another spoon and then tastes a little bit from a second bowl. We watch as she spits it out, then storms into the kitchen. The door slams behind her.

'Do you think this means we get another breakfast?' I ask Darcy.

She shudders. 'If we're really, really unlucky, we might get seconds.' Even Ryan has looked up now and, noticing the dog's distress, he's peering at his own empty bowl with some trepidation.

There are raised voices in the kitchen.

'. . . but I wouldn't feed that to Karma . . . I told you before, healthy food doesn't have to mean . . . well, I'm sorry you feel like that, Hel, but . . .'

'I can't decide if it'll be bad news or good news if they sack the cook,' Darcy says.

Finally, Edie emerges, her face a very unholistic shade of puce. 'Sorry about the porridge. There'll be a *fresh* batch shortly. An army marches on its stomach, after all.'

She scoops Karma up in her arms but he's not having any of it, his paws scratching her skin. She puts him down again.

'All right, Mummy has some delicious treats for you, hungry boy.'

She reaches into the pocket of her stretchy yoga tunic, and takes out a foil pack of smoked salmon. My mouth begins to water. She tears off several pieces and drops them into an empty bowl. Karma sniffs, then tucks in noisily. Edie drops down to ruffle his hair, but he growls threateningly.

That's what Ryan reminded me of when he was eating. An animal so worried someone else wants their food that it wolfs it down without tasting a single mouthful.

It makes me want to cook him a meal he'd linger over.

Yeah, *right*. Annie always says a woman who thinks the way to a man's heart is through his stomach is aiming too high.

After more porridge – an improvement only because it tastes of nothing – we head out of the gates.

'Right, campers. You're about to get your first view of

something that will dominate your lives this week and HAUNT YOUR NIGHTMARES long afterwards.'

We're well away from the hotel grounds now, in a flat field surrounded by bare wintry trees. In summer, it'd be a great spot for a picnic. I imagine a wicker basket packed with Ingram's goodies: our Heather Moor smoked salmon, Taste the World rye bread, Tuck Shop Treats potted cheese, and individual Pure Indulgence raspberry trifles with white chocolate custard. Plus Pimm's, obviously. Anyone who thinks own-brand food is crap would be instantly converted.

But it's more mud than meadow today, so no picnic. The only people who'd choose to hang out here would be flashers . . . or boot campers. And now we're looking for the thing that is going to haunt our nightmares.

'No guesses? Follow me.'

We walk with Pepper, towards the edge of the cliff. Blimey. I hadn't realised how far it is to the shore below. All that's stopping us toppling to our deaths is a rotten fence that's held together by a splinter and a prayer.

'Into two ranks, everyone. So you can get a good view.'

We make a shambolic attempt, whispering as we try to remember the difference between rank and file. A vein is twitching above Pepper's bad eye. Finally, someone whispers that a rank is a line, and then we get in position, still giggling.

He sighs. 'That was pathetic. Next time, do it faster,' he says, but there's a half-heartedness about his fury. 'Right now we have more important things to do. This is what we call . . . the Ladder. Though you could also think of it as *your nemesis*.'

Running directly down the cliff-side is a set of steps that does look exactly like a window cleaner's ladder. The treads are so narrow that they're more like rungs, except your average ladder has, what, twenty rungs? This one has . . . I try to count . . .

forty, *fifty*, sixty, *no*, now they're blurring in front of my eyes . . .

'We've counted for you. It's one hundred and forty-four steps. Going down might give you vertigo,' Pepper says. 'But going up is a different experience altogether. Any of you ever climbed a mountain?'

Agatha, who looks like she should be running a knitting shop, raises her hand.

'I'm not talking a small hillock in the Cotswolds,' Pepper says.

'Nor am I. I was on an expedition in the Andes back in the eighties,' she says, matter-of-factly. 'Peru. Tackled El Misto, El Toro. Nineteen thousand feet each, if my memory serves me.'

Pepper gawps. 'Right. *Real* mountains. Tell us about altitude sickness.'

'Golly. Let me think back. It wasn't pleasant. Symptoms, um, nausea, light-headedness, shortness of breath. One of the gals lost consciousness.'

'Well, we might not be in a mountain range, but the way you're going to feel after a few trips up and down the Ladder will be very similar. On the positive side, it's usually where we get our first case of vomiting.'

That's positive?

'Jog lightly down, single file, then run on the spot till everyone's down. Oh, and Dean. In case you hadn't noticed, it's quite steep. And it involves steps. So try not to fall if you can possibly help it.'

I'm still at the front. Heights never bothered me before, but now there's nothing between me and a fatal head injury. I take a couple of steps forward.

'Dean?'

'Hmm?'

'Dean?' This time he sounds irritated. Very irritated.

'Yes?'

I hear Darcy's cut-glass whisper behind me: 'He wants you to say *Staff*.'

'For the last time. Dean?'

'Yes, Staff!'

'Don't think. Just DO!' His shout in my ear gets me moving.

I begin with my right foot, then left, right, left, right. I start to picture myself toppling over.

Don't think, DO.

I focus on the thumping footsteps behind me. We're a machine. One step after another . . .

Cool! I'm there first. OK, that's only because I'm at the front, and I'm only at the front because I'm the class dunce.

The last girl arrives, Ryan behind her. I notice his eyebrows for the first time. They're all . . . brooding. *Sexy.*

How hopeless am I? At least I'm already purple in the face, so no one is going to notice the effect he has on me.

Pepper sighs. 'Oh dear, oh dear. If you're like that going *down*, it's going to be a complete fucking shambles on the way up again. What do you think, Staff Ryan?'

Ryan shrugs. 'A very long way from satisfactory.'

Haven't they heard that the carrot is better than the stick?

'Let's see if you're still grinning like idiots when you've been *up* the Ladder for the first time. Turn about, then UP! I don't want to see anyone NOT running, or you'll *all* be doing it TWICE.'

Surely it's not fair to punish everyone for one person's lack of fitness? Especially if that person turns out to be yours truly.

This time, I'm at the back. I'm half the age of the climbing pensioner, and there she goes, effortless as a mountain goat, so I should follow her example and . . .

'Bloody well *GO*, Dean. I won't tell you again.'

I launch myself at the Ladder and try to focus on the trainers of the woman in front of me. They have an extra-thick sole that makes her spring up higher with each step. Whereas my new supermarket trainers have lead weights in the soles, and they're rubbing like they're lined with sandpaper.

Stop thinking. Remember to breathe. Try not to topple over.

Ahead of me: feet and bums. Can't even see the sky.

Ooh. Lungs empty. Legs so heavy. Breathe. *How do I breathe again?*

Ugh. What's that taste? Have I bitten my tongue?

In the distance – sounds like actual *miles* away – I hear cheers. One cheer, two cheers, three. People are making it to the top.

'Run, Dean. A leisurely stroll won't shift the fat off that mammoth **bum of yours!**'

Bastard.

Except he's right. All-butter shortbread, goose-fat double-fried chips, Gloucester Old Spot sausages buried in puffy, crispy toad in the hole. Only the finest ingredients have gone into fattening up my mammoth arse.

Stitch in my side like a red-hot poker. How many more steps?

Don't think, Do. This is what you need. This is GOOD for you.

Oh God, I think I can see the top. White flash of trainers is further ahead of me now, way, way ahead. Then, more cheers, HOORAY!

I . . . cannot . . . take . . . another . . . step. No way. Don't have it in me. Falling at the first hurdle. Steve was right. Back to my couch potato dinners for one.

'Come on, Steph. You're almost there. Keep going, keep going.'

The newsreader's voice, the one that announces radiation leaks and worldwide famine and global warming. But she's cheering *me* on. It's not a voice you'd argue with.

And there are more voices joining in and
And
And
And I'm at the top.
'I . . . did . . . it!'

Vicki puts her arm around me and it's like being absorbed into a laundry basket full of freshly washed towels.

When I turn round, even Pepper looks slightly surprised.

'Right, you lot. I've seen one-legged tortoises with blisters on all four feet move faster. Back down again. *If* you put more effort in I might think about letting you get a swig of water before we do it all over again. You first, Dean.'

I open my mouth to protest but realise it won't change anything. So off I go.

Once we're at the bottom, Pepper and Ryan make a big performance of whispering to each other. Pepper says something, Ryan shakes his head, Pepper shrugs, and then finally Ryan steps forward.

'Completely rubbish. But we'll let you off another run up the Ladder *only* because we're behind schedule after the porridge business. Don't expect to get away with that kind of shambolic performance tomorrow.'

Pepper shouts, 'Two files, follow me down to the shore.'

I think I might hate this beach by the end of the week: loathe its fine biscuit sand and its fancy fondant-coloured beach huts and the ice-cream cornet helter-skelter on the stumpy Victorian pier.

Pepper sets us off jogging round him in a circle. 'The bulk of your physical conditioning will take place right here,' he calls out. 'Now we've had a chance to take a look at you, we know there's not so much a mountain to climb as an entire bloody mountain range. Our focus is the three s's: strength, speed and stamina. One or two out of three is no good. It's gonna hurt, but pain is **weakness LEAVING THE BODY!**'

My body must be ninety per cent weakness, as even now I'm struggling to keep up. Running on sand is bloody hard. My wrist itches, and when I look down I remember my elastic band of positivity. If only I had the coordination to run *and* ping.

Ryan nods. 'We're not sadists. To help get the pace right, we're going to divide you into groups, according to ability.'

Uh-oh. No prizes for guessing which group I'll belong to.

He takes out a list of names. 'So, when I call your name step to one side, and keep jogging on the spot. Ste— um, Dean. Step to the right, please.'

OK. So we all instantly know everyone on the right is a loser. He calls out Agatha's name, plus Liz, the mother-of-the-bride, and a chunky posh girl who looks absolutely furious to be lumped in with the likes of me.

'The rest of you will do the tougher exercises. Remember, it's not where you start, it's where you finish,' Ryan says without conviction.

Pepper grunts and picks up a canvas bag. 'To help us remember, we've got some bibs. The fitter ones get green. The four of you –' he reaches into the bag – 'get these.'

He pulls out our bibs.

'You're joking, right?' I say.

'Do I look like I'm joking, Dean? It's purely to *motivate* you.'

The bibs are white, but attached to the front and back are red comedy L-plates. The kind women wear on hen nights. They might as well say D for Dunce. Or L for Loser.

If this is *motivation*, then I dread to think what his idea of bullying is. I'm not doing it.

I look at Agatha and Liz, hoping they might be up for a spot of rebellion too. But instead they pull the bibs over their heads, shoulders slumped. I'm sure it won't be the last humiliation I suffer here. Once I've got it on, I suppose I won't even notice it. I grit my teeth and pull the bloody thing over my head.

Ryan gives me an encouraging smile. 'Let's get moving again! Get back into the big circle and keep running.'

Everything either aches or rubs: my sports bra and my trainers are both giving me blisters. I try to focus on the sky, but it's dank and depressing.

'Now, on your backs, twenty sit-ups.'

All the other girls are in position already. I throw myself down. Ouch. I thought sand was soft, but that's like landing on concrete. Some lands in my eyes, which makes them water.

'Oh my God, this must be a record.' Pepper's leaning over me. 'Hey, Staff Ryan, we have our first case of the water-works.'

'It's not the waterworks; I've got sand in my eye.'

'Never heard *that* excuse before,' he scoffs and then Ryan's there, standing next to him.

'I'll be OK in a minute. It's just stinging a bit.'

'Maybe Staff Ryan should kiss it better for you, *mwah*, mwah,' says Pepper.

Ryan leans over me. His smoky eyes are narrow with dis-approval. 'It's really not good for morale, having someone moan this early. Keep going. It's harder when you stop.'

I try to do a sit-up.

'Come *on*, what's the hold-up?' Pepper demands.

'I'm not very good at this particular exercise.' I am starting to feel slightly victimised. 'But what do you expect? I'm an L-plate. L for lazy loser, right?'

Ryan sighs. 'Stand up.' His arms are crossed to show he's not going to help me.

I push myself up, feeling a thousand years old, my eye

smarting, my hands wet from the sand, my hair blowing in my face.

'Jog on the spot.'

I do as he says. Out of the corner of my eye I can see the other girls watching me. I wonder what the hell I'm doing here. Maybe some women get a kick out of being shouted at by handsome bullies. But I'm not one of them.

'See the groin over there.'

'*Groin?*'

'G R O Y N E – it's the bit sticking out into the sea. Flood defences. Run over there and do push-ups on the wall.'

The words *I can't do push-ups either* are on the tip of my tongue. I wish a freak wave would wash me away.

I ping my elastic band, as a last-ditch attempt to find some backbone from somewhere. Then I catch sight of Ryan's diving watch. Five past nine. I can't take another eight hours of this. That's as long as my working day.

Right now, I should be squashed into the Tube with three million other commuters. Someone usually offers me a seat because they think I'm pregnant, so I move carriages. And I'll treat myself to a latte and a croissant when I get to work to make myself feel better.

'What are you waiting for? Go on, try going outside your comfort zone for once.'

Comfort zone? Weird. Whenever Steve wanted me to do something I didn't, he'd talk comfort zones, too.

'It's just a bit of fun, honey bunch. Things get stale. Since you've put on weight, I've been forgetting how sexy you can be. We have to move out of our comfort zone.'

I stare at the camera. 'I don't think I want to.'

'Do you think I want to spend every Sunday dinnertime at your dad's house, Steph? This is the quid pro quo. Give and take.'

I see his hand reaching out to touch the record button. 'I don't feel good about my body, Steve. And I don't think this is going to help.'

'So, if you ever need reassuring that at least one bloke in the world fancies you, all you'll have to do is press play.'

The red light comes on.

'Did you hear what I said? Move!'

Thank God. I'm on the beach, not inside that suffocatingly hot flat on a Sunday afternoon that seemed to go on for ever.

Everyone's watching. I've got to do this, haven't I? Otherwise Steve will never see what I'm made of.

'Run, don't WALK.' Ryan's jogging next to me.

I position my hands on the bleached wooden surface, my legs out behind me. I couldn't do this yesterday. Nothing's changed.

'This isn't for my sake, you know, Steph,' he says, his voice softer now that we've got our backs to Pepper. 'You came here for a reason. It's our job to get you to achieve more than you ever thought possible. It starts in here,' he taps his forehead. 'Whether you think you can or you think you can't, you're usually right.'

For the first time, I feel someone's on my side, not against me. I breathe out and push up, trying to use my shoulders and my upper arms to force my body higher into the air.

But . . . I'm *moving*. Millimetre by millimetre. Slowly, very slowly, my arms are straightening and even though my muscles are burning, it doesn't feel like pain anymore.

It feels bloody brilliant.

13

Darcy

Lunchtime. Not exactly The Ivy, but then I'm hardly dressed for champagne.

Champagne.

Right now, I'd settle for Nescafé. Healthy living is giving me a crashing headache and a craving for booze and fags and bad men.

Though those are exactly the things that got me into this mess – and this boot camp – in the first place, according to Marian. She calls it tough love, but sometimes I wonder if she has a sadistic streak. I'm no worse than most of the autocuties.

I suppose the difference is, they're still too young for the effects to show on their vapid faces.

'Grub's up,' Vicki says.

'Why doesn't that news fill me with joy?' Steph mumbles.

The food arrives. The best I can say is that it looks better than breakfast. *Marginally.* The cook slaps the plates on the table. The salmon fillet is the size of a matchbox, and the baked sweet potato is hairy, like a dead mouse.

'There's salad too,' the cook says, plonking a Pyrex bowl full of iceberg lettuce and unevenly sliced cucumber in the middle. Is she smirking, or does she always look like that?

'I don't suppose there's any point asking for dressing?' Natalia – the world's most irritating bride-to-be – is sitting at my table, along with her mother, and Agatha the mountaineer.

'Apparently if we don't need to lose weight, we'll get as many hard-boiled eggs as we can eat,' Agatha says. 'You should ask for one, Natalia.'

'No. It's a small price to pay to look my best for my husband.' She curls her hair around her finger, like a five year old.

'Natalia is marrying the doctor who runs the clinic where she works,' Liz says. 'I think she's going to press-gang me into a facelift so I don't show her up in the photos.'

'Mother. Stop making it sound like I'm some kind of plastic surgery obsessive. It's a woman's right to choose.'

She makes it sound as though surgery is on a par with women having the vote in Afghanistan. 'What's the "in" procedure this season, then?' I ask.

'Breast augmentation,' she says.

'Boob jobs,' her mother translates.

'I'm sure Darcy understood me the first time. They never go out of fashion. Boyish figures only work on the catwalk. Men like curves.' She stares pointedly at my lack of cleavage.

I laugh. 'I've never had any trouble with men. What matters is being happy with what you've got, surely.'

'*I'd* pay good money for that,' Steph says.

'That's exactly my point,' I say. 'Clinics exploit people who need help with their self-esteem, not their breasts. You're pandering to their insecurities.'

Natalia smiles a sickly smile. 'You've got the wrong idea. It's a personal decision. I really admire women like you who embrace the aging process. Especially as you're in the public eye.'

Bitch. 'Wouldn't your fiancé be of more use helping people who are really suffering? Some of the things I saw when I was a war reporter really put our obsession with appearance in perspective.'

'*Actually,* he already spends three days a week reconstructing the faces of cancer patients. And why is it less worthy to spend time helping people love themselves more?'

I don't think it'd be possible for Little Miss Natalia to love herself any more than she already does. I sigh. These irritable outbursts of mine have become a bad habit since Afghanistan. You'd think what happened would make it easier for me to see what really matters, but instead I can't seem to get perspective on anything.

Steph looks awkward. 'I wonder where the staffs are?' she says.

Liz leans in. 'I heard them whispering about going for a burger.'

We gasp, scandalised. But as my salmon steaklet disappears in two tiny bites, the thought of a juicy quarter pounder with a side of chips isn't far away.

Outside, it's even colder than it was this morning. I think of Marian in her cosy office, all cow-hide sofas and velvet wall-paper, and resentment bubbles up inside. Though I think my irritation probably warms me up a degree or two.

'This afternoon, we're focusing on teamwork,' Ryan announces. 'If it can get men through the extremes of battle, then it should help you lot survive the week; am I right?'

Pepper and Ryan seem buoyed up by their burgers. 'You're starting as strangers but we're going to make you family,' Ryan goes on.

Which is fine. Until Pepper announces the teams for the 'human obstacle race' and puts me on the same side as the bloody Princess Bride, and her mother.

The rules are absurdly complicated, but focusing on them helps me forget the chill, and the injustice of being here, and the many irritating things about Natalia and Liz. We must leapfrog over, or crawl under, our team mates' bodies, working our way along the shore to the next groyne. It's completely mindless.

I suppose that's the point.

'Remember, don't let your colleagues down,' Ryan tells us. He's 'managing' us in team Bravo, while Pepper is in charge of the Alphas. Both teams have two L-plate girls as a 'handicap'. I still can't quite get over the borderline insanity of the L-plates, or how easily the women have accepted wearing them. Pepper's mad, but there's a kind of homicidal method in his madness.

Pepper blows the whistle. I'm leaning over, ready to be leapfrogged, with my hands gripping the back of my knees. Karen's the first to get going in our team: she has a runner's physique, lean as a whippet.

Thump! She lands on my back and grunts right in my ear, almost toppling me. She's heavier than I thought; it must be all that muscle.

'Sorry!' she shouts, before disappearing under Vicki's legs. The other Team Bravo girls are whooping now, led by Ryan. I do some token whooping too.

'Go, Karen, go KAREN!' we're shouting, and she's throwing herself under and over the other bodies, before stopping nearer the groyne, and adopting legs akimbo position.

I wait for the next person.

Shit. The next person is me.

'Go Darcy!' Vicki shouts, looking round at me.

I sprint towards Vicki, then throw myself to the ground to crawl between her ankles. It's a tight squeeze.

Natalia's my next obstacle. I've got to leap, not sure if I can remember how. The last time I did this was at primary school. In secondary school, it was all about lacrosse and hockey. I made the county team at both.

Instinct takes over, and I vault over Natalia, then crawl

through the gap Steph's made, and then leap over Liz, who has exactly the same petite proportions as her daughter, and finally there's triathlon girl Karen to squeeze under, before I sprint ten paces on and adopt the position, ready to be frogged again.

Hell. That was quite a rush.

As I get my breath back, I sneak a look to the right, where Team Alpha are slightly further ahead. It's only a game.

Yet, I'm surprised how much I want us to win.

'Come *on,* Natalia, you can DO it!'

She can, too. She's fast and determined as she leaps over me. That must have been the fastest circuit so far. Yes, she's young and bloody annoying. But I bet she was head girl: sporty, pretty, bright.

Takes one to know one, I suppose. From the first day at school, I was clearly the girl most likely to pass her exams, win the hockey cup, head for the best uni, do great things in career terms, marry well, produce more baby gals who'd end up at St Hilda's. No glass ceilings keeping us down.

Except, well, it didn't turn out quite like that for me. I avoid reunions in case my classmates did tick all the boxes. Somehow I suspect our headmistress would regard my failure to snag a city dealer husband and procreate as the biggest failure of all.

'This isn't a stroll on the beach, Greer. Shift yourself!'

I look round and see Liz is the next to run. Except it's not really running: her upper body stays upright and her legs kick to the side from her knees as though she's wearing stilettos and an ankle-length sheath dress.

'Come on, Mum, put some welly into it,' Natalia shouts.

She glares at her.

'Go, LIZ, go, LIZ!' Vicki starts up an encouraging chant, and we're all joining in.

Ryan's running alongside her. 'Liz, you're letting us down; work harder, remember there's no I in team.'

Her eyes narrow in irritation, then she lowers her head to try her first leapfrog. She manages – just – though she looks mortified at the indignity. She even brushes imaginary fluff from the front of her tracksuit bottoms.

'Don't you dare stop now, Greer.'

When she gets to Vicki, she looks like a horse about to refuse an obstacle. Then she tuts and moves slowly under those thighs, her face pinched with distaste.

'You're not trying, Liz,' Ryan shouts. 'Being ladylike won't win us the race.'

Her chin is beginning to wobble.

'Speed up. Look at the other team – Agatha is twice as fast and she's got twenty years on you.'

Liz stops running. 'How *dare* you talk to me like I'm an idiot!'

Ryan's speechless.

Liz carries on. 'I'm not an animal. And you have no manners. Part of being a woman is to maintain dignity, though perhaps I shouldn't be surprised that a soldier doesn't realise that.'

Team Alpha's members are rubber-necking now, though Agatha keeps running.

Pepper marches over to our side. 'Dignity? What about *loyalty* to your team members? They've worked hard, but it's beneath you to do the same, is it?'

Liz is silenced by that.

'You must have missed the bit about this being a *BOOT CAMP*,' Pepper carries on, his voice getting louder and his face redder. 'Which means that there are no special cases. There's plenty of time for dignity when you're in your grave, but our plan is to help you live a bit longer. If you don't like that, then you know what you can do.'

She pouts. 'What's that, then? What can I do?'

We wait. Liz and Pepper are so close to each other that you'd think they were about to *kiss*. It's stalemate but one of them has to blink first. I wouldn't be surprised if it's Pepper: Liz has a terrifying steeliness about her.

And then, suddenly, Liz takes a step back. She sighs. 'This is ridiculous. I'm a grown woman. I don't have to put up with this.'

Once again, she brushes down her clothes with those delicate hands, then turns to walk back towards the hotel. She seems to be mocking the staffs with her tiny graceful steps.

Agatha has given up on any pretence of running and we're all waiting for Pepper or Ryan to do something.

This is a turning point. If he lets her go, it could be a *Mutiny on the Bounty* moment. Yet, he can hardly frogmarch her back.

Pepper shrugs. 'One down, ten to go. Anyone else got a hissy fit they need to get out of the way, or shall we do what actually bloody well we're here to do?'

I watch Natalia. Will she go after her mother? But she stares at the sand.

'What are you all bloody waiting for? You won't get fit gawping at me, WILL YOU?' And he blows his whistle and Team Alpha start up again. Here in Team Bravo, we're not quite sure what to do now we're down one member, but then Karen starts running again.

'That's the attitude,' says Ryan. 'We're not quitters, we're winners. Team Bravo to victory!'

Liz is almost out of sight now. Is she leaving for good?

The idea of doing a runner myself is tempting. I could have a couple of facials and a body wrap at the Mandarin Oriental Spa and I reckon I'd look far glowier than I will after a week of this. Marian wouldn't know the difference.

I'd know, though. I made myself a promise two years ago that I'd never run from anything again. God knows, I've come close to running out of the studio, out of strange bars and strangers' beds.

But St Hilda's girls don't quit. I will take my punishment. I owe it to Heela to show I'm learning from the worst mistake I ever made.

14

Darcy

We are trying to be good losers.

'Better luck next time, Team Bravo,' Ryan says. 'We're down but not out!'

'I would just like to apologise on my mother's behalf,' Natalia says. 'She's never been a team player. But I'm not like her. Not at all!'

Karen pats her supportively on the arm. 'We know, mate. We're not going to judge *you* because you happen to share a few genes.'

Except it seems to me that Natalia and Liz are more similar than either of them would like to admit.

'We're the greatest, Alphas,' Pepper calls out, unsubtly, 'and that means we get our snacks first – while the losers clear up the equipment.'

The Alphas strut up the beach towards their leader, who dishes out bags so small they should hold cocaine. Ha! That'd get us moving.

'You don't think you should go after your mum, then?' I ask Natalia as we carry a tyre back to the storage hut.

'I'm no more responsible for her actions than she is for mine.'

'You're disowning your own mother?' I say, smiling to show it's a joke. Except it's not.

'She's not big on loyalty herself.'

'How old are you, Natalia?'

She stares at me. 'Nineteen. What's your point?'

Before I can answer, she drops the tyre – it only just misses my foot – and stomps off back towards the piles of kit.

Nineteen. Only a kid. Perhaps I shouldn't have been so hard on her at lunch. Except Heela was the same age and look what she achieved.

My BlackBerry vibrates in my pocket. Pepper told us anyone who brought their phone would be forced to throw it into the sea and then swim out to retrieve it. But having no signal in the house gives me the jitters. What if there's an emergency?

I take it out, as surreptitiously as possible. *Marian.* Checking up on me, I guess. I reject the call.

'You can have your snacks now, Team Bravo,' Ryan shouts, and the others race towards him, ludicrously excited by the prospect of a handful of linseeds or a segment of satsuma.

I dart behind one of the huts. There are *three* missed calls from Marian, and two texts. The first one was sent at two forty-four.

THERE'S BEEN A DEVELOPMENT RE YOUR NEW CONTRACT. CALL ME URGENTLY.

The second, twenty minutes later, is less calm.

CHANGES AFOOT AT THE CHANNEL. INDIA IS IN THE FRAME. I THINK YOU SHD HEAD BACK TO THE SMOKE. NOW!

As I read, a third text appears.

DARCY. I'D SUGGEST THAT IF YOU ARE AT ALL INTERESTED IN HAVING A JOB TO COME BACK TO, YOU SHOULD CALL ME NOW.

Jesus. It's Monday. I presented my last programme less than seventy-two hours ago, and India the autocutie is already staking her claim on my chair behind the presentation desk. How many blow jobs did she have to give?

Not that I'm in any position to lecture about *that*. It's just I've never used sex as a way to the top. Maybe that's yet another one of my mistakes.

I'm about to press CALL. But hang on a second. Marian's going to expect me to be in full throttle fighting mood, yet right now it all feels so very . . . distant. The idea of getting in my car and racing back to London to appeal to a hanging jury is exhausting.

'You haven't had your snack.' Ryan appears, holding out one of the tiny bags. I throw my phone back in my pocket, though I bet he saw it.

Maybe I need sugar to the brain before I work out what to do. The bag contains five of the smallest prunes I've ever seen.

'You can have a second packet if you like,' Ryan says. 'There's some left over.'

'Is that meant to be a special treat?'

Ryan shrugs. 'You're obviously not hungry enough yet.'

Hungry. That's what Marian wants me to be.

'You're in the top job, Darce, but no one stays up there without putting the work in,' she told me last week over lunch at 'her' table in The Ivy.

'Maybe it's a losing battle, Marian. Everyone knows the shelf life for a newsreader – especially a female one – is longer than milk but shorter than yogurt.'

'Well, you're making sure that your milk is souring faster than most.'

'My *milk*?' I laughed. 'You've lost me completely now.'

She laughed too. 'Maybe I have pushed the analogy to its limit. But you're not doing yourself any favours, are you? I can only keep a lid on things for so long.'

'I told you. I've calmed down. There won't be anything to keep a lid on anymore.'

'I'd love to believe you, Darce. It's not just about your career.

I care about you as a person, too. You've been through a lot. I still wonder whether you'd consider going back to the experts. Professional intervention is nothing to be ashamed of—'

'I'm going on the bloody boot camp; isn't that enough? Plenty of male presenters have gone on benders or fluffed the odd line without being sent off to do penance.'

'You and I both know the rules are different for women. Except if you get your shit together, you could break them, Darcy. You're the dream ticket. Credibility *and* glamour, thanks to your reporting from the field. Think about it. If you prove that female presenters don't have a best-before date, you're striking a blow for all women. Right?'

All women? It's too late for the woman who most deserved a future. 'So now I'm a feminist figurehead?'

She reached out for a bread roll, but then regained her self-control. 'See? You're driving me to carbohydrates, Darce, and I haven't touched them since the millennium. Look. I care about two things. You. And then my commission.'

'In that order?'

'Luckily the two are very closely linked. Well, unluckily at the moment, because you have a very cavalier attitude to both.' She took a gulp of wine. 'It's not like I haven't supported you, is it? Another agent might have let the wolves gobble you up.'

'I appreciate that.'

'Most of the editors are on your side too. They could have sacked you after your Maastricht meltdown. They like you, Darcy, but their patience is wearing thin. And there are plenty of others who are pushing the idea that you're not up to the job anymore . . .'

That stung. Even though she was right, of course. I wasn't up to anything after Afghanistan, except oblivion.

'The trouble is, Darcy,' she whispered after the waiter topped up our glasses, 'I think you've decided you don't deserve success. You don't even seem to like yourself very much.'

Don't I? The public thinks presenters have planet-sized egos, but Marian's right, in a way. Sometimes I do hate myself for reading other people's words, when I can write my own. Or for having my clothes chosen by the channel's personal shopper, or for going to their preferred hairdresser for a focus-group-approved newsreader's bob.

The autocuties are desperate to get their beautifully manicured hands on those 'perks'. Whereas I'd abandon the lot in a flash to go back on the road, where I did, very occasionally, make a difference.

'You all right?' Vicki's standing next to me.

She's got one of those faces that makes you want to tell her everything. But I wouldn't know where to start. And she might hate me for not being more grateful for my dream job. Probably not as much as I hate myself, sometimes.

'Just a bit light-headed. Have you had your prunes yet?'

She pulls a face. Thought I was starving but even I'm not *that* desperate. Agatha will take them off your hands if you don't fancy yours either. Reckons fibre is the secret of her youthful appearance.'

'I'd rather look like a prune than live off them.' I pause. 'I wonder whether someone ought to go after Liz?'

She nods. 'Yeah. When we lost, I was well pissed off with her but it's only a silly race, isn't it? We'll all feel like jacking at some stage this week.'

'I asked Natalia but . . .'

'Not much mother–daughter love lost between those two.'

'You could go, Vicki. You're good at saying the right thing.'

She pulls a face. 'Must be the practice I get stopping World War Three between my boys.'

'This is your one-minute warning, boot campers,' Pepper

bawls. 'Finish your prunes, then we're doing a last hour of circuits to give you abs of steel.'

Vicki smiles. 'Hmm. Somehow trying to find Liz sounds more tempting than ab circuits. Let's go and talk to Mr Team Bravo and see if I'm allowed to bunk off.'

She pats my arm, then heads over to Ryan.

My phone buzzes in my pocket again. This time I don't even read the message. Pretty much every decision made since Afghanistan has been wrong. Marian sent me to this bloody place. And now she wants me running back?

No. Not till I'm ready, and certain. Here on the beach, I realise she can't corner me, force me into doing what she wants, when she wants.

For the first time, when Marian says jump, I'm not going to ask, *how high?*

15

Steph

About the only thing I like about myself – apart from my wrists – is that I never bear a grudge.

So by the time we're lying on the dining room floor, doing stretches so extreme my muscles are about to snap like knicker elastic, the full-blown crush on Staff Ryan has returned. He was only pretending to bully me to help me see my potential. And it worked.

Steve used to do the same. Even though it stung when he said something *cruel to be kind*, I knew deep down he was doing it to help me. The same applies here. Press-ups, lunges, tricep dips; I did them all to Ryan's satisfaction.

With a bit of luck that's my 'breaking down' part of boot camp over with, and now he's going to make it his personal mission to build me up again. I quite like the sound of *that* part.

'Now sit down, let your legs flop out to the side so the soles of your feet meet. Feel the stretch in those inner thighs.'

The two women from the Crab suite can't take their eyes off the bulge in his camouflaged crotch as he demonstrates, but he doesn't notice. He seems so innocent. It's not just those big dark eyes, or the sticky-up hair that makes him look permanently surprised. It's the lack of status symbols. At Ingram's head office, everyone's obsessed with the size of their desk and the length of their title and the cut of their suit: status matters more than anything, especially to my bitch of a boss.

Whereas Ryan would go mad behind a desk – and he probably doesn't even own a suit.

He'd look fantastic in one, though.

I hear a series of loud sighs, and open my eyes. All the others are stretched out on their backs, breathing deeply. I really have to get myself an attention span.

By the time I am lying down, Ryan is telling us to get up again. 'OK. That's it. Don't fall asleep down there. Well done on your work today; you've earned yourselves some R and R time before dinner, followed by a talk from our martial arts coach and massage therapist. So don't miss that. Oh. Almost forgot. One more piece of good news. Monday night is curry night at boot camp.'

There's a half-hearted cheer: after what the cook did to the porridge and the fish, I don't think any of us are getting our hopes up for her chicken tikka masala.

When I stand up, the room's spinning like I've had three double vodkas. It's been the hardest day of my life. Eleven hours of exercise? That's more than I usually do in a year.

I stumble into the hallway, aware that I might be getting a reputation as the woman who is always falling off or over things. Vicki walks through the front door. Why did she miss the cool down?

'What are you up to now?' Vicki says.

'I ought to have a shower, but I don't have the energy to get undressed. Or we could go up to our rooms for a revolting herbal tea. Or maybe we should volunteer to help out in the kitchen?'

'The chef needs shooting, not helping.' Then she smiles. 'Hey. Do you play cards?'

I shake my head. 'Not for years. Mum taught me some games when I was very small, but I can't remember them.'

'You'll soon pick it up. Plus I'm desperate to have a nose

round. I didn't bring my ball gown with me for nothing, Steph. There must be somewhere round here where I can feel like lady of the bloody manor.'

We start our expedition on the ground floor, stopping for a quick sniff outside the kitchen (no promising smells, alas) then to the right of the staircase. There's a step up into a little hallway, carpeted in a pale blue sprigged pattern that would be pretty if decades of dirt were shampooed away.

The large door ahead of us has a ceramic plaque, with *Drawing Room* on it in a swirling typeface, the kind I'd use on packaging for artisan jam tarts.

Don't think of food.

The door's locked, so we go to look for Edie, who is sitting at reception stroking Karma's ears. The dog looks as grouchy as ever.

'Any chance we could have a shufty at your drawing room, Edie?' Vicki says.

Edie eyes her suspiciously.

'It's all right, I don't want to *nick* anything; I just have an interest in historic architecture!'

'It's, um, not looking at its best. Had a bit of a leak, so it's next on the list for redecoration.'

'After the bedrooms, you mean?' Vicki says. 'Only you said they were due to be done as soon as the right wotsits arrived from Italy.'

Edie blushes. 'After the bedrooms. Yes. Absolutely right!'

'In that case,' Vicki says, 'we'd love a go in your hot tub. Didn't the website say it could be enjoyed in all weathers, to *soothe our aching muscles with the healing power of aromatherapy-infused bubbles?*'

'The Jacuzzi is . . .'

'Don't tell me,' Vicki says, 'next on the list for refurbishment?'

'Ye-es.'

'You know, Edie, I reckon *Gossip!* magazine should know about all these refurbishments. I'm recording my blog later. Wouldn't want to mislead the readers, would I?'

Edie opens a drawer. 'All right. You win. You can see the drawing room. But it's probably not a place you want to linger.'

She's not kidding. As the long black key turns in the lock, the door opens with a Hammer Horror creak. It's dark inside, and there's a smell of damp at least ten times more powerful than in the rest of the house. Even when she switches on the light, it's gloomy as a crypt. Half the bulbs are missing on the chandelier and the rest are covered in authentic country house dust.

The shapes in the room get clearer as my eyes adjust. A huge dark-painted fireplace. Chesterfield sofas and chairs, plus a voluptuous chaise longue by the window: once upon a time this room must have echoed with laughter. Oh, and music. There's a piano by the wall, and a rusted music stand.

The wooden bookcases are vast, but empty – perhaps the books went mouldy? A card table and a drinks trolley suggest manly nights talking politics, with a butler keeping the port glasses topped up. And some paintings . . . portraits of a family, or families, mainly men with gloomy expressions and gloomier clothes. It's too dark to make out the details, to guess how long ago they were painted. Perhaps they're Edie's ancestors.

How can she shut them away like this, in a room that also deserves so much better? Edie must be raking it in with what she charges for boot camp. She's *definitely* not spending it on food.

'I keep the curtains closed, to stop the draughts,' Edie says, as Vicki walks towards the bay. 'Can't afford to heat this room.'

But the draughts are getting in anyway. Our breath forms wispy trails in the air which follow us around the room like tetchy ghosts. 'Can I open it? Just for a second?' Vicki asks, her hand touching a deep purple velvet curtain.

'If you like.'

Vicki pulls the drape back, and a cloud of purple dust flies into the air, drifting down onto the dark floorboards like wine-soaked snow.

'Bloody moths,' Edie says. 'They're impossible to get rid of.'

But we're not looking at the remains of the moths' curtain banquet, or even the rotten full-length window frames. We're looking at the view of the sea.

'Wow. That's gorgeous,' I say. Even though the sun set an hour ago, the moon is full enough to light up the landscape, from the frosty hills to the sparkling water below.

Edie steps closer, scowling. She puts her nose right against the pane, which mists up, so she has to clear it with her hand. She stares at the outside world for a long time and when she turns back to us, she's smiling. 'I suppose the view is rather special. Funny. Most of the time all I can see is decay. Work. *Money* that needs to be spent.'

Maybe I was too hard on her. I know how much it cost to get one modern window replaced in my flat. Even all the fees for this week's boot campers probably wouldn't pay for a single pane of that massive bay.

'The fire? Could we light it?' Vicki says.

Edie looks astonished, as though Vicki's suggested setting fire to the chaise longue. 'Um. I suppose there's no reason why not. I did get the chimneys swept last year when a squirrel got trapped. Though the logs are probably damp, so it may not light.'

'I'm an expert fire-starter. My granddad taught me when I was a kid.'

She kneels down in front of the fireplace. The mantelpiece is made from stone, stained black, with a hint of carved flowers under the soot. Edie takes a final look at us, seems to decide we're beyond help, then leaves the room.

'A fire's not going to make much difference, is it, Vicki? It's too cold in here to stick around.'

'Maybe. But . . . I know how wet this sounds, but I feel sorry for the room. We're not the only ones who need a serious bloody makeover, are we?'

I think my hands are turning blue – in this light, it's hard to tell. I crouch down next to Vicki, trying to ignore the pain in my over-worked thighs. She's building a kind of wig-wam from kindling.

'How long before it lights, Vicki? I'm worried they might find us here later, frozen in position like mummies.'

Vicki laughs, then sticks her hand into the chimney. 'That draught will save our lives in a minute; the fire'll catch in no time. All I need now is . . .' She lifts up an old cake tin which is sitting at the edge of the hearth, and opens it. 'Thought so. Firelighters. Granddad would say it's cheating, but these logs won't catch otherwise.'

She takes out what look like blocks of lard. They stink of petrol. 'Here goes.' She puts them onto the pyre, strikes two matches at once, and tosses them into the hearth.

We hold our breath. The first match sizzles, then dies out. We lean in closer, willing the second to light but also trying to catch any heat from its tiny flame.

'Come on, you bugger.'

Maybe it's Vicki's encouragement, but something magical happens. Just as the glow is fading, the white block ignites, a flash of flame so brilliant that for a moment the whole room looks like a different place. A *home,* not a haunted mausoleum.

Vicki smiles. 'That's the job. It's like riding a bike; you never forget how to set fire to stuff.'

Gradually, the flames begin to spread. 'How long before it gets *properly* warm?'

'A few more minutes. But at least no one's going to find us frozen to death. Now I'll teach you gin rummy to take your mind off the cold.'

'Do we get to drink gin at the end of it?'

She laughs. 'I wish. No. But we can dream.'

Gin rummy takes too much mental effort. So instead we settle for *Chase the old woman up the hill*, which should be the official boot camp game.

By the time I've grasped the rules, the fire has caught, and it's so bright that we switch off the chandelier and play by firelight. We're sitting side by side on one of the Chesterfields: the dark brown leather is cracked like a mummy's hands, but it's warm to the touch. Everything looks cosier. Even the portraits seem to have cheered up. I swear the granddad in the picture over the mantelpiece just winked at me.

Must be the lack of food making me hallucinate.

'Curry night, then?' Vicki says, dealing a hand of cards. 'Is that good news or bad?'

'I don't suppose it'll be very authentic. I'm guessing a chicken leg each, a few raw onions and a tub of curry powder.'

'That's my secret recipe,' she says. 'I suppose, to give her the benefit of the doubt, it's bloody hard making nice food with zero calories.'

I think about my day job: the thousands of tonnes of full-fat milk and cream and butter and sugar and eggs and flour that have been blended, whisked or baked according to my instructions in our test kitchen. The nineteen versions of four-cheese pasta sauce I sampled last week. Along with the dozen formulations of chocolate mousse that made me feel like a hot-air balloon.

I've always felt sorry for Jan, the home economist who does the low-fat and low-cal ranges. She seems so apathetic, much more like a scientist than a cook. You are what you eat. My boss once suggested a job swap: Jan and I were both horrified.

'Maybe it'll be more beans.'

Vicki pulls a face. 'Bleugh. Kidney bean tikka masala for us, right?'

'You know, tikka masala isn't really Indian. It's an invention. I know because I was meant to go to India, once, on a research trip. To find out how to make real curry.'

'Wow. What do you do, Steph?'

'I develop recipes for Ingram's. All the own-brand stuff. The ready meals, the ethnic ranges, even the cakes.'

Vicki's eyes widen as only a fellow glutton's would. 'You spend your days eating? Do you need an assistant? I love Ingram's cakes. What's the ad? *Irresistibly Ingram's?*'

I smile at the compliment, then point at my body. 'They really are irresistible. My cellulite is living proof.'

'Get away with you. But what happened to the research trip?'

'My boss went instead. But to be fair, she did show me her holiday snaps when she got back. Mainly of her on the beach, sipping gin and tonic. The research never got done. So I ended up spending a weekend in the kitchen of the six-times winner of Britain's Best Indian Restaurant. In Birmingham, just off Spaghetti Junction.'

'So what is the secret of a good curry? Apart from ordering a takeaway, which is what always works for me.'

'The spices. Serious curry lovers grind their own, so they're fresher. I experimented with all sorts. An old-fashioned pestle and mortar. A mezzaluna, which is a knife shaped like a half moon. But I ended up using a coffee grinder. Less elbow grease.

Hey, it's that kind of laziness that's made me the size I am today.'

'You put yourself down a lot, don't you, Steph?'

'I do it before someone else gets the chance.'

'Hmm. Don't you remember what Edie said about Positive Mental Attitude?'

'I was asleep.'

She laughs. 'I'd forgotten. Never mind. Tell me more about curry. It's weird, but it takes my mind off the hunger!'

'You sure?' I don't normally talk about food outside work: with Steve I felt ashamed to bang on about new ingredients and recipes, because it seemed like proof of my gluttony. Plus, he was only interested in food when he got the munchies from smoking weed.

'Definitely. I could never hear too much about curry.'

'All right, then. Um, the spice mixes are different in every region. My favourites are the sweet ones. Cardamom comes in wrinkly green pods, but when you split them open and crush the tiny seeds, the smell is like perfume.'

Vicki has put down her cards. 'It sounds bloody fantastic. Don't you dare stop!'

I nod. 'OK. Asafoetida is weird. It really stinks, but just the tiniest pinch in a curry transforms it. So, once you've blended your spices, you fry them in ghee, onion and garlic. The colour's amazing.' I look up at the fire. 'Not far off *that* colour. Flame red. I was working on the curry project through the winter and every time we fried up the spices, it felt like summer had come into the kitchen. A hot, steamy Mumbai summer.'

Vicki closes her eyes. 'Yum.'

'You add veg, meat, fish. But not the crap cuts. Curry spices mask cheaper meat, but I always fight for the best ingredients.

112

My boss prefers to pay celebs to put their mug shots on the packaging. But I hope customers are smarter than that.'

'Keep talking,' she murmurs.

I'm not embarrassed anymore: she seems genuinely interested. 'Chicken breast is so anaemic, right, but after a few seconds in the pan, it's the golden colour of the spiced ghee. You could serve it like that, simply fried.

'But we want smoothness, something creamy. Protein makes spices linger in the mouth. Coconut milk, for the southern curries. Or yogurt. Not low-fat; it'd curdle. But yogurt so thick a spoon will stand up in it. It melts into the dish. Like magic.' Vicki's eyes are closed. Maybe I've sent her to sleep.

Vicki sighs. 'Don't stop now.'

'Garnishes make the meal. Sliced coconut. Fresh onion chutney with leaf coriander. Used very sparingly. Oh, and how did I forget the rice? Basmati. Cooked by the absorption method, of course.'

'Of course. Wouldn't have it any other way,' Vicki giggles.

'Some people add a knob of butter or ghee to the pan just before serving, but it's one of the rare occasions where I don't actually believe butter improves a dish. Bon appétit.'

'That's it?' Vicki sounds disappointed.

'That's it. Weeks of research, hours of preparation, four minutes in the microwave, less than ten on the customer's plate. But it's worth it.'

Something's changed. I look up and see a shadow in the doorway. Tall. Spikes of hair silhouetted against the sharp striplight in the hall.

'Who's there?'

Vicki opens her eyes. 'Come on in; we're in the cosiest place in the house.'

Staff Ryan steps into the room. Somehow I already knew it

was him. Surely he didn't hear my curry monologue? Trust the fat girl to be talking about food.

'How long have you been spying on us, Staff?' Vicki asks. 'We do have Edie's permission to be in here. And Steph is telling me fantastic fireside stories, about the food she makes. She's a chef, you know.'

'Not exactly a chef,' I say.

Ryan's skin looks flushed in the firelight. 'Wish you'd give the cook a few lessons.' He looks away. 'Anyway, just a reminder that dinner is served in ten minutes. I'm the human dinner gong. Don't miss it, eh?'

He turns round and walks out.

'How weird was *that*?' Vicki says when we can't hear his footsteps anymore.

'What? He'd just come to tell us it's nearly dinner time.'

She shakes her head. 'No, he was there for ages, listening to your food porn.'

I blush. 'Don't be daft.'

'Why not? He's had years of bloody awful mess food, or those rations in foil packets, and here you are, all saucy and buttery and yummy. You could be the answer to a soldier's dream. Or any man's, come to that.'

You were always my dream girl, Steph, but now you've put all this weight on, no man could fancy you. You don't respect yourself enough not to get fat.

I try to shake the memory away. This is what I'm here for. To become Steve's dream girl again. To learn to say no to second helpings . . .

I stand up. 'You're very sweet, Vicki, but I think I'd only be anyone's dream girl if I stayed in the kitchen, out of sight.'

I expect her to laugh, but instead she walks over to me and puts her arms around me, hugging me tight. 'We've got our

114

work cut out with you, haven't we, Steph? But we'll get you sorted one way or another, and I'm not talking about your muscle tone. Don't you worry, love. My sister doesn't call me Vix the Fix for nothing.'

16

Vicki

Cabbage curry.

Currying cabbage. People have been locked up for less.

'I've eaten worse, my dears,' Agatha announces to the table now we've finally identified the offending veg. 'Though, admittedly, not much worse—'

Agatha looks up, past my ear. I turn round.

Liz is back. Her eyes are wide, almost frightened.

'I . . . uh . . . wanted to say sorry for . . . uh . . .'

Atta girl. Vix the Fix strikes again. When I found her in her car after the obstacle race, and launched into a long stream of unwanted advice, I wasn't sure she'd take it. She seemed so fragile, like if you took away the blow-dry and the perfect manicure, there'd be nothing left of her.

'Come on over, Liz. There's room here if we all budge up.' I pull a chair from the table behind me. 'And I'm sure the cook can rustle up another portion of cabbage curry. It's your lucky night, right?'

But she's waiting for a response from her daughter. Who is bloody-mindedly staring at the curry, the floor, anywhere but at her mother.

Makes my heart break a little bit, watching them. Like when Alastair and Murray fight, or when Rudy told me he hated me, because I made him go to bed earlier than his brothers. Except I knew Rudy didn't mean it. Whereas Natalia . . .

'Come on, Liz,' Agatha says. 'We've all forgotten about this afternoon. Haven't we, everyone?' Agatha tries to catch Natalia's eye and when that fails, she touches her arm, and whispers something in her ear.

I know what *I'd* like to whisper in Natalia's ear. Something like, *stop being a sulky madam and give your mum the benefit of the doubt.*

Natalia pulls a face, but then finally looks up at Liz. 'Come on, Mother. Your cabbage will go cold if you stand there much longer.'

'Here at boot camp, we look after your holistic needs as well as your cardiovascular ones,' Edie says.

She's put a bit of slap on, and looks about a thousand times prettier. Maybe I should make more of an effort for Dave. Last time I went looking for my trusty blue eye shadow at the back of the bathroom cabinet, I thought my memory was shot, as the colour was more green than blue.

Then I realised it was so far past its use-by date, it'd grown fungus.

'And the holistic therapy our campers look forward to most is provided by our massage guru – and martial arts whizz – Frank Walton! AKA Foz the Oz!'

Edie waves towards the door and Frank Walton *leaps* into the room like a Jack in the Box. Everyone starts applauding. I don't know why. Maybe because it's so obvious he's expecting it.

Hang on, though. Not quite everyone's giving him the big welcome. Staff Pepper and Ryan, standing at the back of the room, have their arms folded. And then I remember some of the stuff they said this morning, about someone called Foz . . .

Frank nods a thank-you, and the applause stops. He's tall and blond and he's dressed like a bloke from the Boden catalogue: smart jeans, soft navy jumper with a bright white shirt underneath.

Doesn't do it for me. I prefer my blokes rough and ready.

'Hi, ladies. Forget Frank. They called me Foz when I first landed on these shores and it's stuck.'

I glance at the staffs again. They look like Rudy and Murray when I try to sneak sprouts onto their plates.

'After the build-up Edie's given me, I've got a lot to live up to. But I have been told I have magic hands, which are at your service for the next week.'

Edie is gazing at him like he's Simon Cowell and she's an *X-Factor* hopeful. He smiles back at her. 'Edie, maybe you could go through the schedule now?'

'Yeah, of course. Sorry, girls, miles away. After Frank's given us a *fascinating* rundown of the benefits of massage, you'll get the timetable for your free thirty-minute massages. See me to book extra sessions. Get in quick. It's true about the magic hands.'

'Edie, I'm blushing. But let's move on. Let's talk muscle exhaustion . . .'

I zone out when he starts on about lactic acid build-up. Instead I watch the others. The panthers are trying to get his attention by thrusting their boobs towards him. But he only seems to have eyes for Darcy – and Natalia.

Cradle-snatcher.

'. . . and so my first customer tonight will be . . . Liz Greer?'

Liz waves. When Foz sees his first client, he looks disappointed, but then plasters on the biggest, fakest smile. Betcha he was hoping to get his magic hands on someone younger.

The other girls are looking pissed off. I guess Edie drew up the timetable before Liz's strop this afternoon.

'Great. And the next person will be . . . Agatha?'

When Agatha puts up her hand, Edie's smiling. She's in

charge of the timetable, so she must have given him the two oldest boot campers on purpose.

And there's only one reason why she'd do that, isn't there?

Bloody hell. I thought boot camp was all about health and fitness and feeling better about ourselves.

Turns out that it all boils down to sex.

After dinner, my roomies agree to give me half an hour in the Clamshell suite to record my first video diary.

First I read the 'Idiot's Guide' the journalist sent with it, covering how to turn the thing on, how to record, and how to wander round the hotel grounds in the dark till I manage to get enough of a signal to upload the bloody video back to the magazine.

Wish Alastair was here. He'd have it sorted in seconds.

Ah. At least I've managed to turn it on. Next step, positioning myself so that as few of my chins as possible are on view.

I've written a list of the stuff I'm going to talk about, but the list of stuff I *can't* talk about is way longer:

Boot Camp Groupies
'Deluxe' accommodation consisting of a mouldy shower, a lumpy bed and a door that lost the argument with a guest
A holistic landlady who might have got too close to her masseur's magic fingers
A house that could be beautiful if the landlady pulled her own finger out
A mother and daughter that want to kill each other
A newsreader who could surely afford somewhere a lot nicer than this
Two trained killers chasing fat women round the beach
A cook who'll be lucky to survive the week without being lynched
And the real reason I'm here

119

*

The censored version would be a lot more interesting, but it'd also get me thrown out. And, cabbage curry aside, I reckon this place is the best thing that's happened to me since Rudy came along.

Of course, I know I don't bloody deserve it. But my kids do, so someone up there must be looking after us.

I press RECORD before I let myself think who the someone might be.

'Boot camp diary, take one. Hello world . . .'

The Big Fat Boot Camp Blog, in association with *Gossip!*

....

Dateline 8.23 p.m., Monday, Devon

Well, Vicki, our boot camp guinea pig, was almost too exhausted to chat to us tonight, which suggests the going's getting tougher. But she did find just enough energy to send us a special vlog entry from her phone (we've transcribed it as the sound quality isn't the best!).

Hello, world!

Well, I don't suppose the whole world is watching, but hopefully Rudy and Murray and Alastair are. Hello, boys. What do you think of Mummy TV?

Wish I could give you a great big hug but I'll blow you a kiss each instead, all right. Mwah, mwah, mwah . . . oh, and give Daddy kisses for me, please. Also, when Daddy says go to bed, go to bed. Remember I'll be back very, very soon. With treats if you're good but if you're not . . .

OK. So, if you're watching this because you fancy trying out a boot camp yourself, then I don't suppose you want any more of me bribing my kids, right?

But let me tell you, this is *hardcore*. Started before six, and didn't finish till tea time. Eleven bloody hours.

Whoops. Sorry, boys. Mummy's too tired to remember not to swear. Everything hurts. And the staffs – that's what we call the instructors – say it'll get worse before it gets better. I can't wait.

You know what, though, there was a whole couple of minutes today when I *almost* enjoyed it. Don't tell Staff Pepper.

What else? The food. Yeah. What can I say about the food?

Well, it's mainly beans and cabbage. I could probably run a power station on my natural gas tonight. Yep, boys, Mummy is one big fart machine. Luckily, we're all the same, or we'd need gas masks.

The other girls are keeping me going, though. Best things about it. All got our different reasons for being here, but we're gonna get through it together.

My body's shutting down, now. Up again tomorrow before the crack of dawn for Day 3. Is that really all it is? Feels like we've been here for ever.

No point moaning. The staffs say they want winners, not whingers. And there's no arguing with trained killers, ha ha. Only joking; they're lovely.

Night night to everyone but especially to my three favourite boys. Sleep tight. I know I *definitely* will.

Day 3: Torture Tuesday

How you'll be feeling: achey. You'll be rediscovering muscles you'd forgotten you had.

05:45   Parade and morning run/fitness kick-start

07:30   Breakfast: Popeye's Poached Egg on a Bed of Spinach, Wake-up Tea

08:30   Oh We Do Love to Be Beside the Seaside Circuits

10.15   Combat training with Frank

12:30   Lunch: Fiery 'Chicken' with Tangy Tomato Risotto

13:30   Bike ride along the wonderful Devon coastline

17:00   R&R, massage sessions

18:30   Dinner: Lentil Burgers with Brilliant Buckwheat Prune Surprise.

Please note all activities and meals are subject to change due to circumstances beyond our control

17

Vicki

I wasn't planning to eavesdrop again. Honest.

But my body's decided that quarter to five is time to wake up, and my muscles ache more when I try to stay still. As I tiptoe downstairs, I'm curious. Will they be there again? Boys do love their routines.

I creep into the dining room. There's white smoke against the dark sky. Yeah, they're out there all right.

'. . . not fussy, is he? He'd probably have any of them.' Pepper sounds bitter as hell.

'But will any of them have *him*?' Ryan's playing along.

'The two panthers would.' They both laugh. 'But I think he's after the TV presenter. He hasn't had one of those before.'

'There was that actress last year.'

'*Actress*. I don't think *her* DVDs were stocked in Block-busters,' Pepper says. 'Hey, what about the old bat who nearly did a runner yesterday? I thought we had a record. Earliest quitter so far.'

'No, remember the really big girl who couldn't get up the stairs and turned round before she'd even unpacked?' Ryan says.

'Oh yeah. Edie's really not fussy who she takes on. Or who she takes her clothes off for.'

'Come on. It's only Foz that we know of, and I reckon that's cooled off.'

Pepper sniggers. 'Maybe he enjoyed some special Foz time with his clients yesterday?'

'With *Agatha*?' Ryan sounds appalled. 'She's someone's grandma.'

'If he thought no one would find out, he'd do Agatha, all the fat birds. And Karma the dog. Remember what he told us when he started on the boot camp: *I live to root, boys, and I never have any complaints.*' Pepper's Australian accent is bad, but it kinda works.

'I guess we all live to root in our way.'

'Except you, Ryan. I'm worried you've gone gay or something.'

'People don't *go gay*, you idiot. You're in the dark ages. I'm just bored.'

'With sex?'

'No, no. This. The same old routine. Breaking them down, building 'em up again. How did we end up here? After all we've done. Seen.'

'The good old days, right? Being shot at and bombed and not knowing if you'll survive the next hour every time you step out of the sodding compound. Not seeing a bird for so long you start fancying the platoon goat. I can see why you miss that.'

'Be serious, Matt. Is there *anything* that's given you the same kick as coming out of a fire fight with no more than a scratch? Or having a crack with the lads?'

'Fire fights are one thing, Sammy boy. Fucking bombs are another. Somehow we escaped with our bollocks, sunshine. We should be enjoying 'em, for the sake of them that came back without them. Or didn't come back at all.'

There's an even longer pause and then Ryan says, 'You're probably right.'

'You *know* I am. That's it. No more arguments. This week I am on a mission to get you laid. Let's go to it, yeah?'

I flatten myself against the wall as they come back into the house, Pepper reciting a list of reasons why boot camp is a dream posting: no more insurgents, no more rats, no more ration packs, and no more desert sand scratching your private parts raw.

My boys don't talk about bullets and birds – not yet, anyway – but they tease each other exactly the same. Underneath it all, the staffs are just boys, and it's getting harder to hate them for the dumb things they say because I don't think they mean any of it.

Will my boys be talking about me over breakfast? The thought of them at home, surviving without me, makes me go wobbly for a second. I wish I was there, in my lovely warm kitchen, throwing cereal into bowls and juice into cups.

But David and Chrissie have given up a lot to give me this chance: the least I can do is work bloody hard to get in shape for *their* sake as well as mine.

Didn't think it could get any colder, but when we line up in the car park, all the windscreens are covered in ice an inch thick, and the wind whips through my fleece and body fat, right to the bone.

We're less of a rabble this morning. We even manage to get ourselves into files before either of the staffs appear. Then we realise we're two short.

'It's Liz and Natalia again,' Agatha says.

'With any luck, they might have killed each other,' Darcy whispers.

'I can go and knock on their door,' Steph suggests, but before she can break ranks, Pepper appears. It's freaky to see him looking fierce after hearing him joking with Ryan only a half hour ago.

'Good morning. Except it's not, is it? I spy with my beady eye that two of your boot campers are missing. So you all get a special treat. Two extra runs up the Ladder.'

There's a groan. 'That's not fair,' Steph mumbles, a little too loudly, because then Pepper smiles at her.

'Make that three trips up the Ladder, thanks to Dean here. Every extra complaint, we add another trip. As I'm feeling generous, I might add a few burpees.'

Burpees. My life was that much better before I found out what they are: like the evil love-child of a squat thrust and a star jump. They guarantee pains as powerful as contractions.

Steph stares at the floor so she won't wind him up again. Finally Liz shuffles through the door, followed by Natalia. It wouldn't be so bad if they looked messy. But they're all done up like showgirls. *And* they don't even apologise.

If we were in Big Brother, they'd be voted off right now. Natalia glares at her mother like she hates her, and it makes me want to bang their heads together. Tell them how precious that bond is between mother and daughter: that you never know what's round the corner, when it might be taken from you for ever.

'No more time to waste, shirkers. Stand up straight like you **bloody MEAN IT!**'

We don't need telling twice.

Torture Tuesday. They weren't joking.

We're freezing and we're aching and we're all having our doubts. We've only been up and down the Ladder once so far, but as we start the second trip, I'm a bit bloody tempted to throw myself into that prickly bush and hide till they think I've done a runner.

'I don't want to see any of you lot WALKING! If you WALK, then the lot of you will have to do it yet another time before doing forty push-ups on the beach.'

It's a toss-up which part of my body hurts most. Lungs? Knees? Even my arms feel like they've been battered with an iron bar. The idea of crouching on the freezing sand to push my fat body up and down makes me want to curl up in a little ball.

Well, a big ball, then.

I could just refuse. Tell them I've done enough. But then I remember what Ryan and Pepper were saying about their battlefront experiences and I know they're not going to buy any excuses.

'I said MOVE IT, Adams, or I will come and push your giant backside up there myself. You won't shift all that weight walking, will you . . . you're a bloody disgrace . . .'

He keeps shouting, but I'm trying not to hear. Instead I try to imagine the kids and Dave at the top of the Ladder, cheering me on.

Bet they're not even out of bed yet. It's not even six o'clock and Dave loves his lie-ins, so they probably won't shift themselves till eight, and then it'll all be a scramble and the kids will be lucky to have matching socks on. Or warm coats.

Oh, shit. What if he's forgetting they need warm coats? In this weather?

I'm a terrible mother to leave them, and Chrissie's a terrible sister for putting me in for it.

Except if she hadn't, then what? I get fatter and fatter. Sicker and sicker. Less likely to see my boys play football for the school, pass or fail their exams, break hearts, have their own hearts broken, marry, have kids, be happy.

The doctor said so. Maybe not in so many words. But despite the soft soap – 'your blood pressure is on the high side,' and, 'perhaps at your young age, we'd be hoping for lower cholesterol readings, but then being morbidly obese does play havoc with your HDLs' – his meaning was crystal bloody clear. *You're a fat lump, a heart attack-in-waiting. When something goes wrong, don't say we didn't warn you.*

Except something *has* gone wrong already. I can't tell anyone that it was my fault, especially not Dave. He'd leave me. But I looked it up. The fatter you are, the bigger the risks in pregnancy.

I can't put that right – God only knows, I would if I could – but I won't let my boys down too. There's nothing sadder than a son without his mum.

Except maybe, a mum without her daughter.

'Vicki? You OK?'

I look down the Ladder: even Steph is gaining on me now, though her face is the colour of a ripe blackberry.

'I'm surviving. You all right, Steph?'

'No! Pepper's on his way up,' she pants. 'Don't let him catch you standing still. He's serious about making us do it again. And he says we'll have to run backwards next time round.'

'Come on,' I say, holding out my hand. 'Why don't we do this last bit together?'

'No, Vicki. Seriously. I'll only drag you down. You're like . . . super-fit compared to me.'

I shake my head. 'That was Sunday. Tuesday is a totally different ball game. But we're not giving up. As long as there's breath in our bodies, Stephanie Dean, we're gonna keep moving.'

And that makes her grin, because, let's face it, however much

I sound like that hunky Bear Grylls bloke off the telly trying to tackle Everest, we all know I'm nothing but a morbidly obese housewife struggling to get up the last few steps.

Still. You gotta start somewhere.

18

Darcy

Marian hasn't given up on me – or her commission – quite yet. I think she thinks I'm playing hard to get.

Her latest text, sent at 2 a.m. and lost in the ether till then, said: AM IN SOHO HOUSE WITH ANTON. ALREADY 3 HACKS + 1 BABY BBC PRESENTER HAVE ASKED WHERE U ARE + IF U ARE ON RELAUNCH ROSTER. ANT THINKS U R BEING CHILDISH. IF I DON'T HEAR FROM U BY LUNCHTIME TUESDAY THEN U CAN LOOK FOR ANOTHER AGENT. COME HOME TO MAMA.

Home. I try to imagine myself in Soho House, then remember I can't go back there, not after what happened last time. And anyway, war reporters don't belong there; they head west for the Frontline Club, where no one stares if you're having a bad night.

But I don't belong there either, not anymore. The last brutal battle I witnessed was between two presenters who both wanted to read the top headline. That wouldn't win me much kudos when the war stories start going round.

'Are you girls ready for action?' Foz is posing on the horizon, like a Greek God who's overdosed on sun beds. 'The female of the species can definitely be more deadly!'

But if I ignore the wrinkly Australian, and focus on the waves beyond, then it helps put my stupid industry and stupider colleagues in perspective. The cliffs and the seagulls don't know I'm Darcy Webb, 'the winsome yet knowing face of news in the new millennium', according to that *Guardian* profile, back in 2007. Before I'd even met Heela.

It's taken thousands and thousands of years for this bay to be formed, and for the pebbles to lose their sharp corners. Compared to that, silly profiles and 'what's in my fridge' Q&As in the Sunday supplements seem completely meaningless. As for Soho House . . .

Coming here feels like the first decent decision I've made in months, even though I was press-ganged. Last night I managed my first uninterrupted sleep in two years. I'm detoxing from fame. Here I feel completely insignificant. And that's exactly what I needed.

'Have you ever done martial arts before?' Steph asks nervously.

'Not quite like this. I learned some basic self-defence with work.'

'What, in case the weatherman turns nasty?' she laughs.

'No, no. Before I was a newsreader I reported from all over the world.'

'Wow, that sounds exciting.'

'Yeah, it was. And terrifying, sometimes, when someone's shooting at you. It can make real life seem a bit dull in comparison.'

'Can you . . . shoot a gun?'

I shrug. 'A rifle? No, but they showed us how to treat bullet wounds. Most of the courses were about how to avoid getting into danger. And to be honest, a reporter who picks up a gun stops being a reporter. You try not to take sides.'

Except, of course, if I had been armed, things might not have turned out the way they did.

'But this unarmed combat stuff? You can do that?'

'I found karate isn't much use if people are carpet-bombing, or booby-trapping your jeep.'

'Gather round, girls!'

Foz the Oz has carried the boxing kit all the way to the beach on his own, even though we could easily have managed it between us. But he's one of those pointlessly macho types who has to be the biggest, the strongest, the best. He's trying to impress, and I've got a horrible feeling his performance is aimed at me.

As if I *would*. I'd rather get it on with Ryan or even Pepper. I can't stand a man whose ego is bound to be bigger than his . . .

'Girls, I don't teach aggression. I teach confidence. Knowing our bodies *intimately*, understanding other people's weaknesses, being strong. Right?'

The others are nodding at the pseudo-psychology. What a *bullshitter*. Though at least when we finally get the boxing gloves out, I know *exactly* who I'm going to imagine on the receiving end of my left hooks.

'Right, in your couples, A takes the gloves, B the pads. Quick as you can, girls; no time to waste.'

Steph is still trying to decide if she wants to be A or B, so I give her a gentle shove in the direction of the gloves. We find ourselves a space away from the two Crab women, who are getting seriously annoying. They've already signed up for extra massages with Mr Magic Hands, whereas I'm considering inventing chronic period pain or a highly contagious skin condition to get out of *my* free session.

'These stink,' says Steph, and when I sniff the red gloves, I almost gag.

'Imagine how many people's hands must have sweated in those for them to smell that bad.'

She pokes her left hand in. 'I think they're still wet from the last time.'

'Girls, ignore the whiff of vinegar. In boxing circles, it's a badge of honour, and you can't catch anything from someone else's good honest sweat, right?'

Steph frowns. 'Has he got medical evidence for that?' But she puts on the other glove, and I fasten up the Velcro patches for her, so they're nice and snug. 'Ouch.'

'Did I do it too tight?'

'No, they're full of sand.'

'Exfoliation will give you baby-soft hands,' I say, picking up the two pads. 'You ready to vent your fury?'

She giggles. 'Never really been a furious kind of person.'

'What, not even when Pepper had a go at you in front of everyone on the first day? Or when he added an extra run up the Ladder for daring to disagree with him?'

'I was irritated. But you've either got anger in you, or you haven't.'

'Girls, we'll begin with a few simple jabs. Start with your left foot forward, ready to punch with the right arm. Aim at the pads, rather than your partner. I don't think a broken nose suits any girl. So be careful if you think of any ex-boyfriends, right?'

He demonstrates. 'Step, jab, jab. Step, jab, jab. Step . . . come on, girls, try it.'

Steph is struggling. She's getting her right and left legs confused even before she adds the arms.

'Sorry,' she says. 'Knew I had two left feet. Turns out I have two left arms as well.'

'Don't apologise, you're doing fine. There's no rush.'

Normally, I'd be impatient, but here, on an empty beach in the middle of January, there's no rush at all. I let my eyes drift to the grey sea, wondering if it's looked like this for the last ten thousand years.

'How's it going, girls?'

Irritating men have probably been around for the last ten thousand years, too. This one hasn't evolved significantly since the Stone Age, except for the hair transplant.

'It's harder than it looks,' Steph puffs.

'What's your name, darling?'

'Dean.'

'I prefer first names. None of that army bullshit in my classes. You're a woman. You deserve *respect* for your strength and your femininity.'

'I'm Steph.'

'Much better. Cute name. So, Steph, let me see if I can help.' He positions himself behind her, and pulls a face at me. So much for respect.

'I'm finding it tricky to co-ordinate my legs with my arms.'

'Think of it like a dance,' he says. 'A waltz where you just happen to be punching your partner instead of leading them, right? One, two, three, *one, two, three.*'

'I can't dance either,' she says, sounding increasingly anxious. 'I can't do any of it.'

'Can I *hold* you, Steph?' he asks, as though it's an offer she can't refuse.

'Hmm. Suppose.'

He moves in, so his body is spooned against hers. 'Start with this leg,' he says, pushing his thigh into hers. 'Then punch with this arm,' he says, moving both their right arms, 'then with this one. Try again?'

I hate to admit it, but he's not a bad teacher. Though this kind of *very* hands-on tuition must be a perk of the job.

The fifth time, Steph seems to be getting it, and a girlish smile crosses her face. 'Wow. When you get the hang of the rhythm it feels . . . kind of natural.'

He pulls away. 'Exactly. Now you can focus on getting some strength behind the punches. Though maybe I should just check your partner's technique before I move on?'

The thought of him spooning *me* like that does not appeal. I shrug. 'You're all right. Let's focus on Steph for now.'

'I don't bite, Darcy!'

I smile as charmingly as possible. 'Yes, but *I* might.'

That makes his grin wider – yuk – but he does leave us in peace.

'Do you *fancy* him?' Steph asks.

I pull a face. '*Really* not my type. Why, do you?'

'Out of my league!'

'Don't be silly. You're pretty, young, kind, clever. He's raddled, arrogant and not very bright. It's the other way round. You're out of his league.'

She blushes. 'You don't have to say stuff like that. It's fine. I know my level!'

And she starts punching again, half-heartedly. *Step, jab, jab.*

'Who made you feel bad about yourself, Steph?'

'What?' *Step, jab, jab.* I see her mouthing the words as she punches.

'Someone must have put those ideas in your head. About not being good enough.'

Step, jab, jab. STEP, JAB, JAB.

The punching gets harder and I sense I'm onto something. The two sessions I was made to do with a trauma counsellor seemed to do me no good at all, but maybe I learned more than I thought.

'I don't know what you mean.'

Except she's jabbing so hard now that the force against the pads makes the bones in my hand rattle. 'Steph. You know, everyone has an agenda. In my job, I'm always being attacked by the press for my hair, my dress sense, my voice. And then even colleagues snipe to my face about how tired I look, which is code for how *old* I look.'

'And . . . that doesn't . . . hurt? What people . . . say to you?' She's out of breath but still punching.

'At first, yes. But I had to develop a kind of *shield* to stop the insults hitting home. Like these pads absorb the punches,' I say, pleased at my own wisdom.

'But what if what people say is true?' She stops jabbing. 'Not about you, of course. About me.'

I drop my hands. What if the criticisms *are* valid? What if I *am* too old and the dark shadows under my eyes are distracting viewers from the news I'm reading? Or my dark moods and even darker deeds are making me a liability?

Maybe the management were waiting for me to go on holiday so they could replace me without a showdown.

'Did I hurt you, Darcy? Tell me if I'm hitting too hard.'

'No. No, I lost my concentration. What did you say?'

'I said, what if the negative stuff is *true*?'

Her eyes are dangerously wet. I think she might be about to cry.

'What's the problem, girls? Did I tell you you could take a break?'

Foz is striding over, and there's a hard look on his face this time, maybe because he's realised I'm not going to fall for his charms.

'Get your acts together, ladies. This will only work if you put the flaming effort in, capisce?'

I catch Steph's eye and she smiles guiltily. Foz has made her forget the hurt, and convert it into anger. When she starts punching me again, each blow seems more forceful still.

Or maybe *I'm* feeling it more. Because now there's the most awful realisation that my detractors, my *enemies*, might just have a point about me being unfit for my job. And if I can't even do a convincing job of reading words someone else has written, then I truly am a waste of space.

19

Steph

Violence has given me an appetite.

Obviously, I *always* have an appetite, but this is even more all-consuming than yesterday. And I'm not the only one. We troop back, sweaty despite the cold, and once we've finished our stretches, all anyone can talk about is what's for lunch.

'I keep seeing toasted teacake,' Vicki says. 'Or an old-fashioned crumpet with holes that let butter and honey sink in to the bottom.'

'I'm thinking savoury.' I say. 'Low-fat. And protein-rich. I'm thinking chicken breasts wrapped in ham and sage leaves. With field mushrooms. Oh, and gratin dauphinoise, the top layer of potatoes all crunchy round the edges, and the bottom layers so soft with cream and garlic that your spoon goes right through them.'

'That doesn't sound very low fat,' Darcy points out.

Foz comes back into the room from the kitchen. 'Apparently lunch will be five minutes late, girls.'

There's a group groan.

'But that does give you all time to, um, freshen up a little bit, maybe?'

I can't think *what* he means. My poo-brown trainers actually look better now they're encrusted with sand and dirt, and the scratches on my calves are proof of how hard I'm working.

The sore knuckles are more disturbing. I didn't quite realise how hard I was punching the pads until I saw the pained expression on Darcy's face. That weird stuff she was saying about people trying to put me down made me go all aggressive. And the more I punched, the more I *wanted* to punch.

But I wasn't seeing anyone in particular. Honest. Not my brothers ganging up on me for being a girl, nor the girls who sent me to Coventry at boarding school, my boss when she calls in sick whenever there's a report due, Steve when . . .

No, it wasn't like me at all. I'm very balanced, usually. No point blaming people for stuff that's gone before. It'd be like being angry with Mum for dying when I needed her.

'Can anyone remember what is actually on the menu today, before I die of excitement?' Vicki asks.

'Might have been fiery chicken,' Agatha says.

We turn our heads like the Bisto kids, as an odd smell drifts from the kitchen.

'Is that roasting . . . or *burning*?' Liz asks.

The thought that our hard-earned lunch might just have been incinerated silences us. Hel the chef may not escape alive.

One minute. Two minutes.

Three minutes. The noises our empty bellies make cross the line from comical to disturbing.

Edie emerges from the kitchen.

'Don't panic!' she says, which seems like a bloody good reason to panic. 'We're experiencing a few teething troubles with our new grill. But thanks to our chef's ingenuity and our extensive store cupboard, something equally delicious will served soon. In the meantime, we do have a . . . an impromptu starter. Which is a bonus, isn't it?'

She scuttles off, before we get a chance to complain.

'It's not the bloody grill that's crap, is it?' Vicki murmurs. 'It's the bloody cook.'

The noise of pans crashing and banging almost drowns out

the row between Edie and the chef. But we do hear the odd swear word.

Finally the door swings open and Edie reappears, looking flushed. She's balancing three serving bowls, and a pile of side plates. She puts one bowl on each table. We peer at the contents: it's a pinky-grey sludge topped with sesame seeds.

'Hummus,' she says. 'Made with kidney beans instead of chick peas. Absolutely *packed* with protein and fibre.'

She distributes the plates, then makes another trip to the kitchen, returning with two packets of oatcakes. 'Two oatcakes each should keep those hunger pangs at bay while we wait for the main event. Quite a treat, eh?'

Agatha opens the packet, takes two biscuits, and then passes it along. When we've finished our pass the parcel, there are two oatcakes left in the open cellophane. The oats glisten like jewels.

We spoon hummus onto our plates. It looks like pink slurry. What the hell is wrong with using chickpeas to make hummus?

I spread some onto the first of my precious oatcakes, but the slurry drips off. I bite into the oatcake instead. Yum. That's more like it. It's all crunchy and crumbly. There might even be some – whisper it – *salt* in there . . .

We're like prisoners trying to eke out our rations. Natalia has cut hers into strips. Vicki keeps taking tiny nibbles, like a hamster.

I look down. Shit. Somehow I've eaten one and a half of mine already. My stomach hasn't even registered those few bites.

It's awfully quiet in the kitchen now. I try to persevere with the hummus, in case that's as good as it gets. I've eaten some rank things for work – the *Dragon's Den*-style Pitch Your Produce day we ran last year brought in chutneys and cakes so loathsome I had nightmares afterwards.

But this takes the oatcake.

I might be going a bit mad. Because I'm fixated by those last two oatcakes sitting on the dining table. There's no way we can share them among eleven people. Each person would end up with three crumbs, at most.

So how can we do this fairly? Agatha should get half an oatcake, on the grounds of age. Which leaves three halves. Perhaps it should go to the women with least weight to lose. But then again, us fatties must be suffering more from calorie deprivation as we need more.

Maybe we could divide up the oatcakes based on a secret ballot . . .

It happens in slow motion. Liz's hand is reaching across the table and before anyone can say or do anything, she's picked up *both* oatcakes and is smiling and saying, 'No one minds, do they? It's just I don't need to lose weight and I'm absolutely ravenous.'

The world falls silent. Silent, except for Liz's first bite into the oatcake. It crunches under her teeth. Precious crumbs fall onto the tabletop in slow motion. Everyone's staring at her but she hasn't noticed. She smiles happily as she takes a second bite, and a third, and the biscuit is *gone*.

And then she starts on the second.

Natalia stands up so suddenly her chair falls over with a crash.

'Mother?'

'Oh good, you're talking to me again, are you?' She gestures towards the tin teapot at her daughter's elbow. 'Is that fennel? In which case, I'd like a top up.'

Only when Natalia doesn't reply does Liz look up properly. She looks startled.

'Did I say something funny?' she says, as though we're all about to dissolve into laughter.

'Not funny, no, Mum. You've got no idea, have you? What you've done?'

Liz frowns, like she's trying to mentally retrace her last few actions. Then she sighs. 'Not that again, Natalia. Not in front of everyone. I know I shouldn't have left your father during your A-Levels but there's a limit to how many times I can apologise for the same thing.'

'The *bloody oatcake*,' Natalia grunts.

'The wha—' Her mother's gaze drops to the plate.

The rest of us are transfixed. This would give *Mad Men* a run for its money for pure drama.

'The oatcake. You stole it. We should have . . . discussed what we were going to do with it. Democratically. But, oh, no, not Liz Greer's style to think about what someone else might want to do. She grabs what she wants and fuck the rest of us.'

'Natalia!' She blushes, then looks at the rest of us. 'I am so sorry about my daughter's language, everyone; it's really not appropriate . . .' She tails off. Finally she's noticed the scowls and the fact that the waves of hungry venom crossing the dining table are aimed at her, not Natalia.

'You're the one who's not appropriate, Mum. Why don't you just go? Like you were going to yesterday, right? And just like you did a year and a half ago. You should be absolutely bloody brilliant at leaving by now.'

'I, uh . . .' Liz is about to argue back, but then she runs out of the dining room. Way, way faster than she ran during the race yesterday. She can move when she wants to.

We're all staring at Natalia. Her face is red and she looks dazed, as though she can't quite believe what's just happened.

Neither can I. All that over two *oatcakes*?

Though, admittedly oatcakes I was preparing to fight for myself before Natalia's mother stole them.

'Right, here we are at last, everyone.'

I turn round to see Edie emerge from the kitchen, carrying a huge casserole dish with a lid on top.

'Grub's up, ladies. I'm sure this is worth waiting for.'

20

Steph

It wasn't.

Worth waiting for, that is. We should have realised we were in trouble when the menu put 'chicken' in inverted commas. The mock bird was some unidentifiable grain shaped into cutlets, plus a brown rice and tomato 'risotto' made with canned tomatoes so acidic that I could taste the metal tin. To add flavour, the cook had emptied several packets of chilli flakes into the mix. Steam came out of our ears after the first mouthful. The rest was inedible.

Or, inedible under normal circumstances. We managed to force it down in gloomy silence punctuated by little whimpers, like members of a religious sect performing some act of masochistic penance.

'Look! Liz is reversing out!'

We run to the dormer window in the Clamshell suite and jump onto the bed next to Darcy, who is reporting live from the scene.

'God, her tyres are smoking, she's in such a hurry,' I say, trying to see her face behind the wheel.

'If I was her, I'd be heading for the nearest McDonald's,' Vicki says. 'Which, should you be interested, is exactly six point nine miles from here. I wrote down the postcode before I left. If I get to the end of this week, Dave is going to drive me straight there as soon as he picks me up, and buy me a quarter pounder with cheese. The last one of my life, obviously. But I will savour it, like someone on Death Row.'

I'm about to suggest to Vicki that maybe Death Row isn't the most positive way to visualise her healthier future. But I can't really take the moral high ground when the only way I managed to get through lunch was by fantasising about *proper* risotto, made with equal proportions of rice, cheese and butter. And half a bottle of white wine.

'What about Natalia? What do you think she'll do?'

'The sooner she goes the better,' Darcy says. 'Did you see her face?'

'Well, if her mum left in the middle of her exams, maybe we shouldn't blame her for being upset with Liz,' I say.

Vicki shakes her head. 'It's Liz I feel sorry for. One mistake and she's more or less disowned by her daughter. Can't imagine anything worse.'

Darcy looks surprised. 'I don't like either of them. But Oatcakegate has certainly put the cat among the pigeons.'

'Oatcakegate?' Vicki frowns.

'Oh, it's just at work every time there's some kind of scandal, we add "gate" to it: you know, like Watergate.'

'Oatcakegate.' I try it out. 'I like it. It sounds dramatic. Like regime change or something.'

'If there were ever a case for regime change, it's in that bloody kitchen,' Darcy says.

'Where do you think she learned to cook?' Vicki says, as we head back down the stairs ready for our afternoon roll call. 'Strangeways?'

'No, there'd be a prison riot if people cooked like that there,' I say.

Outside, the whispering is all about hunger pangs and chocolate cravings, too. Someone is groaning that they *wouldn't feed that to a dog*. Actually, the two blondes tried to feed it to Karma, but he ran out and hasn't been seen since.

'Well, I'm taking matters into my own hands,' Darcy says. 'I've got a tenner in my pocket in case we pass a shop on the bike ride. If it carries on like this, we're going to need emergency rations to stay alive till the end of the week.'

My fat reserves would keep me going a lot longer than that but I do see her point.

'Someone should complain to Edie,' Vicki whispers. But after hearing the mad shrieks from Hel's kitchen when Edie went in to sort the mess out, I don't suppose any of us are brave enough to tackle Disasterchef.

Ryan appears, as adorable as ever, though slightly distracted. 'Light jog down to the beach, keep the post-lunch energy levels up.'

He leads the way, but doesn't look back. As soon as we realise he's not bothered, all our pretend military discipline deserts us, and we amble down the Ladder in a formation that doesn't resemble a rank or a file. Finally, Ryan stops next to a long metal hut with a row of bikes lined up outside.

'Right, ladies, this is where I'm going to leave you in the capable hands of our expert, Pam.'

Pam doesn't look like a Pam. She's sharp-boned with padded cycling leggings and about five layers of fleece. She stands in front of her cycles, weighing us up. Perhaps she's worried Vicki and I might bend the frames.

'All right, Sammy boy,' she mutters. 'They know the drill, right?'

He nods at us. 'Remember, boot campers, the idea of this afternoon is that you get R&R after your hard work, but you don't let up on the calorie burning. Pedal hard; don't let the bikes do it all. I'll catch you at the end of the ride!'

And with that, he wanders off along the beach. I'm gutted

he's not coming with us. Riding a bike is one of the few things I can actually manage – Mum taught me. This could be my one chance to prove I'm not completely hopeless.

'Nice arse.' Vicki's watching me watching him go.

'I wasn't thinking about that.'

'No? Won't be the same on the bike ride without Ryan's backside leading from the front!'

'Right, ladies, pick a bike and let's get going. We want to be back before it gets dark at four,' says Pam.

'How far are we going?' Vicki calls out.

'It's the easiest route I do. All on the flat.'

'Great. But I asked how far.'

'Five miles.'

I can manage that, even with my sore muscles.

'Five miles there. And five miles back. But I've had four year olds complete this ride without a peep, so I'm not expecting any complaints.'

Wobble.

Wobble.

Wow!

How *brilliant* does this feel? I'd totally forgotten.

The wind in my hair, the swishing of the wheels, the sense that I can go anywhere. Even the icy rain feels cool against my hot skin. And the flat white sky could be bright June sunshine, I'm so warm.

Somehow, I'm way *way* ahead of all the others. I've never known what it's like to be the leader.

It feels good.

The beach huts and the pier are so pretty, and the sand looks so soft as I speed along. You'd never guess it was capable of inflicting the grazes and scratches and friction burns we've suffered over the last three days.

Three days! Tomorrow we'll be halfway through.

The world whizzes past, and I feel I'm in control. Can't remember the last time I felt like that. The slightest touch to the handlebars and my direction changes.

I *can* go anywhere.

Yeah, the rain is turning into sleet and hitting my face, but I begin to laugh. OK, I'm an overweight, bedraggled woman on a bicycle, cackling away to herself. If anyone sees me, they'll think I've lost it.

But all at once, I realise I don't care what other people think. All that matters is the whoosh of the wheels, the tinkling of the bell and the knowledge that I'm so far ahead of the pack no one can catch me.

The halfway point is a little cove lined with a rainbow of beach huts. They look even more vibrant against a sky that threatens a serious storm.

'How was that?' asks Pam, making eye contact with me for the first time.

'Brilliant!'

'You haven't done it in a while.'

I look down at my lumps and bumps, and then up at her wiry figure. 'That obvious, eh?'

'What?' She pulls a face, then blushes. 'No, I wasn't being nasty. But you've got that glow people get when they get back on a bike and they *remember*.'

I walk over to the water's edge. The snack bag contains four raw almonds and four brazil nuts. Right now, that counts as a banquet. They crunch loudly in my mouth, the flavours earthy and intense.

The others are arriving. Karen first – well, she is training for a triathlon. The others are close behind. I hear chatting *and* moaning: not everyone is loving the sleet. I zone out, focusing on the dark sea and the wind in my ears.

Vicki walks up beside me. 'Hey, you're the Lance Armstrong of boot camp!'

I smile but I don't feel like chatting. 'Might head off, before my legs seize up.'

Before she can answer, I grab my bike – I don't want anyone taking mine by accident – and jump on, leaving the rest of them behind.

The journey back is steeper, but still exhilarating. I'm so high up, I feel god-like: there's the horizon, the beach, and the corrugated roof of the bike shack a long way in the distance. The shore is completely deserted, too cold even for the people whose dogs bark at us when we do sit-ups on the sand.

Wish there was someone waiting at the finish line for me. Steve maybe. Smiling, clapping, calling out. He'd see me differently, realise what I'm capable of. I'm beating some seriously fit girls here. When I look over my shoulder – that made me wobble – the road behind is clear.

I want to tell him. OK, I promised Annie I wouldn't contact him again, but a text would be all right, surely? This isn't Sad Drunk texting, the want-you-back bleating of a lonely heart. This is Girl Power texting!

The path narrows and the wind's blowing so hard now that spray hits my face, even though the shoreline is at least thirty paces away. Bits of me are starting to hurt: my corpse-white fingers, my bum on the hard saddle.

The Wall. That's all this is. Must focus on the next turn of the wheel, on the prize.

On being worthy of Steve.

Now I've got cramp in my thighs, and a raging thirst. I'm not stopping, but I am slowing down. When I drink, the water's so icy it hurts my teeth and I feel it trickling down my throat.

Bad thoughts are taking hold again. I try harder to picture Steve waiting outside the shack. Yes. He's clearer now.

But he's looking at his watch, shaking his head, tutting. *How much longer, honeybunch? Are we going to have to put the bike in for a service, after it had to support your weight for ten long miles?*

Irritation makes me pedal faster. *Cruel to be kind, see, Steph, it works!*

Finally, I read the sign on the shed – Pam's Pushbikes – and it gives me another burst of energy. I pedal as fast as I can, my heart pumping so hard I hear it inside my head, racing, racing, so the beach huts are a pastel blur.

I'm here!

I slam on the brakes and the wheels skid and I almost go over the handlebars. But I control it just in time.

I wish I could bottle this feeling and then take sneaky sips of triumph before work meetings and family occasions and *definitely* before the Valentine's Ball.

I hear someone clapping behind me.

It's Staff Ryan.

'You're the first, eh, Steph? Congratulations!'

I blush. 'Stop clapping! It wasn't even a race.'

He does stop applauding but he doesn't stop smiling. 'Don't do yourself down. It's an achievement. We're all good at different things, right? This could be *your* thing.'

I shrug. He's wrapped up against the cold, which makes him look like Nigel's old Action Man in full Arctic training gear. But those *eyes*.

Most women would kill for eyelashes that long, and those heavy, come-to-bed eyes.

He's reaching into the pack he's brought with him. 'Flapjack,' he says, handing me a foil parcel.

'*Really?*'

Flapjacks are the only thing that could take my mind off his eyes. I tear the foil open. The oats are black, not with molasses, but with soot. The top is uneven, with lumps of incinerated sultana. A lump of coal would be more appetising.

I pass the parcel back to him. 'I don't think I can eat this.'

He opens the foil a bit more. 'That's even worse than usual.'

'Do you know where Edie found the cook?'

Ryan sighs. 'I heard she was working at the young offenders' institution up the road.'

'In the kitchens?'

He pulls a face. 'Edie assumed that when Hel applied. But down the pub, someone said Hel was actually a prison officer.'

'That would explain it. Does Edie realise how bad things are?'

'I . . . Edie means well, but it's a massive task, that hotel. There's so much to do. Always a new leak or damp patch. She's more in tune with yoga and all that stuff.'

'Yoga won't get the roof fixed.'

He laughs. 'No. The boot camp idea was meant to bring in cash fast to fund the refurbishments, because people wouldn't expect luxury accommodation.'

'Except that's what she promises. Comfy beds, tasty home-cooked food.'

'Well, this wasn't produced in a factory, was it?' he says, crumbling one of the flapjacks between his fingers. 'Trouble is, it affects morale. An army really does march on its stomach, I know that much.'

I remember what Vicki said about army food. 'What did you used to eat?'

'On the bigger bases, it's good honest grub. But some of the smaller ones, where maybe there'd be just us and some goats and a few dozen Taliban lurking round the place, it was rations. You know, in packs? We used to say we ate from a bag,

152

showered from a bag, and sh— I mean, went to the toilet in a bag. The only thing we could hope for was that we didn't get to go home in a bag.'

'God.'

He kicks at a stone. 'Sorry. Too much information, right?'

'No. No, it's fascinating. If a bit macabre. So basically, when you're shooting at the enemy, all you're thinking about is what's for tea?'

He shrugs. 'God, I'm not that heartless. No, when you're shooting at the enemy all you can think of is that it's him or you. And don't ask me, please.'

'Ask you what?'

'Whether I ever killed anyone. It's what everyone asks. Drives you mad. As though it's something we'd want to boast about.'

Ryan looks away, and I wonder again what he did in the forces, and what the hell he's doing here now. 'Actually, I was going to ask how old you were.'

'How old was I when what?'

'When you joined the army.'

'Oh. Sixteen.'

'A *kid*,' I say, and as soon as I've said it, I feel ridiculous. 'Sorry. It's just, I think of my two brothers at sixteen and they could barely blow their own noses, never mind blow people to pieces—' I stop myself.

But Ryan just smiles. 'Actually, at sixteen, I could hardly blow *my* own nose, though I could hotwire a car and start a fight in a roomful of pacifists, probably. You wouldn't have liked me when I was sixteen.'

Does he know I like him now?

'Sixteen is a horrible age,' I say.

'And the best age?'

'Seven,' I say, without hesitation. 'Well, for me, anyway. And for you?'

He looks at the ground. 'Gotta admit that so far, there's not one that stands out as being *that* outstanding. Hopefully the best is yet to come, like the song says.'

'Old Blue Eyes,' I say.

'Who else?'

Mum, dancing round the kitchen, singing 'My Way' with my granddad. Or bursting into 'New York, New York'. She never got to New York. She never got to forty either.

'. . . so are you coming with me?'

'Mmm?' I look up. Ryan's staring at me. I think he must have been talking but I didn't hear him.

'I'm going to have to go and find something healthy as a post-race snack. Do you want to tag along?'

'To an actual *food* shop?'

'Yeah. You're into food, aren't you? I need advice on what might fit Edie's stringent requirements.'

'But . . .'

He laughs. 'I'll keep an eye on you. Make sure you don't let the side down by buying chocolate. Unless you want to stay here, wait for the others?'

The sea breeze has turned into a blood-freezing gale. 'I'll come.'

We lock up my bike, and then walk up the Ladder at normal speed, thank God – Ryan seems to have decided he's off-duty – and down the main road. The first store we come to has a big sign saying OPEN ALL HOURS.

And then a handwritten one underneath it saying *Closed, due to the weather forecast.*

'Is it really going to get that bad?' I ask.

Ryan shrugs. 'When we listened this morning, they were talking about a dusting of snow.'

154

My hopes rise. 'Do we still have to work out if it snows?'

He nods. 'Of course. To be honest, it might turn a tad warmer once it snows.'

We march further down the hill to the next store.

'Remember, Steph, sugar is the enemy!' He winks as he pushes open the door to the newsagent's. A bell rings.

'We're shut.' The voice is coming from somewhere further inside.

'The door wasn't locked. And we'll be really fast,' Ryan calls out into the void.

But the shelves are bare, as though we've stumbled on a closing-down sale. A bald head pops up from behind the counter. 'Two minutes. Then I am battenin' down the hatches. Not much left, anyway. They've been hoardin'. Stockpilin'. Like locusts, they are.' The shopkeeper speaks with a kind of awed respect.

The fridge is the emptiest: nothing but sour cream and ready-made puff pastry staring back at us from the brightly lit cabinet.

'Neither of those count as healthy, do they, Steph?' Ryan says, as I reach for them. I don't even know *why* I'm reaching for them: maybe I'm a hoarder too.

'If the weather's going to be that bad, shouldn't *we* be stocking up on whatever's left, Staff?' I suggest.

We both look around the dingy space. It's all instant noodles and dusty packets of custard creams. I rummage around at the back of the shelves. 'There are more oats than Hel could burn here.'

He puts the puff pastry back. His hand hovers over the chocolate display. Then he looks up, those big eyes full of guilt. 'Don't look, Steph. These are strictly for emergencies. In case we all run out of food and have to choose between eating Karma or chocolate.'

But it's too late to look away. I've already clocked what's going in the carrier bag. Kit Kats, Crunchies, Marathons and a last, lone Wispa.

A hunk with a bagful of chocolate. Sweet dreams are made of this.

The Big Fat Boot Camp Blog, in association with *Gossip!*

Dateline 9.01 p.m., Tuesday, Devon

The mercury is plunging to record lows, but Vicki Adams, *Gossip!*'s very own boot camper, is carrying on regardless, in her mission to fight the flab and make the most of her fitness mission. Here's her latest vlog.

Hello world, hello boys, hello lovely husband. How are you coping without me? Don't get too used to it or I'll feel all unwanted.

So, somehow it's the end of Day Three and I'm still here. Surprised? Yeah, me too. Almost halfway now. I'm knack— tired. And hungry. But I'm not going to throw in the towel now I've got this far.

Loads of drama today. People getting a bit grumpy. Plus I got on a bike for the first time since I got . . . big, and somehow the bike and I made it to the end. Ten miles, boys. That's all the way to Granny's. Couple of moments today when I'd had enough, had nothing more in me.

But . . . how to explain this? My sister Chrissie always says we're here for a good time, not a long time. But I wanna be around as long as possible, long enough to see my boys grow up. Normal stuff, right? Not marathons.

Tomorrow's always the worst day, the staffs say. The Wall, they call it. Dunno if it's better to know in advance. I can probably make it over the Wall on one condition – we get something proper to eat.

Otherwise the Wall might bloody well win.

Day 4: Wednesday – The Wall

How you'll be feeling: like you're hitting a solid brick wall at one hundred miles per hour. But every athlete faces this challenge and overcomes it. Till you've tackled the Wall, you can't know what you're made of!

05:45   Parade and morning run/fitness kick-start

07:30   Breakfast: The Guilt-Free Full English, Wake-up Tea

08:30   Staff Pepper's Ton-up Treat

12:30   Lunch: Sizzling Chicken Salad with Rosemary Roast Veg

13:30   Afternoon Jog, then Stretcher Race

17:00   R&R, individual massage sessions

19:00   Dinner: Totally Tremendous Tofu Steaks. Rhubarb Surprise.

Please note all activities and meals are subject to change due to circumstances beyond our control

21

Vicki

Edie reckons it takes sixty-six days to get into a routine, but mine's sorted after three. I'm down the stairs for my daily dose of the staff soap opera. Better than *EastEnders*, these two are.

Pepper is sniggering. '. . . the bikes survived without collapsing, then?'

'The ladies turned out to be tougher than I thought, too. All managed to make good times.'

'That's because they wanted to impress you. Especially your *special* friend Stephanie.'

'Leave it out, Pepper.'

'Thought you could sneak her back in yesterday without me knowing, did you? Well, Edie spotted you. Though she's more worried about what you had in your carrier bags. Did you two really bring *chocolate* into boot camp, Staff Ryan?'

Chocolate? Can't believe Steph would bring some here and then not share it.

Then I remember Edie's talk. She said we should picture the worst that could happen if we don't get fit. This horrible image of my boys in black . . . at *my* funeral, it must be – pops into my head.

I've gone right off the idea of Dairy Milk.

'. . . told you she had a mammoth crush on you, Ryan.'

'Crap. She was just pleased to get to the end of the bike ride.

And it's nice to *talk* to the clients instead of barking at them all the time. You should try it, Matt.'

'Fraternising with the enemy? You've got to be joking.'

Ryan sighs. 'The enemy? They're just women who want to get fit. They're not the Taliban, Rambo. They don't have IEDs.'

I'm wondering what Inter Uterine Devices have got to do with it – the doctor wants me to get one 'because prescribing the Pill to women your size is not advised, and I'm sure no one wants a repeat of what happened with your last pregnancy.'

Then I remember that's an I*U*D. They're talking about Improvised Explosive Devices, like on the news.

'No, but few of them have got room for weapons of mass destruction in their jogging pants.'

'I won't think too deeply about that one, Matt. But give them a break, eh? They're trying to change. *And* they're paying our wages.'

Pepper harrumphs. 'If you let discipline slip, you'll never get it back. They're not here to *like* us. The more scared they are, the faster they'll run.'

'You think? I dunno. I'm not sure military rules quite work in civvy life.'

'That's why you're good cop and I'm bad cop, Ryan. And you know what? Women love a bit of rough.'

'So how do you account for the way they moon over that old smoothie Foz?'

Pepper grunts. 'One of life's great unsolved mysteries.'

'He was on fire yesterday. You need to get in there with the panthers, Pepper, or he'll have them in the sack before you can say Waltzing Matilda.'

'They're tarts, anyway,' Pepper mumbles, and I feel cross on their behalf. Even though, well, they probably *are*.

'Just because they don't seem interested in you?'

I hear the click of a lighter, and flatten myself against the cold wall in case they catch a glimpse of my shape.

That's weird. It feels like my waistband is looser, even though it can't be, not after only three days. It's taken eight years of greedy pig behaviour to get myself this big, so my blubber's not going to melt away overnight.

'. . . forecasters are panicking but it never snows here, by the coast.'

Pepper's talking about the weather, now. Safe territory.

'What about those old photos on the wall in Edie's office, then? I think the sea even froze over,' Ryan says.

'That was the olden days, before global warming. Anyway, it's warmer this morning, isn't it?'

Pepper's right. Definitely feels less perishing today.

'Maybe.' Ryan sounds dubious.

'That lazy lot will warm up soon enough when we get our hands on them,' Pepper cackles. 'They need to be afraid. Very afraid.'

Except the more I hear from Pepper, the more convinced I am that he's actually almost as scared of us as we are of him.

'Good breakfast, troops?' Pepper's standing with his hands on his hips, groin thrust slightly forward, like a camp pirate from one of Rudy's picture books. All he needs is a patch over his dodgy eye and he could do panto.

But amazingly we *are* enjoying breakfast. Horrible Hel over-slept so Edie dished up All-Bran, apologising for the lack of a cooked breakfast. Amazing how brilliant a bowl of All-Bran tastes when you've been living on burned porridge and sawdust stew all week.

Edie's blaming Hel's no-show on the weather, but one of the girls reckons the cook only lives halfway down the hill. We're trying not to get our hopes up, but the idea that she might have resigned is the best news all week.

'Respectable performance on the morning run earlier,' Pepper continues, 'even from the L-plate brigade. You're getting stronger but today will be a challenge. You will be pushed further than you've been pushed in your life. But afterwards, you'll be proud of yourselves. Even if you can't walk no more. Prepare for the . . . **TON-UP.**'

We mumble among ourselves. Ton-up? Is it lifting a ton of weight between us? And how much is a ton, anyway? Is it what an elephant weighs? Even Blonde and Blonder don't know what it's about, and they are paid-up Boot Camp Groupies.

Ryan appears, with two sacks of kit. 'We'll be working out in the park. Please make sure you've got plenty of water. You are going to sweat as you've never sweated before.'

The grass is hard and the soil is frost white. Maybe it's not as warm as I thought it was. Under Ryan's command, we lay out five mini obstacle courses. There are mats, plastic traffic cones, weights, medicine balls. Didn't even know what a medicine ball *was* on Sunday, but now I do. It's heavy and round and about as much fun as a dose of cod liver oil. Nasty medicine, that's for sure.

At the end of the course, there's one of those nets you see sheepdogs crawl under at Crufts. This whole week *is* a bit like a dog obedience trial. We run and we jump and we do as we're told in return for titbits or a pat on the head. We're Pepper's bitches, but he's the one doing the barking.

'Groups of two. A, B, A, B, A . . .' Pepper goes along our two ranks – we now automatically fall into formation – to partner us up. Thank God he puts me with Darcy instead of one of the Blondes or, worse, Natalia. That girl's got a serious temper on her, judging from all that drama over a bloody oatcake.

'All right. The ton we're talking about is one *thousand* reps of a variety of different toning exercises. Plus some aerobic work thrown in for free.'

A thousand? I can't even *count* to a thousand, never mind do that many exercises.

Ryan smiles. 'It might sound daunting. But don't focus on the process. Focus on the end result. This is a month's worth of gym work in a single morning. Laying the foundation for abs of steel, perfect pecs, quality quads. A little pain but all gain, right?'

Silence.

'I didn't hear you. Right?'

'Yes, Staff,' we shout back.

Ryan says we'll be doing ten different exercises one hundred times each. I look at the sky, and pray for snow. Then I look at Pepper and I know hailstones the size of cricket balls wouldn't get us off the hook. He'd probably build snowdrifts into our obstacle course, to keep us on our toes.

For the first time I'm actually a bit afraid.

'Exercise number one. Staff Ryan will demonstrate,' Pepper says.

Ryan gets down on the ground.

'We call it the Devil's Leap. Start off lying on your back on the grass, jump up without using the hands, into a star jump then down to a full push-up, then bring your legs back in to your hands, then roll over. That counts as *one.*'

Even Ryan looks dazed when he gets up from demonstrating.

'Person A does ten of those, then completes the mini assault course to get the heart rate back up, then runs back to person B who does the same. Repeat, ten times. Adds up to one hundred reps. Then we'll find you a new exercise to do. Wouldn't want you to get bored, would we?'

We all look shell-shocked.

'One final thing. If you're tempted to cheat, remember, I'll be counting. Any of you miss a rep, the whole group has to run up and down the Ladder. Backwards. Any questions? Thought not. So, ready, steady, go!'

I gulp. Darcy is A and I watch in horror as she runs towards the patch of grass and throws herself down for her first Leap. If I were her, I'd be pacing myself more than that.

One down. Nine hundred and ninety-nine to go.

22

Darcy

The craving hit me when I was starting repetition number four hundred and three.

No. Craving's too weak a word; it's a *compulsion* to smoke a cigarette. And it's been growing with every exercise, till I am almost speechless with desire for nicotine.

I haven't smoked for three years. I never even liked it that much when I did. It gives you pucker lines round the lips, sallow skin, *cancer*.

'Come on, come on, how many more of these do you have to do before you've finished your ton-up?' Pepper's scowling at me.

'Twelve, Staff.'

But however insanely unhealthy it is, the thought of that ciggie is what's keeping me going.

'Good work, Webb! Two more and then hand over to your partner to get your breath back before your last ten reps. At which point, it will *all be over*.'

I've endured Devil's Leaps, medicine ball sit-ups, reverse curl obliques, burpees, squat thrusts, push-ups and fuck-knows-what other tortures.

And through each one, I've imagined every detail of that cigarette, the way Edie said we should imagine *virtuous* things.

Taking one from the packet, holding it between my fingers, lighting it, that first puff . . . Marian would be horrified. She's the one who paid for a whole month of anti-addictions hypno-therapy. Paul McKenna, no less. God knows what favours she pulled to get me into his diary.

'Put your bloody backs into it; this **isn't** KINDER-GARTEN!'

Good old Pepper's random ranting distracts me from thoughts of Marian again.

I scramble to my feet, my nails broken and blackened, and I do the assault course again: weights, hurdles, then a crawl under the bloody scramble net. I race back to Vicki.

'Doing well, Darcy!'

'Your turn now, Vix.'

I don't even have the energy to be out of breath anymore.

The image in my head is of a battered packet of cigarettes in the inside pocket of my rucksack. Lambert and Butler, the easiest ones to buy Over There. The label's warning of disease and death are like a two-fingered salute to boot camp.

Marian says self-sabotage is my speciality. She's still sending me messages about the grave mistake I'm making, how I'll never work again if people think I've done a runner, that I'm nuts.

Messages that were surprisingly easy to ignore . . . until the one that arrived just after we got to the place on the edge of the cliff where the phone signal kicks in again.

DARCY. THINK ABOUT IT. PUNISHING YOUR-SELF WON'T MAKE YOU ANY HAPPIER. IT WON'T SAVE HEELA, EITHER. JUST SO YOU KNOW. YOUR FRIEND, WHO WORRIES ABOUT YOU. M.

'Webb, your partner's struggling. Don't let her give in.' Pepper shouts. I see that Vicki is on the ground, her face a frightening white. The rest of us are bright red.

I run over. 'You OK?'

She nods, but her eyes are round, the pupils shrunken to pin pricks. I try to remember my battlefield first-aid training. Is she about to go into shock?

'How many do you have left to do?'

She holds up a pudgy hand.

'Four?' I lean in. 'Was Pepper counting?'

She shakes her head.

'Make it two, then, yeah? You can manage two, right, Vicki?'

'I . . . don't wanna . . . cheat.'

Vicki hasn't cheated once, even though I'm certain the rest of us must have shaved off the odd repetition or twenty, when Pepper and Ryan haven't been looking. Yes, she's a big girl – why does that sound like the ultimate insult for a woman? – but she's got the determination of an Iron Man competitor. She hasn't complained, either, even though the exercises must be twice as hard with the extra weight she's carrying.

'I respect that, Vicki. But it's one thing pushing yourself to your limits. It's another making yourself ill.'

To our left, Steph's thrown up twice already. She looked mortified, until Pepper – of all people – went over and clapped her on the back, told her he was impressed. I guess it's a macho thing. The dramatic expulsion of bodily fluids is something to be applauded.

Vicki's head begins to rise, millimetre by millimetre, and eventually it reaches the point where we're meant to pause, breathe, then arch up again. She just keeps on moving, a continuous groan escaping her blue-ish lips.

'All right, then, Vicki, that's far enough. Gently down again, eh?' I lean in further. 'I'm worried about you. You should stop. What's the difference between nine hundred and ninety-seven reps, and a thousand?'

She glares at me, as though I'm being deliberately thick. 'Everything,' she hisses, and that seems enough to propel her up and down in her most energetic sit-up yet.

'Fair point.' You don't argue with a woman who seems determined to exercise herself to death. 'Two more, then.'

As she inhales, she makes an alarming wheezing noise, then forces herself up with a loud grunt.

'How are we doing?' Pepper stands over her as she drops back. 'One from the ton, aren't we?'

I frown: how did he know that? Hope he hasn't been keeping score for all of us, or I'll be sent to bed without any tea tonight.

Though at least I have my cigarettes to keep me warm.

Vicki raises her body to first position: holds. Her eyes look like they're going to pop out of their sockets and land somewhere in Cornwall. Maybe she's glimpsed victory.

'That's it, Adams,' Pepper bellows and she holds that final position for one, two, three seconds, and then falls back down , slamming her head down against the grass so hard she's probably rounded it all off with concussion.

'**ONE THOUSAND REPS!**' he calls out, as he has done for the others who've finished: Agatha, the two dumb blondes, a couple of the other girls I've barely spoken to. I haven't been what you'd call sociable this trip.

Everyone cheers, and I grab Vicki's hand to help her up. She's having trouble focusing and her skin feels clammy.

'You surviving?' I ask her.

'More than surviving. Bloody fantastic,' she says, leaning into me. 'The best feeling ever.'

'Webb?'

I turn at the sound of my name. 'Yes, Staff?'

Pepper's smile twists like barbed wire. 'Don't forget *your* last reps. You wouldn't want to be the only one to fail the ton-up, would you?'

I smile back. 'Of course not. My final ten, coming up now.'

He frowns and I wait for him to tell me that it's not just

sit-ups I've skipped, but also five burpees, four Devils, several pop-goes-the-weasels, and the rest.

He shrugs. Maybe he's taking pity on me; though I can't see Pepper being big on pity.

'Make 'em your best ten, eh, Webb? If you don't, then you're only cheating yourself.'

The scene on the way back to the hotel is like the aftermath of one of the many disasters I've covered for TV.

We stagger back, jaws open, clothes stiff with dirt and sweat. For the first time, Pepper doesn't shout at us for dawdling on the Ladder. I wouldn't say that he looks *impressed* with our morning's work, but he's scowling less than usual.

Even the cool-down stretches he leads us through are half-hearted. Then everyone makes a beeline for the dining room.

Everyone except me. All *I* want is nicotine.

On the stairs up to our room, my body's barely co-operating. If those ciggies aren't where I pictured them, I don't know what I'll do.

I pull my holdall from under the bed, and rip it open so hard that all of the teeth come out of the zip and I know that this bag – my old *lucky* bag that kept me safe in a dozen war zones – is destined for the bin.

'*Shit.*'

I'm emptying the contents onto the duvet. Sun cream (ha, ha), tampons, a copy of a glossy mag that wants to profile me. Sorry, that should be *wanted* to profile me. No one is going to profile me anymore. Why would they be interested in a news-reader who got sacked because she was too old?

A newsreader who got sacked because she was also a drunk, a slut, too weak to fight. Too weak to stand up for her friend.

My hand closes around a hard metal case and my heart does

a little jump as I remember: the packet's safe in a camouflaged cigarette tin one of the lads gave me.

I stash the tin down my bra. There's even more room in there now. If I wasn't a candidate for one of Natalia's breast augmentations at the beginning of the week, I definitely am now.

I head downstairs, slipping out of the fire exit and round the side of the building. As the cold air slaps me round the face, I realise I've forgotten something vital. A light. Not like I can pop into the office and ask Edie for one, is it?

The craving makes me reckless. I hug the building's corners and look for another way in. Yup, there's a door to the kitchen. The cook is possibly the only person in the entire place who might let me light up without giving the game away. Hel looks like a smoker. But as I push the door open, the kitchen is completely empty, the work surfaces clear.

That's not right. Lunch should be almost ready. My stomach growls in protest, but my brain is too focused on nicotine to do anything but search for a light.

I pull open kitchen drawers. No matches. How can you have a kitchen without matches? Ah, but there are gas rings. I fiddle around with the controls until finally a pale blue flame rises from the ring, and I lean down to light my ciggie from it. It occurs to me as I bend over the hob that this would make a fantastic paparazzi image to mark the final moments of my career: ex-presenter Darcy Webb in filthy clothes, hair unwashed, hunched over a hob to light her cigarette.

I take the briefest of breaths to make the flame catch, then go back outside, my hand cupped round the end so the light doesn't go out. I want to savour the first full blast of flavour.

It's the perfect spot for a long, slow drag. The beach opens out below me, and the sea beyond that, both a menacing grey. It matches my mood better than sunshine. I inhale, and wait.

The heat burns my throat and I want to cough and I'm just

wondering why *anyone* does this, and what I was thinking, when the first rush goes through my system, and I remember the companionship and long dark nights and fear and excitement all bound up together.

So, it's not the nicotine that's flooding through me, but memories. There was so much I loved about that life, however chaotic and risky it seemed to outsiders. And smoking was part of it. Lighting up with my colleagues after witnessing the most dreadful things made wherever we were seem like a home from home.

'Webb?'

Shit. Pepper!

'Hi, Staff,' I say, holding my right hand behind my back like a kid hiding a fag from her mother. Knowing that the smoke must be curling up behind me in the freezing air.

He's scowling. I brace myself for a telling off, trying not to laugh. My life is in such a mess that a bollocking from an ex-soldier is going to have no impact whatsoever.

Then he sniffs. And sniffs again. His narrow moustache moves up with each sniff and it makes me want to smile. He looks shocked. 'Is that . . . ?'

'Yeah. I'm smoking. *Sorry*. I know it'll kill me, but the idea of it kept me going through that ton-up, knowing I had this to look forward—'

He holds out his hand, expecting me to hand it over.

'Don't be daft,' I say. 'I might as well finish it. I'll take my punishment afterwards. Like a man.'

'No. The packet. Can I see the packet?'

I shrug. 'Why? Want to read me the health warning?'

But I hand the thing over anyway. Not sure why. He can be quite . . . commanding.

He turns over the tin in his hand. 'Bloody hell. I had one like this.' He opens the tin, raises the packet to his nose and inhales.

'You could actually *smoke* one, rather than sniff it, if you want?' I say, trying not to sound amused.

Pepper looks at me, then down at the tin. Then he snatches one and hands the case back to me.

'I don't have a light,' I say, but he's already taken a chunky silver lighter out of his combat trousers. 'Oh! So you weren't going to bollock me for smoking after all.'

He frowns. 'I've probably breathed in so much desert dust and explosive over the years that one of these isn't going to make any difference to my lungs.' He takes a long, manly drag. 'Bloody hell, they still pack a punch. I never thought I'd—' Pepper's eyes begin to water and his face turns blue.

'You OK?'

He nods, splutters, then takes another drag. 'Where the hell did you *get* these?'

I look at him evenly. 'Probably the same place you last smoked them, I guess.'

'*You* were there? In Afghan?'

I nod. 'In 2009 and 2010. What about you?'

He kicks at the grass. 'Three tours. Last one in 2010, too.' His right eye, the one that's seemed lifeless all week, twitches suddenly.

'It's the little things that take you back, right?'

Pepper still doesn't say anything.

'Can't believe it's dragging on so long out there,' I say. If he doesn't respond to this, I guess I should leave it. Just because he wants a dodgy fag, doesn't mean he wants to swap war stories too.

'Reporting out there, were you?' He looks at me sideways.

'Yeah.'

'Bloody reporters. Always getting in our way,' he says.

'Would you rather no one knew what you did out there?'

He shrugs. 'No one's bothered anyway. Papers are always full of Beckham and bonking and reality TV. No room for our stories in the media.'

'Not all the media's like that,' I say.

'At Bastion, were you?'

'A couple of times. But out in the country, too. Social stories. Educating females. Health care.'

The *girly* stuff. They were meant to be soft, easy assignments. I wasn't right for the front line, they told me, after I'd done my first stint out there. Even though at the BBC, they'd sent me all over.

Different in the satellite world, though, Marian told me. 'You're too pretty,' she said. But my colleagues used to whisper *too lightweight* instead.

They were right; she was wrong. Though gradually my 'soft' assignments did get a harder edge. Until the final one, which proved way too hard for someone as weak as me.

'What did you think of the place?' he asks.

'Apart from the assassins and the religious maniacs and the lack of human rights, I thought it was an ideal tourist destination.'

Pepper stares at me for a moment. Then grins. I hate clichés – like every other journalist, I avoid them like the plague – but his face honestly does light up. He looks like a kid sharing a rude joke.

'Yeah. And who needs the thrills of the National Lottery when there could be an IED out there with your name on it?'

We don't laugh – it's not *that* kind of joke – but we share a look that says, *yep*, that's how it was.

I won't tell him what I did. Or what I *didn't* do. I'm thankful for the unspoken rules of combat: what happens on the front line, stays on the front line, unless you volunteer information. Maybe he's done stuff he's ashamed of, too.

I take another drag, but when I look at my fingers, I realise my cigarette has burned right down. How long have we been out here? I want to stay more than I want lunch. It's a companionable silence, somehow.

'I told myself I'd stop after one,' I say, hoping he'll suggest a second.

'Right,' he says, and he's back to avoiding eye contact.

'Besides, lunch will be waiting, right? And we wouldn't want to miss *that*.'

I walk back round the building, but I can't help turning back just before I go round the corner. He's hunched over his cigarette, as though someone might spot the glow in the gloom. There are no snipers here in the Devon countryside, but I guess old habits die hard.

23

Steph

The kitchen is suspiciously quiet and I can't smell anything burning. But we still sit in the dining room, waiting patiently. It's too terrible to imagine there might not be any lunch. Not after our ton-up. It wouldn't be fair.

'How about a chorus of *Why are we waiting*?' Natalia says, after we've been sitting there for ten minutes.

The others glare at her.

'Joke?' she says, holding her little hands up, so her fat rock engagement ring catches the light. Since Liz left, Natalia seems to have become the camp scapegoat. Luckily she seems too thick-skinned to notice it. But *I* notice it. Bullying makes me sick – but I'm too scared to tackle it head on.

'Can't stand much more of this,' Vicki grumbles.

Hunger has eaten into the endorphin high we had once the ton-up was over. My high was higher than anyone else's, even though I did end up vomiting my breakfast into a bush. Bizarrely, after that, Pepper started being all *nice* to me. Well, maybe nice is stretching it, but he picked up my water for me, and gave me a tissue to wipe my face.

'It's proof you're working at capacity, Dean. Well done.' And he slapped my back so hard I threw up again.

Another three minutes pass. By the time Edie comes out of the kitchen, the mood is murderous.

She gulps. 'I'm afraid we have a problem.'

No one breathes.

'Things haven't worked out with Hel, and she's decided not to return. Obviously I tried to persuade her to finish the week but she said she felt . . . unappreciated and I realised forcing her to work her notice might be counter-productive in terms of food quality.'

So Hel threatened to get the weedkiller out. Though a soupcon of Paraquat might have improved the flavour.

'So what the hell are we going to eat now?' Vicki asks.

'We-ell, we have two choices. Always better when there's a choice, eh? Number one, I'm more than happy to get stuck into making something from scratch. I'm more of a home cook, but I have all the ingredients for a very tasty macrobiotic nut rissole which I could whip up in a jiffy. It'd be ready by just before two.'

We look up at the wall clock. It's only just turned 12.40. If we don't get fed sooner than that, we might turn to cannibalism. Starting with Edie and her overstuffed dog.

'What's option two?' I ask, keen to save her from literally being eaten alive.

'It's not really in keeping with the diet plan but, um, I had a rummage around in the chest freezer and I found . . . *pizza*.' She mumbles the last word, as though it's something shameful.

So she looks pretty astonished when everyone cheers.

'Oh. Is that a vote for Option Two?'

'What flavour?' Vicki whispers, awestruck.

'I spotted four American Hots, five Margaritas and a Four Seasons. There might be more down there if I chip away at the ice.'

The mood in the room has changed completely. You can feel the happy hormones in the air.

'Of course, they're absolutely not in keeping with the boot

camp dietary guidelines. They're not gluten-free, not dairy-free, and not at all vegan. All that *cheese*.'

'I don't think we need to take a vote, Edie.' Agatha speaks for everyone. 'Just get those pizzas in the oven, there's a dear. After all the exercise we did this morning, a couple of slices won't make the slightest difference.'

The smell of baking dough permeates the dining room. Usually I'd probably be able to identify the brand of pizza with just one sniff. But my brain's too distracted: all I know is that the smell of the base toasting and the cheese melting is *heaven on earth*.

We're chattering away about everything and nothing. OK, mainly about pizza: deep-pan versus thin-crust, American or Italian style, the pros and cons of chilli oil, and whether pineapple on a pizza can ever be justified.

'Pizza's never been a favourite of mine,' Natalia announces. 'I hate that bloated feeling afterwards.'

Lordy, she doesn't exactly do much to win friends.

We all stare at her. 'Do you mean bloated or do you just mean not starving?' Vicki asks her.

Natalia frowns. 'One of my clients at the clinic who has had a gastric band swears by *raw* pizza, made with a dehydrator. Tastier than Pizza Express, apparently.'

'Raw?' Vicki's shaking her head. She seems quite agitated. 'Do you even *like* food?'

'What a question! Um, of course—'

'You know what, Natalia? Don't answer that. I was only being polite. What I really want to know is if you've heard from your mother. Did she get home OK?'

Natalia frowns. I thought she'd Botoxed herself into a permanent, expressionless blank. 'That's none of your business.'

'Really? You don't think you *made* it all our business when you screamed at her?'

'She'd taken those oatcakes. She was in the wrong.'

Vicki sighs. 'She didn't think, that's all. You know what I think is worse? Your total lack of bloody loyalty to your mother.'

'Vicki . . .' I say. 'Maybe it's a private matter. A family matter.'

'You don't know anything. None of you do.' Natalia's teetering on the edge of a tantrum. But I know how crap it feels when you look around a room and it feels like you haven't got a single friend.

'I know what disrespect looks like. What did she ever do to you?'

'You really want to know, Vicki? Fine. Where do I start? When I was seventeen, the night before my first A-level, my mother decided it was the right ti—'

'Here we are, pizza to go, senoritas.'

Edie is balancing four giant plates of pizza on her forearms.

Natalia's mouth stays open. The attention of the other campers turns away from her story, towards the American Hots.

Finally, she closes her mouth. I'm pretty sure I'm the only one who notices she's trying her hardest not to cry.

I don't enjoy the pizza as much as I should.

All right, it is the lowest common denominator pizza, the kind that would make the average Roman sever diplomatic relations with Britain. But after the last four days of food hell, it's delicious.

My problem is Natalia. I can't stop watching her. She hardly touches her slice of Margarita, and her face is pinched as she pushes the crust around her plate.

'How's that, Natalia?' I don't care what she thinks of the food. I just want her to realise she's not being ostracised by everyone.

'Nice,' she says, unconvincingly.

But it's obvious no one else is interested. The chatter at the table is happy: the Crab girls are explaining Hollywood waxing to an awestruck Agatha. Darcy and Vicki are talking about flattering camera angles.

I try to catch up with Natalia after we finish eating, but she runs up the stairs like she's being chased up the Ladder by Staff Pepper. I bet she's lonely on her own. I almost consider inviting her up to Clamshell but there's not time.

My sympathy wavers a bit when she's late for the roll call.

'What kept you?' Ryan asks when she finally makes out to the car park. 'You're ten minutes late.'

'The pizza made me sleepy.'

'Well, you're in luck. Staff Pepper hasn't appeared yet, otherwise you'd have earned everyone a trip up and down the Ladder. It's not a good way to make friends.'

I make a space in the rank, and she steps in without smiling.

The wind's as harsh as a blowtorch. I'm actually grateful for my L-plate tabard, now. The fabric's thicker than on the green ones the fit girls wear.

'What did you think of lunch, Natalia?' I whisper, to be friendly.

'I hate carbs. Carb is just another word for sugar, and sugar's a poison.'

Ah.

Pepper appears, and leads us through the gates, down to the beach. By the time we get to the shore, our teeth are chattering. We're doing it in unison, like a military machine: Pepper and Ryan should be proud of us.

'Call this COLD? You should try ops in Norway. But don't worry, we'll soon have you warmed up,' Pepper says.

He and Ryan begin to unpack the kit. There are long poles, and fabric, and . . .

'That looks like a stretcher to me,' says Agatha. 'Which could mean one of us is going to get a nice lie down.'

Staff Ryan shakes his head. 'If you lie down for any length of this time in this weather, you'll risk hypothermia.'

'Right, you losers,' Pepper shouts, trying to project his voice as the wind tears it away, 'no time for dawdling. We have two stretchers and two teams. Mixing those teams up a bit after yesterday's fun and games.'

Ryan takes over. He's not even shivering. *What a man.* 'Each team runs along the beach, to a halfway point we will choose along the way. Then we come back to here. There must be four team members touching the stretcher at all times. Even when you go over the sea walls.'

'That looks easy,' says Natalia.

'Does it? Let's make it harder, then, Staff Ryan.'

Ryan lifts in two huge beer barrels, plus anything else he can think of. His face shows hardly any effort at all though those gorgeous eyes are slightly wider. Medicine balls, free weights, lifejackets. I bet the kitchen sink will be next.

The others scowl at Natalia. The staffs were going to load the stretcher anyway, but now Natalia's the scapegoat; everything's her fault. I just hope Pepper picks the team himself, or she'll be left as the last one standing. And I remember how humiliating that is.

'Right, Team Alpha is everyone this side of Agatha, Team Bravo is everyone else.'

Damn. I'm on Pepper's team, not Ryan's. On the plus side, I'm working with Agatha – along with my room-mates. Plus Natalia. I smile encouragingly at her: this could be her chance to redeem herself. That's the good bit about army discipline. All for one and one for all. Or was that Disney's Three Mouseketeers?

All Natalia has to do is try.

Pepper marches over to us. 'I always lead Team Alpha, for obvious reasons. You don't want to let me down, or there'll be trouble. Winning this takes strength and strategy. So the short arses should go at the back – that'll be Dean and Greer.'

Natalia and I do as we're told and take a corner each.

'You—' Pepper points at Agatha, 'can be the relief when the others get tired, and then Webb and Adams can take the front end. Webb, let's test your leadership skills, shall we? Set the pace, keep the pace.'

The stretcher doesn't feel *that* heavy and the wood is warm against my bare skin. We move towards the start line that Pepper's drawn in the sand.

The pole slips out of Natalia's hand and almost topples all the load.

'Oops.'

'You'll have to take those gloves off,' Pepper says.

Natalia pouts. 'But I'm growing my nails for the wed—'

I don't think Pepper's going to be impressed with *that* excuse, so I talk over her. 'Come on, let me help you, Natalia.'

She glares at me. God, she really isn't helping herself, is she?

'You know something, Natalia,' I hiss, so only she can hear me.

'What?'

'I'm actually on your side. But please give me some sign, just the tiniest little sign, that you're not a total spoiled brat.'

Pepper stands alongside us and calls out advice. 'All right. Go as fast as you can but mind you don't run out of steam. Think about the hare and the rabbit.'

'I think it was a tortoise,' Ryan calls over, and *his* team laugh.

'You won't be laughing when the A Team bust your asses,' Pepper shouts. 'Are you ready . . . steady . . . RACE!'

As we move off, Natalia only just hangs onto her pole.

'Butterfingers!' Pepper shouts, but the word sounds a bit ridiculous in his meant-to-be-scary voice, and I giggle.

Natalia glances at me. And *smiles*. First genuine smile I think I've seen from her in all the time we've been here.

'No laughing. Gigglers don't come first.'

'Yes, Staff,' Natalia and I reply, trying not to look at each other in case it sets us off.

Already we're falling behind Ryan's team.

Darcy turns round: 'How are we doing, team? Don't forget when you get tired we can get Agatha to step in.'

'I'm ready and waiting,' Agatha says.

Natalia and I both shake our heads.

'Stop yakking, Team Alpha. There's a bloody great barrier ahead of you,' Pepper bawls.

Team Bravo are already there, by the flood wall. It seems like there's no beating them . . .

But as we watch, their stretcher topples over, spilling the contents all over the sand.

'Imagine if that was a casualty,' Pepper shouts out, gloating at their error. 'You get a one-minute time forfeit for that.'

'All right, team,' Darcy calls out. 'We're not going to make *that* mistake. Agatha, you spot for us, yeah? Call out so we can co-ordinate our steps over the obstacle.'

Agatha scoots to the front.

I'm breathless, but it helps to imagine that we're carrying a casualty who needs the fastest, gentlest journey back to base.

'Front stretcher bearers, follow my count to obstacle, in three . . . two . . . ONE,' Agatha says, 'UP, one . . . two.'

Darcy and Vicki grunt as they climb up and over, and at the back we try to keep the stretcher as steady as possible.

'Good job, team,' Darcy says. 'Ready at the back?'

'Are we?' I ask Natalia. 'I think we're pretty crucial to this working.'

She nods. We try to mirror each other's movements.

Agatha calls out, 'Approaching the wall in three . . . two . . . one step then *up*.'

We're a team. Steps, legs, bodies, synchronised.

It feels good.

Once we're over, Darcy turns round and grins. 'Good job, team mates. Now, up the pace.'

And Natalia and I share another brief smile. Our feet slap rhythmically against the sand and I feel like we're unbeatable.

'Enough self-congratulation,' Pepper snaps. 'You're not even ten per cent of the way yet. Just one slip, and we'll be the losers again.'

Agatha comes round the back. 'I suppose now's not a good time to tell him that it's not the winning, it's the taking part?' she whispers. 'Anyone need a break?'

I expect Natalia to jump at the chance of a rest, but she shakes her head. 'Nope. What about you, Steph? You've been doing the lion's share of the work back here.'

Pepper looks as surprised as I feel.

'Yes, good work, Dean. And good call by your teammate. Take the break.'

I wonder if I'm hallucinating, till I see the corner of his lips are turned up in an expression that looks . . . well, it looks suspiciously like approval.

And all because I threw up my breakfast.

As we race towards the next groyne, which is glazed with icy seawater, our lead over Team Bravo grows, and Pepper doesn't

183

need to say another word because Webb's got it all under control.

We're not individuals anymore. We're a unit. Me, Agatha, Darcy, Vicki, *and* even Natalia.

And finally I understand why people get into team sports. Because when you're all giving one hundred per cent, you feel on top of the world.

24

Steph

We won!

Really. Even with me to drag us down, Team Alpha are the victors! Suddenly Staff Pepper loves me, loves Vicki, loves Agatha, loves Natalia, but especially *loves* Darcy.

'Fantastic leadership, there, Webb. I'd say you're a natural.'

OK, it's just a stupid stretcher race, but victory tastes better than chocolate.

The only downside is that the adorable Staff Ryan is on the other side. The losers are enjoying a group hug, led by Ryan. While Pepper is too busy gloating to gather us to his manly chest.

Hmm. The downside to being an Alpha is that I'm not on the receiving end of the Team Bravo group hug. Pepper doesn't do touchy-feely and even if he did, it wouldn't be the same without Ryan.

'To the victors, the spoils!' says Pepper. He's holding up bags of peanuts. *Salted peanuts.* They're in those tiny airline-sized packets but those are still at least twice as big as the meagre portions we've been getting all week. 'I know these aren't strictly Edie approved but with the kitchen situation, these are better than nothing.'

Vicki's eyes are on stalks. She tears into the packet, and empties the nuts into her hand. There are *eleven* in total. 'Salt. Never thought I'd be so excited by salt.'

'Better make them last,' I say. 'God knows what's for dinner. I doubt Edie's going to let us eat pizzas for the rest of the week.'

Vicki sighs. 'No. I guess it's gonna be Edie's knit-your-own macrobiotic rissoles from now on. I don't even know what macrobiotic *is*.'

'I've a feeling we could be out of the frying pan, into the microwave.'

'If you weren't on holiday, you should do it, Steph. I bet you could make even tofu taste edible.'

'No, I can't cook without butter—' I say, automatically. Then Staff Ryan catches my eye and smiles. And I wonder whether Vicki has accidentally stumbled on the one way I could impress Ryan. 'Or maybe . . .'

Don't think. DO!

I corner Ryan before I can change my mind. Does he smile more broadly for me than for them? Or am I deluded?

'Hi, Steph.' He whispers my name, so Pepper doesn't hear he's using Christian names. It makes it sound surprisingly naughty.

'Do you have a minute?'

He steps away from the others. 'Is it about the chocolate?' he says. 'Because I'm not going to give you any extra rations, even if you did win the race.'

'No. No, I don't want that. But it's sort of connected,' I say, blushing madly. My crush really is spiralling out of control. 'The thing is, I can cook.'

He nods vaguely, distracted by the blondes, who are putting on quite a show as they bend over to put the gym kit away.

But then he realises what I've said.

'*Cook?*' He sounds so impressed, as though I've told him I can levitate or tell the future from tea leaves.

'Hmm. My day job *now* is designing supermarket ready

186

meals, but before that I did full Cordon Bleu training. Patisserie. Butchery. I can even bone a fish or humanely despatch a lobster.' *Wish* I hadn't said that. My ability to kill crustaceans is hardly likely to cut the mustard with a war veteran. A *trained killer*.

'Handy skill to have.' His eyes twinkle in a very un-trained killerish way. 'Are you suggesting what I think you're suggesting?'

Is he *flirting*?

'We *could* keep eating frozen pizza,' I say. 'But it does defeat the purpose of boot camp.'

He thinks about it. 'You'd be happy to cook for everyone?'

'I can't promise a banquet, but I reckon I could do a better job than Hel.'

'But this is meant to be your holiday.'

I try not to laugh. 'Believe me, what we've been doing is not my idea of a *holiday*. Anyway, I love cooking.'

Do I? Over the last few years I've started to hate it: the cost-cutting and the office politics at work, and the constant nit-picking from Steve at home for using too much cream or sugar. Oh, and the sheer boredom of cooking the same dishes every Sunday for my family. It's not that Mum's recipes aren't delicious. But food's about experimentation, as well as the comfort of the familiar.

'Well, it's a very generous offer, Steph. Edie will want to kiss you all over.'

It's not *Edie* I want to kiss me all over. I look down so he won't see how fiercely I'm blushing. 'It'll be enough of a reward to know I've rescued my fellow campers from starvation.'

'Only your fellow campers? Don't me and Staff Pepper get a taste?'

'If you stop sending me up and down the Ladder . . .'

187

'Let's see how well you cook before I agree to *that*, Stephanie Dean.'

Edie doesn't *actually* kiss me but she does look super-relieved.

'Seriously? You think you can cook for everyone?'

I look round the kitchen, which is basic, but has all the essentials for mass catering. 'I won't win any Michelin stars, and I doubt I'll have time for pudding, but we won't go hungry.'

'Wow! You're a saint! Saint . . . Delia of Boot Camp!'

It always amazes me how people get so excited about something as basic as breaking eggs, sifting flour and melting butter. For me, it's about treating the ingredients with respect, tasting as you go, and the rest . . . well, it's as easy as pie.

She backs out of the kitchen and almost curtseys as she leaves.

'Right!' I say, to my new domain. 'Let's see what you've got.'

I'm in uncharted culinary territory. Kitchens tell you a lot about their owners. Mine would tell you I'm indecisive, prone to mad crazes and ridiculous experiments. And *so* messy. My old tutor would weep into her coq au vin.

But I hope my kitchen would also tell you I'm generous. The cupboards are groaning with home-made biscuits and cordials, to be pressed on guests as a farewell gift in case they get hungry or thirsty on the way home. In the autumn I smell of pickling vinegar. By November, it's the brandy I use when I'm mixing my Christmas puddings.

The Windy Hill Hotel kitchen is harder to read. The pans are marked by years of cooking, baking, braising. I wonder how many breakfasts have been fried on the hob there. When the house was first built, there'd have been a range, and a sturdy Victorian cook with her platoon of kitchen maids, their Sunday roasts and grand dinner parties warming the whole house.

There are two wooden bar stools tucked under the counter,

and a stack of puzzle magazines on the shelf where I'd expect to see recipe books. I pick one up: the word searches are all done, and the crosswords filled in with spidery capital letters. I guess Hel was too busy doing these to cook.

I open the fridge and sigh with relief at the stack of butter and the huge bottles of milk. Then I remember I'm supposed to be cooking dairy- and fat-free. Hmm. We'll see. There's a wilting iceberg lettuce the size of a cow's head, a brown paper bagful of hard tomatoes, and one of the smallest chickens I've ever seen. Plus a brick of bean curd, and a range of other unidentifiable ingredients.

It's like a nightmare version of *Ready, Steady, Cook.*

The walk-in larder is bigger than my entire kitchen, but the cupboard is almost bare of regular ingredients. Maybe Hel nicked anything tasty before she went. What's left is baffling. Quinoa and flaxseed and hemp. *Hemp?* I thought they used that to make T-shirts for hippies. Soy and rice flour, with one life-saving box of wholemeal. On the bottom shelf are cardboard boxes overflowing with gnarled, uninspiring winter veg: carrot and swede and onions and something that may or may not be sweet potato.

Potato. My heart skips a beat. Was there ever a nicer word?

Plus beans, of course. This is *Windy* Hill, after all. Ink speckled borlottis, hard red adukis, flat butter beans (how anyone could think they taste of *butter* is beyond me), and three different kinds of lentils. On one shelf, there's a collection of luminous liqueurs: banana, fig, something purple with the label missing.

Then I see it, a battered old box on the top shelf, like something shameful.

Maldon. *Come to Mama.*

The sea-salt crystals sparkle like diamonds under the strip

light . . . if I grind it up small enough, Edie never needs to know.

'How's it going, Steph?'

Ryan's behind me. When he's not shouting orders, his voice is mellow, like the moors. I've always hated being called Steph – it sounds like a boy's name. Or like an old man clearing his throat.

But not when Staff Ryan says it. I'd love to record him saying my name. Use it as my mobile ringtone. *Steph, Steph, Steph.*

The sooner I get back to civvy life the better.

'Are you spying on me, Staff?'

'No! No, I just wanted to come and thank you.'

'You haven't seen what I'm making yet.'

He comes round to face me. 'Can I lick the spoon?'

Again, I wonder if he's flirting. I never can tell. Maybe he does just want to lick the spoon.

'I don't actually *know* what I'm making yet, so there's nothing to lick.'

I really wish I hadn't said the word *lick.*

'It can't be worse than what Hel used to make. I've suffered five boot camps with her cooking and each time I worry I'm going to be the one losing the most weight.'

'I'll try to make sure that doesn't happen.' He doesn't need to lose a gram. I swear his body is *perfect.* Funny, I always thought men like Steve were my type: tall, rangy, slightly raddled.

But Staff Ryan's reassuringly manly: he'd make even *me* feel small and protected. And those hands . . .

I'm fighting the urge to ask him to sit down and chop some carrots or something, just so I can watch his muscles work. 'You're distracting me.'

He hesitates for a second. Then he nods. 'Sorry. Well, if you need any help . . .' He smiles. 'Don't bloody ask me. I can't even make toast without burning the kitchen down.'

'Better stick to what you do best then, eh, Staff?'

'And what would that be?' He raises his eyebrows. Waits. Is he fishing for compliments?

'Ordering around defenceless women. And push-ups.'

And looking like the sexiest man to come out of Yorkshire since Heathcliff.

They're waiting out there. I hear laughter. Maybe this is how an actress feels on a first night.

My Posh Grain Bake is either going to be disastrous or delicious. As I lift it out of the oven it smells OK but then baked things always do.

Ah well. This lot are so hungry they'd probably eat the porcelain.

I take a deep breath and push my way through the door, holding the enormous gratin dish out ahead of me.

'Wow!'

'That looks *amazing*.'

'Bring it over here right now. I want first dibs.'

Half of me wants to chicken out even now and beg Edie to order a takeaway. But I think the campers might lynch me if I take the food away again. There's a lot of barely suppressed frustration in this room.

So I put the dish down and race back into the kitchen, pretending I have to fetch something else. But it's really so I don't have to see their faces when they take a first mouthful.

I wait.

Silence.

It's inedible.

They *hate* it. They hate *me*.

Everything Steve ever said about my food is true – how

my meals are a triumph of expensive ingredients over slapdash cooking.

I'm not hungry myself. I only had a mouthful of the raw mixture to check the seasoning. It was very . . . solid. I'd hoped it'd taste better when it was cooked, but . . .

'Steph?' Ryan again, behind me.

'Look, I'm sorry if it's awful. I tried, but, you know, low-fat cooking isn't my area of expertise. My muffins are great, though. And my—'

I feel a hand on my shoulder.

His hand.

I think I might faint.

He turns me around. In a movie, this would be when we'd kiss. But in that movie, I'd be blonde and a size eight and irresistibly cute in a white frilled apron and not a lot else.

'Aren't you coming to have some?'

'I . . . I'm not hungry.'

Ryan grins. 'You're joking!'

I shake my head. 'Is it OK?'

He keeps smiling. 'Well, I must admit that it's not my kind of thing . . .'

The disappointment makes me dizzy. He *hates* it.

'I'm more a bangers-and-mash boy. But it seems to be going down pretty well out there.'

And he ushers me out towards the dining room – he's not touching me anymore but he *almost* is – and I peep through the crack between the door and frame.

You could hear a pin drop. Or a fork . . .

'They're eating it,' I whisper to Ryan.

'They are,' he says.

'Doesn't mean they *like* it,' I say.

'They're smiling.'

And they are. No one looks up. They're all too busy scoffing to notice me.

'But it's not *your* sort of thing, though, Staff?'

He pulls a face. 'Normally I wouldn't touch anything I can't identify. It's a kind of self-protection mechanism. But you know what?'

'What?'

'It was absolutely *bloody* delicious. I only came out here to see if you've saved any seconds for me and Pepper.'

The Big Fat Boot Camp Blog, in association with *Gossip!*

....

Dateline: 10 p.m., Wednesday, Devon

Our very own Private Benjamin, Vicki, gets hot and bothered in her latest posting from boot camp.

Evening, world and especially my boys. So much for the Wall. Today I'm a happy bunny.

My belly's full of our first decent meal in four long days, thanks to an angel. Well, she's actually my room-mate, but now we're calling her St Delia. I swear her cooking has turned me into a new woman. I never knew that low-fat food could taste nice.

Yes, the portions were half the size of what I eat at home, but, you know, my stomach must have shrunk because I felt *totally* full up afterwards. Bloody brilliant. And if my stomach's shrinking, well, hopefully the rest of me will follow before *too* long.

Night night, everyone. But especially Alastair, Murray and Rudy. Missing you more every day. See you Saturday. If you recognise your brand-new Mummy.

Day 5: Thunderous Thursday

How you'll be feeling: moody! In our experience, this is the day when the adrenalin rush hits the buffers and happy hormone levels take a nosedive. So we've got fun activities to keep you smiling – and a protein-packed, all-veggie menu!

05:45   Parade and morning run/fitness kick-start

07:30   Breakfast: Bootylicious Baked Eggs, Wake-up Tea

08:30   Body Combat Gets Sexy with Foz

12:30   Lunch: Home-Made Bean Curd Burgers with Calorie-Burning Chilli Salsa

13:30   Animal Crackers on the Beach: Crawl like a Caterpillar, Lunge like a Llama, Feel like a Fox!

18:00   Talk

19:00   Dinner: Asian-infused Aubergine on Roast Peppers. Fig Surprise.

Please note all activities and meals are subject to change due to circumstances beyond our control

25

Vicki

'. . . you could do worse, mate. All women get fat in the end so at least you know in advance what you're getting with Dean. And bloody hell, can she cook!'

I slide along the cold wall. Why didn't I drag myself out of bed sooner? Well, I know why. Getting up was hard this morning. My muscles felt like lead, and the world outside the blankets was icier than ever.

But if I'd got here just sixty seconds earlier, I might have heard what Ryan said about Steph before Pepper's back-handed compliment. More piss-taking, probably. Except . . .

Except I remember Ryan's face after he snooped on us in the drawing room. Maybe he's after something more than her recipe for chicken tikka masala . . .

And why not? She's very pretty, and she'd only have to get shot of a few pounds to be even prettier. Maybe it's disloyal of me to think that about another big girl, but it wouldn't take much effort to turn her into a total stunner.

I'm so convinced I'm right that in my head, I've married them off – with a boot camp guard of honour – by the time Ryan sighs. 'Stop it, Matt.'

'Stop what?'

'Taking the piss.'

'I'm not.' But I can hear Pepper chuckling. 'You know I'm

an old romantic at heart. What's the matter with her? Not your type?'

Yeah, Ryan, I think, what exactly is the matter with my new mate? She's smart, she's nice to look at, and she cooks dinners that could change your life.

'It's nowt to do with *her*. It's *you*, Matt. Why does everything have to be a game? The women we can pull, the ones we can reduce to tears, how many times we can make them throw up. It's like living in an episode of *The Weakest Link*.'

'It's called *fun*, Ryan. A laugh. God knows, I need something to take my mind off what a bloody misery you can be.'

My mum and dad bicker exactly like this, and they've been married thirty-six years.

'Fine, Staff *Pepper*. You won't have to worry about that soon.'

There's a pause that lasts *way* too long before Pepper says, 'What?'

Another pause. 'Forget it. I wasn't planning to . . . not now.'

'What weren't you planning?'

Ryan sighs. 'This isn't working for me, Matt. I've tried but, I dunno. I can't seem to adapt to *normal*. I know you've gone out of your way for me and I'm bloody grateful but . . .'

'You're leaving me?' Pepper's voice has lost its bluster. 'I mean, leaving boot camp?'

Ryan says nothing.

'You can't.' Pepper sounds so sure that I think there must be a contract Ryan has signed in blood to keep him here for ever.

'I can, though. Look, I appreciate all you've done, but it is my decision. You can't pull rank on me anymore.'

'And who else do you think will employ you, Ryan? With *your* record? There's a recession out there, in case you hadn't noticed. Last time I checked there wasn't a massive demand for loony ex-soldiers, even pretty ones like you.'

Loony? If I'd had to put money on which one of these two was unstable, I wouldn't have chosen Ryan.

'Thanks for that, *mate*.'

'You're welcome. Mate.'

I can hear Pepper smoking, taking short, angry puffs.

'Can I have one?' Ryan asks.

'Help yourself.'

The lighter flares.

'Listen. Me leaving, right? It's got nothing to do with you, Matt.'

Staff Pepper laughs. 'It's not you, it's me, is that it? Save your breath. Write me a Dear John letter instead. Base it on the ones women have sent you, eh?'

'Sticks and stones, Pepper. Makes me more sure I'm doing the right thing.'

'I thought it *wasn't* my fault. Make your fucking mind up, Ryan.'

I can hear how hurt Pepper is, but he's never going to admit it, is he? He's a bloke.

'It's not you,' Ryan says, softer now. 'It's *them*.'

'The women? They can be a bit irritating, but—'

'They're not irritating. They're *normal*. That's what I can't stand about them. Their stories about their kids and their wedding plans and their ordinary jobs. I hate it. Knowing I had my chance and I blew it.'

'With *Jackie* you blew it,' Pepper says. 'But that doesn't rule out all the other women on the planet, does it?'

'You said it yourself, Matt. I've had a postbag full of Dear John letters over the years. I don't *get* women.'

'They get you. They *love* you.'

'It's the uniform. The muscles. But I can't talk to a girl unless I'm correcting her sit-up position, or I'm pissed out of my skull. Might as well join the Foreign Legion.'

'They wouldn't have you. You're out of condition.'

'Plenty of other places where that wouldn't matter. Iraq's nice this time of year. Or Afghanistan.'

'You wouldn't go back *there*?'

'Like you said, not many grand opportunities for loony ex-soldiers here. I'm gonna have to go somewhere that doesn't need references.'

'Ah, I'll give you a reference, mate.'

'The kind that'll help, or the kind that'll mean no bugger will touch me with a bargepole?'

'You really think I'm that vindictive?'

'No. No, I – I don't make much sense this time in the morning. You should know that by now, Pepper.'

'Or the rest of the bloody time, now you mention it,' says Pepper.

And then they stop talking. They can't admit they'll miss each other any more than they'd admit to impotence or crying at the end of *Bambi*.

I'd bloody hate to be a man.

On the dawn run, you'd never know anything had happened. And at breakfast, everyone is too distracted by Steph's amazing porridge to notice that both staffs look pretty glum.

Karma the dog's glum, too. He's worked out he's not going to get any food from us, because we don't want to waste a single spoonful. Even that silly cow Natalia is all but licking her bowl.

'This is incredible,' Edie says, when Steph finally sits down to enjoy her breakfast. 'I mean, obviously I did promise sugar-free food this week. But it's not a criticism. We'd be going hungry if you hadn't stepped in so magnificently. What did you use? Honey? Agave nectar?'

Steph shakes her head. 'Actually, I didn't sweeten it at all. Just used ground almonds to thicken the porridge. But the flavour fools the tastebuds, and the protein content of the nuts should help us feel full for longer, too.'

'Genius,' says Edie, and when she puts her bowl down, it's scraped clean. Karma starts to whine and she pats him guiltily. 'Better get you fed, now, boy or you'll be calling the RSPCA dogs' hotline, won't you?'

The food's on a different plane, but Steph's got one thing in common with Hel: the tiny portions.

'I know they're small but there's not much to work with. Plus I don't want you lot coming after me on Saturday if we haven't lost weight, do I?'

Are we losing weight? Now the food's so good we don't need to fantasise about that; we've moved on to obsessing about whether boot camp is going to work.

'My body feels the same,' Steph says, 'but my trainers feel too big for me. Can your feet lose weight?'

'Definitely,' says Natalia, who is finally making an effort. 'I'm not going shopping for shoes until a fortnight before the wedding, in case mine get even smaller. I might have to resort to the children's range; I'm only a size four to start with.'

You'd think she's the only woman in the world who's ever got married. God help her when she gets pregnant. She'll call Sky News. It'll be like a second virgin birth.

Blimey. That's a bit nasty, even for me. She's just a silly kid I'll never have to see after this week. Can't even blame hunger for my bitchiness anymore.

Maybe it's envy? Wouldn't I love to start over, undo all my terrible mistakes?

'I'd love to lose weight on the outside,' I say, making the effort, 'but what matters to me is what's going on under all the fat. I just want my body to work better.'

'Hoorah to that,' says Agatha, raising her cup of mint tea. 'Here's to living for ever.'

We sniff the air like dogs as we step outside. Despite the grim forecast, I don't think it's going to snow. I'm almost disappointed – Team Alpha would be bloody good in a snowball fight, and Pepper would be on hand with battle tactics.

But instead of winter sports, it's kick-boxing with Foz. Now there's a bloke that loves himself. I wonder whether the panthers love him too.

'Till now, you've been working on your upper halves, but today we're kicking off. Your quads form your most powerful muscle group, so it makes sense to use 'em when you're under attack.'

I pair off with Steph.

'Who are you going to imagine kicking today?' she asks as she puts on the pads. 'Natalia?'

'God, is it that obvious? No, I just wish she'd make it up with her mum. I don't *hate* her. You?'

She frowns. 'It's a bit odd. The other day, I ended up imagining a whole line-up of people I fancied throwing a punch at.'

I laugh. 'None of us lot, I hope?'

'No. People from my past. Mainly my ex, if I'm honest.'

'What did he do to you?'

'Nothing. Well, he dumped me, which I'd have preferred him not to have done. But he didn't sleep around, didn't beat me, didn't steal my money. Yet when Darcy asked me to think who I wanted to hit, Steve's face kind of . . . appeared on the pads. Like a hallucination.'

I pull on my gloves, the sand inside scratching my skin. 'There've been times when I've felt like slapping my husband, but I can't say I've ever wanted to *punch* him.'

'Oh,' she says. 'I guess I'm a violent psychopath. The even weirder thing is that despite the punching, I'm actually here at boot camp because I want him back.'

'Yep. That is *officially* weird.'

Foz begins to demonstrate his latest moves – choosing Darcy as his model, surprise, surprise. She doesn't look happy.

'Why did he dump you?' I whisper.

'He said I was holding him back.'

'Really? You don't seem like a holder-backer to me, Steph.'

Frank is grunting his way through a routine that involves more groin-thrusting than a pop video.

'I tried to make it work. To support him. But Steve wanted adventures and, well, do I look like the adventurous type?'

'I'd say that anyone who comes on a boot camp has to be a little bit adventurous.'

Steph shrugs. 'I only booked because I want to show him I've changed. There's a Valentine's Ball coming up and Steve will be there so . . .'

She stops abruptly and I see Foz staring at us. 'Girls, you're not going to burn any fat gassing away.'

'Keep talking to me while I kick,' I say. 'Oh, and lower those pads a bit, or I'll do my hip in!'

She drops her hands. 'I really do want to be in shape for this ball.'

'Why? If he finished it, why not look for someone who wants you for *you*? Shouldn't be any shortage; you're fantastic.'

Steph groans. 'Yeah, right. Well, first of all, I love him. And second of all, my whole family love him too. He's always sending tickets for the hottest gigs to my brothers, and he even took my dad to the Grand Prix. He's a concert promoter. Rock god. I mean, imagine. Me, dating someone that cool?' Her face drops. 'Lost cause, isn't it?'

I'm starting to get puffed. 'Fight . . . if you . . . want.

But . . . maybe the two of you . . . you just weren't . . . meant to be.'

'Except I want to change, Vicki. Be less boring. I don't want to spend my life inventing TV dinners. Or sitting alone in my flat, eating them. I want drama.'

I think about Ryan and Pepper, and the *dramas* they must have had. 'Drama can be overrated, Steph. Plus, you don't have to climb mountains to have adventures. The kids have been mine. Changed everything.'

'Steve doesn't want kids. Says they'd hold us back.'

'Time to swap over, my Amazonian tribeswomen,' Foz announces.

I pull at the gloves – bloody relief to get the sweaty things off – and get my breath back as I fit the pads instead. 'No kids is fine if neither of you want them. But don't waste your life on someone who doesn't want *you* either, Steph. I was lucky, I met Dave without having to kiss hardly any frogs. But you're still young—'

'Thirty in two years,' she says, throwing a first wild kick that almost catches me on the wrist.

'Thirty! Oh, wow! Better book that retirement home. Or start paying into your funeral savings fund.'

She smiles sadly. 'My mum died in a car crash when she was thirty-four. Only six years older than I am now.'

'Shit. Steph, I'm sorry, that joke—'

'Don't be sorry. All I'm saying is, you never know what you've got till it's gone. I lost my mum. I don't want to lose Steve too.'

She throws another couple of kicks at the pads, but they barely register on my hands. Her heart's not in it.

'But your mum and this Steve, they're not connected, sweetheart. Losing your mother is terrible. But losing a bloke who isn't right, that could be a good thing.'

'No.' She stares at the pads, eyes glassy.

'Oh, Steph, babe, you mustn't be sad. If a man makes you sad, he's not worth it—'

'Vicki? VICKI?'

Edie is calling me. I look up and see she's on the beach path with Phil the photographer.

'Shit. I'd forgotten all about him. What do you reckon, Steph? Am I ready for my close-up? You can be in the picture, too.'

She manages a smile. 'You're beautiful inside *and* out, Vicki. But however much I love you, there's no way *I'm* going to pose. I don't want to break the poor man's camera.'

26

Darcy

Breaking news, courtesy of my voicemail.

Hi Darce. I'm guessing this will be no surprise to you but they've finally lost patience. As of 9 a.m. tomorrow, you no longer have a job. They're planning to issue a press release with the new line-up first thing Saturday, for max coverage in the Sundays.

Am assuming you're happy with this as you haven't returned any of my calls, or texts. Either that or you're having some sort of breakdown by the beach. Sorry, perhaps that was uncalled for. I respect your decision. You're a grown woman. Just wish I could shake the feeling that you haven't actually made a decision, but that you have rolled over and let it happen.

OK, here goes. I'm not one to beg, but call me, please, Darcy. If only to agree what you want me to say when the calls come in from the press, as you know they will. It's not about my commission now. Just about your dignity—

'Darcy . . . I don't suppose I could ask one little favour, could I?'

Edie has snuck up on me. I end the call, then turn round. 'What?'

'It's just . . . well, you're so good at the combat work, and I wondered if you might agree to be in the photo with Vicki. You're so photogenic, and I'm also thinking that if you've enjoyed yourself, it might encourage others of your *stature* to give us a try . . .'

Stature. I manage not to laugh out loud. 'I thought this was the celebrity's *best kept beauty secret?*'

Edie smiles fixedly. 'Secrets aren't always very helpful when it comes to marketing.'

I sigh. 'Sorry, Edie. I . . . don't think it's the right time.'

She shrugs, and walks off to ask Natalia. Edie must think I'm some kind of stuck-up celeb who won't get out of bed for anything less than a *Hello!* centrespread. But she'll be grateful later. It won't do Windy Hill any good to be known as the place where I was hiding when I literally got my marching orders. Lightning won't strike twice, but your average dim celeb is superstitious about that kind of thing.

Natalia doesn't need asking twice. She stands with the boxing pads raised as Vicki kicks. In the background, Frank is ducking and diving, trying to get into the frame.

'Look like you're enjoying yourselves, if you can,' the photographer calls out.

It's surreal to be on the sidelines. But this whole week has had a surreal quality, like I'm watching myself from a distance. There's been the odd moment when I've actually felt something – exhilaration after the stretcher run, extreme cold on the morning jogs, the desperation for a ciggie.

But that phone message from Marian has had no effect at all.

What was the word the trauma therapist used? *Disassociation.* Maybe this is what a nervous breakdown feels like. Hey. Pretty painless so far.

'That's it; we're done for the time being,' says Phil the photographer.

Natalia's expression doesn't change. Perhaps her face is frozen in that unnatural smile – the temperature *has* dropped by several degrees since we came down here.

'Stay for lunch, won't you?' Edie says, fluttering her eyelashes so hard at the photographer that it looks like she's dislodged a contact lens.

'I'm more of a beer and burger guy,' says Phil, slapping his huge belly. 'Porridge isn't my scene.'

'Ah, but we've had something of a breakthrough on the food front,' Edie says. 'One of our boot campers turns out to be a gourmet cook. You *must* sample her food for yourself. I think she might be the Next Big Thing.'

Hunger breaks through my numbness. As we traipse up the hill and through the curly gates towards the hotel, I'm looking forward to being back in the cosy dining room. Now Steph's dishing up miracles, it's like coming home.

'I had to break into the rations for tonight for this,' she says, as she brings in a roasting dish full of veggies in earthy Mediterranean colours.

'I didn't even realise I *liked* aubergine,' Agatha says, taking a first taste of the ratatouille, 'but this is divine. It's like eating an autumn bonfire.'

Steph sits down at the table, her skin red and sweaty from the heat of the kitchen. 'Is a bonfire really something you'd want to eat?'

'Undoubtedly, my dear. It takes me back to nights under the stars in the Girl Guides. In fact, you know, my only disappointment with boot camp so far is that it lacks an actual *camping* element. Staff Pepper?' she calls over to his table.

'Hmm?'

'Have you considered including a camp in your courses? I do think that there's nothing *quite* so invigorating as sleeping in the great outdoors.'

'Even in January?' he says.

'Absolutely! Come on, girls, hands up who'd want a night in the open with our two dashing instructors?'

No one puts their hands up. Having slept under canvas – and under fire – I don't have any romantic ideas about it myself.

'Look!' Vicki shrieks, before jumping up and racing towards the French doors. 'It's snowing.'

I'm expecting a half-hearted sprinkling. But when I get to the window, the flakes are as big as fifty pence pieces, and they're already turning the grass white.

We're all looking now. Ryan gazes up at the skies like a little kid, while Pepper is pushing open the door to stick his hand out.

'It's only bloody snow,' he says.

We follow him out. Snow disruption led the bulletins for two weeks running the Christmas before last, and our poor forecaster spent the month on outside broadcasts in various snow drifts, because the producers had this theory that the public held her responsible and wanted her to suffer as much as possible.

But out here in the wilderness, with no buses or trains to derail, there's something magical about this first fall, like watching a spell being cast on the countryside.

We're shivering, even though snow usually warms things up a bit.

Agatha frowns. 'Rum sort of snow, if you ask me.'

She's right. The stretch of drive leading up to the house is changing from snow white to a glassy grey.

'Brilliant effect,' says the photographer, and he grabs his bag and heads outdoors. 'Vicki, will you come with me? Boot camp frolics in the snow would make a great shot.'

Vicki pulls a face but follows him anyway. I won't miss demanding photo shoots, the snappers determined to try out some new idea, to get 'that' definitive shot of me.

Is it really all over?

Pepper and Ryan huddle together in discussion for a few seconds.

Then Pepper claps his hands. 'Right. The Animal Magic afternoon session is delayed by fifteen minutes while we suss out the weather. But don't expect an easy ride. Staff Ryan and I have spent seven nights on exercise in Norway without a sleeping bag or a single word of complaint, so we'll still be expecting one hundred and ten per cent.'

As the others leave the room, whooping about their extra fifteen minutes of freedom, I catch Pepper's eye, and he nods.

Outside, Vicki's trying to make snowballs for the photos, but the flakes turn to ice as soon as they hit the ground. I go out the back way, and the cold makes my eyes hurt. I pull my hooded top up over my head, and reach into the pocket for the cigarette tin.

But it seems rude to light up before Pepper joins me.

'So has snow really stopped play?' I ask, when he finally appears. I offer him the box, but he lights my cigarette for me first, holding his hand protectively around the flame till he's sure it's caught. When they're not turning the air blue or firing RPGs, most soldiers have impeccable manners.

'Snow's fine. Ice is our problem. Forecast is for temperatures to keep dropping, which could make it treacherous. If this was real basic training, it'd be business as usual but with you lot . . . might have to be indoor circuits. Don't expect an easy ride, though.'

'I'm confident you can inflict every bit as much pain on us as you can outdoors,' I say. 'Out of interest, when was it that you discovered your sadistic streak?'

He looks at me. 'Might have been when I started decapitating sparrows for fun. Or maybe when I water-boarded my best mate in reception class so he'd tell me where the Easter bunny had hidden his eggs. What about you? When did you realise you were vain enough to become a TV presenter?'

'Ha, ha. For your information, I always hated the limelight. I was the only media student who refused to do a piece to camera in my graduation film.' In the distance, the snow clouds are darkening, making it seem much later than lunchtime. 'Funny how things turn out.'

'I checked your joining questionnaire. I'm curious about something.'

'What's that?' I suppose he's entitled to read it, and yet I feel oddly exposed. I was in a bad mood when I filled it in. Well, I've been in a bad mood for the last two years.

'You already work out regularly. You planning a marathon or something?'

'Me? Christ, no. I don't have the stamina. Or the inclination.'

'Going back to Afghan on assignment, then?'

'They wouldn't let me. They say the insurance would be too high.' Even though they're always sending the other top billing anchors to present from war zones. I reckon they just don't trust me anymore. Well, that's one less problem for them now I've been replaced.

'Why come here, then?'

'You read my questionnaire. You tell me.'

'To look better,' he says, sounding baffled. 'Isn't the fact you're on telly night after night a sign that you might look pretty . . . respectable already?'

'Are you paying me a compliment, Staff Pepper?'

A pink tinge spreads across his ruddy skin. 'Don't take the piss. You're a TV star. Of course you look good.'

'Ex-TV star.'

He frowns at me. 'Ex? How do you work that one out? I saw you on the telly last week.'

'Bong!' I say, doing my best Big Ben impression. 'My agent just left me a message confirming that the company have terminated my contract. Bong! They're bringing in an autocutie who is ten years younger. Apparently, my wrinkles are distracting viewers from the serious issues of the day.'

'They said that?'

'No. I made that last bit up. But they *have* ditched me, and it's pretty obvious that's why.'

My mouth has gone dry. Telling Pepper makes it real, and I feel light-headed. Free? Or frightened of going back to London to . . . nothing.

He's still staring at me. 'I'm no expert but I can't see any wrinkles. Are you sure it's because you're older?'

'How old are you, Pepper?'

'Thirty-two.'

No guessing games, no bullshit. That's why I prefer the company of men. I look at his face, try to work out why he looks older than that. There are hardly any lines but there's a wariness in his eyes. He's seen things he wishes he hadn't.

Maybe that's why I've aged too fast as well.

'Do I look old for my age, then, Webb?'

'I never thought *you'd* be the vain sort, Staff Pepper.' I smile. 'You don't look old. Just *experienced*.'

'So do you!' he says, then laughs when I pull a face. 'Don't tell me. That's the wrong thing to say to a woman, right?'

I nod. 'It does have . . . connotations.'

'I apologise, Webb. Can you take a thousand previous insults into consideration? I'm not good at dressing things up. But what will you do now? You're not going to take it lying down?'

I shrug. 'No point fighting once they've made their minds up.'

'Is it that easy to find another job with a different channel, then?'

211

'As a woman approaching –' I hesitate, then decide that I don't want to bullshit either – 'forty, I'm more likely to marry the Pope than walk into another presenting job.'

He breathes out bright white smoke. 'And you don't care?'

Do I care? Right now, the rejection hurts more than the practicalities of losing my job. I know the newspaper columnists will stick the knife in, that there'll be the unbearable shots of *her* posing with the rest of the presenting team in *Hello!*

'Obviously I'm upset—'

'Then do something about it. I mean, I've met a few hacks over the years and there are two categories.'

'That's funny. I always think the same about soldiers. Type one are good guys. Type two are psychos.'

'Which am I?' he asks.

'Jury's out.'

'All right. Well, there are two kinds of journos. First sort, I wouldn't have trusted to use a bloody latrine. But second sort were grafters. Didn't expect special treatment, rolled with the punches. I reckon you're one of those.'

If only he knew. 'Thanks. But I don't know what makes you think that.'

He looks up at me. 'A hunch.'

'Right.' Our eyes meet.

And I see in *his* face what I think he's seeing in mine. Not strength, but loss. Once you've stared death in the face, you're different. You inhabit a place where true goodness seems as unlikely as a fairy tale.

He takes a deep drag on his cigarette. 'Tell you another thing. What all those hacks had in common – the lazy bastards and the good ones – was they loved a fight. Our lads are the same. Two thirds excitement, one third shitting themselves. But like us, the journos had chosen to be there. No one gets sent to the field against their will, right?'

'No.' Most of the proper war reporters I knew – the ones with special extra-thick passports which read like a combat history of the world – would rather lose their wives than their jobs. And they did. During late, whisky-fuelled nights, divorce stories were swapped as often as battle tales.

There *was* something incredibly seductive about it. A life where what mattered most was the now, where every minute could be our last, where the graveyard humour kept us laughing when really we should have been crying.

'So you had the guts to go to a war zone, Darcy. And the ambition to become a big name presenter. But you don't have the bottle to fight for your job?'

'It's not like that—'

'Matt? MATT?'

Ryan comes round the corner, and the look on his face when he sees me is a picture. 'Hi,' he says. 'I need to talk to Matt—Pepper.'

'Just cadging a cigarette from our war reporter friend here,' Pepper says. 'She's been to Bastion. We were comparing notes.'

Ryan barely looks at me. 'Great. But we need to talk about the weather warning they've just issued.'

'It's cool,' I say. 'I'm done.'

Pepper reaches out as I go past. His hand catches my sleeve. 'Think about it, will you, Darcy? The one battle tip I always gave to my boys before their first time. Trust your instincts. Doing nothing ain't an option. Move forward, move sideways, duck. Anything. Better to do *something* than die because you turned into a sitting duck.'

As we grind our way through sit-up after mindless sit-up on the hard ballroom floor, I can't stop thinking about what Pepper said.

Trust your instincts? But what if your instincts got someone killed?

'You should be getting to the point of failure, now, boot campers. Your muscles very nearly giving up. But you can push for the last five.'

What will life be like as a failure? I've *always* been busy. I edited the college newspaper, did shifts in dead-end radio stations in my holidays, wrote freelance pieces for the broadsheets instead of sleeping. I lived and breathed the news.

Yet I've survived this week so far, haven't I? No telly, no radio, no papers. I'm still alive.

In London, though, there's no escaping the news. My apartment mailbox will be filling up with magazines: *Private Eye, The Economist,* the *Spectator.* My Sky Plus is lining me up dozens of shows to watch, from *Newsnight* to *The One Show* to subtitled despatches from forgotten war zones.

What is the *point* of Darcy Webb if she's not reporting, informing, telling stories?

'No bad going, boot campers. We'll switch to reverse curls, now.'

The other women groan. Ryan's running this class, while Pepper makes contingency plans for the weather. From my position on the floor, I can look up through the window but I can't tell if the snow's still falling: all I can see is heavy cloud that seems to promise another three or four inches before dusk.

'All right, we're beginning with twenty. And UP . . . down . . . UP . . .'

If I'm not working, will I still read every single paper over breakfast? Have the radio *and* TV on at the same time? Pile up political biographies and terrorism reports next to my bed, so I can use my insomnia to stay a step ahead of the competition?

It sounds like a sad life, but I don't like novels, I loathe watching soaps, and glossy magazines leave me cold. I'm a journalist.

It's in my blood. News is oxygen. Without it, I'll suffocate.

I sit up suddenly, and despite the dizziness, everything is crystal clear.

Ryan frowns. 'You OK?'

'Very much so,' I say, standing up. 'I'm really sorry but I need to make a phone call. I'll make up the sit-ups later on.'

'So you've remembered how to use your phone?'

Marian answers at the first ring – something she never does – and despite the sarcasm in her voice, I can tell she's relieved to hear my voice.

'The signal in the sticks is intermittent. I've had to go way beyond the hotel gates just to get two bars.'

'Well, it sounds perfectly clear to me. Anyway, my messages have said it all. The press enquiries are already burning out my BlackBerry. And I warn you. The protection that being a name gave you won't last for ever. Don't be surprised if the new presenter line-up isn't the only story with your name in it on Sunday.'

I shiver. 'I know that. I . . . I've made a mistake. Not calling you. I was confused. But I'm not confused anymore.'

'Oh. Do tell.'

'Is it really game over, Marian?' I've phrased my question like that on purpose. If there's one thing my agent loves more than Missoni, it's a Mission Impossible.

'We-ell. Any other agent would have sacked you already.'

I don't remind her that she has ditched me several times this week. 'You're not any other agent.'

'Hmm.' She's waiting for me to say something else. To apologise, maybe, or to come up with a convincing excuse for my behaviour. But if it was easy to explain, I wouldn't have been hiding from her for the last three days.

'So what would be your strategy?' I ask.

'*If* I agreed to try again, then it would have to start with you getting your newly toned arse to London and preparing to grovel as you've never grovelled before.'

It's what I was expecting her to say, of course. 'How soon can you fix up a meeting?'

'Well, I'm meant to be going to Milan tomorrow night but I might be able to squeeze you in pre-lunch.'

'That might be a struggle from here. It's a long way.'

She tuts. 'Do you *want* this, or not?'

'I want it.' *I think.*

'Well, then, another early-morning start won't do you any harm. Despite your appalling behaviour, you still have your defenders in the network, though the chances are if you do get your job back, you'd have to work graveyard shifts again for the next year. But you must *promise* you won't stand me up.'

'Of course. I'll leave first thing.'

Another pause. I know she wants me to say how lucky I am to have her, but perhaps the back-slapping should wait until we've got it in the bag.

'It'll be a fight, Darcy.'

'Yeah, but you always win, Marian. That's why you're my agent.'

27

Steph

I've fallen in love all over again.

Not with a man, obviously. My crush on Ryan won't change my life. But my rediscovered love of cooking just might. After so long producing conveyor-belt cook-chill compromise food, with no idea what the 'end users' (ugh) thought, it's so energising to get immediate feedback.

'What are you doing for us tonight, Steph?' Edie's behind me. She's so tiny that I can never hear her footsteps: it's like sharing space with a fairy.

'Depends on what shows up on the farm van.'

She frowns. 'It hasn't been yet? They usually come by midday at the latest.'

We both look up at the kitchen clock. Ten to four. It should have been here by now, especially if I'm going to get something on the table by six.

'Maybe the weather held them up . . .' I peer out through the window. Dusk is falling earlier than usual, thanks to the snow clouds. It makes the kitchen feel extra-cosy but I guess it's not much fun on the roads.

'I'll chase them up,' she says. 'If by any chance they don't show, do you have enough to pull something together? With two extra for dinner. Foz usually does massages late on Thursdays and Fridays, and the photographer's worried about the ice, so I said he could stay over. I'd send him out for fish and chips but I don't think he'd make it down the hill without a sledge.'

I open the fridge, scrutinising what's left. 'I can just about manage tonight. It might end up being a bit . . . well, fusion, if you see what I mean.'

'Fusion? Wow! You really are a culinary genius, my darling Steph. You know, when this week is done, perhaps I can make you my nutritional consultant.'

I pinch more than an inch around my belly. 'Because I'm such a good advert for healthy eating, right?'

'Don't! I'd die for a cleavage like yours.'

'Trouble is, you'll have to have the fat arse to go with it.'

Edie scowls. 'Dear me, we need to do some more visualisations, don't we?'

'So long as I manage not to fall asleep this time?'

'Well, you're definitely coming on boot camp again. I'll give you a free week for this. As many free weeks as you can handle till you feel comfortable in your own skin.'

'Thanks.' I won't tell her that I wouldn't come on boot camp again if she paid me. 'I'd better . . . get cracking, I guess.'

Edie gives me a final thumbs up and then leaves me wondering how exactly I'm going to fill fifteen empty bellies (sixteen if I include Karma's) with a brick of dried-out tofu and a large bag of basmati rice.

By six, the kitchen is all steamed up. It feels safe. Outside is a different story. I've pulled down the blind because the snow gives the world an odd orange glow, and I keep imagining there are wolves circling the hotel.

'Need a hand?'

My heat levels shoot up another twenty degrees. It's Ryan. 'You could take some plates through in a minute once I've dished up.'

When I turn round, he's enough of a gentleman not to recoil. I bet I look like Mrs Bun the Baker's wife: a sweaty roly-poly whose cakes you'd want to eat but you'd never want to undress.

Undress? Who mentioned undressing?

'What's this?' He goes over to the paella pan where the dish of the day is undergoing a final searing.

'If I tell you, you won't want to eat it.'

'Well, it smells bloody good. Double rations for me, please, chef.'

Oh, what I wouldn't give to give *him* double rations . . . 'It's almost there. You can take the salad out to the troops, if you want.'

He picks up the two glass bowls and leaves the kitchen with the last of the fresh veg. I grated two seen-better-days cabbages till they cried for mercy, then added poppy seeds and an improvised creamy yogurt dressing that disguises their limpness well enough.

I dip my finger in the dressing. What does that remind me of? Something about the flavour unsettles me . . .

Germany. Rain and rows. Steve was there promoting a thrash metal group. The weather was awful, the band even worse.

'Couldn't you have made a bit more effort, butterball? Your face is going to make a wet weekend in Munich even more depressing.'

We rowed at the airport, in the hotel lobby, our room, the venue – and the things he said were so horrible that I stormed out, something I'd never done before. I didn't have an umbrella, or even a coat, so I took refuge from the rain in the very first restaurant I found, a backstreet place full of families who hadn't expected to see a young, plump English girl come in on her own and stuff her face.

But the food was perfect for my mood, comforting country

stodge: thick-sliced potatoes and paprika-loaded goulash, with a poppy seed and cabbage salad on the side.

He got back to the hotel room at three, or it might have been four in the morning. He woke me up to say sorry and then we made up properly, as we always did, even though I felt about as sexy as a dumpling drowning in stew. Who can blame him for leaving me?

'What can I do now?'

I blink, surprised to see Ryan there again. 'Oh. If you carry the warm plates, I'll take the paella in.'

'Paella,' he says, careful not to pronounce the 'll'. 'I've never had the real thing. Spanish, right?'

'Mine's . . . more inspired by the East,' I say, which is a cheffy way of preparing him for the fact that there's no chicken, no prawns, no saffron. At least there's rice. Thank God there's rice.

When we get into the dining room, I remember they're all so hungry that they won't care about gastronomic faithfulness. 'Boot Camp Paella,' I say, then dart back into the kitchen before anyone can complain.

In the kitchen the smell seems more intense. I'd become used to it while I was cooking, but now it hits me full-on: warm, rich, spicy. OK, so the 'meat' of the dish is the tofu, but after the roasting I've given it, it should be almost impossible to identify. Then there's about two heads of garlic in there, and a slosh too much oil for it to be truly low fat.

But my top secret ingredients couldn't be more basic. Salt, and pepper. Absolutely *loads* of both. On Edie's banned list of course, but beggars can't be choosers. The flavour was pretty good when I checked the seasoning, but now it's time for a proper tasting. Last night, I forgot to save myself any and ended up going to bed hungry: tonight I've kept a small portion for me.

I blow on the spoon to cool it down.

Wow.

That's possibly the best tofu dish I've ever had in my life. Not that I'm a bean curd connoisseur, but *wow*. The sauce is rich and the curd is crispy and delicious. It's not pretending to be meat, but when it tastes this good, I don't think it has to. For the first time, I begin to wonder whether I might actually be a culinary genius.

But the proof of the pudding isn't what *I* think. It's what the end user . . . sorry, *diner* thinks.

I open the kitchen door and look through to the dining room. Edie, Ryan, Pepper, Foz, the photographer and the other boot campers are hunched over their bowls like workhouse orphans in *Oliver Twist*.

No one's saying a word. But they're all grinning from ear to ear.

After dinner, they have to manhandle me out of my cosy kitchen.

'You should put your feet up,' Edie says. 'Plus, don't forget your massage with Foz. It's thoroughly well deserved!'

I *had* forgotten, and the idea of getting my clothes off in front of someone doesn't feel like much of a reward. Vicki drags me off into the drawing room in the meantime. Compared to my kitchen, it's like the North Pole. But then she lights the fire and the room is splashed with red and orange light. What with that and the snow outside, I feel even more like a character in a Dickens novel.

'Ever thought about leaving your job, Steph?'

'Only about twice a day.'

'Come and be my live-in chef, then.'

I laugh. 'I'm flattered, but what would your boys think? Do small boys eat tofu?'

'If anyone could convince them, you could. That was amazing. The only thing that would have made it even better is a bloody great glass of wine. '

'Or port,' I say. 'All sweet and syrupy and—'

'Stop it! I reckon we should play cards, to take our minds off the booze.' Vicki picks the pack off the table and begins to shuffle. 'Didn't think I'd miss drink *this* much. I've spent thirty-six months pregnant over the last eight years so it's not exactly new, but even so . . .'

I'm adding up numbers in my head. 'You've got three boys, right?'

She keeps shuffling, but drops a few cards. 'I . . . I've been *pregnant* four times, though.'

'What happened?'

She leans down to pick the cards up, shuffles again. Bites her lip.

'Sorry. It's none of my business,' I say.

Vicki begins to deal, making two piles on the table alongside us. 'She died. My last baby.'

'Jesus, Vicki. How?'

She doesn't look at me. '*I* killed her.'

'What do you mean?'

'It was me. Greedy, you see,' she pinches her belly. 'I was too fat to carry a baby this time. Too selfish to see that stuffing my face meant I didn't deserve her.'

'No. Vicki. I'm sure that's not right. Babies die for lots of reasons. It's awful but it's no one's fault.'

'Everyone says that. But they don't know.'

'Have you talked to anyone about it?'

She shakes her head. 'No. Dave's the keep calm and carry on sort. For the sake of the boys. Doc said he could refer me, but I don't want to sit opposite some drippy counsellor who'll end up hating me because it *was* my fault. Plus, I'm too much of a coward. If I start talking about her, I'm scared I won't be able to stop.'

I reach over to touch her, but she shrugs me off. 'You could tell me about her. What was her name?'

'I don't . . . I won't . . .'

She jumps up, and rushes out of the room.

'Vicki, wait. Sorry if I said the wrong thing. But please. I'm sure you weren't to blame.'

I run after her and catch her by the front door. She's fighting to get it open, but Edie's already fastened all the latches and so we end up in this ridiculous battle, with me trying to close the locks as she tries to open them.

'Leave me *alone,* Steph!'

'You're not even dressed to go out. Look at your feet.' She's wearing those fluffy socks with non-slip plastic paw marks on the bottom.

'Let me go. It's nothing to do with you!'

Finally she wrestles the door open, and pushes me out of the way, running out into the snow. Should I follow her, or leave her or—

'What's going on?'

Ryan appears, a tea towel in his hands.

'It's Vicki. She got upset about . . . about something and ran off outside. She's only got slippers and a tracksuit on.'

We both gaze at the white landscape outside. The footprints are tiger-shaped, and go round to the right of the building.

'We could follow her trail,' I say.

'Did you have a bust-up?' he asks.

'Us? No. She's upset about stuff in her own life.'

'Tonight's usually the night when the women fall out. That's why we call it Thunderous Thursday.'

I stare at him. 'We're that predictable, are we?'

'We've run a few of these now, and Thursday's always when

the stress kicks in. Guests start worrying about whether they've shifted enough weight.'

Poor Vicki's got a hell of a lot more on her mind than her waist measurement. 'And soldiers never come to blows on *their* boot camps, then?'

Ryan looks surprised. 'Oh. I'd never thought about that. There were more than a few punch-ups, but at least the blokes got it out of their system. I remember one time—'

'I'd love to hear the story, Staff, but shouldn't we be going after Vicki?'

We step further into the porch, and then jump backwards, startled by the cold. 'I think she'll be back of her own accord soon, don't you?' Ryan says.

'Maybe . . .'

He puts a hand on my arm, and I feel a tingle. 'I'll do you a deal; if she's not back in five minutes, we'll send out the search party.'

'She could freeze to death in that time.'

Ryan smiles. 'You women are better at endurance than us, right? She'll be fine. I'll make you a herbal tea while we wait. You deserve it after that amazing dinner.'

I should be out there looking for poor Vicki, but it's rude not to respond to a compliment. Especially one from *him*. 'You liked it?'

'Are you kidding? I *loved* it. So did Staff Pepper. He loathes veggie food, but now he's talking about refusing to do any more camps unless Edie chains you to the kitchen. Though I said it'd be only fair to let you have the odd day off.'

I laugh. It's a stupid idea, but for a minute, I let myself imagine working somewhere I'm appreciated. 'You couldn't afford me.'

'Shame.'

It is. I'd be no great loss to the world of supermarket ready

224

meals. In fact, I wonder how long it'd take them to notice if I didn't turn up for work on Monday morning.

The front door rattles, then creaks open.

'Vicki—'

Her hair is flecked with snowflakes and her skin is waxy from the cold.

'Don't. Just . . . don't.'

And she pushes past me and Ryan, and back up the stairs. I consider following her, but Ryan touches my arm again. 'I don't claim to be great at understanding women, but I'd say right now she'd like to be on her own.'

28

Steph

Vicki has locked herself in our room. I knocked on the door, but she just told me to go away.

The only positive spin I can put on this woeful situation right now is that, as the Clamshell suite is under occupation, I'm safe from Foz's magic fingers.

But Edie's not having any of it.

'We'll set his couch up in my flatlet, so long as you turn a blind eye to the mess!'

I smile. The people who go on about mess usually live in laboratory conditions. Though in Edie's case, the laboratory probably smells of lavender oil and enough incense to mask any macrobiotic flatulence.

Foz is ahead of me, bounding up the narrow staircase behind the kitchen, with his massage couch under one hairy arm. He seems to know the way.

'Right you are, Steph. Let's just find a space to pop this up . . .'

That's going to be easier said than done. Edie's quarters are tiny – and *definitely* nothing like a sterile laboratory. In fact, I'd quite like a plastic pinny and rubber gloves to protect me from whatever's growing on that cluttered kitchen worktop.

Maybe that's unfair. The room isn't *dirty*, but it is ferociously overcrowded with *stuff*. Edie must live, eat, work *and* sleep here, when she's not on duty downstairs. The space doesn't even have the faded grandeur of the rest of the hotel, unless seventies curtains and woodchip ceilings count as faded grandeur. There are stacks of books, files, paperwork. And I can't smell incense, or lavender oil. Just the whiff of Karma: as in dog biscuits, dog hair and a vague aroma of fart. Can't tell if it's macrobiotic or not.

'There we go,' says Foz. 'Upstanding and ready for action.'

He's put the couch up next to the sofa bed. 'Do I . . . undress?'

'It's going to be a bit bloody tricky doing the massage if you don't, Steph,' Foz says, and I cringe. His tone softens. 'I'll make myself scarce to give you a chance to get down to your bra and pants, and then just pop yourself under the sheet, face down. Oh, and take that thing off your wrist too. Is that the latest line in friendship bracelets or something?'

I look down. I'd forgotten all about my elastic band therapy. And I only realise now that my Compare-o-meter has been on standby since I started cooking again.

'I don't know what that's doing there,' I say and as I pull the elastic off, it snaps.

Foz has arranged his bottles of massage oils so they're perfectly aligned. I wish I was looking forward to this. Could I ask him to go up to Vicki instead of me? I hate to think of her in our room, alone, except for the ghost of her lost daughter. I don't believe in the supernatural, but I do think grief can haunt you.

I shiver.

'Tell you what,' he says, 'I'll stick a blanket on top too, Steph. It's the coldest January I can remember. But once we get your circulation going, you'll feel hot to trot! Right, back in two shakes.'

He leaves via the only other door. I hear water running, so I guess he's in the bathroom. Yes, he's *definitely* been here before.

I sit on the sofa arm and take off my shoes and socks first. The last time I undressed for Steve was five months ago and I've put even more weight on since then. What will Foz think of my awful body?

Maybe it was a bit too soon to take off the elastic band.

Still, Foz can't think any worse of me than I think of myself . . . and I've missed being touched. I fold my clothes up on the sofa arm, then climb onto the couch and wriggle under the blanket. From here, I see one corner of the room is cosier than the rest. There's a huge armchair, a crocheted rug in rainbow colours, a collection of soft toys, a water bowl and a series of plates with a few scraps of food left on them: cooked sausage, chicken, cheese.

Then I realise. It's Karma's corner. That animal is so spoiled.

'Ready!' I call out.

He smiles professionally as he comes out of the bathroom.

'Let's get going, Steph. You've bloody earned this with that knock-out grub, so I'll give you an extra special going over. For you, I think, a warming aromatherapy blend. Black pepper, mandarin, in a grape seed carrier oil.'

I twist my head round. Close up, he's older than I thought, with crow's feet and blotchy freckles, as though he's beginning to rust from the inside out.

He lays his hands on my neck, puts me back in position so my head's sticking through the hole in the couch. I can see a pile of paperwork on the carpet. 'Just relax, Steph.'

Relax? I'd prefer to relive the moment when they applauded me at the end of the meal, as though I was an alchemist who'd turned cans of slop into gold.

When Staff Ryan told me he wanted seconds.

'So how are you finding boot camp, Steph?'

His fingers dig so deep into my muscles, it's almost painful.

'Hard going.'

'Yup. That's normal. But, Steph, I do think Pepper and Ryan are tough. They take no prisoners. One of the highest client drop-out rates in the business.'

'Really?' I feel quite smug not to have dropped out. 'How do you know?'

'There's quite a big circuit of camps out there now. I talk to clients. Some are addicted to boot camps. They might do five or six a year. This camp has a reputation as one of the hardest. So you're doing well to stick it out, Steph.'

'I'll try to remember that when I'm on my way up and down the Ladder.'

'Your first time on a boot camp, is it?'

'Isn't it obvious from the shape I'm in?'

'Ha, ha, ha.' His laugh is too hearty. Of *course* it's obvious to an expert like him, who must have felt thousands of bodies in his time.

I should change the subject, to distract him from my cankles, and those strange stretch marks behind my knees. 'So, um, how did you get involved in this particular boot camp, then?'

'Ah, that's a long story, Steph. And a story that might involve too many indiscretions.'

'Right.' Not sure I want to hear about Foz's conquests. I open my eyes: through the breathing hole in the couch, I can see the floor. There's a gnawed bone, and a couple of bills. Red bills. I squint till I can see the figures. Bloody hell. No wonder Edie's not got round to the decorating if that's what she owes the gas board.

'Let's just say that Edie and I go back a long way and when she was launching, she needed the old Foz magic touch. I attract people, if that doesn't sound too vain. If those two staffs are the rough, then I'm the smooth.'

As he kneads away, I have to admit he's a pretty wonderful masseur. My body seems to float somewhere in space, with waves of pressure and warmth passing over me. I smell citrus trees and earthy spices. It's better when he's not talking, and when all I can hear is breathing. Mine and his. He knows where to push and where to be gentle. I wonder what he's like in bed: whether he shows off there, too.

I'm blushing. What the hell? I don't even fancy him. Maybe he has hypnotic powers. Either that, or boot camp is releasing hormones I'd forgotten I had.

I start talking again, about anything, to fill the silence. 'What about Staff Ryan and Pepper? Did you know them?'

'Not before I came here. They're new to the game. Might explain why they're on the tough side. Plus, of course, they're super loyal to each other. Maybe too loyal. Go back a long way, those two.'

'How long?'

'They were in the army together. Pepper's older than Ryan, right, had served longer. I gather Ryan was his protégé and so Ryan won't challenge Pepper even if he's too tough on the guests. Plus, of course, they were in the field together. An experience like that can screw you up. Make you lose sight of how far you should push people.'

'You think they go too far with the clients?'

'Ha, ha, ha. Naughty Steph! Not for me to say, though going too far isn't exactly unknown in camp circles. Some of the campers would be disappointed if the staffs *didn't* go too far.'

'Eh?' For a moment or two I can't work out what he's talking about. Would anyone come here *wanting* to be bullied, or made to wear L-plates?

Then the penny drops. He thought my *going too far* meant something else entirely. 'You mean sex?'

'Ha, ha. You won't catch me telling tales, Steph. All I will say is that on the last night, the beast with two backs sometimes makes an appearance, if you get my drift.'

Every muscle in my body tenses up as I *do* get his drift.

Ryan and Pepper screw the clients.

'Oh,' I mumble. Is that what Ryan has been doing – buttering me up for a *basting* later in the week? But then I realise how ludicrous that would be. Why would he choose *me*, when he could have Darcy or the blondes or even Karen the triathlon girl?

'I'm deadly serious, Steph. Though –' he coughs – 'maybe I shouldn't be gossiping. People in glass houses shouldn't throw stones, eh?'

His hands leave my shoulders suddenly. '*Shit.* You got me all distracted talking about the fun and games. I'm late for my next lady.'

I begin to get up, shell-shocked by what he's said about the staffs. Especially Ryan.

But Foz pushes me down, quite forcefully, as though he's horrified by the idea of seeing my saggy belly. 'No, no, Steph, don't get up too fast; just stay down on your front. Let me check my list so you can tell me which room to head for and then you can dress in private. It's . . . Karen Regan?'

'She's in Barnacle, I think. She does Iron Man challenges and stuff,' I say. 'I bet she has outstanding muscle tone.'

Foz chuckles. 'Now, now, Steph. Anyone would think you see me as some kind of lech. I'm more of a connoisseur. I've massaged thousands of bodies in my time and I assure you, if you dig deep enough, every female form has something wonderful about it. You've got gorgeous firm, creamy flesh, for example. Bet you never sunbathed, right?'

'I burn.'

'Well, it's something that makes you very special in this age of deep orange tans.'

'Thank you.'

'My pleasure, Steph. Just part of the Foz service: to try to leave every lady understanding what makes them uniquely wonderful.'

Whereas all Pepper and Ryan care about are the bits of the body that make every woman exactly the same.

The Big Fat Boot Camp Blog, in association with *Gossip!*

Dateline: 10.45 p.m., Thursday, Devon

The snow's come down in the West Country, and Vicki's caught a chill and gone to bed early, so our photographer, Phil, who is stranded in darkest Devon, has recorded his own 'boy's own' vlog for us.

Hello and, um, welcome to the Phil Channel. It has been said I have a face for radio, but I'll do my best on this side of the camera for one night only.

We appear to be cut off from the rest of the world, mainly because Windy Hill Hotel is at the top of a ruddy great, ungritted hill. I've just got myself a seriously nippy new Audi and I'm buggered if I'm going to risk—

Anyway, chances are you're more interested in boot camp than my car bodywork. You know, I'm impressed by the ladies. They've embraced the Blitz spirit and the weather's no excuse to slack. There are sit-ups in the sitting room, stair races, indoor circuits.

Poor Vicki's so keen to keep up the good work that she took a brisk walk in the old sub-zero temperatures outside and came back bright blue. Don't worry, boys, your mummy's gone back to normal colour now, and is tucked up in bed after a hot shower. She says night, night to everyone. And I'll wish you all good night, too, and sorry you had to see my ugly mug. Normal service will resume tomorrow, I'm sure.

Day 6: Thank F It's Friday

How you'll be feeling: exhausted but finally seeing the light at the end of the exercise tunnel. But beware of complacency. Today is no easy ride. By this evening you'll be on your knees, or flat out on your back. Or we want to know the reasons why!

05:45   Parade and morning run/fitness kick-start

07:30   Breakfast: Passionate Porridge, Wake-up Tea

08:30   High-Energy Hike – Let the landscape take you to new heights!

12:30   Lunch: Flavour-Packed Pickled Peppers

13:30   Super Power Circuits: Channel your Inner Spiderwoman, Catwoman or Wonder Woman

18:00   Talk: Goals to keep the 66-day habit

19:00   Dinner: Surf 'n' Turf – Boot Camp Style. Gooseberry Surprise.

Please note all activities and meals are subject to change due to circumstances beyond our control

29

Vicki

I go to bed ashamed and I wake up ashamed. I'm a grown woman, but last night I behaved like a little kid. Except that's unfair to little kids: even Rudy's outgrown that kind of tantrum.

One minute I'm fine, belly all full, hands warming up, ready for a card game and a gossip with Steph. Next I'm running outside the bloody hotel in the snow, my Lion King socks soaked through, my hair frozen solid, and my eyes blurry with pointless, stupid, angry tears.

I'm not a crier. But there I was, leaning against the hotel building because I'd come over all weak, howling at the moon like a ruddy werewolf.

Weird, though, crying felt quite . . . good. My throat hurt and the tears made icicles on my cheeks. But inside I felt like I was defrosting. The more I howled, the better it was, as if the moon was listening, and the sky, and the countryside out there. I howled because I was all alone.

Except, I wasn't alone, was I?

Between howls, I heard a twig crack. I crept round to the corner of the building, and saw the silhouettes of two people. The staffs. A gossip at that time of night? My cheeks burned red hot when I realised they'd probably heard me.

But it wasn't Pepper and Ryan. It was Pepper and *Darcy*, both smoking. At first, I couldn't make sense of it. The hoity-toity TV star, and the rough, tough soldier?

I watched them from my corner. Felt relieved when I saw Darcy lean in as Pepper lit another cigarette. They hadn't heard me at all.

'. . . will you do it for ever?'

'What, be like Frank Walton, oiling up women into my fifties because it's the only way I can get a cheap thrill? Please God, no, Webb.'

'Maybe you should settle down.'

'You offering?'

'Not me. I'm not a settling-down kinda girl.'

'Pipe and slippers and a wife and kids? Not for me, either. Tried it once. Not the kids bit, we didn't get round to it, but the rest. Then Afghan changed me, I guess. All some of the lads wanted was to get home, screw the missus, take the kids to the swings, make everything normal. But normal's overrated, in my book.'

'I'm with you there.'

I couldn't work out what Pepper and Darcy meant. Normal was all I ever wanted. Normal equals happiness. I *had* normal, till I messed up.

Then I realised I wasn't crying anymore, but I didn't feel better either. And my feet were going numb, so I had to get inside again. I pushed the front door, and Steph and Ryan were there. Last thing I needed was a reception committee, so I raced past, up to the room.

But I saw the look on her face as I pushed her out of my way. I'd hurt her. I almost turned back but I was about to collapse from the cold. Threw myself under the shower upstairs, then hid under the duvet, shutting everyone out.

I thought I wouldn't sleep, but I did. Didn't even wake up to my alarm. The other girls are moving around, so it's too late for me to eavesdrop on the staffs. But I don't think I want to know anyone else's secrets now. My own are enough of a bloody burden.

Steph sits down on my bed. 'Coming out for the run?' she whispers.

At least she hasn't asked about last night. I don't want to tell her any more about my daughter. She probably hates me enough already.

'I don't know . . .'

'Yes you do! You're doing this to make your boys proud of you, right?' Her eyes are puffy from the early awakening.

I grunt, but how can I say no? I can't change the past. But I can shift my lazy arse and try to change the future.

There's a queue out of the hallway, because everyone's nervous about walking out onto the frozen car park.

But as I take a careful step out, I realise . . .

'Bloody hell.'

It's not the black ice that's slowing us down: it's the view.

I'm a warm-weather person. All right, the fatter I get, the more I sweat, and I end up with rashes in places nobody would guess. But if I could, I'd live in Spain, and be slim and pretty in cotton dresses. It's the cold that makes me want to eat.

But this different. Special. The hills are white, with lines of trees at the top, heavy with snow. The sky's still dark but there are no clouds, just a hint of pink where the horizon is.

It's going to be a beautiful day.

Pepper marches out onto the tarmac but even he marches more carefully. 'Come on, you lot; let's get moving. Dean, goes without saying that ice is slippery so watch yourself. Once we get down to the beach, it'll be fine.'

Ryan follows. I wish *he* hadn't seen me in my hysterical state last night. I guess I'm just the kind of crazy woman that's made him want to leave boot camp.

We set out down the path towards the Ladder. The air feels like a penknife stabbing my lungs, but I'm not as out of breath as I was before. The thud of the other girls' footsteps helps me pick up speed.

'Everything OK?' Steph.

I nod. 'Freezing but fine apart from that. You?'

'The same. Well, better since I realised this is our last dawn run.'

Bloody hell. She's right. 'I thought this'd be the longest week of my life, but—'

'You're not going to say you'll miss it, are you, Vicki?'

'Not miss it, but—'

A horrible scream, from somewhere lower down the ladder. I look down, and see Natalia falling arse over tit down one, two, *three* steps before grabbing hold of a shrub to break her fall.

'Shit! That must have hurt,' says Steph.

'STOP! Everyone, stay exactly where you are,' Pepper commands, then runs towards Natalia. She's lying on her side, whimpering like a kitten.

'God, that was a nasty fall,' I whisper to Steph.

'Do you think she might have broken something?'

Pepper kneels down next to her. 'I promise I won't hurt you,' he's saying, and his voice is so gentle I hardly recognise it. 'Where does it hurt the most?'

She mumbles something and he touches her ankle, which makes her squeal. Ryan supports her head while Pepper continues his examination. When he's finished, he stands up, then turns to Darcy. 'Webb, get back to the hotel and call an ambulance.'

Natalia squeals again and he holds her hand. 'It's all right, Natalia. I don't think it's broken, but we need to make certain.'

She's so surprised she stops squealing: I didn't think he'd bothered to learn any of our first names.

'As for the rest of you, you're about to get some real life stretcher practice. Just keep your minds on the job and your feet on the ground, and we won't slip up.'

Our journey back to the hotel is slow, but steady. Ryan carries Natalia up the Ladder in a fireman's lift – they'd never have managed it if I'd been the one who'd fallen – and then Pepper sets up a stretcher from his bag of kit, and positions me, Karen, and the two panthers at the back and sides. It makes me feel a little bit proud, that I'm one of the ones he chooses.

'You'll be more comfortable this way,' he tells Natalia as he lays her down.

As we walk, dawn is breaking, but the weather's turned again. Grey cloud is covering the pink horizon.

'More snow coming, I reckon,' Steph whispers.

The staffs are at the front, setting the pace. There's so much tension in my shoulders and back – even Natalia feels heavy going uphill – but I won't let go.

Our casualty is white as a sheet, despite all her fake tan. Her eyes are shut tightly, as though she's trying to block out the world and the pain. She's mumbling something to herself.

I strain to hear what it is. Then I realise.

'Mum . . . I want my . . . mum.'

Suddenly, she looks so different to me. All week I've been cross with her for being so self-centred and immature. But she's only nineteen. She's *meant* to be immature. Lying there, so vulnerable, she could be one of mine.

Edie comes rushing out of the car park, and we all screech, 'DON'T RUN!'

She does a comedy freeze. 'Oh. Whoops. Bring her into the drawing room; there's a sofa big enough to lay her on, and maybe Vicki can light the fire?'

Pepper frowns. 'No. Better aim for the hallway so we can

wait for the ambulance. Save having to move her more than necessary.'

'The thing is, Matt . . .' She hesitates. 'Well, ambulance control are overwhelmed at the moment. Plus, they're not entirely confident about getting up untreated roads unless it's life or death. And the hill up to here definitely won't have been gritted.'

'Bloody Britain,' Pepper grunts. 'First sign of ice, and we grind to a halt,'

Natalia moans.

'Don't worry, sweetheart,' I say, 'we'll soon get you sorted.'

'Shall we put Britain's shortcomings right *after* we've got Natalia inside?' Ryan suggests.

I catch sight of Pepper: he looks slightly shamefaced. 'Stretcher team, proceed to the drawing room. Lurft, roight, lurft, roight!'

The room is chilly, but not quite as chilly as the rest of the house. We lower the stretcher very, very slowly, and the staffs lift their patient onto the sofa. Then Edie covers Natalia with so many blankets that you can hardly see anyone is underneath them.

I set about lighting the fire, though my hands are rigid from the cold. Someone made a complete pig's ear of this last night, but I guess as I went off in a hysterical huff, I shouldn't complain. There's just enough heat in the embers to help my fingers thaw. I build my usual tower of newspaper and fire-lighters at double-quick speed.

'Can I take another quick peek at that ankle, Natalia?' Pepper asks, and she sobs a yes. He unlaces her trainer and removes it and her sock. The foot is already swelling, but it's not twisted. When Alastair broke his ankle playing football with a house brick, it was bent over at such a freaky angle it made me want to throw up.

'Reckon it's a bad sprain, Natalia.' He replaces the blankets, one by one, so the sudden pressure doesn't hurt her ankle. 'Though we'll need an X-ray to be certain. For now we'll stick to RICE: rest, ice, compression, elevation. Though maybe leave out the compression just in case. Steph?'

It's Steph's turn to look bemused at him using her first name. 'Yup, Staff?'

'Reckon you could locate me some frozen peas or similar from your kitchen?'

'Um, Steph, just before you go, um, while everyone's together, I'm afraid we do have another little, well, challenge to deal with,' Edie says.

We wait. Challenge is Edie's word for Bloody Great Problem. 'We appear to be having a few issues with the, um, gas supply.' She pauses to let this sink in.

Everyone seems to lean in towards the fire without realising they're doing it.

'I haven't got through to the gas board yet but I'm sure it's a temporary thing. Demand rises when the whole world's snowed in, right? The good news is we have lots of firewood and a couple of fan heaters for in here so none of us will freeze. In fact, it could be extra-cosy!'

'The hob and the oven both run on gas, though,' Steph says.

'Um. Yes. It really is turning into the ultimate cookery challenge for you this week, eh, Steph? But the microwave and the kettle and the toaster don't run on gas, luckily!' Her smile doesn't quite reach her eyes.

'What about hot water for the showers?' one of the Crab girls asks.

Edie laughs nervously. 'There might be a little bit left, but I think we should save that for kitchen work and emergencies. Just till the supply's restored.'

Edie heads for the door. 'Can't stand here all day, must get onto the gas board. I'm sure we'll be a priority. In the meantime, perhaps you'd like to stay together in the drawing room. Honestly, ladies, between us we could probably survive for months up here. Nothing like a spot of weather to bring out the British stiff upper lip, right?'

No one smiles.

Steph can only find broad beans to treat Natalia's ankle, but Pepper accepts them without his usual snarl. I follow her back to the kitchen.

'What's for breakfast, chef?'

She groans. 'I was *planning* on doing a healthy fry-up.'

'Ah. That's going to be interesting. Though at least *the microwave and the kettle and the toaster don't run on gas*!' I say, parroting Edie's fake positivity.

'Yeah. And a toaster's a lot of use on a wheat-free boot camp, isn't it?' Steph shrugs. 'Looks like it's porridge or porridge, then.' She opens a cupboard door and pulls out two large glass bowls.

'The one you did yesterday was delicious.'

'Really? I hate porridge. Couldn't work out why till yesterday. Then I remembered we had it at boarding school.'

I stare at her. 'I never knew you were a posh girl.'

'Not posh. Charity case. Was sent there after my mum died. I got some kind of lost-cause scholarship. Which didn't help, because all the proper posh girls knew my dad was broke.'

'Your mum died?'

'Long time ago,' she says, like it's nothing. She goes to the larder and brings back a sack of oats. 'This is way past its sell-by date. But if there are weevils, it'll add protein. Just don't tell the others.'

'How old were you?'

242

'Eight.'

'You were sent to boarding school when you were *eight*?'

'Sounds worse than it was. My dad was terrified of bringing up girls and he had his hands full dealing with my younger brothers. A great aunt suggested her old school.' She wrinkles her nose. 'I was a curiosity at first, and the girls tried to be nice to me, but I was rubbish at sport and I had terrible clothes so pretty soon they moved on. Except they still noticed me in domestic science. I always seemed to have friends when I was cooking.'

'Oh, Steph, what a nightmare.' I take a step forward to hug her, but she rips open the porridge packet before I get close, and the oats cascade into the bowl.

'Like I say, it was two decades ago. The good thing was that after almost a year away, I was so pleased to be home that I'd sort of forgotten to be sad about my mum.'

'Really?'

I imagine my three without me. Dave would try his best but he's not the most practical. By the time I get back home tomorrow, the four of them will have generated a month's worth of washing, and mess so bad I'll have to spend next week cleaning.

But dirt is no big deal. What breaks my heart is imagining them growing up without me. Alastair would retreat into his shell. Murray would get an ASBO, and probably make several girls pregnant. My baby boy, Rudy, might cope best, but only because he wouldn't remember me well enough to miss me.

Steph is adding water to the porridge, and checking the back of the packet for microwave instructions. She disappears into the larder again, and brings out a huge handful of dried apricots, which she chops so rapidly I worry she'll cut off her fingers. Then we really *will* starve. She takes a pot of honey off the shelf and mixes it with the fruit, adding a tablespoon of cinnamon.

'I know honey's cheating, but there's no almond left and I think we all need some sugar, right? Never fails to perk people up.'

'That's why you learned to cook, isn't it, Steph?'

'What?'

'For your dad and your brothers? To make things better.'

She bites her lip. 'It was more practical than that. Dad couldn't crack an egg without getting it all over the kitchen. When I was away at school, they all lived on KFC and food parcels from neighbours.' She looks up at me. 'They still love junk food. I like it myself. But my brothers are still thin as rakes while I . . . well, there's no justice.'

'Vicki?'

Phil the photographer is behind us, aiming his camera at me. The shutter clicks before I can protest.

Steph growls. 'You're not going to use that, are you?'

'Just trying out some reportage.'

'Well, you'll be reportaging your own close encounter with a frying pan if you don't stop taking pictures of me,' Steph says.

'OK, OK.' He backs away, then turns to me. 'But while I'm stuck here, Vicki, I wondered if I could do your After shots. Save me having to come back here again tomorrow. You do look better and if you suck your cheeks and belly in, no one will know. Plus I'll use the extra time to airbrush your pictures. By the time I'm finished, you'll look like a supermodel.'

'You saying I don't already?'

Phil laughs. 'Give me the choice between a supermodel and a woman with a bit of flesh on her bones, I'd choose you any day of the week. So would most red-blooded males.'

Bless him. So saying I'm his ideal woman is meant to make

my day? Even though he's even bigger than me, and his beard has had that same bit of egg white stuck to it all day?

No wonder most boot camps are women-only. Men have got it made.

30

Steph

Alone in the kitchen, at last. *My* kitchen, Pepper called it, which gave me a little lift, even in the midst of all the drama about Natalia.

The house is quiet, because everyone else is crowded into the drawing room. I could almost believe I'm the only person in the whole building.

But I don't feel lonely. I love working here. The chopped apricot is in a glass bowl, and I heat that for a few seconds in the microwave, till it turns jammy. It tastes really good, though if I were making this for myself, maybe I'd add a little slosh of brandy . . .

Brandy? For *breakfast*? Dear lord, Stephanie Dean, is it any wonder you're in the state you're in, if you eat like you're in a Marks and Spencer advert? *This is not just porridge, this is alcoholic porridge, just the thing for staving off the shakes first thing.*

This time tomorrow, boot camp will be over except for the dreaded weigh-in – and after that, perhaps there's a fork in the road. I can step back on to the old path, the full-fat lifestyle that didn't make me happy. Or turn in a new direction, of bean curd and no-fat yogurt.

A life where no-fat yogurt is the highlight of my day doesn't sound worth living. But maybe there's a third way. I can't get what Vicki said out of my head, about me *cooking to make things better*. I was going to argue back that it's what everyone does, surely? We bake cakes on sad days. Eat cheese when it rains. Keep calm and eat up.

Doesn't work as well as it should. Cakes and cheese haven't stopped me feeling sad and empty.

It's chilly, so I warm my hands on the outside of the first microwaved bowl of oats while the second one cooks on the turntable.

My fingers . . . they don't look quite like mine anymore: is it possible *they've* lost weight?

Steve always says I have fat girl's fingers. 'We couldn't get married, honeybunch. We'd never get a ring to fit. The skin would bulge over the sides. You have spinster's fingers.'

Maybe when he sees me at the ball, with newly slim fingers, he'll change his mind. 'Will you be my wife, now, Stephanie? You have the prettiest fingers here.'

Steve's jokes always made me smile. Even though, now I look back, I don't know how funny they actually were. Like the fingers remark. I let a simple joke get out of proportion, started staring at my hands, wondering if I should wear gloves, even Googling *finger slimming exercises*. But you're kind of stuck with your hands, aren't you?

Would it have hurt him to think occasionally before he made a joke at my expense?

'That looks almost ready.'

I jump. Did Staff Ryan catch me scrutinising my fingers for signs of fat loss? 'Not far off. Are they ravenous?'

He nods. 'Yep. And stressed out. It's like one of those detective movies on telly at Christmas. Where everyone's stuck in a country house and there's a body in the library.'

'And a Belgian detective happens to be among the guests and solves the mystery in time for afternoon tea?' I sigh. 'Not that there'll be afternoon tea. Though I might be able to rustle up afternoon porridge. It's about all we've got left.'

We watch as the bowl keeps turning under the glow of the microwave light. 'How do you know how to make all these delicious things, Steph?'

Is he buttering me up again for *later*? I look at him, and he looks sincere enough. And anyway, why would he pick me?

No. He's just after bigger portions. 'It's not hard, honestly.'

'Hel proves it is very hard indeed. And I'm in awe. On exercise, we used to take it in turns to make the food. I almost started a riot when I was on cookhouse duty. After that they kept me on pan bashing.'

'I thought they were meant to teach survival skills in the army?'

He shrugs. 'I know how to open a foil ration pack. And I can iron shirts with knife-sharp creases, and polish boots to a mirror shine. But I can't cook.'

'Ha. I can't stand ironing; we'd be the perfect couple.' I can't believe I just *said* that. I move on quickly, hoping he'll forget it. 'And your mum never even taught you to make beans on toast?'

'I don't think she knew how. Plus, I wasn't really around long enough to find out.'

'How come?'

'She wasn't the mothering kind. So the nice social workers found me somewhere else to live.'

'You were adopted?'

Ryan shakes his head, grinning. 'No, I wasn't nearly cute enough for adoption. By the time everyone realised Mum preferred the bottle to looking after me, I was six going on sixteen. They tried fostering but I wasn't very co-operative. So I went into care.'

There's an angry little boy hidden somewhere under those

camouflage fatigues. A little boy who doesn't get why he was moved around like a parcel no one wants to sign for.

I'm wondering exactly how to tell him I understand, when the microwave pings: the porridge is ready. Ryan looks relieved. 'I'll take the bowls through, shall I?'

I nod, and watch him go, at least six foot in his stocking feet with a six pack to match. And I think, *poor kid.*

Breakfast is eaten in silence. It reminds me of camping, as we huddle together in the drawing room, rugs over our knees, porridge bowls keeping our hands warm.

Or maybe it's more like being in an old people's home. Except that Agatha, the only pensioner among us, is the one trying to liven things up.

'Right!' she says. 'I sincerely hope we're not going to be moping around here for ever, especially with no heating on. What's the plan for this morning, Staff Pepper?'

He looks shifty. 'We, er, are still working on that one. This morning's incident with Natalia . . . I mean, Greer, has made us conscious of the extra risks the weather poses to untrained civilians.'

'I'm feeling much better,' Natalia says, her voice high-pitched. 'My ankle feels all floaty and tingly, like it's healing up.'

'That might be down to the double paracetamol and quad-ruple brandy that Edie administered earlier,' Vicki whispers to me. 'She must be high as a kite after the teetotal week we've just had.'

'Hopefully Natalia's had a lucky escape, but as things stand, we can't risk letting you out until the weather improves,' Ryan says.

I'm groaning as loudly as everyone else. At the beginning of the week, I'd have been over the moon that snow had stopped play, but now I've got this yearning to feel the chill wind on my skin, run along the shore, push myself harder and harder.

'The weather's *not* going to improve,' Phil the photographer says. 'My iPhone signal's out so I resorted to local radio. They reckon the snow might not clear till Sunday at the earliest.'

'But we're going home tomorrow!' Vicki cries out, and the others nod.

I'm more worried about whether there's enough food to keep us going till then.

'It'll be media hype,' Darcy says. 'I should know. Newsrooms latch on to a story, whether it's war or the weather, and next thing we're fuelling mass panic. They'll be exaggerating.'

'The sea's frozen over,' Ryan says.

'*What*?' Even Darcy looks gob-smacked by that.

'First time in about forty years, according to the local radio,' Pepper chips in. 'Motorways are at a standstill till they dig cars out. And in the sticks, well, we're stuck.'

'And the trains?' Darcy sounds panicked. Whereas I'm relieved. Anything to avoid going back to work on Monday.

'Probably not. It's bound to be the wrong kind of snow,' Pepper says. 'Of course, it's only like this because of the mad health and safety culture we live in now. If I had my way, we'd start a military coup with compulsory national service to drum in some bulldog spirit, so we don't all give up as soon as the first flake of snow falls.'

Ryan's face is twisted; I think he's trying not to laugh. 'But until El Presidente Pepper stages his revolution, you'd best accept that boot camp might last a little longer than you'd expected.'

250

31

Darcy

I don't care what they say. I can't stay here. Even if I have to yomp cross-country to the nearest road with traffic on it and hitch a lift with a serial killer, *I'm going to get to London.*

Which is funny. I've already changed my mind about this bloody meeting ten times since getting up this morning. As we set out for the Ladder, I was getting angrier with my bosses. If the channel management were willing to ditch me for *that* dim bimbo then maybe I didn't want to work for them after all.

But then we got cooped up here, and now I feel like a battery hen.

'We'll be running circuits in the ballroom in fifteen,' Ryan says.

The other battery hens don't seem to mind being stuck. Maybe Edie laced their porridge with sedatives. But then they don't have a terrifying agent pacing her office in London, drumming her talons against her Conran walnut desk. Despising me because she thinks I've let her down *again*.

Pepper throws me a look that says he needs a ciggie as much as I do.

We RV in the usual place.

'I've only got six left,' I say, showing him the almost empty tin.

'That's the second worst news I've had all day,' he says, taking one.

'The worst being the weather, right?'

Pepper lights up, then hands the cigarette to me and takes another for himself. 'The weather's bloody fantastic for training. But Edie was too scared of being sued to let you lot out again. So instead we run workouts that are as tough as a bloody tea dance.'

I breathe in the nicotine. It tastes horrible, suddenly. Another sign that I don't know my own mind – or proof I've come to my senses about everything? 'I wish I was going to be around to take part but . . .' I pause. Why don't I want to say the words?

He grunts. 'You're off?'

I nod.

'Back to London, I suppose.'

'Back to London. Back to . . . well, I took your advice. I'm going to fight, like you said I should.'

'*Did* I say that you should?'

'You said something like, *don't you have the bottle to fight for your job.*'

'Trust a reporter to make notes. And trust a reporter to misinterpret what I meant. I wasn't giving you advice, Webb. Wouldn't dare. It was more of a rhetorical question. And before you say it, yes, I know rhetorical is a long word for a soldier.'

'That wasn't what I was going to say.'

'What were you going to say, then Darcy Webb?' He hasn't used my first name before: I guess it's because he knows I'm definitely leaving his 'platoon'.

'It's what I *should* do though, right? I can't let them win.'

'Must be the weather. Everyone's deserting the bloody ship. Ryan thinks *he* wants to leave, too.'

'What? Today?'

Pepper shakes his head. 'No, he'll see this camp out. But then he's had enough of you whinging women.'

'Fuck off. I haven't whinged once.'

He looks at me. 'No? You can come off my hit list, then.'

'That's a relief. I was pretty sure I'd end my days courtesy of you and an AK47.'

'Nah. My psychopathic sergeant major thing, it's mostly an act. At least ninety-five per cent. There's barely five per cent of ruthless terminator left.'

I smile. But I hadn't quite credited Pepper with so much self-awareness. 'What's the real reason why Ryan's leaving?'

'Me, I guess. We're like brothers. Brothers who argue all the time and want to kill each other.'

'Is that because you served together? Went through . . . stuff together?'

He thinks it over. 'Possibly. Though it could also be the fact that he's not very bright and feels intimidated by my superior intellectual prowess. And my success with women.' His moustache twitches. He's taking the piss out of himself.

I laugh. 'Could be. So when are you going to tell him?'

'Tell him what?'

'That you don't want him to go?'

'What makes you think I don't want him to go?'

'Come on. It's obvious.'

He scowls. 'I'll find another partner. I'm not going to try to stop him.'

'Why not?'

'No point trying to force someone into doing something they don't want to do.'

'I'm not talking about forcing him. I'm talking about telling him you'll miss him, that you appreciate his company, that you're good together.'

'Bollocks to that.' He stubs out his cigarette.

I shake my head. 'And that, Staff Pepper, sums up what's wrong with men.'

'If you say so. Anyway, good luck with the drive back to

London.' He says it with contempt. 'Shame you're going to miss the weigh-in.'

'I didn't come for weight loss.'

'No. You came for perspective, right?'

I nod. 'Yup. Thanks. You helped with that.'

'Right. You realised you preferred a job you hate to being shouted at by a washed-up old soldier, right?'

'It hasn't been *that* bad.'

He shrugs. 'No? I think boot camp works most of the time because women are so terrified that they'd have to come back. It's a deterrent.'

'Oh. And I meant to say, you're not washed up either. Or old.'

He smiles. 'Final word of advice, Webb? When you're in a hole, stop digging.'

'Right, Staff. Thanks for everything.'

As he walks back into the building, I feel like I could have, *should* have, said something more, because there's a loneliness about Pepper, behind all the bluster and the bullshit.

Or maybe I'm just projecting.

I'm rubbish at goodbyes, so I leave business cards on my two room-mates' beds, and then dart downstairs with my rucksack.

It feels warmer outside than it does in the hotel. My car starts first time and the heater blasts through the ice on the windscreen. Instant satisfaction. I'm on my way back to the city that never sleeps, where I can get the cuisines of fifty countries delivered to my door within half an hour, where my name and my face get me free entry into any club or restaurant, not to mention free clothes, free hair dos *and* free Botox. Never bothered with the Botox before, but I guess I've got to get my forehead around the idea now, if I'm going to hang on to my job with my freshly manicured fingernails.

I hold my breath as I steer my way out of the car park onto the icy track. My car is solid, Scandinavian, winter-proofed. I wouldn't trust an Italian car to get me back, but these boys are built like tanks, for heavy weather. Which is what lies ahead of me in London, even if there's not a millimetre of snow at Westminster.

I stop at the gates, braking carefully. Unbolting these for the last time should feel like I'm making a break for freedom. But as I glance back up at Windy Hill, it's more like leaving things unfinished.

I get into the car again. No going back. I thought I loved a fight as much as the next reporter. So why does my belly feel like it's full of acid?

Shouldn't have left without saying goodbye to my room-mates. Except promises to keep in touch mean sod all. We used to swear lifelong friendship to all the other journos whenever we left the latest hell-hole. Yet how many of my former colleagues have contacted me since I screwed up?

They're superstitious. It's like bad luck is catching.

I take a left, and the view makes me gasp. Beautifully bleak. I'm a sucker for wild landscapes: one of the reasons I loved Afghanistan, until it all went sour.

I try to commit this landscape to memory, so I can call it up and calm myself down instead of screaming at the director who keeps coughing into my earpiece or the idiot who wrote a news script so clunky I sound like Steven Hawking.

Yes. I'll close my eyes and I'll be back here, where none of it matters.

I turn the radio on. The only station I could get when I drove up here was a local one, with awful music and worse presenters. But at least it'll drown out my doubts.

'. . . and that's a reminder not to call the emergency services unless there really is an emergency, ladies and gents. Might sound obvious, but people are calling about colds and chil-blains, and taking resources away from proper emergencies. So, coming up, we're live from traffic control, and from a snowball fight in the back garden of your favourite morning presenter, Davey Drew, whose sledge wouldn't start when he tried to make it into the studio this morning . . .'

On second thoughts, I prefer silence. The radio's staying off till I'm back to civilisation and can get Radio Four again.

The sat nav hasn't picked up GPS but I remember the way. A twist in the road, a long lane, then downhill for at least a mile, then through the village towards the bypass. There's petrol in my tank, and fire in my belly. I'm coming, Marian, and I'm not going to let them sack me—

Shit

I slam on the brakes.

Nothing happens.

COME ON! Brake, bloody useless car

Fuck

Don't skid, *please*

Brake

I'm spinning scarily fast and yet in slow motion the weight of the car that felt so reassuring now feels like a coffin and there's no chance of stopping the momentum as it does this wild dance towards the edge of this mile-high hill—

I'm going to die, I'm going to—

Thank *fuck* for trees.

Without trees I'd have gone over.

I clamber out of the car, so pleased I'm alive that I forget all about the ice, and trip, falling on my backside. I cling on to a bush, my bum safely on the ground, and bottom shuffle as far away from the car as I can.

It doesn't *look* like it's about to burst into flames, but I've seen the movies. Pouf! I am not going to push my luck. Two near-death experiences in one life is enough.

I stop shuffling once I'm a hundred metres away. My heart's beating harder than it did on those runs up the Ladder. The medics on my battlefield first aid course told us adrenalin can disguise life-threatening injuries, so I work methodically from head to toe, checking gingerly for anything that might be missing or fatally compromised.

Barring hidden internal injuries, the worst I seem to have suffered is a bump where my arm hit the steering wheel, and a bruised backside from my fall out of the car. My trousers are wet where the ice is melting beneath my backside, and my palms are dirty and numb. As the adrenalin wears off, I begin to shiver.

Then I notice the silence. Before, the distant rumble of traffic was still present. Not now. Now, nothing stirs. Even the birds are struck dumb by the weather. And anyone with any sense is huddled indoors, watching the news, relieved they're not out there where it's dangerous.

Which must make me someone with *no sense at all.*

The nearest help must be back at boot camp, a mile up a hill that's as slippery as glass. I find my phone in my pocket, undamaged. But there's no bloody signal.

'Work, you bastard,' I hiss at the phone. Because that's *really* going to make a difference. I can't call for help. And I can't call Marian either. I bet it's positively balmy in Soho. She'll think I've bottled it again.

Hypothermia is a more urgent threat than Marian. So I can either try to crawl to the hotel, seek shelter in the potentially explosive car, or freeze to death.

I giggle. It sounds eerie against the silence. To think I survived Afghanistan – just – and countless other riots and small wars, and here I am, in danger of succumbing to exposure on the outskirts of a Devon village.

Except I don't give in that easily. The hotel it is. Right hand first, grasping for something that isn't ice. There's a shrub, frosted like glacé fruit on a Christmas cake. It looks just about sturdy enough to hold my boot camp-reduced weight.

'Shit.'

Thorns pierce my skin, but I don't let go. I pull myself up, feeling the thorns go deeper, trying to convince myself that it's a good thing I can still feel pain. It means I'm not dead.

When I look back, I've travelled the length of my body. What am I? A metre sixty? If the distance to the hotel is a nice round kilometre and a half, that means I've got, what, nine hundred of those pull-along movements before I get back.

All right. Let's try *walking*. Even if I can only manage a few steps before falling over again, it'll be faster. I'm going to be black and blue anyway.

I manage three steps before the ground comes up to meet my chin. I move my face just in time, so the hard earth grazes my left ear. I feel a whole new empathy with toddlers. Learning to walk is bloody hard work.

For a moment I think the rushing sound is concussion. Fantastic. Now I really *am* screwed.

Either concussion . . . or a *car*?

Perhaps hallucination is a symptom of exposure. Next, I'll be ripping off my clothes, convinced I'm boiling, in the final stage of hypothermia, as the body tries, and fails to keep brain function going.

Hmm. Or it might just be a car.

The noise is coming from further down the hill. Maybe I ought to warn people that the road is a death trap, stand up and wave my scarf like in *The Railway Children*.

Except I don't have a scarf. And, of course, I can't stand up without falling over again.

I turn towards the noise. It's not a car but . . . well, a *serious* country 4x4, possibly the only vehicle except a tank that might be able to tackle this icy slope.

At last, some bloody *luck*. Already I'm rehearsing the anecdote in my head, for when I finally get to London. I'll flutter my eyelashes at the driver – surely some light flirtation is justified under the circumstances – and hitch a lift to the nearest train station that's working. The train will be faster anyway.

The 4x4 is coming towards me. It's a farmer's car. Or a vet's. Perhaps he's on his way to rescue some animals. He'll offer me hot tea from a flask, or maybe a slug of whisky, and—

Oh no.

Of all the people in the world . . .

Still, beggars can't be choosers. All that matters is getting back to civilisation as quickly as I possibly can.

I plaster a smile onto my face, as the 4x4 stops right alongside me. The window whirrs down, and a horribly familiar voice says:

'Darcy. What's a nice girl like you doing in a place like this? No. Don't tell me. You were in such a hurry for my massage that you thought you'd come looking for me, make sure you were front of the queue. Am I right?'

My smile falters. 'Hello, Foz. It's good to see you.'

'Jump in, then, gorgeous. I can promise you a *very* smooth ride.'

32

Vicki

The bottom's dropped out of boot camp.

Since the snow and Natalia's accident, the staffs have stopped scowling, but they've also stopped trying. Darcy was last seen scuttling off to her car (she can't *really* have left without saying goodbye, can she?). Steph's in the kitchen trying to conjure up lunch out of the remaining porridge oats and a freezer full of ice cubes. Agatha's on nursing duty, as she used to run a WRVS tea stall. And Edie is now so paranoid about her guests freezing to death that I've been given permission to skip this morning's classes to keep the home fire burning.

So there are only five boot campers left taking Ryan's Arm Blaster class in the ballroom.

'Everything's *so* nice,' says Natalia.

At least, I think that's what she's said. Since Edie administered that emergency brandy with paracetamol, Natalia's speech has been slurred. I wouldn't mind some myself: might take my mind off being stranded for another day or more instead of getting to see Dave and the kids.

'That's good, dear,' Agatha says, patting her hand. 'So, nothing hurts anymore, then?'

'Why should it hurt?'

Agatha throws me a worried look. 'You fell, Natalia. Don't you remember?'

Natalia frowns. 'Oh. Yes. My ankle. It feels . . . fuzzy.'

'Well, you let me know if that changes for the worse.'

I add another couple of logs to the fire. Ouch! My thighs ache as I stand up. And when I collapse back into the chaise longue it creaks under my weight. Oh dear. Perhaps Steph's been lying about cooking without butter. I'd better not go home heavier than when I got here . . .

Natalia's singing to herself now. I think it's 'All the Single Ladies'.

'Do you think she's OK?' I whisper to Agatha.

'It does seem to have gone to her head, doesn't it? We had a girl who fractured her wrist when she was halfway up El Toro. We kept her going with Irish whiskey and coca tea. So I don't suppose a little local anaesthesia will do her any harm till the ice thaws.'

'Let's pretend . . .'

We look up at Natalia. 'What was that, dear?'

'Let's pretend. You're the groom, I'm the bride.' She stares at me, cross-eyed. 'You can be the vicar.'

I shake my head at Agatha, who puts a hand on Natalia's forehead. 'Doesn't seem to be running a fever. It's a while till the wedding, isn't it, Natalia? You'll be right as rain by then, I'm sure.'

'Four weeks tomorrow.'

'No time at all,' Agatha says. 'You must be so excited.'

'Yes. But I'm too young, you know. Nineteen is too young to get married. Everyone says so.'

Agatha and I exchange another glance. 'I was young when I married Dave,' I say. 'Couldn't wait. I hate being the centre of attention, normally, but as soon as he asked me, I couldn't stop thinking about that day. Not a single doubt. Not for a second.'

Natalia thinks this through. 'I do *love* Lucas. But he's almost old enough to be my father. People think he is, sometimes.

When we go to wedding venues and things. They're ever so embarrassed when they find out he's not giving me away but taking my hand.' She giggles, but there's something slightly bonkers about the way the giggle goes on and on . . .

'Did you marry young, Agatha?' I ask.

'It might surprise you, but I've never taken the plunge myself.'

'Oh. Never met Mr Right, then?' I ask.

'I met the right person, dear. Eventually. She just happened to be a woman.'

It takes me a second to work out what she means. 'Ah. Right. A woman.'

'Should have planned ahead a little better,' she continues, 'realised that if I'd married young, I could have had a baby or two, divorced, then met a soul mate. I'd have loved little ones. But while most of the world was swinging madly in the sixties and seventies, my provincial backwater saw things in black or white. Hey ho. I've had a super time teaching, climbing, seeing the world. *Je ne regrette rien*, not really. But I'm concerned that Natalia here might end up regretting things.'

A log shifts on the fire, and Natalia looks up at the mention of her name: I think she zoned out of the bit about Agatha being gay. 'I do *love* Lucas.'

'Yes, dear. You said so before. What do you love about him?'

'He loves me.'

'That's a good start, Natalia. But what makes him worthy of *you*?'

She blinks. 'Of me?'

'Yes. You. You're a very bright young woman. A little short-tempered, perhaps, but a catch nonetheless. So why choose Lucas?'

Natalia's eyes are clear blue, her pupils huge. 'Because . . . he's handsome.'

'Good. But looks fade, Natalia. Hard to believe now, but they do. What else?'

I lean forward. I'm a sucker for a romance.

'He's rich.'

'Hmm. Not a bad thing in itself, but money doesn't buy happiness.'

'Makes the bad times pass quicker, though,' I say.

Agatha tuts. 'Come on, now, Natalia.'

'He . . . he won't leave me. He promised.'

That wasn't what I expected at all.

'Why in heaven's name are you worried about him leaving you when you haven't even married him yet, my dear girl?'

'Because that's what my mum did.'

And then hard as nails Natalia begins to sob like her heart is breaking. I get up and fling my arms around her, because I can't bear the sound of it.

I half expect her to struggle, but instead she reaches round my shoulders and squeezes hard.

'There, there, Natalia, everything's going to be all right.'

The story spills out faster than the tears. Not everything she says is a hundred per cent clear, but we gather her mum left her just before her exams.

'I sat in the exam hall and . . . my mind was full of *them*. Mum and revolting Roger and my dad at home trying to pretend his eyes were red from hay fever. I couldn't write a thing. I failed every exam.'

'Jolly bad timing on your mother's part,' Agatha says. 'But, my dear, you're not the first to fluff your exams. You could resit.'

'You don't understand.'

'What exactly don't I understand, dear?'

'It was so . . . humiliating. All the other girls at school were on the front page of the local paper, holding up their result slips. A A A A A A A A A A A A . . .'

She's beginning to sound like a broken record. I pat her on the back, like I'm winding a baby. She stops repeating herself.

'Then they disappeared off to college and I was left behind. I was finished. Eighteen. And finished.'

I hug her tighter. I was never top of the class, but I remember what it was like being her age. Everything was life or death. No in-between.

'It was worse after they went. They'd come back at weekends, full of stories about uni. And they'd ask me what I was doing. They were laughing at me behind my back. But not Lucas. Lucas adored me from the first moment he saw me. When he proposed, I felt like the old Natalia. The one who always got the prize. None of my school friends had a handsome doctor who wanted to marry them. When they came back at weekends, I had something to show them. My Tiffany engagement ring.'

Agatha raises her eyebrows at me. 'It's not a competition, darling Natalia. Or a sprint. I mean, sometimes people do meet their soul mates at your age, but—'

'I did,' I say, feeling protective towards Natalia. 'We met at school.'

'Hmm, but there's quite an age gap between Natalia and her beau.'

Natalia's eyes narrow. 'It's not that much. Sixteen years. He's one of the youngest but most gifted surgeons in his field. And it'll seem like less, the longer we're together. Everyone says so.'

I pat her hand, but I'm beginning to wonder about this Lucas. What's to say that he's not taking advantage of her vulnerability? I bet Natalia would be quite the trophy wife.

'Why did your mother leave?' Agatha asks.

264

'Because she's a selfish bitch.'

'Did she ever explain it to you?'

Natalia shrugs. 'Said something about feeling trapped. About her and Dad being different people from when they married . . .' She looks up at Agatha. 'Oh. I see. You think we're the same.'

She might be drugged, but she's still sharp.

Agatha sighs. 'I just . . . worry that you might be trying to prove a point to your mother and your school-mates, rather than being one hundred per cent certain you want to spend your life with Lucas.'

The fire's spitting now. Maybe it's snowing again and coming down the chimney.

'Maybe you were never in love, Agatha. Maybe that's why you don't understand.'

'On the contrary, Natalia, I was in love for thirty-seven years. Still am. I love the very bones of my soul mate, even though I buried her three years ago. But she wanted me to have everything that the world could offer, and I wanted the same for her. Seems to me that marrying someone you barely know could be an awful waste.'

That sets Natalia off crying again. 'Sorry,' she mumbles. 'Sorry. I don't know why I say things, sometimes.'

'Because you're a teenager, love,' I say.

She shakes her head. 'No. I never used to. Not before the pills.'

I turn her face towards me. 'What pills, Natalia?'

'The . . . happy pills.' She laughs sarcastically. 'They're not working very well, are they? I'm not supposed to drink with them. This *always* happens when I drink.'

'My dear Natalia. Pills aren't the answer. Who gave them to you? Your fiancé?'

She shakes her head again. 'No. No, Lucas doesn't know. He'd hate it. He'd hate me. We want a family straight away, you see. But he wouldn't want the mother of his children to be some kind of . . . *head case*.'

This sets the tears off all over again.

'I think someone needs to have words with this not-so-young man,' Agatha says.

'It might be fine,' I say. 'I married young. Had babies young. I'm happy.' But I'm not convinced there's a happy ending for the girl sobbing into my sweatshirt right now.

'What had you planned to do, Natalia? Before you failed?'

She looks up from my armpit. Her pretty face is purple and snot is running down her chin. 'You'll laugh.'

'I bet I won't.'

'I wanted to be a physio. I broke my leg when I was eleven, climbing a tree. It was a mess, the bone sticking out at a horrible angle. The doctors put it right but it was the physio who fixed it for me. She was . . . scary but good. I know I can be grumpy too. The patients at the clinic drive me mad. But Dad thought being a physio would be perfect. *You'd boss people back to health*, he said.'

'And what does Lucas think about it?'

'I haven't mentioned it. I wasn't realistic at seventeen. Now I know what I want. A nice house. A husband. Children to love. I know what you're going to say but just because Mum messed it up, doesn't mean I will.'

'A family is delightful, of course, Natalia, but is that really enough for you on its own?'

Part of me wants to protect Natalia from Agatha's questions, but this is too important. 'We're not saying you shouldn't marry Lucas, Natalia. But you don't seem a very happy girl right now.'

'*Am* so. All brides get stressed. I'm having six bridesmaids.

A five-course sit-down wedding breakfast. It's a lot to think about.'

'Not all brides need to take anti-depressants, though, do they, dear?'

But Natalia doesn't seem to have heard her. 'We have the photographer who's done most of the celebrity weddings. Our honeymoon is in the Turks and Caicos. We have our own private pavilion with a plunge pool and butler service.'

'Even so, it's not too late to postpone, Natalia. Just till you're sure?' Agatha's voice is soft, but persistent.

'Of course it's too late,' Natalia snaps back, and pushes away from me, before I can stop her. 'Oww.'

She must have forgotten about her ankle. She slumps back against the sofa, trying not to touch me.

'You could even blame your injury if you're worried what people will say, you know, dear. Not that you should care.'

Natalia laughs. 'It's not about other people. You have no idea of how much this matters to *me*. No one has.'

'Your mother might,' I say. The look on her face makes it clear what she thinks of *that* but I can't let her do this alone. 'I know she did something that's hard to forgive, Natalia. My mum and I argued like cat and dog when I was a teenager, but when I got married, we started to get close again. She was the only one who understood.'

She scowls. 'I won't be asking for *my* mother's help. Not now, not when I get pregnant, and definitely not for baby-sitting. Never.'

I have to have one last try. 'Never's a long time, Natalia. And husbands can be adorable and supportive but no one can ever replace your mother. You can be the bigger person. Don't throw the relationship away unless you're sure it's what you want.'

'I'm sure, thank you.' It comes out more like a snarl than a statement. 'I'd actually like to call my fiancé right now, and as I don't seem to be able to move from this sofa, I wonder if it'd be possible for the two of you to give me a little privacy.'

I'm about to remind her that there's no phone signal here, but then perhaps she's so far gone that it won't matter.

Agatha and I leave the room and close the door behind us. Agatha sighs. 'I really am worried she's making the most awful mistake.'

'Mistakes are what teenagers do best. And as parents, we just have to watch from between our fingers and hope they don't hurt themselves too badly,' I say.

'Hmm. In that case, it's probably a good job I never became a mother.' She frowns. 'No. I can't be a spectator. I'll wait till she's finished her pretend phone call, and then I'm going in for round two. It's not as though she can run away.'

'And hold there. Do you control your triceps or are you gonna let them control you? Work them! We're holding to a count of ten, nine, eight . . .'

Ryan's voice drifts into the corridor, even though the ball-room door is closed. Sounds from all over the house are floating up through the floorboards, on cold draughts. There's Ryan barking orders. Steph chopping veg. Natalia whispering sweet nothings to a fiancé who can't possibly be on the other end of the phone. Agatha pacing outside the drawing room, planning what to say to convince Natalia to think again.

Is that the hardest lesson to learn about having kids? That it's one hundred per cent responsibility, zero per cent power? That however hard you try with the anti-bacterial sprays and the Green Cross Code and the Stranger Danger talks, you don't really have any control because fate won't treat your kids any differently from how it treats everyone else's.

Except I can't blame fate for what happened to my baby. That was *my* failure, my responsibility to keep her safe.

Natalia needs to know the truth: that you can't rely on there always being a second chance.

33

Darcy

After two minutes in my rescuer's car, I'm beginning to think an excruciatingly slow death from exposure might have been preferable to spending time alone with Foz.

'You don't have to be in a war zone to change people's lives, do you, Darcy? Sometimes it's just a matter of being ready, in the right place, at the right time.'

'Right. Did you ever actually fight in a war, Frank?' I ask.

His deep-fried face twists, though I can't tell if he's annoyed at being called his proper name, or at having his bluff called over his military credentials.

'You know, it was all about timing, Darcy. Not saying there weren't moments when I missed being called into battle. But I happened to serve during the good old days when it was only the Ruskies that bothered us. And I'm grown up enough now to know you don't have to kill someone to become a man.'

'Even so. All that training and you never got to fight.'

'You've only gotta look at that Neanderthal Pepper to realise that fighting doesn't equal becoming a better person, right?'

Maybe my silence tells him who *I* think is the real Neanderthal.

Once we get to the hotel, Frank grabs my hand. 'We can't have you slipping on the ice, Darcy,' and then he drags me into the office where he tries to impress Edie with his heroics.

'Of course, you could say it's a coincidence I was passing

when Darcy was in her hour of need. But then sometimes I think there's no such thing as coincidence—'

I can't take any more of this.

'I hate to interrupt – and I really am very grateful to Frank for giving me a lift up the hill – but I need to make a phone call, and we couldn't get a mobile signal anywhere. The snow must have made reception even worse.'

'Oh dear,' she says. 'Is it urgent?'

I try very hard not to scream at her. 'Well, it *is* the whole reason I risked life and limb to drive down the hill in the first place. I have a meeting in London in . . .' I check my watch, 'fifteen minutes' time and I need to explain why I won't be there.'

'I'll leave you two girls to it,' Foz says, backing out of the cramped office.

Edie studies her fingernails. 'The problem is, Darcy, the landline isn't, um, strictly operational at the moment.'

'What? Fine, I can Skype them if you let me use your computer.'

'We've been having a few connection issues with the Wi-Fi too.'

'Don't tell me, it's the wrong kind of snow.'

She blushes. 'It rather pre-dates the weather conditions. The company have been promising to come out and upgrade all the wiring but . . .'

Or you can't pay the bill, I think. 'Your website promised wireless broadband.'

'Um. Yes, well. The website is one of the things I haven't got round to updating. On account of the, um, lack of broadband. I do go into the village twice a week to do my emails but, well, other stuff has tended to take priority.'

'Jesus Christ, it's worse than the dark ages. I've reported from disaster zones with better comms.'

'I'm very sorry,' she says, beginning to sound ever so slightly chippy, 'but people do tend to come on boot camp to get away from it all.'

'Hang on, though. You said you'd called the gas board.'

'Just a little white lie. To avoid panic. I'm sure it'll be back on soon.'

'Unless you haven't paid the bill for that either!'

She says nothing.

'And what about the bloody ambulance you were meant to call for Natalia? Are you seriously running a hotel – not just a hotel, but a fitness boot camp – when you can't even reach the emergency services without smoke signals or carrier pigeon?'

'I didn't lie about that, Darcy. My mobile will do 999 calls if I stick my head out of the loft window. Honestly. I'd never be so irresponsible.'

I don't know how to answer that, so I leave her office, to see if anyone in this godforsaken place has a mobile with a signal powerful enough to connect to the outside world.

Not that I believe in miracles.

Ryan's leading a class in the ballroom, so I go outside for a smoke. Only two left.

Parts of me are beginning to throb and ache from the crash. I'd like to smoke both cigarettes, but there's no way of knowing how long we're going to be stuck here, cut off from civilisation. I have to ration myself to one.

With the first gasp of nicotine, my hands stop shaking. But the aches in my body multiply about a thousand times over. I'll live, though. God knows, I've survived worse than this.

'Decided you couldn't miss the final weigh-in after all?'

Pepper's behind me. I hold out my cigarette box, and he's about to take one when he changes his mind and takes out a crumpled pack of ordinary B&H.

'Don't panic, Webb. I managed to raid Ryan's secret stash, and there are plenty more where these came from. We might perish from starvation but we won't be denied a last cigarette before dying.'

We look down. From here, you can twist your head to gain an oblique view of the seafront. I hadn't even noticed the water before because I was so desperate to leave, but Ryan was right: the sea *has* frozen. Not all the way to the horizon, of course, but there are huge chunks of slushy ice moving noiselessly against each other, like white whales.

'It's like being at the end of the world,' I say.

'What have you got to say about global warming, now?' Pepper says. 'You're always on about it, you newsreaders. So how come this is the first time in my life I've seen an ice storm?'

I laugh. 'That's one thing I'm not about to take responsibility for. I only read the news. I don't make it.'

'You almost did make the headlines this morning with your daredevil escape attempt. You all right?'

'Black and blue. But in one piece.'

He nods. 'How far did you get?'

I laugh. 'Halfway down the hill. My car was in an even bigger hurry than I was. I guess I'll have to get it towed at some point. Might be a write-off.'

'Good job our all-Australian super-hero was around to step into the breach, eh?'

I glance at him. 'Now, now. Soldiers aren't supposed to be bitchy.'

He shrugs. 'He's a fraud.'

'A fraud with a four-wheel drive is better than nothing when there's no mobile signal and no way up a hill without the crampons I'd inexplicably forgotten to pack for my mini-break in Devon.'

He sighs. 'So what did your agent say?'

I look at my watch. Twenty past twelve. 'No idea. All comms are down, with the exception of semaphore, and I've been struggling to get a line of sight to Soho from here. The car's probably not the only write-off.'

'But you're a star, aren't you? They expect diva behaviour. It adds to the mystique.'

'My mystique is on life support. I'm guessing they'll be turning off the machine in around about ten minutes' time.'

'Ah.' He takes an extra-deep drag on his cigarette. 'Not good.'

'Filthy habit, Darcy.'

We look round: Frank is watching us from the patio doors. He takes a step towards me. 'I didn't save your bacon for you to smoke yourself to death.'

'Oh, come on. We all have our vices.'

His laugh is filthy. 'I can't think *what* you mean by that. All right, Pepper. Hardly setting a good example to the clients, are you?'

Pepper grunts in reply.

'It's boot camp that's driven me back to the ciggies, Frank,' I say.

'There are less toxic ways to relax.'

'Who says I *want* to relax?' I say it to be contrary, but it comes out flirtatious. Pepper looks disgusted with me. Not as disgusted as I am with myself.

'Well, I think you could do with chilling out, Darcy. You look as jumpy as a kangaroo with a funnel web in her pouch.' Frank grins at his own joke.

Pepper grunts, throws his half-smoked cigarette onto the earth, and grinds it into the ground. He stomps back inside without a word.

'Bit short on the old conversation, Staff Pepper, isn't he?'

'You know, Frank, this Australian act is a bit OTT. Are you sure you're not from Essex?'

'No, I really am the original red-blooded Aussie male. Can I help my colourful turn of phrase?'

'It does seem fairly pathological in your case.' I shiver. 'Christ, it's cold.'

'I can think of a way to warm you up.'

'Ah, Frank,' I sigh. 'You really don't take a hint, do you?'

'Straight up. I'm the original winter warmer. My massage technique definitely improves the circulation. Just you wait.' He grins and then turns round to go in for lunch. 'See you later, alligator.'

Not, I think, if I see you first.

Even Steph's culinary genius can't compensate for the dwindling ingredients in her kitchen.

She comes into the drawing room carrying a huge gratin dish between oven-gloved hands. 'Apologies in advance, ladies and gentlemen. This was *meant* to be a root veg and tuna bake. But we're all out of tuna. So I had to stick cheese on top, or this would be an entirely protein-free lunch, which seemed unwise when we're in a cold, cold house.'

Natalia sticks up her hand. 'Is there any alternative? I don't want to put weight *on*.' She seems to be having trouble focusing.

'Understood. Well, if you don't want to bugger your diet, I can offer you stock-cube soup. With dried onion flakes.'

I can see the other boot campers making the calculation – do they eat the bake and survive, or go hungry to maximise results at the weigh-in tomorrow?

Even Natalia chooses the bake in the end. There's not much of that to go round, but it tastes wonderful. Almost wonderful enough to distract me from the thought of how much Marian must hate me right now.

Almost.

It's packed in here, with extra chairs brought in from the chilly dining room to seat the staffs, and Phil. After my encounter with Edie earlier, she's decided to skulk in her office to eat her dinner. Scared I might spill the beans on the 'little gas supply problem', I suspect.

The firelight flickers and contented sounds fill the room. It'd be almost cosy if it weren't for Frank, perched on a pouffe by the fire, providing the cabaret. 'So, ladies, I was there in my bed this morning thinking, ha, I could easily award myself a duvet day today, given the ice-age conditions. But I couldn't bear the guilt of leaving you all in the lurch. There are massages to be done, right? We might be down but we are *not* out.'

Ryan and Pepper are glowering at him. I once did a report on a group of male gorillas who'd been illegally captured to be sold to zoos. They tried to tear each other apart in their cage. Not all of them got out alive.

The resemblance is striking.

'Give it a fucking rest, will you, Walton?' Pepper growls.

'*Someone* got out of bed the wrong side this morning. But whose bed?' Foz says, and the two Crab women laugh inanely. He starts telling some story about doing commando training in the heat of the Australian outback.

Ryan places a hand on Pepper's shoulder, but he shrugs it off.

Pepper stands up so suddenly that his dining chair topples over. He's towering over Frank on his pouffe, poking him.

Poking has to be one of the world's most incendiary acts.

'I said, give it a rest, you Aussie twat. Some of us prefer to eat without some wanker giving a running commentary.'

Frank stands up. As they square up to each other, it's like

276

trying to predict the outcome of a fight between two of those gorillas. Pepper is shorter, but he's more wound up.

Ryan steps between them. 'Come on, lads, calm down, eh?'

I may not be an expert on the workings of the male brain but I do know that telling men to *calm down* rarely has the desired effect. The other women are gawping. The Crabs look excited by the prospect of a fist fight.

'Come on, then, Pepper, let's see what you're made of.' There's a new aggression in Frank's voice.

'Staff Pepper . . .' I say, not wanting him to get flattened. 'Fancy a fag?'

But he isn't listening.

'I asked you politely. Will you keep it shut, Walton?'

'Maybe it's different here, but where I come from, telling someone to *give it a fucking rest* doesn't count as polite, *Staff Pepper*.'

'Maybe you'd rather I shut you up myself?'

'Oh, *please* do, sunshine. No woman would touch you with a bargepole, so I guess you need some way to get rid of all that pent-up testosterone.'

Pepper throws his arm back, ready for a punch, but Ryan catches hold of him. For a few seconds, they're wrestling. Pepper's shouting, and Ryan's shouting, and that's enough, finally, to bring Edie out of her lair, followed by Karma, who is yapping with delight.

'What's going on?' she says.

The staffs stop for a second.

'Boys, this kind of vibe isn't going to help us out of a crisis, now, is it? I set Windy Hill up as a strictly aggression-free zone.'

That must be why she decided to recruit two ex-soldiers to run a military-style boot camp.

Pepper and Ryan seem to have lost any interest in Frank. They're about to kick off again, but Edie is shaking her head.

'No. No! If you must behave like animals, then take it outside. Go. Shoo!'

Bizarrely, they do what they're told, still jostling and mumbling as they twist past the sofas and into the hallway. I can hear shouting, but I can't make out the words.

'Well, ladies,' Foz says, 'that is yet more proof of why I left the military. Working with women is just *so* much more civilised.'

34

Steph

Maybe it was the cheese. After a week of wholegrains, bird food and bean curd, the cheese could have pushed the staffs over the edge.

In a funny way, it's a compliment; I don't think my food has ever started a fight before.

I'm tidying up after lunch – I'm now so possessive over this kitchen that I don't even want help loading the dishwasher – when I hear someone behind me. I smile – but the smile fades when I hear scrabbling paws, and realise it's not Ryan.

'How are we doing for supplies, Steph?'

Edie's pixie face is tired, with deep shadows under the eyes. After seeing the red bills piling up in her room, I can understand why.

'I haven't really had a chance to look since I finished lunch.' That's not strictly true. The cupboard really is bare, now. But I don't want to add to her worries. I might have a brainwave between now and dinner time. 'We'll survive.'

'So long as it thaws overnight. Otherwise it's going to turn a bit *Lord of the Flies*. Even on an average week, people are going stir crazy by now. We regularly get people staging a break out to the pub two miles away.' She sighs. 'Not that I blame them. Sometimes I wish I could break out too.'

I put down the tea towel, and put the kettle on. 'Must get lonely up here.'

'Thank God for Karma.' She lifts the dog up and tickles his huge pink tummy. 'Though I worry about how much I talk to him. And spoil him. But he's my only company, half the time. Apart from boot camp weeks, I'm hardly overflowing with bookings.'

'Brave of you to take on somewhere like this, alone.'

Edie frowns. 'I wasn't meant to be alone, but *someone* got cold feet once we realised what a huge job it was. My only mistake was not doing a runner too. I thought it was karma that we found this place, won the auction. Hence the name of the puppy we bought together. Turns out it was *bad,* bad karma. I must have done something truly dreadful in a previous life.'

'Oh.' I don't quite know what else to say.

'Sorry, I shouldn't be moaning to the one person who has gone out of her way to help me this week. Forgive me, Steph. I'm sure you have troubles of your own to deal with.'

'I'm a bit stressed by tofu levels right now, but I'm happy to listen, if it helps.'

And then it all floods out. The London life, the dream of a rural holistic escape, the coked-out City boyfriend who bought into that dream, the inheritance from a favourite uncle that made the hotel affordable – just. And then the terrible first winter, the bill for a knackered roof that swallowed up the entire refurbishment budget, the boyfriend's urgent business meetings back in London. And, finally, the realisation that they weren't business meetings at all.

'The worst thing is that it's all such a cliché,' Edie says. 'I didn't even miss *him* that much when he'd gone. But I missed having someone to share the worries. This house is like a hydra – you know, the many-headed monster. Whenever I think I've chopped one problem down to size, another one leaps out of the darkness and goes right for the jugular.'

'Wow. You've done well to survive this long.'

'Thank you. I'd like to say it's down to my spiritual side, but really I think it's sheer bloody-mindedness.'

'Would you consider selling?'

Edie sighs. 'No one would want the place, would they? Not if I told them the truth. Only after I bought it did people in the village start telling me about the people who owned the place before. You know the portraits in the drawing room? Half of the subjects died mysteriously, suicides, deaths behind enemy lines. And one of those guys lost the entire hotel to a rival in a game of canasta.'

'Maybe you could build on the mystery,' I say, aware that I'm clutching at straws. 'Tourists like ghosts, don't they?'

'I've never seen one. I mean –' she looks heavenwards – 'help me out, guys? Please? A little light haunting could be our last hope.'

I laugh. 'It wouldn't take much to make the place feel more cheerful, you know. Look at how much nicer the drawing room looked once Vicki lit the fire. Plus, shabby chic is all the rage again.'

'You're sweet, Steph. But I don't think I've got the energy anymore. I've got some agents coming to view it next week. If I can get anywhere near breaking even then I'm selling up.'

Karma has started to snore in her arms.

'Wouldn't it be a shame to give up now?'

'I've nothing left.' She smiles wearily. 'Good luck with dinner. And thank you. If only you'd come along sooner, Steph. You're a fairy godmother. But I'm too far gone to go to the ball.'

The compliment makes me glow. Until I remember that the fairy godmother is a fat, round woman with terrible dress sense.

Karma and Edie have been gone less than five minutes when I get *another* visitor.

'Can I come in?'

I give Ryan my dirtiest look. Which isn't very dirty, to be honest, unless by dirty I mean lustful. 'So who won your punch-up, then?'

His face is pink, and his spiky hair even spikier than usual. 'No one. We pushed each other around, shouted a bit, and then realised we were bloody freezing. Sorry if we spoiled your latest lunch triumph.'

'I grew up with brothers. It takes more than a barney to rattle me. But Edie's definitely rattled. I don't think you helped her bio-rhythms.'

Ryan pulls a face. 'No. Though if you ask me, Pepper won't be the last one to flip. The longer we're iced in, the more likely it is we'll turn on each other.'

'We might have to, because there's nothing else left to eat.'

He grins, then reaches into his pocket. 'I have a secret weapon to raise your morale, though, chef. Tea!'

He's holding two sachets.

'I can't drink any more herbal, Staff.'

'Good job this is English breakfast, then.'

I take a step forward, unable to believe my eyes. 'Wow.'

'Edie gives us a supply each week before she clears the guest rooms of the hard stuff. It's in our contract. Shall I put the kettle on?'

'I'll do it.' I don't want to risk any mistakes with my first cuppa in almost a week.

'It's all right, Steph. I can't cook for toffee but I *can* brew up.'

'Sorry. I've turned into a bit of a control freak.'

He pulls out a chair at the kitchen table and puts his hands on my shoulders to guide me into it. I feel faint and it's not because I didn't eat enough root vegetable gratin.

'You deserve a rest, Chef Steph. The others have started taking you for granted.'

Story of my life, I think. 'So, what was it about, then?'

'What?' He fills the kettle and washes out two dirty mugs, first with Fairy Liquid and then with water. I could watch a man do housework for hours . . . especially this particular man. In twenty-four hours, it'll all seem like a dream. Maybe I'd like to stay snowed in: the view here is the best.

'The punch-up. I don't believe it was just cabin fever.'

He pauses. 'It's a man thing. We can't be cooped up.'

'OK. Pepper wanting to punch Foz, I can almost understand. But Pepper seemed to want to punch you even more. That's what *I* don't get.'

Ryan makes the tea like a child following a recipe for the first time. But when he puts the two mugs on the table in front of me, they're the perfect shade of golden brown. If he can make tea like this – it's an underrated skill – then I bet I could teach him to cook.

I dismiss images of steamy kitchens and my favourite soldier in an apron, a chef's hat and not a lot else. He sits down opposite me.

'We've fallen out.'

'Soldier's tiff?'

'No. More serious than that.' He sighs. 'I want out.'

'Out . . . of boot camp?'

He nods. 'Told him a couple of days ago. He didn't take it right well.'

I sip the tea. It tastes incredible. 'Why do you want to leave?'

'It's . . . tricky. We go back such a long way. OK, he was the search team commander, but after months in the middle of nowhere, the ranks didn't matter so much. We became mates, too. That happens, when you go through that amount of shit. Yeah, it's awful. But it's also like being, I dunno, two hundred per cent *alive*.'

'Even though you're killing people?' I'm shocked by how disapproving I sound. 'Sorry, I don't mean to be harsh, but—'

'But it's natural to wonder. Some people think we treat it like a video game.'

I blush. That *is* what I was thinking.

He looks past me. 'It's not like that at all. Apart from anything else, I wasn't out there to kill people. My role was defusing bombs. But whether I was on my stomach waiting to be blown to pink mist, or returning fire in the middle of a dog fight, it was the most real time of my life. The fear. The risk. Everything's more colourful, louder, brighter. Psychedelic. I've never done LSD but it couldn't be better than battle. Some of the lads say they'd take it over getting laid any time.' He seems to remember I'm here. 'Sorry. Went a bit far, then, eh?'

'No, I mean—'

'It's fine. I'm used to people's eyes glazing over. Which is why I don't talk about it, especially not to women. Nothing puts a girl off more than the idea that her date is an adrenalin-crazed psychopath who prefers killing to being in bed with her. Rubbish, of course, but once a girl's started thinking that way . . .'

I force a smile. Maybe it's a compliment that he can share all his anxieties and doesn't feel the need to censor himself, as he would with a girl he actually fancies. 'I don't think you're a psychopath.'

'Maybe not, Steph, but I'm not much good at real life. When I first came out, I was wrecked. My girlfriend booted me out and I don't blame her. Then Matt asked me here. I'm bloody grateful, but staying put is the easy option. Like a halfway house.'

'Sometimes I think the easy option is underrated,' I say. 'I've taken it my whole life and I'm not unhappy.'

Ryan frowns. 'Not unhappy? I guess that's better than

nothing. But this place,' he looks around him, 'this is making me unhappy.'

'And have you ever been happy as a civilian?' I ask gently.

He scowls. 'A few times. On leave. But it wasn't real.'

Somehow I know he's talking about the girlfriend again. 'So what will you do?'

'God knows. There's work. Private security contracts. Here. Abroad. Loads going in Iraq and Afghanistan. The more troops pull out of there, the more work there'll be, protecting the people who still think there's money to be made.'

'And will that make you happy?'

Ryan says nothing for a while, and I wonder if I've gone too far. 'After some of the things I've seen, Steph, I think maybe we expect too much of life.' His eyes drift away.

'Unless the things you've seen mean you have a duty to use the freedom you have got?'

He sips his tea. 'Maybe I should apologise to Matt, stick around, till something better occurs to me.'

I sip my tea. 'What made you decide you had to go now?'

Ryan fiddles with the teaspoon. 'Something about this particular camp has got under my skin. I realised that when the rest of you leave, you go back to real relationships and families and friends. It's . . . richer, somehow. But me and Pepper stay here, bickering about Foz and whose turn it is to run the abs class.'

I struggle to see the richness in my own life: the empty flat, the pile of work my boss will have ready for me. Even the thought of presenting the New Me to Steve doesn't make me smile. 'Funny. I've been loving my time in this kitchen so much that I haven't missed my so-called real life at all.'

'No?' He leans forward. 'I'm bored talking about me, Steph. What about you? Has boot camp delivered what you wanted?'

'I might have lost some weight off my fingers,' I say, and he thinks I'm joking.

'Why did you come? It's not about weight loss, surely, because you're great as you are. Some women aren't meant to be all sinewy and skinny.'

'Is that a nice way of saying that being obese suits my personality?'

'Obese?' He shakes his head. 'Bloody hell. *Women*. You're curvy. Where did you get this warped idea that you're *obese*?'

Steve's mocking face pops up. I blink him away. 'Everyone knows curvy is just a *Daily Mail* word for grossly overweight. But boot camp's been great. I'll be going home with an encyclopaedic knowledge of what to do with bean curd.'

'Don't laugh it off, Steph. You're a great girl. You shouldn't be down on yourself.'

'It's not weird to want to improve yourself, is it?'

He shakes his head. 'No. But it's weird to want to punish yourself with words like obese when you're lovely as you are.'

I remember what Foz told me during the massage. Perhaps Ryan's hedging his bets for tonight, in case someone else says no to his night-time manoeuvres. 'You sound like a shrink.'

'Ah. Guilty secret. When I left the army, I hung out in the library to search for jobs online. Librarian suggested some self-help books and that was it. I was addicted. I know men are from Mars, that women love too much, and I should be brilliant at winning friends and influencing people. Then Pepper tracked me down and told me to stop being a Nancy Boy. Tough love, he called it.'

'Tough love.' I laugh. 'Yeah, I know all about that. My last boyfriend . . . he could be quite tough. God knows I need a bit of *encouragement* to stop me eating all the pies.'

'Tough, how?'

'Just the usual.'

'Such as?'

'Um . . .' I rack my brains, not for Steve's zillions of

criticisms – they come easily enough. But for something Ryan won't take out of context. 'Well, for example, he used to say that if I kept eating like a pig, my eyes would get even piggier!'

Ryan stares at me. 'Your *boyfriend* said that?'

'Well, my eyes *are* quite piggy, aren't they? I'd said that to Steve myself, so he was only helping me to see I wasn't doing myself any good by overeating.'

'Very supportive. Not.'

'It wasn't just superficial things. He wanted me to make the most of myself. So he told me to read the classics, rather than the thrillers I like. And that going out of the house without make-up probably wasn't doing my confidence any good because people would ignore me.'

'He sounds a right charmer.'

'I'm not telling you the *nice* things he said. They don't stick in your memory, do they? Not like the tough-love stuff?'

Though I'm struggling to think of a single compliment he paid me that might not have a double edge.

Ryan just looks at me, the doe eyes all sympathetic.

'Come on, Staff. Pepper does the same. The way he told you to stop being a Nancy . . .' I can't say it. 'He's good for you, isn't he? The same as Steve was good for me. A bit cruel, yes, but definitely cruel to be kind. Motivating.'

Ryan puts his mug down, and looks at me. 'Cruel, sure. I'm not hearing much kindness from your boyfriend.'

I scowl. 'Well, you don't know him. I do. And if you want to know the real reason I came on boot camp, it's him. To prove there's more to me than . . . I don't know, root vegetable and tuna bake. Without the tuna.' I get off the bar stool, and go to check the dishwasher, even though it's still rumbling away.

'Steph.' He stands up too, his hands outstretched in an apology. 'You're right. I'm sure your boyfriend will be as impressed as we are. Take no notice of me. I can do a thousand press-ups but I know absolutely bugger all about relationships.'

And he leaves the kitchen.

I don't move. I'm searching my memories, going all the way back to the first days of my relationship with Steve, the ones I see in a golden haze. He said wonderful things, then. I *know* he did. I wouldn't have fallen in love with him if he hadn't, would I?

'Sorry.'

Ryan's back. Maybe he's going to say Something Significant, something he's learned from battlefield encounters with life and death.

Maybe he's going to tell me I'm lovely again. I'd settle for that.

But instead, he darts across to the table, picks up his mug, and rinses it under the tap, washing away the stains with his fingers, before setting it back on the draining board.

'I like to clear up after myself. Army taught me that, at least,' he says, and then leaves for good.

35

Vicki

Learned a new word today. Discombobulated.

Darcy says it's how she's feeling after her accident. Confused. Upset. Knocked off course.

I'm feeling it too. It's dusk, and there's no sign of a thaw. If it doesn't warm up soon, we've got no hope of making it down the hill and then back home tomorrow. My texts to Dave – sent by hanging out of the window or venturing down to the gates at high risk – have become a lot more needy.

The ones that come back, hours later, are reassuring. The boys are wrapped up like Eskimos, they're loving the snow, and if I can't get back tomorrow night, it won't be the end of the world.

It will be to me. Plus, everything's gone a bit wild west round here. When Pepper almost knocked out Ryan, we could have been in a saloon bar. And Steph bit my head off when I asked if she needed help chopping or peeling for dinner.

Then later she came to apologise, and admitted there's nothing left to peel, chop *or* eat. And begged me not to tell the others.

'You're not asleep already are you, Vicki?'

Foz has set up his couch in the Clamshell 'suite'. I'm lying under a blanket, and the clean smell reminds me of ironing. And that reminds me of home yet again.

'No, I was thinking of my boys.'

'Ah, sure thing, Vicki. Nothing more important than family, right?'

'Do you have kids, Foz?'

'No. Haven't met the right girl yet, Vicki. I know it's late, but there's always hope. So, you'll be reunited with your sons tomorrow, right?'

'If we can get through the snowdrifts.'

'Vicki, if there's any problem, I will personally transport every camper to a snow-free zone in my Fozmobile. All part of the service.'

His hands find a tender spot between my shoulder blades, and dig in. 'How's that feel, Vicki?'

'Sore. But good. Is that how it's meant to feel? I've never had a massage, unless you count my kids walking up and down my back to get me up on a Sunday morning.'

'Bet they can't wait to get their mummy back.'

The thought of seeing them makes my throat tight. Foz is very good at what he's doing, but I'd rather be pummelled and wrestled by *my* boys. And then taken to bed by my husband . . .

Jeez, who knows, he might even be able to *carry* me there now.

'That was a big sigh, Vicki. But don't let homesickness spoil your last hours here. Friday's usually a fun night, you know? We call if Thank F It's Friday.'

'I can guess why.'

He laughs. 'Can you really?'

'The F stands for . . . you know. Because we're all effing relieved we've got this far.'

'That's right, Vicki. Though Friday's also traditionally when things go bump *and* grind in the night.'

'Eh?'

'Come on, Vicki. You've got three kids. You know about the

birds and the bees? Remember the game, musical chairs? Here we prefer to play musical beds.'

I remember the staffs' gossip at dawn. 'Do you play?'

'A gentleman never tells tales. You'll just have to wait and see.' He laughs again. 'Right, let's turn you over and give your front some attention.'

The massage has left me even more discom— muddled than before.

I'm lying on my bed half-asleep when the special phone the magazine lent me buzzes. Probably a text reminder to file my video diary – they were well pissed off that I didn't do it last night.

But when I look at the screen, it shows a video camera, not an envelope. I press the picture and it asks me:

Do you want to play?

Didn't even know I could get video on this phone, but I say yes.

The tiny screen goes black and I wonder if it's a virus thingy. Great. The magazine will probably charge me for messing up their precious phone.

But then it comes back to life.

My boys, filling the screen.

They're dancing around a snowman, a spindly version with eyes and a mouth made from the slate chippings, and a beef tomato for a nose. He looks . . . drunk. Alastair is finishing him off, while the other two hold snowballs so big you could bowl with them.

'Say hi to Mummy, like we practised.'

Dave's voice sounds tinny on the speaker.

'Hello, Mum!' they chorus.

'Now line up in height order.' Dave's really getting into the director's role.

The boys line up. Funny – I always think they're the spit of Dave, but now I can see me in them, too. Alastair has my toothy smile, Murray my eyes, and Rudy is standing on one foot, exactly the same way I do in all my childhood photos.

'We miss you, Mum, and we especially miss your dinners,' says Murray. 'Dad burned the oven chips last night. And the baked beans.'

'Oi, Murray, no telling tales,' Dave says from behind the camera.

Next it's Alastair. 'Mummy, there's been no school today! And we can't wait to see you tomorrow. Daddy says you're coming back all skinny but I like you all fat and squishy for cuddles.'

I look down at the phone resting on my still extremely squishy thighs. 'No danger of skinny, sweetheart.'

And finally Rudy stares at the camera, biting his lip. 'You are coming back, Mummy, aren't you?'

I gulp.

'Course she is, silly,' Murray says. 'Mummy lives *here*, with us. You're such a baby.'

'Well, he is only four,' I tell the phone.

'Boys, I'm going to stop filming now, so smile nicely for Mummy,' Dave says.

'Not finished yet,' Murray shouts. 'Three, two . . . one . . . THROW!'

And they throw their snowballs straight at Dave, hitting the camera so hard that the screen whites out and I hear a yelp before the movie ends abruptly.

Would you like to play again? a little message suggests.

I click yes and watch it once, twice, three times. Each time I notice something new. I'm laughing, but there's a ginormous lump in my throat, too. Never mind thank F it's Friday. Whatever it takes, I'll be back with them for Super Saturday.

Picking up after them, feeding them, washing them, loving them. As though I'd never been away.

Maybe I should try to savour these last few hours of peace and quiet.

But peace – and especially quiet – makes me nervous. Noise is reassuring. The squelching of the heartbeat at the first hospital scan is the most reassuring sound of all.

The sonographer wasn't even supposed to tell me I was having a girl, but Julie had scanned me with all three boys and she couldn't resist giving Dave and me the good news.

'Hey, you two are going to be just like the Beckhams again. Three boys and now . . . a little girl.' She pointed at the screen. I couldn't quite see what I was meant to be seeing, but I knew Julie wouldn't tell me unless she was sure.

It was what we'd wanted, of course, but I hadn't got my hopes up. My body seemed to be good at making boys.

Dave kissed me and I kissed him back. But then I had the weirdest daydream. I knew I was lying on the hospital couch, bursting for a wee, but at the same time, it was like I was zooming forward in time. Next to me, there was a girl who looked a lot like me, except with Dave's slim arms and slim legs.

My hand was resting on *her* belly, and I just knew somehow that my first grandchild was in there. It was like I was a little part of this long line of mothers and daughters going all the way back into the past and as far as you can see into the future.

Never told anyone. Way too weird to share with Dave or Chrissie or *my* mum. But I thought that maybe, just maybe, when she was older, I'd tell *her* what I'd seen.

I chose her name when we got home after the scan. Both Dave and I had Scottish ancestors, and we'd toured the lochs on our honeymoon. So it felt right that our kids should have Scottish names. I'd made a list late in each of my pregnancies. A female Rudy would have been Rowena, and Murray could have been Morag and Alastair might have been Aileen.

But this time I scanned the list on the internet, and one jumped out at me. It meant *Jewel*. Much softer than the no-nonsense names Dave and I usually went for. But I knew it was right. I used to whisper the name to her when she danced inside me. The boys kicked like footballers. She was like a ballerina.

And then . . . and then I screamed her name when I woke up one morning and she wasn't dancing. That lunchtime, Julie held her sensor over my much bigger belly and said nothing. That silence will haunt me for ever.

I tried not to cry out in labour but her name echoed round my head. When I saw her, she was beautiful. They say every mother thinks her newborn is beautiful, but Rudy wasn't. Rudy was angry. Alastair was serious, his face all folds like a little old man. Murray had pink lips and a full head of hair. But even he wasn't as beautiful as she was.

That wasn't the only difference, of course. All three boys came into the world with loud screeches. Only my baby girl was peaceful.

We named her, as we'd planned, on the death certificate. We could have had a funeral, too. Were advised to by the midwives. They were so kind. But Dave wasn't keen, wanted to move on, to bury the hurt. I've hidden the hand- and footprints the hospital gave me, too. Never looked at them, though knowing they're there reassures me she existed.

And I've never said her name out loud since the day of that last, silent scan. I've even tried not to think it.

My eyes are closing. I'm so tired. But I fiddle with the phone so the video plays again and again, my kids' voices at full volume. It comforts me.

Noise means life; it's as simple as that.

36

Steph

Dinner for *sixteen* is going to take a loaves and fishes-style miracle.

From the jaws of victory, you're about to snatch defeat, right, honeybunch?

Steve's voice is back in my head. With a vengeance. It's a shock: since I've been busy with exercise and cooking, I haven't been hearing him at all.

Good job I'm back. Without me to motivate you, you'd never get anything done.

I turn on the radio, to try to drown him out. The only station we can get is a local one, which is keeping up a constant stream of doom and gloom and high-pitched phone calls from listeners stranded across the county.

But it's still better than Steve.

OK, I must concentrate. I've laid all the food that's left in front of me on the Formica countertop. There is: quinoa, Tewkesbury mustard with horseradish, a jar of cranberry sauce, a packet of six quail's eggs (so not even half each), a catering tin of custard powder, three cans of condensed milk, a tray of apples and pears in various states of mouldiness, and a frozen Veggie BBQ Party Multi-Pack I exhumed from the bottom of the chest freezer.

At least we have protein, but the 'No Beef Burgers' and 'Chicken-less Breasts' are made from flaccid, beige meat substitute. I might be able to force it down if it was fried in half a pound of butter, but with no hob *or* oven working, all I have is the microwave.

Which is *so* not going to work.

Sod 'em, Steph. Not your problem. Get Edie to cook what's left. Soon you'll be back to your old ways anyhow. Better warn your local Dominos to stock up on your favourite garlic bread.

Shut up. Shut UP, SHUT UP!

It's all going wrong. Tonight I wanted to give everyone a meal they'd remember for the right reasons. A dinner prepared with love and friendship. Nourishment to make Natalia forgive her mum. To help Edie see the hotel could have a future. To soothe Pepper's temper, and heal poor Vicki's broken heart.

But the person I most wanted to please is Ryan, of course.

It doesn't take one of Ryan's self-help books to realise the reason I see the little boy lost in him is because there's a little girl lost right here, under my layers of woolly jumpers and my thirty-two per cent body fat.

Off you go again, honeybunch. Self-pity won't get dinner cooked but it's par for the course, right?

For the first time I can remember, the voice is saying something useful. There must be more food, *somewhere*.

And then I remember Ryan's shopping trip. Chocolate, and sour cream. If only he hadn't made me put the puff pastry back.

Not that puff pastry in itself would have made for a gourmet dinner. But the memory has given me one last brainwave . . .

Most of the group are in the drawing room now that the day's sessions are over. It's too cold in the bedrooms, and there's no hot water for a shower anyway.

I step into the room, and immediately three of the campers shout out, 'Shut the door, Steph! It's cold!'

Bloody cheek. They're all lounging about in front of the

open fire, while I single-handedly slave away in a chilly kitchen, trying to save the day.

'Well, I'm *very* sorry to bother you, but I need some help. Supplies are running at a critically low level. However, I know that before the snow fell, some of you had been making illegal trips to the local shops to buy forbidden foods. And I wouldn't be surprised if others brought a few little extras from home in their suitcase.'

No one looks at me. I think I've hit the nail on the head.

'So I am offering an *amnesty* to salve your conscience. I need any food donations you can spare. No questions asked. Bear in mind that, if we're lucky, we'll all be off home tomorrow so you'll be able to eat whatever you want. But till then, we're going hungry.'

Still no one moves. 'All right. I know no one's admitting anything publicly, so I'll stay away from my kitchen for the next five minutes. All donations should be left on the counter, and anything is welcome. Otherwise it's half a microwaved veggie sausage each for dinner and I promise that'll be even more disgusting than it sounds.'

I head upstairs. Darcy's lying on her bed, her eyes wide open. She must be freezing.

She sits up slightly. 'Everything all right, Steph? I thought you'd be cooking.'

I open my mouth to tell her about the amnesty but I can't see her being the type to hoard Cheese Strings or Cadbury's Fruit and Nut. 'Long story. Short version is, there isn't much *to* cook. But we'll live.'

Darcy sighs. 'You sound cross. Are you pissed off at me for trying to leave?'

I shrug. 'Up to you what you do. Though I'm surprised you didn't say goodbye.'

Darcy looks away. 'I hate goodbyes.'

'I hate the dentist but I still go.'

'Fair point. Sorry.'

And that's enough to make me like her again. 'Must have had a good reason to head off in this weather. What was the hurry?'

'There was this meeting about my future. Make or break stuff. I didn't get there, obviously, so I think it must be break.'

'Don't be daft. They can't blame you for the weather, can they?'

'I can tell you've never worked in the media, Steph.'

I ignore her slightly superior tone. 'Besides, you're a household name. The rules are different. If they got rid of you, there'd be letters. Petitions. A protest march.'

Darcy laughs. 'Oh, I think you'll find I'll be forgotten within hours of another girl taking my place behind the news desk.'

'You don't sound that bothered, if you don't mind my saying so.'

'No. I can't work out if it's the worst thing that could happen, or the best.' She laughs again. 'Forget I said that. However bad it gets, losing a job is chicken feed compared to the worst life can throw at you.'

I feel like she wants to confide in me. But I'm running out of time before dinner.

'Um,' I look at my watch. 'Darcy, I'd love to talk some more but I'm scared I'll be lynched if I don't put *something* on the dining table. Sorry. Later, right?'

'Later. Sure.'

I hesitate outside the kitchen door, in case someone's still in there, off-loading a family pack of Snickers. But I can't hear anything. As I push the door open, I have absolutely no idea if I'm facing a feast, or a famine.

*

298

Thank St Nigella and St Delia and St Jamie!

We're *not* going to starve. In fact, I'm in danger of completely derailing everyone's boot camp progress before tomorrow's weigh-in, unless I exercise serious portion control.

Because alongside the shameful little heaps of sinful booty – a giant pack of Maltesers, a kilo of Bombay Mix, a bag of Oreo cookies and a half-drunk red wine box that has the Crabs written all over it – there is enough raw flesh to keep Lady Gaga in meat dresses for the entire winter season.

Steak.

Sausages – *real* sausages, stuffed so tight with marbled meat and flecked green herbs that they'll burst the minute they start cooking.

Bacon.

Oh. And not just meat. Farmhouse cheese in sunshine yellow bricks so firm you could build a house with them. Un-pasteurised milk in old-fashioned bottles, with a layer of creamy top-of-the-milk below the foil caps. And a tray of three dozen eggs, feathers still attached to the shells like tiny Red Indian head dresses.

There's a note attached, on the back of a pizza flyer: *DOES THIS HELP?* And alongside it, a small camping stove, and an industrial-sized blowtorch.

I can definitely do something with this.

Maybe this is how Picasso felt, or Michelangelo. I dive straight in, too inspired by the freshness of the ingredients to worry about who has been hoarding enough protein to keep an army going till Easter. I set up the camping stove on the worktop, and the blowtorch next to it. I'm not entirely sure this blowtorch is kitchen-safe, though I've used a miniature chef's version for burning the top of a crème brûlée and I guess the principle must be more or less the same.

There's a clear and present danger that I'll end up with singed eyebrows, but this is a time for courage in the face of almost insuperable odds. My fellow boot campers are depending on me. I will not fail them . . .

37

Steph

Dinner is either going to be disgusting or a triumph. Maybe I'm too arrogant for words, but I have an inkling it might be the latter . . .

Who are you kidding? You're not exactly Gordon Ramsay, are you?

'Why would I want to be a sweary, wrinkled bully with bad highlights?' I answer out loud.

Ooh, who rattled your cage?

It shocks me that I'm talking to the voice. But for the last hour and a half, I've been getting crosser and crosser with my imaginary ex-boyfriend. This evening, I've worked harder than I ever have in my life. I've cooked by toaster, kettle, microwave, primus stove *and* blowtorch. Even though there's no gas, the kitchen is like a furnace. I'm sweating harder than I did during any of the boot camp sessions.

But the nasty comments keep coming. Yes, I'm imagining them, but all the same, they're just as hurtful as if he really were here, sitting on the worktop, those skinny legs getting in my way, and those fatuous remarks stinging like lemon juice in a papercut.

I'm mixing up a dressing, and the movement of my hand is getting faster and faster. '*You* rattled my cage, Steve. Did it ever occur to you that most boyfriends try to support their girlfriends, not undermine them?'

Always knew you had no sense of humour, honeybunch.

'It's not a case of having no sense of humour. It's the fact that you've always been so busy using me as the butt of your jokes that you've stopped seeing me as an actual human being.'

I stop mixing. The dressing has thickened, almost to the texture of mayonnaise. But it's not that stopping me.

It's the utterly unarguable truth of what I just said.

All week I've been playing that whole 'if he could see me now' game, trying to convince myself that if I lose weight or slimmed down, he'll change his behaviour, give me his approval.

Yet for years – maybe even the whole bloody time I've known him – Steve's regarded me as an appendage. One to laugh at and joke about and manipulate, to make him feel better about himself.

The boot camp has been a total and complete waste of time. He was never going to recognise the new Steph because, put simply, he's not interested in anyone but himself.

I slump down on the bar stool. What a sucker I am. What a fool. What a bloody fool.

Don't know whether to laugh or cry. Feel like doing both. Because a part of me admires him for fooling me for so long. But the rest of me is so angry I want to smash everything in sight.

'You fucking bastard *fucker*, Steve fucking Ellison. What was the fucking point of that, you arsehole? Ten years. TEN YEARS. For what? Your ego?'

I lift the bowl of dressing off the counter.

And then smash it down onto the tiled floor.

It seems to take several seconds to land. Then the bowl smashes with the loudest crash, sending splinters of dressing-covered glass skittering across the tiles.

For one mad moment, I picture the kitchen when I've finished. Shards of crockery and glass carpeting the floor.

Scraps of food sticking to the cupboards, sauce all over the ceiling.

Carnage.

But then I start to giggle to myself. Smash up my kitchen? When I've had such fun here? I feel calm again, now. Though I wouldn't trust myself not to commit GBH if Steve walked through that door right now.

'Looks amazing.'

For a split second, I think that my imaginary Steve has suddenly fallen into line. If I'd stood up for myself years ago, could it all have turned out differently?

Except there's nothing imaginary about the voice, or about the lips that almost graze my neck as I spin around. The temperature in the kitchen has just shot up by a thousand degrees.

'Oh. It's you, Staff. Thank you. Though I seem to have had a bit of an accident.' *Did he hear me swearing?* I feel quite ashamed of myself. Ryan hasn't sworn once in all the time I've been here.

I reach out for the broom, but he's there before. 'Soon have that sorted out.'

I watch for a second as he sweeps up the glass. Handsome *and* house proud. How could any woman resist?

'I can't believe you've managed all this *and* transformed the dining room too.'

'Ah.' I'm almost disappointed he's seen it before I've finished. I decided to lay the table properly; I don't know why it hadn't occurred to me before. At Dad's I've given up making an effort, because no one seems to notice.

But tonight, it's going to be different. Tonight I want my fellow campers to take their time, to feel the love I've put into their food. Edie agreed to give up her tiny fan heater – 'I've only kept it to keep Karma warm in here' – and I've borrowed the other two from the drawing room so we won't freeze over dinner.

It's amazing what a difference a few nightlights and jam jars full of evergreens make. I unearthed some rather beautiful lacy napkins from the dresser. They're yellowing with age, but they are so delicate and so fine that I can easily picture the days when Windy Hill was a grand home rather than a run-down hotel. The dining room is set for a midwinter feast.

I haven't stopped with the table settings. I'm not a qualified food stylist, but I've picked up the tricks on packaging photo-shoots: even a budget-range tikka masala looks like a feast fit for a maharajah by the time we've dished it up in light-reflecting balti dishes, spritzed it with cooking oil, added half a coriander bush, and arranged the very strictly limited number of chicken chunks to their best effect.

Tonight, I've prepped and primped and posed like never before. Even a supermodel doesn't get this much attention before her big moment.

'Right. All cleared up. Is there anything else I can do, chef?'

'I'm nervous.'

'Why?'

'I don't want to disappoint people.'

He squeezes next to me. 'Are you *kidding*? It's all amazing.'

'Really?'

For a moment, he says nothing. I become suddenly pre-occupied with his lips. How full they are. How *close* they are.

'Can I . . .' He stops. 'Um, can I call the others in? This time I really do wish I had a dinner gong. It would be very fitting.'

He leaves the room, and I run a hand through my hair, which is damp and ratty. I must look like a scarecrow. But, weirdly, it doesn't seem to matter right now.

There are noises in the hall outside.

Karma trots in first, followed by Edie. I watch her face.

Whatever the guests think of the food, I want this room to give Edie in particular a glimpse of how gorgeous her hotel could be with the tiniest bit of effort.

She blinks. 'Wow. I wouldn't have recognised the place.'

'Amazing what candlelight will do,' I say.

'Candlelight *and* a little love. You know, you've made me feel quite emotional.'

At least that's one of my missions accomplished. I wanted to give the house the care and attention she deserves.

She? I don't think I've ever given a building a gender before. Steve would have laughed at—

Bugger Steve.

I see more delighted expressions on my fellow campers' faces as they file in, and I make a silent wish that the food lives up to the surroundings.

Agatha helps Natalia into her seat, but the two don't speak to each other. Vicki sits closest to where I'm standing and gives me a huge smile. Darcy is opposite Pepper, and then the two blondes plonk themselves between Pepper and Ryan. Hedging their bets?

Can't believe it's less than a week since we arrived. Has everyone lost weight, got fitter?

Or are the changes happening on the inside? So far, I only have thinner fingers to show for all that work. But what really matters is that I've fallen in love with cooking again. And fallen out of love with someone who didn't deserve me.

There's a silence, as if they're expecting someone to say grace. I'm suddenly self-conscious. A chef's place is in the kitchen, not the spotlight.

Vicki nudges me. 'Go on. Tell us about the menu.'

I stare at her. 'Eh? Why?'

'Well, it's that much more formal, tonight, isn't it? This feels more like a banquet than canteen grub.' She smiles.

'It's what all the top chefs do,' Darcy says.

'Oh. OK.' I get to my feet again. 'Um. Well, what can I say? I hope you like the food. And thanks for the many generous donations. I must admit I didn't find a use for the Bombay Mix . . . or the Maltesers. You'll thank me at the weigh-in, but both will be available for collection in the kitchen tomorrow morning.'

I scan the faces. Up till now I've been too busy to worry where the food came from. But now I'm intrigued. Agatha smiles when I mention Maltesers, and I think the Bombay Mix might belong to Triathlon Karen. Too healthy for any of us fatties.

'But the meat . . .' I sigh. 'Apologies to the veggie contingent but the sausages and the steak were a protein-packed godsend. I shan't ask what kind of a secret binge the donor was planning, but thanks for sharing.'

Another glance around the room. None of the campers seems to know what I'm talking about. The staffs are both frowning. Has one given away the other's meat stash? Did they keep that primus stove in their bedrooms, for secret fry-ups?

'So, let me introduce you to dinner, before it goes cold. In the earthenware dishes here we have campfire sausages in healthy-hearty onion gravy. And in the white casseroles, there's blow-torch-seared fillet steak, cooked medium, with a herb crust.'

I *should* call the dishes Trial-and-Error Steak, and Boy Scout Sausages, because neither quite do justice to the quality of the ingredients. I set up the mother of all production lines to get everything at least partially caramelised, but it was impossible to wield the blowtorch and fry the sausages at the same time without setting fire to the kitchen, so they're not as *evenly* browned as I'd have liked. Though thanks to the dim candle-light in here, I might just get away with it.

'On the side, there's fat-free harissa sauce or, if you aren't bothered about the weigh-in tomorrow, Moroccan spiced butter.'

Oh, how I salivated making *that*. Maybe I shouldn't have made it at all – Edie is scowling as though offering butter is a crime punishable by death. But those steaks were so good they cried out for a little pool of butter and smoked paprika melting in a gooey pool on the top.

I'll admit, I tasted. And swallowed. But only the tiniest amount, the thinnest sliver off the edge of my knife, to check the seasoning. It was delicious – but weirdly, it was also enough.

I hope I'm not turning into one of those women who takes two salad leaves and a cherry tomato from a buffet, consumes half, and then insists she's *absolutely stuffed*.

'Then for the vegetarians, we have Mediterranean Frittata.'

Otherwise known as all the limp odds and ends of veg from the bottom of the fridge drawer, turned in a glorified omelette in the microwave. Also blow-torched, though, for a nice caramelised finish.

'Plus for everyone, there's steamed winter greens with juniper berries – those might taste a bit like gin, though I promise you there's none in there – plus there's fiery lentil hash, to warm us up. Those of you who suffered from some of the um, *beanier* casseroles earlier in the week might be relieved to know that these lentils are the least wind-producing of all the pulses.'

They're still staring at me.

'Um. That's it, really. Well, apart from pudding, but . . .'

Vicki leans over to whisper to me again. 'They're waiting for you to give them permission to tuck in.'

'Oh. Sorry. Bon appétit.'

I don't enjoy any of it.

I'm in hypercritical mode, as though I'm evaluating a new range at work. So . . . Flavour comments: the Moroccan butter lacks sweetness, the onion gravy's slightly too thin, could do with corn flour, a dash of real ale for depth of flavour. The sausages might work better baked. Or served as toad-in-the-hole to make the most of the glorious juices that escape during cooking.

Tasting panel comments: none. Reaction so far seems muted.

Appearance comments: irregular browning on sausages. Lentils neither whole nor fully pureed, texture dubious (add low-fat crème fraîche for a creamier edge?).

Potential customer appeal: difficult to gauge. Untapped market. Couples? Her on a diet, him wanting something more substantial than a salad. But range would require higher quality ingredients than we'd usually use so costings might be prohibitive—

Everyone's finished already. All that food and I *still* misjudged the portion size?

Worse, they're getting up, without a word of thanks. OK, so it wasn't Michelin-star standard. And I'm not Gordon Ramsay. But I'd challenge any of that lot to do what I did, and on a primus stove!

Vicki and Ryan nod at the others, and then they start—

They start applauding. Applauding me. *Me?*

Are they being sarcastic?

But I think they're smiling too broadly for sarcasm. It's a bit like . . .

Well, a bit like a standing ovation.

The Crabs, Agatha, even Natalia is applauding as she leans on Agatha. They're clapping and clapping, holding their hands up in front of them like I'm the sixth member of *Take That*. Rather than an overweight, moderately good cook from Zone Three and a Half.

My cheeks burn. Thank God for candlelight. I flap my hands

for them to stop, but they ignore me. Their palms must be stinging by now.

Their plates are so clean they look like they've already gone through the industrial dishwasher. *My* cooking did that.

And then, all at once I'm not embarrassed by the attention. In fact, I think I might rather *like* it.

Finally the applause dies down.

'Thank you. Thank you. But I nearly forgot. Tonight . . . well, tonight there's pudding too. And it's definitely *not* Prune Surprise.'

38

Steph

This time they give me no choice: they lift me up and throw me out of my kitchen while they clean up.

Edie is especially forceful. 'You haven't stopped all day. You need to put your feet up.'

The thing is, I don't want to put my feet up. The more compliments I get, the more I want. So maybe I *had* better leave before I turn into a complete egomaniac.

No point going to the freezing Clamshell suite, so I head for the drawing room instead. There's a smoky smell, because the wood fire has been burning all day. Natalia has been carried back to the big sofa, where she's dozing away. She has such a sweet face. I tiptoe, trying not to wake her up.

I walk over to the window seat. The burgundy velvet curtains are threadbare, but when I open them a sliver, I feel a whole winter's worth of chill hit me. Out there the sky is dark as earth and the ground white with snow.

Being snowed in doesn't worry me anymore. Even after that dinner, the fridge is still packed with enough goodies to keep us going well into next week. Courtesy of the secret meat and dairy hoarder.

I hear a creak on the floorboard outside. A ghost? No, too solid for a ghost. Natalia murmurs, but doesn't open her eyes. I look up at the doorway.

Ryan. *Somehow I knew that already.*

He heads towards the window.

'Tired, chef?'

'No. Wide awake. You?'

'Same. Usually by Friday I'm knackered but it's been different this week.'

He sits down on the edge of the window seat, but the cushion sags in the middle bringing us closer together. Too close.

'Different in a good way, or a bad way?'

Ryan gives me a curious look. 'Not sure yet. Camp's not over, after all.'

'No,' I say. But it will be soon. I shiver at the thought of heading back to my empty flat. I used to be able to pretend that the emptiness was a temporary state of affairs, till I persuaded Steve to come back. But now I don't want that bastard anywhere near my flat ever again.

'Anyway, I wanted to tell you in person, Chef Steph, that that was the best dinner I have ever had in my life. Better than burgers, better than fish and chips. And the pudding. Those apricots with the tiny little almond clouds.' He stops. 'I'll never forget your food.'

I try not to frown. 'It's great to know *something* about me is memorable.'

He's silent. What a bloody dumb thing to say.

'Steph, that bloke of yours? Was he . . . I dunno . . . George Clooney?'

I think of Steve. His fair, slightly too-fine hair creeping slowly backwards, as his hairline shrank. Vampire-pale skin from late nights in smoky clubs and his life-long 'allergy' to vegetables.

'Maybe he was the next Bill Gates, then? Or a surgeon who restored people's eyesight on one of those hospital ships in Africa?'

I smile at the idea of Steve wanting to do anything for anyone else. It wasn't his thing. Neither was making money, mind you. He didn't believe in pensions, or savings, or mortgages.

Life's too short, honeybunch. I rely on my wits and my magnetism to keep me fed and watered.

Plus there's no need to save for a rainy day, or organise the direct debit to the water board when your girlfriend does it all for you.

'I thought I told you, Staff. He was a creative type. A promoter. Music, you know.'

'Made a lot of money, did he?'

I laugh. 'He was more into spending it. Why?'

'I'm just curious. Well, more than curious. I'm waiting to hear the reasons he could have had for wrecking the confidence of the lovely girl sitting opposite me. Because I can't see anything that would give *him* the right to judge you . . .'

lovely

I'm about to tell him that I was the one who put up with it, so I'm equally to blame. But I don't get time to form the words before

he kisses me

One second he's on the other side of that sofa and the next his lips are on mine and it takes me a moment to make sense of what's happened.

And once I do . . .

Bloody hell.

The man can *kiss*.

Seriously. He really, really can. Forget all that stuff about, *I don't understand women* and *I've never had the chance to learn.*

Either he's a natural, or he's been talking porky pies . . .

He's stopped.

Damn him.

'Is this . . . OK?' he asks me.

My brain's not really up to small talk right now. So I nod.

'I can't believe it's taken me till Friday to do this,' he whispers, and leans in to kiss me again.

Except . . . even though this second kiss is as astonishing as the last one, something's wrong.

Friday. I remember what Foz told me when I was having my massage. About Fridays. The staffs getting their fringe benefits. Maybe he's taking pity on me.

Am I this week's charity case?

I pull away.

'Are you all right, Steph?'

'Fine.' I sound strange to myself, my voice breaking like a teenage boy's.

'Really? Sorry. Maybe I shouldn't have— '

'No, it was fine. Honestly.' I shift back into my corner of the window seat.

No Man's Land lies between us. Unbreachable.

He blinks. 'Is that genuine *fine* or is it the female version of *fine?* I'm just a simple squaddie, right? You can't expect me to understand the complexities of a woman's mind.'

'I'm not very complex. But I didn't come to boot camp for . . . I mean, I know some do, and good luck to them but me, well, that's really *not* what I wanted.'

Ryan looks at me. 'I didn't think— '

'Don't misunderstand me, it was . . . very flattering. Lovely, even.' I fall back on his word and I realise how tame, how *all purpose* it sounds when I say it, and I laugh at myself for reading anything into it before. 'But I don't want to lead you on, and I'm very tired, so I'm off to bed. Alone. But thanks. I mean, that was a nice end to the evening. But that's all.'

Nice?

I get up from the window seat before I die of embarrassment. There's a bloody big indentation where my bum was. Yes.

Definitely a charity case. It's only as I walk past Natalia that I realise her eyes are half open. She must have heard everything we said.

Sod it. What do I care? I'll never see Natalia again, or any of them.

A little voice – definitely not Steve's this time – whispers, *All the more reason to grab the opportunity – and Staff Ryan – with both hands? Isn't he just perfect rebound material?*

I stop in the doorway. Ryan's looking up at me, bewildered.

So what am I meant to do, voice? Go back and say, *oh all right then.* Try to be all seductive and sexy, even though he's seen me up to my neck in sand, covered in sweat and even vomiting from too many press-ups.

Some things are better left in the imagination.

39

Darcy

'Wakey wakey!'

I keep my eyes shut. All I want to do is sleep in front of the open fire and forget about everything.

'You're not *hiding* from me, are you, Darcy?'

I turn away, but then someone paws my shoulder. I open my eyes and the world's most annoying Australian is there in front of me like a leathery mirage. I wonder if they had him deported after a mass petition by the nation's women.

'No. Not hiding. Just sleepy after dinner. Why?'

'It's massage time! Not a moment to waste. Most of my clients are counting off the hours to their slot.'

The Crab women are watching, with gimlet eyes and hang-dog expressions. *Impressive.*

'Then maybe you should give it to someone more deserving. I'm not really feeling like I need a massage right now.' But as I shake my head, my neck freezes. 'Ow.'

'Ah. The dreaded whiplash. You did climb out of the wreckage of your car only a few hours ago, Darcy. A spot of massage could be just what the doctor ordered.'

'It was hardly wreckage,' I say, but as I try to twist my neck back into position, I *am* incredibly knotted and bruised. Surely he's professional enough to stick within boundaries? 'All right, all right. But it won't hurt, will it?'

'Not unless you want it to,' he says, with a preposterously lascivious wink.

'OK. Five minutes then. Let me make myself decent.'

'You know, that's *really* not necessary,' Foz says.

The Crabs give me the dirtiest of looks as I leave the room. I'd find them scary if I hadn't faced down the Taliban morality police *and* the leaders of no less than three drugs cartels in my reporting days.

The Clamshell suite is empty, though Vicki's bag is packed on her bed. I guess she can't wait to get home to her sons.

What's waiting for me back home? I walked down to the gates before dinner, and managed ten seconds on the phone to Marian before the signal died completely. She was so incandescent she could barely speak. Which is unusual, to say the least. Among the few words she did get out, I heard *disrespect*, *disloyalty* and *permanently unemployable*.

Home. I don't even know how I'll get to London, now the car's smashed up. Hope my RAC renewal payment didn't bounce. Only Marian knows how parlous my financial situation is. After Afghan, I couldn't keep on top of anything. And I could hardly rock up at the Citizens' Advice Bureau and ask for debt advice. The story would have been online before you could say shopaholic.

Though I dread to think what stories are circulating about me now. I can't be sure any of my special friends won't kiss and tell.

There's a knock at the door. 'Ready for action, Darcy?'

'Go on, then.'

Part of me wonders if I should just go ahead and sleep with him. It's not as though I've been that choosy in the last couple of years. Most guys with a pulse and a friendly word would have passed muster.

But when he comes through the door, I realise another

one-night stand isn't the answer. I wish I knew what *was*, but ruling out one form of bad behaviour is a kind of progress, I suppose.

'I'll make myself scarce while you're undressing, Darcy.'

'I hadn't taken you for the coy type, Frank,' I say, and it's only when I see the expression on his face that I realise I've given the old boy hope. 'I mean, you must have seen thousands of old bodies in your time?'

'Not many as famous as yours, Darcy.'

I should tell him I *wasn't* flirting, that he shouldn't get his hopes (or anything else) up. But it's all too complicated.

'Make yourself scarce, then.'

I lie down on my front. After the accident, it feels as though my skeleton has been thrown in the air and all the bones have landed in slightly the wrong order.

I call Frank back in. 'I'm still quite tender so be gentle or I'll scream.'

'I never push it any further than a client wants to go, Darcy. Even if she doesn't always know that ahead of time.'

'You know that makes you sound quite creepy, Frank?'

He laughs louder. 'You tell it how it is, right, Darcy?' And then his hands grip my back like they mean business.

'Bloody hell.'

'Too much?'

'I'm in a worse way than I thought.'

'You're looking in pretty good shape from where I'm standing, Darcy.'

'Can I be frank, Frank?'

He chuckles. 'Do I hear a brush-off coming?'

'Don't take it personally. I'd turn down George Clooney.'

'Do you have something against silver foxes?'

'No. I'm just suggesting that you focus your attention elsewhere. I never led you on.'

'You sure about that?'

Am I? Perhaps flirting is my way of managing most men: however close they get physically, they never reach the real me. The only man I haven't flirted with lately is Pepper. I don't know what that says about me . . . or him.

'Tell you what, Frank. I'm feeling too tender to take much more of this. So if you like we can pack up early . . . and you can go to pursue other avenues.'

'Any ideas?'

'Well, I think you know the way to Edie's room. Or I hear the Crab Suite is very hospitable to men without a bed for the night.'

Steph knocks on the door a couple of minutes after Frank leaves.

'Thought I'd have a quick cold shower. I'm sweating like a pig after cooking dinner. Then I'm packing in case we do actually get to go home tomorrow.'

'You sound even less keen to leave than I am, Steph.'

She shrugs. 'I quite *like* being snowed in, miles from real life. Don't you?'

Her shower lasts about thirty seconds and she comes out hopping. 'Bloody hell, that's almost as unpleasant as the bloody Ladder.'

She opens her bedside drawer, takes out her garish sweat-pants-and-top combos, and begins to stuff them into the tiny waste paper bin. They don't fit, so khaki and orange sleeves and legs keep escaping, as though her exercise gear is determined to fight back.

'Er, Steph? What are you doing?'

She looks up. 'Won't be needing these anymore.'

'That's a bit drastic, isn't it? You shouldn't give up!'

She goes back to the drawer, takes out a purple sports bra.

'I'm not giving up. It's the opposite. I'm definitely going to keep exercising. But I am never going to wear any of this kit in public in London, where I *know* people.'

'The clothes are a bit . . .' I can't think of a polite word. 'But you promise me you *are* going to buy new stuff, right? You didn't do the crack-of-dawn runs and that terrible bloody ton-up to go back to a life of doughnuts, did you?'

'You really think my life revolved around doughnuts?'

I feel myself blushing. 'No, no, sorry, it was a joke.'

'Because I can tell you now, Miss TV Star, it took a lot more than doughnuts to get into this state. There were chocolate éclairs, sticky toffee puddings, steamed jam roly poly . . . and don't even get me started on the savouries.'

I stare at her for a moment before I realise she's joking. And then we both burst out laughing. 'I knew you wouldn't give up, Steph.'

'I'll try not to. What else was it Edie said? It takes sixty days to establish a habit?'

'Sixty-six. Hey, maybe we should all get together on the sixty-seventh day? Check we're on track.'

'Not sure I'm bothered about the others, Darcy. Maybe just you, me and Vicki.'

That touches me. 'What about Staff Ryan, too? Make it a foursome.'

'Definitely *not* Staff Ryan.' She winces.

'Come on. Whenever the two of you get together, I can see the electricity.'

'He's very good-looking, but you know it's what they do every Friday, don't you? Pick a girl each and give her the "ultimate" workout.' Steph's smiling but her eyes aren't.

'Are you sure about that?'

'Of course I am. It's what Foz told me.'

'I can believe it's what *Foz* does,' I say, 'because he was

319

offering the same to me. But Ryan and Pepper seem better than that.'

'You didn't go for it, did you?'

'No way! It'd be like having sex with a shop dummy. But Ryan is a sweetheart under that *very* well-toned exterior, and even Pepper has his sensitive side.'

'I'll have to take your word for *that*,' Steph says. 'God, I'm so, so knackered.' She lays out the one pair of leggings she hasn't thrown out, neatly lining up her trainers underneath, as though she's expecting a kit inspection.

'Listen, Steph. If you wanted some advice . . .'

'Sorry?'

'With new trainers and stuff. If you wanted someone to come with you, well, I know some quite good places.' I feel self-conscious saying it. It's been a long time since I tried to make a friend.

'Oh. Thanks. That'd be great. If any of your designer stores do gear to suit a plump blimp with a lemonade budget.'

'WALTON!'

A male voice – bar-room drunk – blasts through from the corridor.

'WALTON, I know you're in there; come out or I'll come in and drag you out, you BASTARD.'

Pepper.

Steph heads towards the door, her eyes wide. 'Should I open it, or lock it?'

'Come on, you treacherous TOSSER. I'll count to three and then I'M COMING IN.'

I *know* drunks. God knows, in the last couple of years, I've been one myself often enough. But I'm surprised that Pepper's an angry drunk: if I'd had to guess, I'd have thought maudlin was more likely.

320

I lean against the door, holding the handle. 'Pepper? What's the matter? Walton's not here.'

There's a pause and then a grunt. 'Thought you were smart, Webb. Never thought you'd fall for Walton's BULLSHIT.'

'I haven't fallen for anyone's bullshit. The only person here in the room with me is Steph. And your tone is making us feel threatened.' Short clear sentences. Calm voice. Drunks and rabid dogs respond to the same treatment.

'You expect me to believe that?' he calls back. But there's a trace of self-doubt in his voice now.

'Yes. I do. Frank Walton gave me a massage. Then left. What else would we be doing?'

Of course, I can guess exactly what he *thinks* we've been doing.

'If he's not there, can I come in?'

'What, to check up on me?' I say.

'No. To talk.'

I look at Steph. She raises her eyebrows, then nods.

'You can come in, but you have to behave.' I turn the key in the lock and open the door.

Pepper is slightly cock-eyed, though his body's still parade-ground rigid. He's in civvies, which make him look . . . well, almost normal. Except that under the jeans and black fleece, there's obviously a fiercely honed body.

'Come on, then, Staff. Search under the bed if you like, but he's not here.'

'You're all right,' Pepper says. He smiles nervously as he steps into the room. 'I, um, don't know quite what came over me.'

'I'm guessing whisky, from the smell of your breath?'

He coughs. 'So Walton didn't . . . there was no . . . funny business? It's obvious he's been after you all week. Then I went looking for him and I couldn't find him,' Pepper mutters. 'I was worried.'

'Very touching, but I can look after myself.'

For the first time, he smiles. 'Maybe I have been barking up the wrong tree.'

'Or pissing up against it. You boys are very territorial, aren't you? I don't see why you can't live and let live.'

'He's still missing. And Edie's in the drawing room, so he can't be there.'

'So they are . . . together?' Steph asks.

'They go back a long way,' Pepper says. 'On off, on off. Though me and Ryan thought it was more off than on right now.'

At the mention of Ryan's name, Steph blushes. Bizarre. I thought an all-woman boot camp would be free of sexual tensions and craziness. Instead, it's like a cross between *Private Benjamin* and a Carry On film.

Was Pepper jealous? I thought he was the one man in the last two years who respected me as a person, rather than saw me as an easy lay. 'Why the fascination with what Frank gets up to?' I ask. 'We're all adults.'

Pepper shrugs. 'It does seem a bit sad, now I think about it. Been a rum week, all things considered.'

'But if he is on the pull, then that's normal, isn't it?' Steph looks embarrassed but ploughs on. 'Sorry, but that's what he told me. Foz. He said that every Friday night, there tends to be a bit of . . . well, nocturnal activity.'

Pepper stares at her. 'What?'

'You know. The, um, beast with two backs. That's what he said.'

'Bloody hell.'

She nods. 'And Vicki said she overheard you. Talking about . . . well, us.'

He cringes. 'Ah. We joke about it. Me and Ryan. But we don't go through with it. It's not . . . ethical. You know what we're like,' he says to me, almost like he's apologising, 'all talk. No action. It's the same with the sergeant major bollocks. It's an act. Didn't realise we were that convincing.'

I wonder whether he'd talk about this if he wasn't drunk. 'And Frank doesn't sleep with the clients either?'

Pepper shrugs. 'Well, he sees things differently. Not just Edie, but . . . they fell out before Christmas when he bedded half of the Aylesbury Amazons who were here to prepare for a marathon. Foz promised her he'd behave after that.'

'Just a hunch, but I'm not sure he's keeping his promise.'

'Why not?' Steph asks.

'He was last seen heading for the Crab suite. Thought he might get luckier there than in Clamshell.'

'Poor Edie,' says Steph. 'She deserves better.'

'That's debatable,' I say, but I keep forgetting how soft-hearted Steph is.

'I think we should find out,' Steph says.

I laugh. 'What, go and knock on the door?'

'No, but the walls are paper thin round here. It wouldn't take much to work out if things really are going bump in the night.'

Pepper takes the lead and despite being drunk, he's stealthily quiet. Me and Steph seem to step on every creaky floorboard on the landing by the Crab suite. I'm in the middle, and when I look back, Steph's eyes are bright. She's trying not to laugh.

I guess that's what happens when you're trapped in a country house. You begin to act like kids. It's so *stupid*.

And *infantile*.

I suppress a desperate urge to giggle.

And really quite funny.

Another floorboard creaks under my feet, and Pepper turns round, scowling. We freeze, like cat burglars. In the dark corridor, a narrow strip of light shines out from under the door. And there are voices. A high-pitched squeaky one. An even higher-pitched squeaky one.

And a guttural, Australian growl.

'What now?' I whisper.

Pepper takes a couple of steps closer to the door and then beckons us towards him. Then he kneels down on the floor.

Have I somehow missed the fact he's religious? Is *that* why he's after Foz – to save his soul?

But then I realise what he's up to, and I kneel down too. Steph looks nervous.

Pepper leans forward, so his chin almost touches the musty carpet, and then peers through the gap. So do I.

I can see feet. Three sets. A pair with crimson-painted nails at the end of toes that look blue from the cold. A bronzed, hairy pair, planted wide apart on the floor.

And a pair with its back to us, so only the soles are visible because the owner appears to be kneeling down and facing . . .

Oh.

'Don't stop, Caz,' the man grunts.

'*I'm* Caz,' a voice corrects him. 'That's Cat, as she'd tell you if she didn't have her mouth full. Least you can do under the circumstances is get her bloody name right.'

'Sorry. Cat, you're the best.'

'What's going on?' Steph whispers. 'Let me see.'

Pepper crawls away from the door, looking slightly queasy.

I move back, too. 'We should leave them to it. I think Frank's magic touch is in for a busy night.'

'Seriously?' Steph whispers. 'He's cheating on Edie in her own hotel?'

Pepper is backing away faster now. 'To be fair to bloody Walton, which are words I never thought I'd say, I doubt he ever promised her *exclusivity*.'

We tiptoe backwards along the hall. The whole situation is

super-tense, yet completely farcical. We get to the top of the
stairs, and head down, rather than up. Pepper and I are trying
not to laugh, but Steph's looking super-serious.

'We should get Edie. She can't waste her life on him.'

I put my hand on hers. 'Steph, it's not really our business.'

'If someone had shown *me* the truth about my boyfriend
years ago, it'd have saved me so much heartache.'

Pepper stares at his feet. I get the feeling he'd rather be on the
battlefield than in the midst of *this* kind of conversation.

'Sounds like she might already have got the message with a
bit of help from the Aylesbury Amazons,' I say.

She sighs. 'I just wish people could be up front with each
other.'

Pepper raises his eyebrows and gestures smoking a cigarette
at me. I nod.

'Steph. Forget Edie, and the Crabs. Just enjoy your moment
of glory tonight. There's a roaring fire in the drawing room. I'll
be there in two ticks.'

It feels warmer *outside* the house than in. When we step out of
the kitchen door, the ice is slushy.

'Is it thawing?'

'That desperate to get away, are you, Webb?' He passes me a
cigarette, lights it, then lights his own.

'Just an observation. Vicki'll be pleased. And the others with
someone waiting for them back home.'

'Warm enough yet?' He holds his cigarette between his lips as
he takes a hip flask out of his pocket, and unscrews the cap.

'What is that?'

'Brandy. I'm the camp St Bernard, me.'

He holds the flask up to my nose. It smells of caramel. I
shake my head.

'Not teetotal, are you?' He takes a swig himself and winces.

'Hardly. But haven't you had enough, Staff?'

Pepper shakes his head. 'Normally I can hold my drink. But something came over me.'

'It's obviously not Walton you want to thump, anyway. It's Ryan.'

'Is it?'

'Come on. It's obvious. And it's him that's driven you to drink, too. Him leaving – I bet it's as bad as a divorce.'

'I've had one of those, too, Webb. At least he won't take my house off me.'

The metal of the hip flask flashes in the moonlight. I take it, take a swig. It hits me immediately. 'It's really hard to imagine you married.'

'Which is why I got divorced. And you? You're a bit old to be single, aren't you? You should be married to a footballer or something.'

'Cheers for that. I've had a few proposals. But then they usually want kids and a nice wife keeping things in order, and it's bloody hard being a war reporter with babies. Some women manage it, but they get a lot of stick.'

'Except you're a presenter, not a war reporter, Darcy.'

'Not in here,' I say, clutching my hand to where my heart should be, then suddenly feeling self-conscious. 'Face it. I'm neither, now.'

We stand there in silence. There's a rustling in the trees: a bird, perhaps, or a squirrel. And the sound of our breathing, as our lungs pull nicotine into our bodies.

'Why did you really give it up, Webb? The reporting?'

Tightness spreads across my chest. 'You can have too many adventures. Can't you?'

He nods. 'Got that right. But then, close shaves. They make you feel alive.'

'Because you're not dead?'

Pepper says nothing for a while. 'Nights like this. We used to fantasise about frost and ice when I was in the middle of an Afghan summer. Try to remember what a British winter felt like. Wasn't sure I'd see one again.'

I wonder whether he wants me to ask more. In the darkness it seems easier somehow. 'I'm guessing not everyone you went with did?'

'No. And they're still dying, poor bastards. More of them than ever. I try not to watch the news. So fucking pointless. Could have been me, should have been me instead of one of the boys with a life. Look at me now. Not exactly making the most of surviving, am I?'

'Did a lot of your guys die?'

He screws up his eyes. 'We were a search team. Went with the territory. Sometimes thought they were the lucky ones, you know. We'd talk about it – would you rather go home without your balls, or your legs, or not go home at all? Not that you got a choice.'

I think of Heela. She *was* there by choice. Did that make what happened to her worse, or better?

'Survivor's guilt,' I say.

'Eh?'

'That's what my counsellor called it. I call her *my* counsellor; I only went twice. She was getting a hundred quid an hour. I got nothing out of it. Except a label to give to my nightmares and my chronic indecisiveness.'

He casts a sideways glance at me. His cigarette is almost burned out already, so he crushes it under his foot and lights another. 'That's what you're doing here, is it?'

'What?'

'Punishing yourself for something.'

I wasn't expecting that. 'I don't understand.'

'You do, though, Webb. I recognise it. The guilt. Like when

327

someone talks in the accent of your home town. You know because it's your country.'

Or because you're suffering the same way. 'I hadn't realised it was so obvious.'

He shrugs. 'Did it happen in Afghan?'

I'm about to say that I don't want to talk about it – it's been my standard response for the last two years – when I realise that I do. I nod. 'It wasn't a soldier.'

'Another journalist?'

I smile. 'No. Heela wasn't chasing the story. She was part of the story. Well, she became the story, but not in the way she intended.' I close my eyes and I see her. Stern face and smiling eyes. Pretty, but in a way that you had to look closely to see. And anyway, she wasn't interested in anything as trivial as men. They could come later, once she'd changed the world: made sure women had full rights, education, healthcare. For a young girl, she had grand ambitions.'

'How did she die?'

'We don't know. We don't even know if she did die but nothing has been heard of her and it's been two years since—'

'Since?'

Since I showed my true colours by hiding from her killers. 'We were on assignment. She was my guide. Not a fixer, but an interviewee, an interpreter. The perfect example of the new Afghan womanhood. She wasn't even born there; her family fled to England when her mother was pregnant. But as soon as the war was declared over, Heela volunteered. She could get me to places no one else could. The women and the girls who'd suffered, they trusted her, and so they trusted me.

'I interviewed her two, three times. We became friends. There was always a tremendous viewer response when she was on screen, because she sounded like a Londoner, someone they could relate to. She made the place feel normal. Salvageable. To me, too. We dropped our guard. Stayed in the same place one too many nights.'

Pepper lights me another cigarette.

'I was the target, I'm pretty sure about that. But I was the lighter sleeper, too. I heard noises that could have been exhausts firing or . . . I went into the room we used as a kitchen, to see through the window. That's when they broke into our bedroom. The noises had been gunshots; they'd killed our two guards.'

'Jesus.'

'There was screaming. Not from her, from them. Men – five or six, or it could have been fewer. I've relived it a million times but some things get *less* clear.'

'How did you get away?'

'I didn't get away. I knew there was a space under the kitchen floor with just enough room for two or three people. We'd filmed it the day before. It had been used as a hiding place by the family who lived there before.'

'But she didn't get to the hiding place in time?'

'No. The first room they searched was the bedroom. I didn't hear Heela's voice so I hoped . . . perhaps she'd found somewhere else to hide. I stayed there, crouched in my hole, trying not to breathe even though panic made me want to pant like a marathon runner. Tried to convince myself that she was safe. But I think I knew. Especially when they left. They came into the kitchen but they didn't seem to look very hard. Heela was a pretty good consolation prize.'

'Taliban?'

'Maybe. Or some enterprising kids who thought kidnapping a Western journalist would bring them a good ransom.'

'How long were you hidden?'

'Hours. Hoping there'd be a voice in the dark, Heela telling me what a *fucking close shave that was.* I crept out after dawn.

There was nothing but the bodies of the guards, and Heela's rumpled bed sheets. They'd taken the goodies, though. Sat phone, laptops. There was nothing I could do till the camera crew came back for me in the morning.'

'So there's a chance she could be alive?'

I shudder. 'It might be better if she isn't. We tried. Ran lots of pieces about her, put the word out that a hefty ransom could be up for grabs. But nothing. That's why I think she might have died on the first night. The idea she survived as some trophy . . . it's worse than thinking she died straight away.'

'And you think it would have helped if you'd come out of your hiding place?'

'Pepper, I was wrong to hide.'

'What? If they'd got *you*, they would have let *her go*? Given her a pat on the head and a brand new burkha, told her to behave herself in future?'

I say nothing. He reaches back into his pocket, passes me the hip flask. I take a swig and it travels down my body like a tiny flame.

'Do you believe in fate, Darcy?'

I shake my head.

'Plenty of soldiers do. You know, that whole *if a bullet's got my name on it,* thing. Or, in Afghan, more likely an IED's got my name on it. Somehow it's easier than thinking if I'd done this or that differently, been ahead of the guy that died, or next to him, taken a different route.'

'And you?'

He kicks at the ground. 'Nah. Believing in fate is the easy way out.'

'What do you feel guilty about, Staff?'

'What *don't* I feel guilty about?' He laughs bitterly.

'War's indiscriminate, though, and IEDs are the most

indiscriminate of all. So I'm sure you have nothing to feel guilty about.'

'No. How about sending the youngest kid in our team as Vallon man on his birthday?'

'Vallon?'

'It's the name of the metal detectors we used. First line of defence.'

'Ah.'

'Nineteen that day. But Rocky looked about twelve. We called him that because he was so weedy, however hard he tried to build himself up.' He talks fast, as though it's something he has to do, but wants to get it out of the way as quickly as possible.

'Didn't you all take turns?'

'The lads did, yeah. Was Ryan's turn that day. But we had planned a surprise for Rocky when he got back . . . except he never got back. Ryan feels shit about it too.'

'An IED?' I ask.

'Such a fucking unfair fight. Cowards. Rocky should have been crawling, of course. Down on his belt buckle. That way you're more stable, run less risk of triggering the fucking thing. But he was too excited or too much in a hurry and . . . took the full force of it.'

I try to think of something to say. Then I decide to stay silent, because Pepper must know, as I do, that sometimes words, however well-intentioned, make things worse.

'But life goes on, eh, Darcy? Fate's got nothing to do with it. We're just pawns in other people's games.

I nod. Games. Heela and Rocky make the stupid hoops I have to jump through with Marian seem even more ridiculous. India and the other autocuties act like presenting is the be all and end all. Well, if that's what the network wants – zombie

331

presenters who couldn't give a shit – then fine. Maybe the viewers want more. Maybe they'll vote with their remotes.

Standing in the dark with Pepper, I know I'm not going back to that world. It should be a bleak thought, scary, everything that's waiting for me in London. Debts. Scandal. Gossip.

But right now I feel less alone than I did when I talked to the counsellor, or took some unknown man home to try to dull the pain.

It's been a very long time since I've felt anything but a freak. Yet I make sense to Pepper and he makes sense to me. And somehow that helps the world make more sense, too.

40

Steph

Low voices drift into the hall from the drawing room. I'm about to push the door open when I realise that, actually, I don't want company.

I go left instead of right. To the kitchen. For the next twelve hours at least, still *my* kitchen. My favourite place in the house.

Only the lights under the cupboards are on, giving the space a yellow glow. There's still a little residual warmth from the cooking I did, and from the dishwasher. I open the door and the steam hits my face, hot and clean-smelling.

Then I run my hand along the worktop. In contrast, it's deliciously cold, like dipping my fingertips in ice-cream.

When he steps out of the shadow I don't jump, or even feel surprised.

'Hungry?' I say.

'No.' He takes another step away from the larder. 'But I thought you might come here. And even if you didn't, it feels nice here, because of you. Smells nice.'

'I smell of garlic and steak?'

'God, I'm crap at compliments, aren't I? I meant that it smells of home cooking.'

He can't be a Casanova with a line like that.

'Thanks.'

'Steph? What you said before, about . . . about why I kissed you. I haven't *ever* hit on a girl at boot camp. Never had much success outside boot camp either, to tell you the truth.'

No man would *boast* about not pulling women to impress, surely? It makes me want to smile, but I try not to. 'How come?'

'Because I'm rubbish at pretending to be something I'm not. Clubs are the worst. Trying girl after girl till one is pissed enough to say yes. I mean, it worked when I was sixteen, but not now. Not when it's more important to find someone who likes you sober.'

'OK, Staff. You've convinced me. Though I can't believe many people would not like you when they sobered up. You're lovely.'

Lovely. That bloody word again.

'So you believe me, Steph?'

'Which bit? The bit about you giving up on nightclubs, or the bit about you not hitting on me?'

He gulps. Shuffles his feet on the lino. 'Um . . . well, the thing is, I actually *was* hitting on you. But just you. Especially you. Because you're so . . .'

Lovely? Don't say *lovely.* Or nice.

'. . . amazing.'

I let that word swim round in my head for a bit. *Amazing* and *Stephanie Dean* don't seem to go together at first but maybe I should keep trying the combination in my head.

'Am I?'

Ryan frowns at me. 'I don't say things I don't mean. Another one of those things that makes me crap at dating.'

Am I amazing enough for you to want to kiss me again?

For a moment, I imagine saying those words out loud, and I giggle. Darcy could get away with that. Or Vicki. But not me. I try not to think about the number of kisses I will miss out on in my life because I don't have the courage.

Ryan is crossing the room. He looks . . . purposeful. Could he be a mind-reader, or something?

Or, even worse, did I say the words out loud?

Before I have to work that out, I feel his lips on mine, hot compared to the wintry air around us.

Oh

My

God

I don't think I care about the kisses I've missed. Not when this one was *so* worth the wait.

How can he be so gentle but *so* sexy at the same time?

Outside it's still below zero but in here . . .

'Amazing,' he whispers.

His hands are on my hair, my face, my neck.

My *neck*. In *that* place, the little point where he accidentally touched me on that first day, when he was meant to be re-arranging my posture.

'Did you realise?' I whisper.

'What?'

'The effect it had on me. When you touched me *there*?'

He shakes his head. 'No. I hate all that hands-on stuff. Especially with someone who'd already made quite an impression on me.'

'By ending up on my backside twice in my first ten minutes?'

'It's a very nice backside, though.'

'*Nice*? It's been called a lot of things but never *nice*.'

'Lovely, then.'

I smile. 'Better.'

'Sorry. Never went to university so I'm not one for fancy words. But it's very, very, *very* nice.'

'Yours is pretty lovely too, then, Staff.'

'I think you can call me Sam, now.'

I don't call him anything, because he kisses me again. He seems to want to kiss me for ever.

But I don't think that's enough.

I close my eyes, then open them again. Just to check this is real.

It is. Bloody hell.

OK, so it's probably just one night.

So what?

What happens on boot camp stays on boot camp.

I want my skin against his. I don't remember ever feeling like this before. This . . . *wanton*. This sexy.

I open my eyes. And reach for those hands—

Can I do this? I came so close to missing out on this kiss and it gives me courage . . . I place them on the zip of my top. He looks startled.

Hussy, I think. But it makes me giggle.

His eyes ask the question. I answer it with a smile.

The zip makes an incredibly loud noise as he pulls it down, little by little, like unwrapping a Christmas present. We both giggle now.

The top's on the floor and next it's my T-shirt. Only my sports bra is left. The one that leaves bright pink weals in the places where it's too tight.

He doesn't seem to notice the marks as he unhooks it.

'Your turn,' I whisper, How come I'm not embarrassed at sitting three-quarters naked on a chilly marble countertop?

Ryan pulls his T-shirt over his head. His body looks too perfect in the yellow light. Smooth and irresistible. I've never been this close to a six-pack before.

And then suddenly, I'm shy again, like in one of those dreams when you realise you're running down the street in the buff and you've no idea how it happened.

I know how *this* happened. But what I'm struggling with is how can he possibly look like *that* and want *me*?

'What is it, Steph?'

'Me.'

'What about you? Amazing Steph. Let's talk all about you.'

'You're all toned and . . . and I'm all . . .'

He touches my lips with his finger. 'Shh. You're all *you*, Steph. Amazing. Smart. And absolutely gorgeous.'

I let him kiss me again, his skin touching mine. I reach down towards his belt buckle.

'Don't you believe how much I fancy you?'

Bloody hell. That is *very* convincing, actually.

'I believe you.'

'Shall we go to bed?'

I kiss him my answer. And he lifts me off the worktop, as though I really am the slip of a thing he seems to think I am.

My hero.

Day 7: Saturday-yay-ya-y-hip-hip-hooray

How you'll be feeling: thrilled to have got this far.
Nervous about the weigh-in. Ready to face a fitter,
feistier future. Remember – it's not just about this
week; it's about the rest of your life.

07:15   After a lie-in, time for fitness tests and
         timed run, followed by weigh-in

09:30   'Champagne' Breakfast and Boot Camp
         Awards

10:30   Departure

41

Vicki

When I wake, I don't know where I am at first.

The room rumbles. With snores.

Ah. The drawing room. The air is cold, but the fire is still smouldering, just. I did a bloody good job, there.

Don't think we're all here. Bodies or blankets, it's hard to tell the difference. Natalia is on one side of me, Agatha on the other. Karen was here when we all snuggled up for the night, I think. But not my two roomies. Or Edie. Or the *panthers*.

A log collapses in the fire, sending splinters flying onto the tiles of the hearth. The other pieces of wood shift to fill the gap, and the flames lick round the new log. Like they're working up an appetite.

It's dark, except for the embers. I can't tell if it's still Friday, or already Saturday: the *last* day. If we're very lucky . . .

I lean forward but I can't get warm. Draughts whirl up from nowhere in this room. Like the house is haunted, or ghosts are whispering in my ear.

It's the stress of not knowing if I can go home. I'm seeing things that aren't there. Thinking freaky thoughts.

But the harder I try to concentrate on reality – my kids, Dave, whether my belly has shrunk and some of my chins have disappeared – the less real things seem. Shadows grow. There are shapes at the edge of my vision. No, not shapes. *People.*

Except when I turn my head there's nothing there except the other boot campers, snoring and dreaming of home.

My head keeps filling with strange questions. Who else has sat where I'm sitting? In our house, there's no history. We were the first family to live there.

But this place is full of other people's memories. I see little girls with legs dangling over this sofa, whispering secrets to their dolls. Little boys playing marbles on the rug. Dads worrying about financial meltdowns and world wars and hoping their sons won't have to see what they've seen. Housemaids clearing the ashes at dawn with chapped fingers, morning after morning, year after year . . .

I've been watching too much *Downton Abbey*. But it's freaky how real it seems. My eyes sting from the smoke, and my lids are heavy. I close them.

It wasn't your fault.

I open my eyes again, whip round, but there's nothing behind me. Only the dark. I don't even know if that's where the voice came from. If there *was* a voice.

This is turning into the longest night.

I never dream. When I sleep, I'm out for the count, till I'm brought back to reality by loud demands for toast or missing football boots.

You'd have been the best mum.

My eyes are heavy, but the voice is clear. A child's voice.

But it wasn't to be.

I force my eyes open. I catch a glimpse of movement by the fire but it's only wind whipping up the ashes. No one else stirs.

I wasn't to be.

'Are you there?' I feel silly whispering to thin air, but the voice sounded so *real*.

Nothing answers, of course. I stare into the hearth.

340

Is that a *face* smiling back from the flames?

This is mad. Like those crazies in the paper who think they've seen Michael Jackson's face in their tea leaves or Madonna in a slice of marble cake.

I rub my eyes, hard. When I look again, the embers don't look like a face at all. I feel disappointed. There was something comforting about that voice, that face.

If they came from my imagination, then I should be able to summon them up again, surely?

'Enya?' I whisper, but it sounds like a shout in the silence of the room.

I haven't spoken her name for so long.

No one stirs.

'Enya?' It's the most beautiful name in the world. Jewel. My jewel.

Still no one in the room moves. Maybe I'm not even speaking out loud. I can't tell anymore.

'You had perfect rosebud lips. And little puffy curls of blonde hair on your head. I have the same, in my baby photos. I touched your hair. It was so soft. Like . . .' I can't think of anything as sweet. Then I remember the beach.

'Like candyfloss. There's a stall here, at the seaside. You'd have loved it. Of course, your brothers like sweet things, but they think candyfloss is too girly, too pink. But you and me, we'd have wandered down the seafront with sugar beards on our chins.

'I wanted to teach you my mum's foolproof sponge recipe. It's in the sifting. The boys like baking, but only because they can make a mess. They won't remember the tips. The tricks.

'*Enya*. I wanted that so much. To share what my mum shared with me, and then see you make the world your own. Meet your first boyfriend. I'd have hated him, probably. And later meet the man you'd marry, hoping you'd made a good choice, like I did with your dad.

'Your wedding day. And your graduation, too. I'm not old-fashioned. I'd have been ambitious for you. Wanted whatever would have made you happy . . .'

I stop. This is crazy.

The room is still, except for the fire. No face there now. A trick of the light.

'I'm so sorry, Enya. I'd have swapped my life for yours in a second.'

My eyes feel gritty so I close them again.

Sorry, sorry, sorry, sorry, sorry, sorry, sorry, sorry.

The word bounces round my head, louder and louder.

And then I hear something else, from a long way away.

No more, Mummy. No more.

My eyelids are too heavy for me to open them. I listen for a voice beyond the crackling of the flames.

Nobody's fault.

But that's not true. It was mine.

No blame. No point.

I argue with the voice in my head. *My* fault. *My* blame. But somehow the other voice is stronger.

I wasn't to be. It's all right. It's all right.

'Vicki? It's all right. Please. Please, stop crying, everything's all right.'

The voice is louder, more insistent. I open my eyes and I realise it's lighter in the room now. The face next to mine is young, beautiful, *real.*

Natalia.

'Vicki, what's wrong?'

She reaches out to brush tears off my damp cheeks. The fire's gone out and my face is numb with cold. But the rest of me feels different.

Warmer.

'I'm OK,' I say.

'Well, you don't look it,' she says. Even when she's trying to be sympathetic, she sounds ever so slightly sarcastic.

'What time is it, Natalia?'

'Almost six-fifteen.'

'Shit. I've overslept. I've let everyone down.'

'No, no. We get a lie-in this morning, remember? I wouldn't have woken you up, but you were sobbing so hard. Was it a bad dream?'

'No.' It was a good one. If it was a dream.

I squeeze Natalia's hand, then walk over to the window, and pull the curtain aside. It's darker than yesterday out there. Hardly morning at all. Then I realise why: the snow is melting, and the landscape has lost the diamond brightness.

There's still a gale whipping through the gaps in the wooden frame, but it feels less bitter. I pad back across the carpet and towards the door. When I open it, more warmth hits me.

Staff Pepper's coming towards me, smiling.

'Ladies,' he bellows. 'Wakey, wakey, ladies!'

I wonder why it sounds so weird and then I remember the first day when he said he'd never call us ladies again. He's grinning, too. What's put him in such a good mood? Maybe he got off with a panther. Or perhaps he's just relieved that he'll never have to see us again once we leave.

'Ladies, I am pleased to announce that we have heating and hot water again. So when you're back from your fitness tests, there'll be showers and a proper breakfast to look forward to. But only *after* your last boot camp run.'

He claps his hands, and the girls groan and yawn and check

their watches and groan again. But they're all moving. There's no point making it this far only to fall at the final hurdle.

I'm the first out of the door. For Dave, for my kids, but for me too.

For the future.

42

Steph

'Come on, sleepyhead. Time to show them what you're made of.'

It takes me a few seconds to remember where I am, and who the voice belongs to.

I reach out for Sam, but he's not there. The side of the single bed where he slept is still giving off body heat, and I want to burrow underneath the sheets again, to hold onto the moment a bit longer.

'No slacking!'

He pulls away the sheet and blanket and I lie there, starkers, feeling exposed in the cold light of morning. Not that this morning is all that light. Or cold. The gas must be back on.

Sam watches me and I watch him. I wait for his smile to falter. He can see me clearly now, every extra inch and every excess pound. But he just grins and says, 'I'd much rather stay here, but Pepper will only come looking for us.'

Pepper. That brings me down to earth with a bump. Could he have heard us? Sam's Spartan room is smaller than the larder, and separated from Pepper's by a plywood wall.

Last night, it didn't matter. Last night, it was like primeval forces came together: steak, winter darkness, fire.

Wasn't just the primeval forces that came together. I blush at the thought, and the recent memories.

'You look . . .' I can tell he's trying to think of a different word than *amazing* after I took the piss out of him about that word last night. '. . . adorable when you blush, Steph.'

Sam reaches down to pull me up: like on the first day, when he pulled me up from the cold tiles of the hall floor. The muscles in his arms tense. He looks like an anatomical drawing, he's so perfect.

'Let me look at you for a moment,' he says, when I'm standing up.

Why don't I feel shy? Perhaps it's a dream. I'm hallucinating due to lack of food.

He leans forward to kiss me. No. Definitely not a dream.

Sam tuts, as though he's cross with me, or himself. 'I shouldn't have done that, should I? Not when we should be on parade in –' he checks his watch – 'ten minutes.'

'We could have a shower together. To save time,' I say, and then giggle.

'That is *not* going to be a timesaver, and you know it.'

I lean down, to lift up my clothes. The carpet is purple, and slightly damp. It's a horrible little room: tidy, but depressing. There are no photos, or shelves for anything personal. And no wonder it's dark: the tiny window is half-below ground.

Last night, I thought this was a one-off, a crazy rebound moment that would give me nice memories but nothing more.

But now, more than ever, I want to save Staff Ryan.

'I'll go to my room to shower, then.'

He puts his hand on my shoulder. His skin is red hot. 'About your room-mates, Steph. Would you mind . . . um . . . not telling them? It's a small world and the last thing we want is gossip, right? Especially if it got back to Pepper.'

I stare at him. 'Oh. Right. Of course.'

'It's not that I wouldn't want people to know. But . . . well, it's nice to have secrets. Pepper has a habit of making things seem less than they are. Grubby. This is one secret I want to keep, to keep it special for as long as I can.'

That's when I realise that even though I am wide-awake now, I was dreaming. *Day*-dreaming.

I was nothing but a Friday night conquest after all.

When I creep into the Clamshell suite, Darcy is packing, and Vicki is in the shower.

'All right?' Darcy says. She must know I didn't spend the night here.

'All right.' I wait for her to ask more, but she doesn't. Probably just as well.

Vicki appears. There's something about her that's different. Her body is slimmer, but her face looks lighter, too. She must be a candidate for biggest loser in the weight department. And she deserves it, the work she's put in.

'You go,' Darcy says. 'I already have.'

As the hot water crashes on my body, I try to cling onto the good bits of last night. The feeling of being alive and, well, a tiny bit amazing. The sense that suddenly I knew what my body was *for*. Not burpees and circuits but . . . love.

Ridiculous, of course. A man like him and a girl like me? Jeez, I'm too old for crushes, aren't I?

What did you expect, honeybunch? Men always lie to get into a woman's knickers. Even your enormous ones.

But the words wash over me as fast as the water does. They don't hurt, because what happened last night doesn't change the fact that Steve is, and will always be, a Grade One Arsehole.

'We're almost late, Steph. You need to get a shift on,' Vicki shouts.

Or what? What can the staffs do to punish us now? It's time to send us back out into the world, and now the ice is melting, we're free to go.

But I should make the effort, one last time.

We jog down the stairs, as though these final few flights will make a difference to the outcome of our fitness test. Outside, everyone but Natalia is ready to go, and even she's limped to the back door to wave us off. Our breath no longer condenses in the air, and there's a patch of pink morning sky between the clouds. As I step onto the snowy tarmac, it turns to slush underneath my trainers.

'We're going home,' Vicki whispers to me as I fall into line. 'Can't bloody wait.'

Pepper's first out, and I remember the crazy Hunt for Foz last night and I smile. Pepper's gruffness is an act. Even his dodgy eye looks less dead this morning.

He looks at Darcy, then looks away. I glance at her. *Hang on.* Did she ever go back to the suite herself? Maybe that's why she didn't ask where I was all night.

The Crabs are looking blameless. Maybe we imagined the whole thing. Maybe Cat or Caz were just mending a rip in Foz's trousers. While he was still wearing them . . . then again, perhaps they have the right idea. Treat them as mean as they treat us. Meaner.

Then Sam appears. I can't think of him as Ryan anymore, not since I whispered and *screamed* his name roughly a thousand times during the night.

Almost don't recognise him with his clothes on . . .

He blushes, and looks away. I peer down at my horrible velour tracksuit and I realise he might be regretting what we did.

'Right, you lot,' Pepper shouts. 'Just because you had an easy day yesterday doesn't mean we're not expecting five hundred per cent effort from you today. In fact, the unscheduled down-time will have given the muscles time to recover so we should be on target for improvements in the run and circuits. Let's get going. Oh, and Dean?'

What have I done now? Surely he's not going to humiliate me in front of everyone? Hint at my nocturnal activities?

'Yes, Staff?'

'Keep your eye out for branches, right?' But then he winks. 'Warm-up run down to the beach, starting now.'

As we run, the snow melts under our trainers. The temperatures are rising as quickly as the sun is coming up. It feels like a glimpse of spring. The Ladder is no longer treacherous, though there are still icy lumps floating in the sea, big as whales.

Remind me *never* to come on a boot camp in the summer, when we might have to swim. Another hangover from my one year of expensive private education is a horror of being seen in my cossie.

But hang on. I'm never going to come on a boot camp again, summer *or* winter.

Except, as we warm up on the cold sand, I have to admit to myself that there's been something *huge* about this week. And I'm not talking about Sam's most vital statistic. Well, not *just* that, anyway.

'Time to run like your life depends on it,' Pepper shouts. 'Give it all you got!'

'But don't forget you're not competing against anyone except yourself,' Sam says, and he risks a look at me. 'Be the best you can be.'

'Pansy!' Pepper mutters. 'On your marks, set . . . GO!'

I go.

This time, I know I'll come last. What I want is to keep going. Agatha's running at her own pace; so will I.

Don't think. Do.

Which is what I did last night, eh?

'Keep your eyes ahead, race towards your destination,' Pepper calls out.

Sam is my destination, waiting at the halfway point, shouting encouragement, smiling at everyone. We're all the same to him. Fat birds, thin birds. Women who'll return to their paper clip empires and reception desks as soon as breakfast is over.

'Hey, what's got into you?' Vicki says, and I realise I'm running level with her, even though I'm not out of breath.

'No idea, but it's working!' I say. A week ago I couldn't speak when I was at this stage of the run.

The proper athletes are way in front, and good luck to them. Sam was right about one thing. I am doing *my* best, and it doesn't matter what anyone else thinks. Not Pepper, not Ryan, not Steve.

Especially not Steve.

Karen is already heading back the other way, giving me a high five as she passes. She's winning the race, but so am I, in my own way. Edie will be proud of my Positive Mental Attitude.

I'm close enough to see Sam's face. He looks tired. It's almost sweet to see that a night on the tiles (and the worktop . . .) catches up with him in the morning. If it's true what he said about never normally pulling girls, then maybe he's twinged muscles that haven't been in use for a while.

Though something doesn't quite add up, and not just the fact he's disowned me this morning.

Focus, eh, Steph? Concentrate on the running, not the paranoia.

'Hey, you're doing brilliantly.' Sam's smile gives me a flashback to last night, and I almost trip over my horrible trainers. He grins. Maybe he's remembering too.

'Don't stop now,' he says.

I was the one saying that last night. It amazed me how well

we . . . worked. Him built like a Greek statue, me like a plump cherub with a very naughty streak.

'Go on, almost halfway,' he shouts. And then he whispers, 'You're amazing,' so softly that Agatha can't hear even though we're almost neck and neck.

Amazing.

That word fires me up again and it's as though my legs are longer, or my feet springier. I'm pulling ahead. At last my body is working properly. No tripping. No stupid heavy breathing. I'm a well-oiled machine: heart pumping, lungs pulling in oxygen, muscles propelling me along the prom, so the beach huts are almost a blur and the other women are getting clearer with each step. Their smiles, their shouts.

'Come on, Steph, you're almost there!'

'Chef Steph is our champion!'

So much praise for a silly one-mile run! So why do I feel tears in my eyes? I focus on the last few metres . . .

I'm racing through the line of people, and the others are hugging me, and I feel hot and sweaty and *cared for.*

'You've done it; you've finished your last boot camp run! Hoorah!'

Despite the abuse I've given my body and the disrespect: moaning, and groaning, and comparing, and punishing, and hating, and wishing I had someone else's ankles or fingers or nose.

I turn in time to see Agatha cross the line, too, and we huddle together to share our great victory.

Have I impressed Sam? As I get my breath back, I replay last night in fast-forward in my head, with the help of these fabulous endorphins. I'm wondering if he could actually be telling the truth about why he doesn't want Pepper to know. That he's keeping it a secret because it's the beginning of something that he doesn't want to be spoiled.

I hold the thought, like a secret of my own. Warm and wonderful, like a buffer between me and real life.

But then as I watch him, Sam reaches into his pocket for his phone, where our original times were recorded. And I remember him reaching into his pocket last night.

For condoms.

That was the niggle, the part of the puzzle I couldn't solve. Because if Saint Sam the Celibate never kisses the girls and makes them cry, then what the hell was he doing keeping a packet of three ready for action?

43

Darcy

Steph obviously slept with her soldier. So why didn't I sleep with mine?

I have form when it comes to one-night stands, after all. I can hardly pretend to be a blushing virgin. Other people drink to forget.

I drink to—

'How many?' Pepper is leaning over me as I try to catch my breath.

'Six.' Oh, God, it might even have been seven guys.

Then I realise that that's not what Pepper's asking. 'Sorry, what's the question?'

'How many sit-ups this time round?'

'Oh. Thirty-nine.'

He checks his clipboard, nods. 'Twelve more than when you started. Outstanding. Especially considering how little sleep you got last night.' He winks at me.

Bizarre. He's acting . . . well, he's acting as though we *did* sleep together. And I guess we did, but not in *that* way. After Steph left, we went down to his basement room, poured bigger tots of whisky, and talked and talked. Not about Heela and Rocky. I didn't want to say any more about that, and he didn't seem to want to either.

But we did talk about what's happened since. About going on living when you shouldn't even be here. About that strange mixture of euphoria and guilt at cheating the Grim Reaper. And the knot in your stomach that says, he'll come back to get you . . . that he won't give up that easily.

Pepper admitted it's the first time he's discussed about Rocky's death to anyone properly. He said they talked technicalities in his platoon: what went wrong, what to tell Rocky's parents, the practicalities of getting his body home. Oh, and now and then they'd laugh about the things Rocky did.

But he'd not been able to tell a single other soul that he blamed himself.

Maybe that's why he's so bright this morning.

I get up and into position to count Steph's sit-ups. I manage to resist making a joke about *her* practising overnight.

'Get ready, ladies,' Pepper says, and it strikes me that he's dropped the macho act this morning. What a difference a night makes.

Different for me, of course. My boss, the counsellor, the girls, Marian, they all offered me shoulders to cry on, and felt variously pissed off, professionally irritated and hurt when I went off and pulled cute men in clubs instead of baring my soul. I did try with the counsellor, or pretended to, so I could get the all-clear to go back to work after my meltdowns. Both of us knew we were only going through the motions.

Her report was perfunctory but it did the trick. I was in front of the camera again, though safe in a studio, far away from the field where I could do more damage to my reputation or the channel's.

Or get someone else killed.

'Put the effort in. Remember this is your very last sixty seconds of boot camp effort so give it your all!'

Do *I* feel better now, for telling someone how I really felt? Around three this morning, or maybe four, I *almost* cried and Pepper held my hand.

Though I didn't tell him about my bout of sleeping around. I doubt he'd approve of *that*.

'Come on, Steph.' She's staring at me, instead of even bothering to attempt a push-up. 'You haven't managed one yet.'

She smiles. 'I couldn't do one at the beginning of the week either. It'd take more than a few yomps to develop the right muscles, right?' Then she whispers, 'So?'

'So *what*?'

'What happened?'

Pepper's passing along the line so she adopts a face of extreme distress and I shout encouragement.

'Come on, Steph. Shift yourself.' Once he's out of earshot, I say, 'All we did was talk. Whereas you, young lady, well . . .'

She blushes. Collapses back onto the cold sand and grunts. 'Is it that obvious?'

'Uh huh.'

'Ah well,' she says, trying to push back up again. 'It was fun while it lasted. And it did last quite a long time.' She giggles.

'No more than fun?'

Her smile falters. 'Better to be realistic. That wasn't real.'

Pepper blows the whistle and comes along the line to ask for numbers. When he gets to us, I butt in before Steph can speak. 'Five,' I say.

'*Five*?' he sneers, then looks at his chart. 'Oh. Actually, that's four more than the one you managed on your first day. That's an impressive percentage increase. Good progress, Dean.'

'You didn't have to lie for me,' Steph whispers when he goes.

'I didn't do it for you,' I say. 'I did it for them. If you did their job, what do you think would be the one thing you'd get out of it?'

'I take it the answer to that isn't shagging the clients?'

I shake my head. 'Hmm. I suppose that might be a bonus. But I think it's simpler than that. They want what we all want. To think we've made a difference to someone else's life.'

44

Steph

I'm hiding in my kitchen. Trying not to remember what happened on this very countertop eight hours ago. Hoping no one will notice that I haven't been weighed and measured.

I don't want to have failed in front of Pepper and Sam. Especially Sam.

Breakfast. That's what I am focused on. Not inches or pounds lost. Or condoms. Definitely *not* condoms.

Eggs. I go to the fridge and take them out. *Twenty-four left*. There are so many super-healthy things I can do now I have gas again. I could scramble them, poach them, bake them in the oven . . .

Bugger the healthy options. I have aching limbs and a serious case of morning-after regret. And after the week we've all had, I think we deserve them fried. Two each. If anyone objects, they can come here and make their own sodding soya milk porridge.

I turn on the gas. The blue flame that shoots up from the burners seems a magical thing. I turn it off again, find six frying pans. Slosh in oil. Bung the plates into the oven to warm. Break all thirty eggs into six bowls, four each, so that I can pour them into the pans simultaneously to make sure they'll be ready all at the same time. Switch on the grill. Line the sausages up in the pan, squeezing them in skin-to-skin.

Busy, busy, busy.

There's a shriek outside. A happy shriek from either Cat, or Caz. I wonder how it works with those two when one loses more than the other. They can share men, but sisterhood only goes so far.

I open the door so the smoke from the sausages doesn't make the kitchen fuggy. There's a coil of cigarette smoke drifting round the corner. I follow it.

'Darcy?'

She's standing against the wall, texting someone with one hand, holding a lit cigarette in the other. In her dirty kit, with her unwashed hair in sweaty tendrils from the run, she couldn't look *less* like a celebrity.

'Finally we have a signal. When it's too bloody late,' she says.

'What have we missed in the big wide world while we've been cut off from civilisation?'

'One of the tabloids has got a story about me doing a runner and being sacked.'

'You did a runner?'

Darcy shrugs. 'No. I booked holiday two months in advance. But that's not a story, is it? I tried calling my agent but she's texted back, *not my problem anymore,* so I suppose that's that.'

'You don't sound that bothered yourself.'

She shrugs. 'Maybe I'm not. Maybe being here . . . well, it's given me some perspective. Last night, me and Pepper . . . we just talked about stuff. Turns out me and Sergeant Scary have a lot in common. Reckon we'd both lost the plot a bit over things that have happened to us.'

'Really?'

Another text comes through. As she reads it, I swear Darcy shrinks.

'What is it?'

She groans. 'Just more details of what they're planning to print. They've got a file on everyone, the papers. It's a tit for tat thing. Either I give them an interview about the trauma of being replaced for a younger model, or they publish all the crap they've collected about me over the years.'

'Like what?'

'Sex and drugs and rock and roll. I don't care, really, but I don't want my parents to have to read about my private life. So I'll probably do the weepy interview. Make up some line about being burned out. Pose in a bikini or a burkha. Whatever they want . . .' She sounds defeated. Not at all the girl I've got to know this week.

'But if they've got this stuff on you, what's to stop them publishing it in future if you don't do everything they want the time after this?'

'Honestly? There's nothing to stop them.'

'Maybe you could—' But I can't think of a good suggestion.

'Is that smoke . . . ?' Darcy says. We both turn round to see it pouring out of the door to the kitchen.

I race back inside. It's not as bad as it looks, just the inevitable result of two dozen sausages spitting fat onto the red-hot grill.

Darcy follows me in. 'Can I help?'

'You could keep an eye on the sausages and the eggs, while I make the toast.'

'Toast as in . . . actual, real-life bread? With wheat and carbs and all the evil in the world?'

I smile. 'The weigh-ins are over. No one will care.'

'Have you had yours done yet, Steph?'

'Um . . .'

'Steph?'

'I don't think I'll bother.'

She shakes her head. 'All those dawn runs and burpees and sucker punches and you don't want to find out how you got on?'

'It might sound dumb but I've already proved what I wanted to prove to myself by seeing the week out. If I find out I haven't lost anything, I'll be a failure.'

'Bloody hell, girl. Anyone can see you've lost weight.'

'Maybe a bit,' I admit. 'Off my fingers.'

She laughs. 'Never mind your fingers. You had a pot belly when you arrived. Now it's more like an ironing board.'

I look down. It's true that my horrible tracksuit bottoms aren't quite as tight on my thighs. But my belly . . . 'Ironing board is pushing it. More of a pudding basin bump.'

'Come on, Stephanie Dean. If you can't face a set of scales, then you're not the woman I thought you were. I'll do the eggs.'

She's wearing her stern newsreader's face. I don't argue.

The queue for the scales has gone right down now. Only Vicki and Agatha are ahead of me. The others are standing in huddles. The posh girl I never really spoke to has gone white and seems on the edge of tears. Cat is comforting her, though she's finding it hard not to smile. Caz is standing in the porch, smoking furiously and muttering under her breath. I can guess which of the Crabs lost the most weight.

Vicki goes into the room first. 'Wish me luck.'

'You don't need it,' I tell her. 'You look like a different woman.'

'Sad, isn't it?' Agatha says, nodding at the posh girl, who is now sobbing openly. 'I'm at that age now where losing weight is less a cause for celebration and more a sign of advanced osteoporosis. I wish I could tell her none of it really matters.'

'Why come here, if you don't care about your weight?'

'For the challenge, dear. And I do love being around young people. So much vitality.'

'I think you've got more vitality than the rest of us put together.'

Vicki emerges, looking puzzled.

'What did you lose?' I ask.

'Um . . . it's in kilos so I don't quite know.'

I take the Post-it where the staffs have written out her results. 'Total weight loss for the week: four point eight kilos. Bloody hell, Vicki, that's over half a stone.'

She blinks, then looks down at her own body. 'That's good, right?'

'Not just good. It's brilliant!' I give her a huge hug. 'There's nothing left of you.' I feel her laughing.

'I do feel . . . lighter.'

I check the note again. 'And you've lost two per cent body fat. Amazing.' The word reverberates in my head.

Amazing.

She pretends to shrug it off, but I can see she's glowing.

Agatha steps out of the office. 'I am delighted to say that I haven't lost a single pound! My bones are still gloriously dense.'

How did she manage that on so few calories? I wonder whether Agatha might have been the secret meat hoarder. With everything else that's happened in the last twenty-four action-packed hours, I haven't had a chance to solve the mystery.

My turn. Pepper smiles when I go in. Sam doesn't look up.

Perhaps I need to try harder to think of him as Staff Ryan again. Fibber and condom carrier. Still annoyingly gorgeous, obviously. But not to be trusted.

'Hop on to the scales for Staff Ryan, will you, Dean?' Pepper says.

The metal is cold under my bare feet. I daren't look down. Or up at Ryan. Instead I stare at the scuffed chintz wallpaper.

Ryan scribbles something on a Post-it, then I stand in front of Pepper while he wraps the tape measure round various parts of my body, then adds his figures to the note.

'Right, Dean, let's see, this week you've lost—'

I shake my head. 'Don't say it. Let me read it alone.'

He shrugs. 'Whatever you prefer.' He hands me the note and I leave the room without looking at Ryan.

I can't face the truth. What if after all of this, I've only lost a pound? Or less? Maybe I am destined to stay a fatty for ever. But a confident one. That's better than nothing.

By the time I get back to the kitchen, Darcy has started cooking the eggs. What she lacks in technique – those frilly edges are too browned for my liking – she makes up for in enthusiasm.

She tries to make me sit down in the dining room. 'You deserve to be waited on for once.' But I don't want to join in the chatter about who has lost what and why. I've actually missed having time to myself this week. All at once, my empty flat and my single life seem a little less terrifying.

I take the plates out of the warming rack and we arrange the food on the plate.

'This is a joint effort by me and Darcy,' I tell the other boot campers.

I don't think they hear me. The minute they see what's on their plates, the mood changes. Weight lost or gained is forgotten. Darcy's even managed to find some ketchup and brown sauce and there's almost a punch-up over who gets them first.

'I have never seen anything so delicious in my life,' Vicki says, and everyone mumbles in agreement. I try not to feel hurt that the rough fry up is scoring better than my lovingly made low-fat creations.

Sam . . . no, he's not Sam. He's Staff Ryan and he's walking towards me. This time he's smiling.

I can't deal with this. One minute I don't exist to him, the

362

next we're sharing secret smiles. I sit as far away from him as possible.

Everyone's tucking in already. I stare at my plate. The oil round the eggs is flecked with black and the sausages look obscenely plump. Even though it was my idea to cook this, I've lost my appetite. I push solid pieces of egg white around my plate like someone with an eating disorder. There's a first time for everything, I guess.

Agatha is sitting next to me. I offer her my food and she accepts happily. 'Terrible waste, otherwise.'

I look at the clock. Quarter to ten. So when did I go from wanting to celebrate completing the boot camp with a hearty breakfast, to counting the minutes till I can leave?

When I let a boot camp instructor choose me as *his* end-of-week treat.

As soon as everyone finishes, Edie stands up, claps her hands together and smiles. 'The moment we've all been waiting for.'

The staffs and Foz appear next to her, holding bottles of sparkling rosé wrapped in pink cellophane. I recognise it from a wine fair last year. Talk about bargain basement. I remember it tasted of bubble bath.

'Our boot camp tradition is to give three awards. One for most weight lost, one for most inches lost and then one for Boot Camper of the Week. Of course, everyone gets a completion certificate to take home, too, so we're all winners. But I know you're *dying* to know who made the grade, so I'd like to ask Staff Pepper to do the honours.'

If only I'd sat at the end of the table, I might be able to sneak away now, but I'm wedged in. Please let this be over soon.

'Is everyone **PAYING ATTENTION?**' Pepper shouts. Then smiles. 'You made it. We've had one of our more dramatic weeks here on boot camp. Accidents, snowdrifts, emotional outbursts, hissy fits . . .' Pepper looks at Ryan when he says that. 'But, despite all that, and my very low expectations at the start of the week, you've turned out to be one of our better groups.'

The others smile – from Pepper, this is bloody high praise.

'So, the totals. In the last week, between you, you lot have lost a total of . . .' He pauses. 'Forty-four point seven kilos. Or, in English money, just over *seven* stone. Which happens to be just about a whole Natalia!'

We all look at Natalia, who seems slightly irritated by the comparison. People whoop and applaud.

'In lost inches, because I know some of you really cannot get their heads around centimetres, it's two hundred and five. Which is equivalent to a person measuring seventeen feet tall!'

This gets an even bigger cheer. Sure, it's impressive, though I have a feeling Pepper pulled his tape measure that bit tighter today than he did on Monday, to make us seem slimmer than we are.

'Let's get down to the real business now. Our biggest loser this week, with an incredible five point one kilos – or eleven pounds – shifted is . . .'

We wait. I look around. It has to be Vicki, doesn't it? She isn't quite sylph-like yet, but she's an awful lot slimmer. Her face looks about five years younger, too.

'Karen REGAN!'

No one reacts for a moment. Karen? As in super-fit Iron Woman Karen, already leaner than a Quorn sausage Karen?

The applause is muted as Karen steps up to take her certificate and a glass of revolting pink fizz. Pepper kisses her on both cheeks, then Ryan does the same.

I'm *jealous*. And in desperate need of getting a grip.

Karen looks gobsmacked. 'Um. Well, thanks. Don't know what to say. Or where it's gone. But I think we're all winners, really, right?'

The two Crabs are whispering. I catch the words, 'weights in her bra'. But I don't think Karen was that bothered about losing weight. She was here to prepare for some super-human feat in Finland next month. She returns to her seat.

'Now for the most inches lost. The winner, with a total deficit of an amazing nineteen inches is . . .'

It *must* be Vicki this time.

'Stephanie DEAN!'

At first I don't recognise my own name. Then I shake my head at Pepper. He's wrong. He must be. He didn't measure my *fingers*, which are surely the only area where the change is noticeable.

But Agatha is pushing me up from my chair and I stumble forwards. Pepper hugs me. 'You proved me wrong, Dean. I hate it when people do that. But well done anyway.' He gives me my certificate.

I hesitate before turning to Ryan. He hands me a glass of fizzy wine, then as he leans in to kiss my cheeks he whispers, 'Told you you're *amazing*, Steph.'

I step back. Why did he have to say that? It's like he wants me to like him again. Perhaps so he doesn't have to feel guilty.

The other campers are waiting for a speech. 'Right. Well, like Karen, I can't believe this. Though I was obviously much fatter than her to begin with, so I had plenty to lose.'

There's a groan from the room. Edie frowns at me. 'Steph, that isn't the kind of talk we expect at the end of your trans-formative week. If you're not careful we might have to keep you here for a second week of boot camp, just to get you thinking straight.'

'I take it back, then. It has been an amaz—' I stop myself using the word. 'A life-changing, incredible experience. But I can't say it's one I want to repeat.' I look at Ryan, so the meaning is completely clear.

I head back towards my seat, but Edie touches my shoulder. 'Where do you think you're going? We haven't finished with you yet.'

I freeze.

'Right, boot campers,' Pepper says. 'I usually do this spiel now about how much deliberation it's taken to work out who should win Camper of the Week. Remind people of a few highlights, and low points. But I don't think there's any point this time round. Because it was obvious from Wednesday onwards who should win.'

They're chanting something. Quietly at first but getting louder.

'Chef *Steph*, Chef *Steph*, Chef *Steph*!'

I gawp at Pepper. He's grinning like a Cheshire cat. Did Darcy *really* not sleep with him last night?

Foz and Ryan are moving round the tables handing out glasses of pink peril.

'The Camper of the Week could *only* be our emergency Gordon Ramsay, our St Delia of Windy Hill, our very own . . . Chef Steph!'

Pepper steps forward and this time he's holding a bottle of *real* champagne. The decent stuff, with a gilded label and glass as dark as a limousine's windows. I only take it so he doesn't drop it. As the others watch, I fumble with the foil round the cork.

'No! You are definitely not allowed to share that,' Edie says. 'We'd only get a dribble each. That's to be enjoyed when you're back home, celebrating your amazing achievement.'

She begins to clap, and everyone else stands up and holds their glasses out towards me.

'To Chef Steph. We thank you from the bottom of our bellies!'

I take a sip of the sickly rosé, and smile as graciously as I can. It *does* mean a lot that they all think I deserve this. But I'm a backroom girl, always have been. Being the centre of attention now is every bit as overwhelming as it was on day one, when I catapulted myself to notoriety on a broken plastic chair.

But they keep clapping and I keep smiling and gradually I start to like it. It's strange to know that on Monday morning, I will be back at work, where no one notices me, never mind appreciates me.

Except, maybe I don't have to put up with being ignored. Perhaps what boot camp has really taught me has nothing to do with waistlines or burpees.

Perhaps it's time to make the rest of the world see what I'm made of. Starting on Monday.

After the presentation, the hugging goes on for ever. We pose for a group photo, and I force myself to look away when all the girls line up to have their picture taken individually on Sam's knee. Everyone's swapping email addresses and mobile numbers, and Edie's signing us all up for motivational Tweets from @TopBootCamp till the vital day sixty-six, 'to keep you on the right track until your fab new habits are completely established'.

There are only two people I'd like to stay in touch with. Well, OK, if I'm honest, there are three, but that's not going to happen.

I hug Darcy. 'What you said? About running shops?'

'What?' She moves back.

'You were talking about helping me buy new gear.'

'Eh? Oh, that. Sorry. Of course, we'll definitely make a date. It's not like I have anything else to fill my days.'

I pull away, hurt that she didn't remember and suddenly certain she has no intention of staying in touch. What would she have in common with me away from here? The tabloid darling and the pudgy supermarket home economist? We were *never* going to be best mates.

Vicki might turn into a real chum, though.

She notices I've brought my bag downstairs. 'You off early?'

I nod, and she follows me outside to the car park, and gives me such a warm embrace that I don't feel the cold at all.

'Promise me something, Steph?'

'So long as it doesn't involve burpees.'

'No more slagging yourself off. You didn't get that award just for cooking, you know. You got it for being the nicest person on boot camp. And the prettiest, too.'

'Yeah, and when was the last time you had your eyes tested, Vicki?'

'You underestimate yourself, gorgeous. You deserve someone lovely.'

Lovely. I haven't had a chance to tell her about Sam . . . Staff Ryan, and right now I don't feel like confiding something that I want to put behind me. 'We will stay in touch, won't we, Vicki? You're fantastic. An inspiration.'

She kisses me on the forehead, the way a mum kisses a child goodnight. 'You betcha. Drive safely, sweetheart.'

I load my bag into the boot. It's almost empty now I've got rid of all that horrible velour and acrylic workout gear. But at the back of the boot I spot an Ingram's carrier bag, and I wonder what it is. Then I remember: I packed emergency packs of flapjacks, almond slices and chocolate sponge rolls, 'just in case' they didn't feed us enough. I'd forgotten all about my stash.

Or maybe I didn't forget, exactly. Maybe it was my *subconscious making better choices on my behalf*, like Edie kept saying.

Well, except for one choice that probably wasn't for the best.

Vicki's still waving as I reverse out and down the lane. Her round body gets smaller in my rear-view mirror, and so does the Windy Hill Hotel.

I stop the car to unbolt the gates. Six days ago, it felt like I was going to prison. And now it does feel a bit like I'm being released for good behaviour.

The gates shriek when I open them, a horrible sound that sets my teeth on edge. I look back at the house. I didn't say goodbye to Sam.

No, it's better that way. It is what it is. I definitely won't let myself feel guilty or duped.

But after ten years with Steve, I probably deserve a break from the wrong kind of man.

One last look in the rear-view mirror, then I put my foot down and drive back towards my cosy, singleton flat. And towards a better life.

DAY 33:

Motivational Tweet of the Day from @TopBootCamp:
UR halfway to a lifetime of good habits, and it's Feb 14, so love yourself, celebrate the progress you made so far but don't veer off course!

45

Steph

All that work. The circuits, the sit-ups, the boxing, the squats.

They were all about tonight.

By tonight, I was supposed to be two stone lighter, and ten times more gorgeous. I was supposed to sweep into the Valentine's Ball, ugly duckling no more, to claim Steve as my 'prize'.

'Hey, you scrub up well, considering, sis.'

My brother Nigel is standing in the doorway to my bedroom, watching me as I try to tame my bushy hair. Half the spray just went in my eyes, which are now the same pink as my blusher. Of course, all *he* had to do was throw on the tux and the bow tie and run a hand through his hair to give it a rakish look.

'Do I?'

I've only lost eight pounds, and seven of those went during the week of boot camp itself. Progress has slowed since.

'Seriously. You look knockout. *Lady in red.* Steve will see you across a crowded room and then wham. Bam. Realise what he's missing. Race over. Ask you to marry him or whatever it is girls want. Bingo. Next thing you're trending on Twitter.'

'Um. That's great, Nige, but I don't actually want to get back with Steve, remember?'

He hands me his Corona, and I take a swig. 'Then why are we going, exactly?'

The billion-dollar question. My official answer is that I'd

already paid seventy-five pounds a head for the tickets so I am going to get my money's worth.

But unofficially . . . I guess I do want to show him I've changed. Maybe there's an element of *look at what you could have won, sucker.*

At least, I hope that's what I'll think when I see him again. That I won't go all weak-kneed and needy. That I'll finally be immune to the old Steve magic.

'For the free booze. Anyway, I know you want me to get back with him so you start getting comp tickets again.'

He thinks it over. 'I think, on balance, that I miss the freebies more than I miss Steve. What about you? Singledom suits you better than I thought it would. You seem . . . happy.'

I'm getting there. Since I survived boot camp, I've been kicking rather more ass in all directions. On Sundays, I now cook new recipes, and so far Dad and the bros haven't said a word. Dunno if they even noticed.

It was trickier at work. My boss didn't take me seriously at first.

Until I threatened to resign.

The look on her face was priceless. She could tell I wasn't bluffing. Before the meeting, I kept a running total of the times she'd dumped work on me with no apology, made me cry because *she* had PMT, blamed me for some fuck-up that happened while I was on holiday.

I decided that unless things changed, and sharpish, I was off.

'But where would you go, Stephanie, dear? I mean, your whole career has been here. And with retail under the pressure it is, well, I wouldn't rate your prospects outside. You're not exactly essential to requirements.'

B.C. – Before Camp – that would have been enough to put me back in my box. But now I have a secret weapon: the memory of the standing ovation they gave me at the last supper.

Instead of being scared by the idea of leaving Ingram's, I can imagine finding a job where people would love what I made, whether I was cooking in a greasy spoon or a boot camp kitchen.

After all, I am *amazing*.

However hard I try not to think of that word, it keeps coming back. Along with a memory of a man who kept saying it.

'So I told my boss straight. Miss Pendleton, I'm twenty-eight years old and I have no intention of staying chained to the Ingram's test kitchen for the rest of my life just because there's a recession on. People will always need good food. Food made with love. That's what I do. If you don't want me, someone else will.'

And she knew. Since then, I've gained an office and a hyperactive intern called Drew who is as loyal as he is camp. I've also had the go-ahead to develop my own range of 'Boot Camp Bistro' ready meals for the fitness-conscious customer.

Maybe I'm more *essential to requirements* than she was admitting.

'Steph? Are you ready yet? Only if you're really only going for the booze, then the champagne will already be flowing. And we want to get our money's worth, right?'

On the Tube into town, I notice them for the first time.

Men. Looking at *me*. At different bits of me. My legs in my new glossy tights. My cleavage, till I pull the raincoat over my bust like a flasher in reverse. Even my face. A couple of the guys smile. I'm too gobsmacked to smile back. One is *really* good-looking.

Nigel's even more surprised than I am. 'Are you wearing a new perfume, Steph? Something extracted from the musk gland of a beaver or something?'

I'm sure the dress is too small for me. It's tighter than

anything I've ever worn, two sizes smaller than I was wearing Before Camp. I've only really lost enough weight to go down one dress size, but the girl in the shop said I was being stupid.

'Darl, the whole *point* of this dress is that it clings to your best bits. Why hide 'em?'

B.C., I wasn't sure I had any best bits. But there's another image that keeps coming back to me however hard I try, and that's of Sam's face when he pulled back the covers that morning, before he spoiled everything.

For that single moment, he looked at me as though I was nothing *but* good bits.

It's raining when we get to the hall, but I hesitate outside. My world revolved around Steve for so long. What if one glance at him is enough to make me go back to being the Steph B.C. who depended on him for what little self-esteem she had?

'I'm getting soaked out here, sis.'

And Nigel pushes me over the threshold. I think it's meant to be a light, encouraging shove, but it sends me off balance, and I slip on the shiny flagstones and fall down, my legs akimbo and my beautiful, too-tight dress straining at the seams. It's a miracle they hold.

Someone reaches down to help me up. For a split second, I imagine it's *him*. My soldier. I can't help grinning.

Then I recognise the long, thin fingers curling around mine.

'Well, hello there, Steph! Falling for me all over again?'

I let Steve pull me up, and I wonder if he's noticed how much less plump my fingers are. I've bought a ring for every one: only costume jewellery, but together they look like a sparkly knuckleduster.

'Phew, a bit of weight-lifting always gets the evening off to a good start,' Steve says as I dust myself down. 'How are you, honeybunch?'

I'm about to say, *eight pounds lighter, mate,* when I look at his face for the first time. It stops me in my tracks.

So much shared history. So much high drama. So many sleepless nights.

Over *him?*

In his too-loose tux, he looks like a pallbearer in a Dickens novel. Tall, thin, sallow, with his top lip curled up permanently from so many years feeling contempt for everyone but himself.

I'm sure he was good-looking. *Once.* But now he's as desiccated as a ten-year-old coconut. It's actually quite sad. And what's sadder still is I didn't see it.

'I'm . . . really well, thanks, Steve. And you?'

'Stormingly good.' He looks behind him, and beckons to a girl in a long off-white dress with all the shape of a Victorian nightgown. 'You haven't met Rosie, have you?'

The girl takes a few steps forward and reaches out for his hand. She reminds me of someone.

'Rosie, this is Steph. Steph, Rosie. And this is Steph's brother, Nigel. Good to see you again, mate.'

Instead of taking Rosie's hand, he slips his arm around her waist and squeezes. As I watch, he pinches some of her skin between his thumb and finger. Her smile gets wider, more forced.

I can definitely pinch more than an inch there, honeybunch.

He used to do that to me all the time. Not teasingly, but hard. It *hurt.*

'Hi, Steph,' she says. She's weighing me up.

Yes, Rosie, I am older. Ten years older, at a guess. And even now I've lost the weight, the Compare-o-meter judges that you're slightly thinner than me. Though my ankles are slimmer, and my face is less chubby from puppy fat and . . .

I stop. How long since I did that compare-and-contrast

routine? Around the same time I told my inner Steve to sod right off.

'Rosie, it's great to meet you. That dress looks gorgeous on you.'

OK, it's an off-white lie. But God knows, she'll be getting few enough compliments from Steve.

'Thanks. I think it makes me look a bit fat, but then I am a bit fat, so I suppose that's normal.'

Steve laughs. 'Don't be silly, Rosie.'

Do I say something? Like: *Get out while you can, Rosie, and mind you don't trip over the shroud he's made you wear. Take a long, hard look at him. Ask yourself what gives him the right to make you feel bad.*

But will she listen? Would *I* have listened?

'We've bagged a table, right by the stage,' Steve says. 'There's room for you two as well. Unless you've got a date for the night, Steph?'

The way he says it makes it sound a preposterous idea.

'Maybe later. Nigel, we should go and get ourselves a drink,' I say. 'Before the bubbly runs out.'

'Trust you to worry about the booze running out, Steph,' Steve says.

I turn around and walk, before he starts his little riff about drinking too much being unladylike, because it makes wobbly girls dance, when dancing should be against the law for anyone over a size ten.

Looking back, I think it was simply his way of making sure I was always sober enough to drive us both home.

By the time I've got to the free bar, I've made three decisions.

One: I'm going to give Rosie my card, just in case she wants to compare notes.

Two: I'm going to get drunk and unladylike.

Three: I'm going to dance all night long. Apart from anything else, it's fat-burning. I take my first glass of free champagne, and turn back towards the hall. It's been decorated with sugar pink hearts and garlands. In the bottom of my glass, there's a hibiscus flower just starting to open out, as though the bubbles are making it bloom. I think I'm the only girl here with her brother on her arm, instead of her boyfriend.

Across the room, I see Rosie and Steve deep in conversation. Or, rather, Steve is talking *at* Rosie. She's nodding too vigorously, and I wonder if he's taking something out on her.

Of course, I realise it's *me* she reminds me of. She doesn't even look like me, but what's familiar is her body language. They can only have been together a few months yet already he's wearing her down.

I hope she emails me. I might suggest a boot camp.

'You all right, sis? Never good to come face to face with the younger model, I guess. Don't let it spoil your evening.'

I laugh. 'You're all heart, Nige. But I'll survive. Though I have a feeling you're going to have to make do without free tickets in future.'

'No hope of a reconciliation, then?'

'That's the last thing I want.'

'So you meant it? I thought you were pretending, in case your new dress didn't have the desired effect.'

I shake my head. 'Honestly. Word of advice from your wise big sister, Nige.'

'Yeah?'

'There's only one thing worse than not having a date at the Valentine's Ball.'

'And what's that?'

'Having the *wrong* date at a Valentine's Ball.' I clink my glass against his. 'Let's drink to the worst night of the year to be single. To us, and billions like us.'

DAY 66:

Motivational Tweet of the Day from @TopBootCamp

You did it! There's a word for people like you – and it's WINNER! Celebrate with the people you love. Love & congrats from Edie & Karma.

46

Steph

Late. *Again.*

What's my excuse today?

There are no riots at the young offenders' institute – it's a beautiful sunny day, more like May than March.

No malfunctioning alarm clock to blame.

No detour to pick up hideous exercise gear.

Edie would say it's my subconscious at work. That I didn't want to come here back in January and that I don't want to come back for the reunion either.

When the invite came, I was torn. I know I've let the side down. My new habits are certainly a lot more virtuous than the old ones, but I have been a slacker. It wasn't exactly practical to fit eight hours of hardcore physical activity alongside a full-time job.

Never bought the funky designer clobber, either. I tried texting Darcy three times for advice, but she didn't even bother to reply with an excuse. I kept watching the papers, too, but nothing appeared, no topless centre-spreads or kiss and tells. Sometimes I have to look at the final team photo, to convince myself that I heard her stomach rumbling in the wee small hours, watched her sweat, and told her what happened on that last night.

The more time passes, the harder it is to believe that *anything* happened between me and Staff Ryan. But, weirdly, it doesn't make it any easier to forget him.

The hill seems less steep this morning. Along the banks on either side, there are zillions of snowdrops. I keep catching glimpses of the sea, mirroring a cloudless blue sky.

Suddenly, I'm looking forward to getting to the top. The house might be damp and decrepit, but the view from Windy Hill will make the journey worthwhile.

It won't be quite the same without the staffs, but I don't think I'd have come if they might have been here. Vicki checked with Edie for me, and Ryan's long gone. As is Pepper, which surprises me more.

I climb out of my car to unlock the gates. They look less forbidding in the sunshine.

No. It isn't just the sunshine. They've been restored. All the rust has been scraped away, and they've been painted silver, so that the curls and the flower petals glow.

Must have taken *days*.

When I open the gates, they move gracefully, and there's no more screeching of iron against iron. Less like a prison, now.

As my engine strains up the final, steep stretch, I'm slightly giddy. Who is going to be there? What's happened to the others – did Natalia get married? Has Vicki lost even more weight since I met her last month?

And will I finally solve the mystery of the meat mountain?

Uh, oh. *That's* not good.

The hotel has turned an ugly grey. The white render must finally have crumbled off. The week after we left, the winds turned hurricane force, so perhaps Windy Hill finally met its match, after over a century battling the elements. I hope Edie's OK.

In the car park, there's a messy people carrier with a Truckers

Do It Long Haul sticker. Today I get to meet Dave and her boys. It'll be worth the journey just for that.

I walk round the front of the building. Chips and chunks of white paint and render cover the ground and the path. What's underneath looks more solid. But she can't be having it re-plastered. Not when she was struggling just to pay the gas bill . . .

The ballroom window has brown paper taped to the panes. I have a flashback to the first time I saw the staffs, through the glass. I was terrified. Yet in the end they were about as scary as Karma. In fact, I'd rather take on Pepper than a hungry Karma any day.

At least today there'll be no star jumps, no press-ups, no planks.

I raise my hand to push the bell, but before I can, the door opens.

'Chef Steph. The one and only.' Edie comes towards me and holds me in her little arms. She smells of patchouli and jasmine and . . . paint?

When she lets go, she steps back to survey me. 'Hmm. You've lost more weight, definitely. Excellent work.'

I nod. 'A little. I'd have lost even more if I hadn't been testing out a new range of boot camp-inspired ready meals.'

She nods. 'Hmm. Interesting. Might have a commercial proposition for you there, but that can wait. Come on through.'

The hallway is dark, till my eyes get used to it. And then it looks far, far worse than I remember: the walls are dark brown with damp, and there are massive holes in the plaster. 'Shit. Did you have a flood?'

Edie smiles at me. 'We did. Talk about good timing! This is the before, obviously. For the after, you'll have to come and see the artists' impressions.'

That's it. Being on her own with Karma has finally sent her

over the edge. If I hadn't seen Vicki's car in the car park, I'd be running away before Edie lures me into captivity as her *special friend*.

She leads me through the hall, avoiding huge stacks of cement bags, and bundles of thick cables hanging from the ceiling. I pass the kitchen, but the door is closed, and it'd seem rude to go back in there before I see the others again. Even though it's where I want to be.

I hear Karma growling and when I look down, he's in the corner, half a very fine-looking Cumberland sausage poking out of his mouth.

Hang on. A Cumberland sausage . . .

'Is that who I think it is?' Vicki's voice is coming from the drawing room.

I can smell the wood fire burning. It's so warm today that it probably didn't need to be lit, but it's hard to stop Vicki setting fire to things.

'Steph!'

She jumps out of the shadows. As we hug, I put my hands round her midriff.

'There's nothing left of you, Vicki. You're a waif!'

'Yeah, right.'

When we separate, I look at her properly. She's wearing a wrap dress that goes in at all the right places. And she has a seriously good pair of legs. 'I take it back; you're way sexier than a waif.'

'I'm just happy to have a waist again,' she says, and puts her hands either side of her tummy. They almost meet.

'How much have you lost?'

'Just under two stone. Pretty good, huh?'

'Bloody brilliant, Vicki. You'll be as skinny as Posh before you know it.' Behind her, I spot three little boys playing tag behind the giant sofas. 'Aren't you going to introduce me?'

'If they'll stand still long enough. OK . . . that's Rudy . . . behind the curtain. And Alastair under the windowsill. And Murray – MURRAY ADAMS, will you get off that table this minute!'

A tall guy in tight jeans lifts the protesting boy off the table. 'That'll be Dave, then? Handsome!'

'Oi, Dave, come here. Steph reckons you're handsome.'

He comes towards me with a boy under his armpit, and holds out his other hand to shake mine. 'Sorry, love. I'm taken. But I do have a brother.'

'Don't worry. I'm a confirmed bachelorette.'

Vicki frowns. 'Which I've told her is a waste. All that hard work getting as gorgeous as you're looking today, and you're staying single? I don't believe it.'

'You're meant to think I look like this naturally.' OK, so I did spend half an hour in the loos on the M5 services, perfecting my make-up so it looked like I wasn't wearing any.

'I meant all the work at boot camp, you silly girl.'

'Yeah, yeah. So . . . where are the others? Nobody else turned up?'

'Well, I'm sure you'll be gutted that Natalia hasn't made it.'

'Did she get married?'

'Yup. Though not before Agatha organised some kind of intervention with Natalia, Liz and the mystery fiancé. Only when she'd banged all their heads together did Agatha promise she wouldn't stand up in the back of the church and tell the vicar they shouldn't do it.'

'And is Lucas as adorable as Natalia says?'

'Surprisingly, yes. Agatha says she went along fully expecting him to be the world's creepiest cradle snatcher, and actually, he was an intense bespectacled Harry Potter lookalike who worships the ground Natalia walks on.'

'Wow. And Agatha? Is she here?'

'You'll have to wait and see. There's a bit of a reunion workout going on by the Ladder. I thought we'd go down there once you got here.'

'But I'm not dressed for a workout.'

Vicki gives me a knowing look. 'No. Didn't think that dress came from any kit list I'd ever seen.'

I'd bet a thousand pounds that there isn't a better view than this anywhere in England. Sea and sky and the promise of spring. Even the seagulls are beautiful, though as they scope us with tiny yellow eyes, there is a hint of the pterodactyl about them.

Vicki's boys tear ahead, so fast that I'm worried they won't brake in time to avoid going over the cliff. But she and Dave are oblivious, too busy making eyes at each other. How fab would *that* be, still to feel that way about someone after ten years, three babies, one tragedy?

'Come on! Get a move on! Use it or lose it, girls!'

Pepper. He's barking from somewhere further down the Ladder.

And where there's Pepper . . .

'Staff Pepper's right, ladies. Fitness is a battlefield.'

His voice stops me in my tracks.

Has he been here all the time? Maybe I misunderstood what Vicki told me. Maybe he never left Windy Hill at all.

Would it have made any difference if he hadn't?

I feel a tug on my arm. Vicki's littlest boy is staring up at me. 'Mummy says you have to come and look.'

I let him drag me along, and try to pull my happiest face, the one that says I've moved on from that night, thank you very much—

I peer over the side. Pepper's near the top of the Ladder, looking super-grumpy. And Darcy is puffed out in dark-grey fatigues, running up the steps backwards.

'She came because she wanted to see you before she goes,' Vicki says.

'Goes where?'

'Her and Pepper are going into business together, reporting from all the dangerous places in the world that most news crews don't dare go to. He's bought a camera and everything.'

'But what about . . . ?' I don't say it.

'His dodgy eye? Cured, apparently. It was psychological. Though I can't help wondering if Darcy has been kissing him better.'

I'm about to ask if she's got any proof, when I see Ryan, right at the bottom.

Oh, boy.

Has he got better looking? Or did my memory make him uglier, to help cure me of my mammoth crush?

If you can have a crush on someone you've already slept with . . .

I step back from the edge of the cliff. He hasn't seen me, so I've got time to get a grip. There was always a chance he'd be here. And much as I like and respect the other girls, would I really have had my hair done *and* bought a new dress just to impress *them*?

I peep over again. My boy soldier.

'You should go down there,' Vicki whispers.

'In these shoes?'

'I'm sure you'll manage.'

It's only as I walk down the steps, gripping the metal hand-rail, that I realise I can't see *anyone* else. Or hear them. Darcy waves at me as she finishes her backwards run but then darts out of sight. Pepper has disappeared. There's just Sam at the bottom of the steps.

I get almost all the way down before he sees me. But I haven't worked out what the hell to say to him yet. His face is tanned, and his eyes look even darker as he squints in the sunlight.

'Steph. You look . . .'

I wait for him to say amazing.

'. . . spell-binding.'

'Oh. Thanks. Weren't you planning to join the Foreign Legion or something?'

'I considered it,' he says. 'It's what men do when they've had their hearts broken.'

I nod. There we go. I knew I was a rebound thing, though I can't complain, because he was the same for me.

The difference is that he probably rebounded with another dozen boot camp girls.

I force a light laugh. 'Heartbreak's a bit like measles, I've heard. It only happens once, then you're immune.'

Wish I hadn't said that. It makes it sound like he did break *my* heart. Which is definitely not true. Steve was the shit. Sam was just . . . the right guy at the wrong time. Or the wrong guy at the right time. Or something.

'You never said goodbye, Steph.' He sounds quite cross with me.

'Lucky Edie sorted out this reunion, then, isn't it?' I say, trying to lighten the mood. 'Goodbye. Oh, and hello again!'

'There is no reunion.'

I stare at him. 'Of course there is. That's why I'm here. And Vicki and Darcy and . . .' and then it occurs to me that the only people I can see on the beach are Sam, and a lone dog walker about half a mile along the coast where the line of beach huts begins.

'I . . . um . . . organised it. I asked Edie to lie, and Vicki. And Pepper. You're the only guest.'

'But . . . why? Just to say goodbye?'

'I can't stop thinking about you, Steph.'

I shrug it off. 'What? I suppose I am the most *amazing* girl you've ever met.'

Sam laughs but his eyes don't join in. 'Yeah. Even though you take the piss out of my vocabulary. Anyway, just for your information, I think you're pretty awesomely stupendously outstandingly astonishingly . . . amazing.'

I blush. 'God. That bit about taking the piss makes me sound like a right bitch.'

'*I* don't think you're a bitch. Wary, maybe. After all the nasty things that ex of yours told you, that's understandable. But I got you here today to tell you I'm the real deal, Steph. Yeah, I'm a bit short on long words, but what I do say, I mean.'

I'm about to fall into his arms. Those arms. He's gone to all this trouble to get me here. Got Edie and Pepper and Vicki and even Darcy involved in the secret. Why would he do that if he wasn't for real? My heart is thudding so loudly in my chest that he can probably hear it. I *want* this to be true.

But one thing stops me believing in him.

Condoms.

'The trouble is, one thing doesn't add up, Sam. Here you are all handsome and muscly and buff, yet you say you can't get the girl. OK. If that really was true, then I suppose you might deign to try an ordinary girl like me—'

'Steph—'

'No, let me finish! I'm trying to make sense of it. So if you did decide to settle for a girl like me, well, I can make myself believe that I have special qualities. But then . . .' Suddenly I feel embarrassed. 'Well, you came . . . prepared . . . for our night together.'

'Prepared?'

'Condoms. You had *condoms*, Sam. You said you hadn't tried to pull a girl in years and yet they were in your pocket. I mean, obviously, I'm not going to slag you off for wanting to be safe.

But why were you ready for action if you don't make sleeping with boot campers a regular thing? You must have been lying.'

He looks away. *Got him.*

'I . . . uh. I wasn't lying.'

'What did you do then? Nip out to the nearest twenty-four-hour chemist even though we were in the middle of nowhere *and* cut off from condom-selling civilisation by an ice storm?'

Sam kicks at the sand. 'That's why? You left without saying goodbye because you thought I was . . . some kind of stud? Like Foz?'

'No, I left early because boot camp was over and I wanted to get back to real life,' I lie. 'But I did feel slightly . . . taken in. It's not a nice feeling.'

'It was bloody Pepper, all right?' Sam says. 'Pepper got it into his head that you really fancied me. That you'd be *up for it.* Not that he's an expert on women, but he kept pushing me to take the pack of three and in the end it seemed easier. I never expected to *use* them.'

I say nothing.

'And then when it *did* suddenly seem like things were going in that direction, I couldn't believe my luck. A lovely girl like you—'

'Oh, don't tell me. Now you think less of me because I wanted to sleep with you?'

'No. No, I mean, I'd never felt a connection with anyone like I did with you. It felt . . . right. But it was still a surprise. I actually had to try to read the back because I was so sure Pepper had been hoarding them so long that they'd be past their use-by date.'

I won't let him see me smile. 'They weren't, were they?'

'No, they weren't. And I was bloody grateful to Pepper in the end. Not just for the condoms. But . . . well, if he hadn't encouraged me, I would never have kissed you. Never have dared.'

He kicks the wall. 'Taliban? No problem. Defusing a pressure-plate IED? Complete doddle. Kissing the girl I like? Petrifying. But, actually, now I wish I *had* taken it slower, because if it hadn't been for those bloody condoms, well, you might have given me the benefit of the doubt.'

I've been so cross with him for so long that assimilating a brand new version of events is hard work.

'There. I've embarrassed myself completely now. Why would I lie, Steph?'

Because . . . because . . .

I begin to walk towards the water's edge, and he comes with me. 'Tell me about what you've done, Sam. Since boot camp.'

'You mean, apart from thinking about you and swallowing a dictionary in case I ever got a chance to impress you with my word power?'

The sun is blinding against the sand. 'Vicki said you left.'

'I did. But Edie's asked me back. For a new project. I'm still thinking about it.'

'You hated it, though, didn't you? Why would you come back?'

'I was unsettled that week. Because of one particular boot camper . . .'

I ignore that bit. 'So what's the new project?'

'It's a bit embarrassing.'

We're at the water's edge, now. His boots are giant-sized next to my little court shoes. 'Embarrassing?'

'It was Darcy's idea. She's got contacts at a TV production company that's developing a real-life boot camp show. Based here. It's got through to the final stages, and Edie's over the moon. They suggested Frank as the main instructor but the TV people said he was too old, so he's left in a huff. And Pepper's off to bloody Syria with Darcy.'

'Are they *together*, then?'

He laughs. 'I asked him before you got here. He was trying to talk me into going with them so I said, what am I, a gooseberry? He told me to mind my own fucking business. Which I took as a no. Or he'd have been less bloody grumpy about it.'

'So. This TV show . . .'

'That's the embarrassing bit. I did a, um, screen test. And they want *me* to do it. I can just imagine what the lads from my regiment would say if I was on telly.'

He doesn't know how cute he is, how much better a show would work with him as the star instead of Foz.

But do I really want him to be idolised by millions of viewers?

'What other offers have you had?'

Sam picks up a stone and throws it as far as he can off shore. I lose sight of it until it hits the water. 'Not exactly rolling in. I have been seriously thinking of doing private security. Or retraining. I've even been teaching myself to cook. Probably sounds daft but it's what I wanted to do. It makes me think of you. My very own, um, Naked Chef.'

I blush. 'What can you cook?'

'I'm quite good at scrambled eggs.'

'Watch it or Edie will have you cooking as well as training.'

'I think she has someone else in mind for that.'

I realise suddenly what he's hinting at, but I ignore it. 'You should go for it, Sam. The TV thing. It could take you anywhere.'

'I guess it depends on whether there's anything for me to stay in the UK for.'

'You want me to say whether you should leave the country? That's a lot to ask of someone you hardly know.'

'I think I know you better than anyone I've ever known,

Steph. And you know me, too. It's not about the trivial stuff. Favourite movie, favourite colour. Maybe this sounds even more wet, but I reckon we'll be all right, even if you love cowboy films as much as I love rom coms.'

I've been single for less than seven months. Everyone says I should lick my wounds, play the field, enjoy my new freedom. *Make a better bloody decision next time* – that's what they really mean.

But what if Cupid's feeling bad about my ten wasted years with Steve and is throwing me a lifeline? Haven't I earned this?

'Sam, I think—'

'Your shoes,' Sam says.

I look down at my feet: seawater is lapping around my new suede courts. They're ruined. I couldn't care less.

He kisses me.

Oh

My

Oh

My

Sixty days of kissing time lost. How could I have been so stupid?

I pull away from him. 'I have a question. A *motivational* question, about Edie's sixty-six day rule.'

He frowns. 'Fire away.'

'If you kiss me for sixty-six days – and don't miss a single day – do you think that would establish a habit that could last a lifetime?'

Sam smiles lazily. 'Tough challenge. But I'm willing to give it a go, if you are . . .'

As I wait for his lips to touch mine again, I taste the brininess of the sea, and the mintiness of his breath, and I'm certain that kissing him is a habit I will never, ever want to break.

Acknowledgments

Atten-SHUN!

When I first thought of the idea for *The Boot Camp*, I planned to write it without actually *going* on a boot camp. I have a lifelong loathing of exercise, especially exercising outdoors. Not to mention a major problem with authority . . .

However, I soon realised that there was no substitute for hands-on experience, so I packed my sports bras and headed for the English seaside. In November.

Nine hours of exercise every day was never going to be my idea of fun, but as in the novel, my fellow campers kept me going. Thanks for everything, ladies and gents!

It goes without saying that none of the characters in the novel bear even the slightest resemblance to the lovely folks I met at Boot Camp Beach in Bournemouth – though I heard tales of *other* camps that would make you wince in pain or weep with laughter. Special thanks to 'Corporal Cuddles' Gary, the slightly less cuddly Luke and the fantastic Hannah for making the process *almost* painless.

Team Orion is the ultimate in crack publishing platoons. Many thanks to the top brass – Susan, Lisa and Jon. Shiny medals to Angela for comms and propaganda; to Juliet and Julia for re-engineering; to Jemima for logistics; and to Sidonie Beresford-Browne for the glorious cover design which has a hint of khaki chic about it. Field Marshal Kate Mills is commended as usual for outstanding intelligence and leadership. Though I'm not sure those high heels are entirely appropriate for yomping.

Over at LAW (the SAS of the agency world), they're always ready for action. Thanks to Harry and Sophie for outstanding operational duties, Peta for stopping the Cavalry, and Araminta for being the best.

My brothers- and sisters-in-arms – other writers – are there on the ground when it gets tough. Especially the Board.

I must mention Emily Kubec, who won the Autistica Auction to choose a name for a character in *The Boot Camp*. Emily asked me to use her sister's name in the book – and so, Karen Regan, triathlete and all-round superwoman, was born. Hope you enjoy the story.

I'm very grateful to friends and family and Rich for not laughing too loudly when I told them I was writing a book about fitness. Especially my parents, who know just how hard I used to work to get a note to skive off PE. Thanks, Mum, for giving in to me occasionally.

Finally, and most importantly, many thanks to *you* for picking up the book. If you want to talk boot camps, burpees or books, do get in touch via my website, www.kate-harrison.com or say hi on Twitter – I'm @katewritesbooks.

Kate Harrison